STORIES *from* ETHIOPIA

Also by Charlotte S. Gray

Fatima's Room: A Novel

STORIES
from
ETHIOPIA

HISTORICAL & CONTEMPORARY

Charlotte Schiander Gray

Arc Light Books
Portland, Oregon

CharlotteSGray@gmail.com

Gray, Charlotte Schiander, 1944—
Stories from Ethiopia / Charlotte Schiander Gray

ISBN: 9781939353313

Published by Arc Light Books
Portland, Oregon
www.ArcLightBooks.com

Cover and book design, Jan Camp

Cover image, Debre Birhan Selassie Church, Gonder, Ethiopia

To my wonderful family: Nathanael & Priscilla
and Alexandra, Warren, and Leif;
Adam & Alexandra and Addison;
Jonah & Sara and Solvej and Viggo;
and my beloved husband of fifty years, Kenneth.

ACKNOWLEDGMENTS

Thanks go to Kenneth Gray and his work that took us to countries unlike our native United States of America and Denmark, and to the many friends who visited us in those foreign lands.

To the United Nations Woman's Organization, which I chaired while living in Ethiopia. Through that volunteer work, I met many wonderful people and became familiar with the ongoing aid work. Much of the material in my contemporary stories derive from my experiences there.

To the Doe Library, University of California at Berkeley for the wealth of material I found in its stacks, from which I created my fictional and yet historically based stories.

Thanks also to Vicky Elliott in Oakland, California for her editorial support that did not change the voice of my writing, and to book designer and publisher Jan Camp in Portland, Oregon for her visual and technical expertise in making this book available to readers.

CONTENTS

The Dreamer

I. The Dreamer

I OBSERVE THE GREAT PRESTER JOHN in his flaming, salamander-woven garment, looking into his magic mirror, which shows him everything that goes on in his kingdom. He nods to me and points, and off I go on my white steed, to combat the enemies of his lands. As I gallop down the hill, I turn and wave to the princess in the window of the crystal tower.

She waves back with her kerchief.

Flying along on my white steed, I fight the one-eyed monsters, the centaurs, the Amazons and the bloody-mouthed cannibals. With my faithful unicorn alongside, I charge the enemies of Prester John. Together, we confront the most feared invader of them all, the Black Rider. The emissary from Satan.

I am the Christian crusader fencing with the infidel Mussulman. I may seem small, but I'm agile. The Mussulman will underestimate my prowess and suddenly … there. There he goes. (Oops, I almost fall off the branch.)

Where was I? Yes, I return to the King's crystal castle and pass under the ceiling of precious stones with the head of my adversary under my arm. Prester John rewards me with golden goblets and rare emeralds, sapphires and chalcedony. We walk across the floors of shiny crystals, past the open windows and the twenty-four columns of gold and rubies and carbuncles.

He takes me with him for a walk in his wondrous garden, together with his beautiful daughter, under the filtered light of the tree of life, down the slope towards the fountain of youth. We don't go too close to the tree—the serpent is on his guard—before we bend down to the fountain to drink to eternal health.

On the other side of the river, the phoenix rises towards the sky with his colorful plumes gliding out of the red flames.

There is no end to the wonders.

In contrast, here in Portugal, we are so poor. Not the King and the nobles, but my parents and I. That's why I have convinced dear Father Alvares to take me along with him to Abyssinia.

Now I can't wait to get away from my father's orders. "Pero, chop the wood while your sisters are fetching the water. Pero, even if you are small, you can lift that pail. You don't get stronger if you don't do your best."

What has it helped my father to be strong? He is still poor, in a small cottage with seven children.

Never can I be left alone here on my branch in my favorite pine tree. This is the only place I can think in peace about the wonders out there in the big world. The only place where I can rub the resin off the bark and smell and dream. And look down to my dear Caro wagging his tail down below on the soft pine needles.

Then I love my mother better. She is an angel. She sneaks extra bread and oranges to me and tells us fairy-tales and stories and saints' lives. St. Sebastian. St. George. It will be very hard to leave her. But I will bring her back great treasures. That I will—even if it was she who threw me out of our house to work as an altar boy. She said it was time to stop dreaming and there were too many children in the house.

I guess she had her reasons, and if it weren't for her, I wouldn't have sung for father Francisco Alvares and he wouldn't have discovered my voice and taken an interest in me and taught me to read and write Latin and Portuguese.

And if it weren't for Father Alvares, I wouldn't have heard about all the Portuguese explorers and heroes like Dom Henrique, Bartoloméu Dias, Pêro da Covilhã, Afonso de Paiva, Vasco da Gama, Afonso de Albuquerque, João Gomes and João Sanches. I especially like Pêro da Covilhã—my namesake. (That Pero went to Prester John in 1493, and he never came back. Why did he stay there? What was he doing there in that other world?)

And if it weren't for Father Alvares telling me about all these people and their adventures and travels to make Portugal great, I wouldn't have known. And I wouldn't have learned that Prester John's emissary, Matthew, arrived this year—the Lord's year of 1514—and that Father Alvares was to accompany him back.

Now I will serve Father Alvares as his personal valet and secretary. It is true that his first answer to my request to come along sounded rather doubtful, but then he grew to like the idea. He had said that he didn't feel sure my big, dreamy eyes could be of much help, but at least I showed I had some imagination. And then I could sing.

He thought that could be helpful.

II. The Dream

It already seems like an eternity since we sailed out of the estuary—out onto the big, open sea. Standing on our majestic galleon under those towering masts, we waved goodbye to our countrymen. Below us, our ship rocked gently with its heavy belly, filled with the gifts for Prester John. I saw them already in the procession to the ship before we left:

the large canopy bed trimmed with blue and yellow taffeta curtains. The cart with a tall load of mattresses, bolsters and pillows stuffed with the finest merino wool. The dining table and chairs—silver-studded. Fine china and tablecloths and napkins embroidered with gold thread. More carts with shiny silk and gold attire, armor and swords, shields and harnesses for horses. But also, devotional pictures, candles, vestments, organs, bells, missals and holy books.

Yes, I can imagine a life with all those luxuries.

How beautiful the water looked in the twilight of the setting sun as we took off. How the red glow turned the water into the Mar de Palha (Sea of Straw).

I could see the small figure of my mother far up on the hills, waving with her kerchief.

It made me cry.

But back to our ship, where the hours pass into days and days into nights and weeks and months, as our convoy of noble galleons plows through the waves down along Africa, past Cape Bojador, Cape Blanco and Cape Verde, around the Cape of Good Hope. Then we'll be heading north to Malindi on the eastern side of Africa, before the long crossing of the Indian Ocean to Goa in India. From there, we will embark on a ship going from Goa back to the Red Sea.

Life here on the galleon hasn't been so great yet. Dysentery, scurvy, typhus, malarial fever. I had a bad case of diarrhea, and Father Alvares gave me medicine and wiped me with a cool cloth and emptied the potty for me. And he prayed for me. Without him, I might not have made it. He says so himself. What he said was he didn't think such a runt (why must I always hear about my size?) would make it, but that I was more resilient than he had thought at first.

It seems to me that sailing isn't much different from my daily life at home—only worse. Also, I miss my pine tree, where I could sit and dream in peace. Now and then I sneak in a moment or two to contemplate the wonders of Prester John's Kingdom.

If only we were there!

Padre Francisco Alvares is a very capable man. He seems to know everything, from the holy writings, languages and medicine to cooking, sailing and fencing. They are quite a remarkable lot. Lopo de Vilalobos, Lourenço de Cosmo, not to mention our Abyssinian ambassador, Matthew. But above them all stands the leader of our mission, Duarte Galvão. He is knowledgeable, brave and pious. But if I should say one thing about my companions, it would be that they all seem to think very highly of themselves. They believe they can do anything.

They will not only bring Portugal to the world, no, they will turn the world into Portugal.

But these are all the old guys. Especially Duarte Galvão, who is ancient. The good thing is that I have also made some young friends. There is Galvão's son, Jorge, and Matthew's young helper, Jacob. I must admit this has been the best part of the trip so far. When we aren't working or eating our salty soup, we play games and cards on the deck of the ship, in the shade of the sails. Jorge and Jacob are two rascals, who always cheat to win. They tell me not to daydream so much and remember my hands.

Our favorite time, however, is when we sit under the starlit night and talk. (Sometimes we manage to steal a little rum to share.) Then we fantasize about Prester John and his Christian kingdom, surrounded by cruel Mussulmen. We declare how we'll give our lives to defend the Christian banner.

After the rum, we talk about the beautiful women in Portugal and wonder if there are pretty damsels in Abyssinia. We agree that they cannot be as wonderful as the Portuguese ones, for they are the best in the world.

We also talk about the women we wish to find for a wife. I extol my preference at great length (for I have given a lot of thought to this) about how beautiful and perfect and angelic I expect her to be. To which Jorge suddenly says, "But wasn't she supposed to be your wife?" I ask him what he means and he says something like "somebody you can live with on this earth." Sometimes people just don't understand.

That's when we are called in to do our night duty of emptying the latrines.

Alas, our voyage at sea already seems to belong to a previous and more innocent life. Before I had the great sorrow of losing my two best friends.

Before we finally reached Goa, Jacob fell seriously sick and died, because our wretched leader refused to sail back to the harbor for a doctor. After some days, we entered a terrible storm, and because our captain refused to listen to Duarte Galvão to anchor the ships at night, Jorge's ship was lost. Against all hope, we waited for it to return. It broke Duarte Galvão's heart, and he followed his son to the other world after we had landed on the hot, barren island of Kamaran.

Now I have lost my two best friends, and although Abyssinia is within sight, the wind refuses to take us there. And it isn't a good sign that the magnificent gifts for Prester John have rotted away. The bed and table and precious materials and holy books have decomposed—destroyed by hot dampness, salt water and burning sun.

How can we meet the great Prester John without the appropriate gifts? How can he believe in the marvels of Portugal if we come empty-handed?

To and fro is the same distance—is that what you say? Anyway, that's what we do. We go back to Goa and make the best of our time until another captain can take us to the Red Sea in January of 1520. This time, we land at Massawa in a little bay with stone houses and a mosque—similar to Karaman's dry land, with sand and rocks and wilted, wild shrubs under the scorching sun.

Finally, the representative of Prester John, Bahr Nagach, makes his appearance on the beach. We are astonished. This poorly dressed representative of the glorious Abyssinian land doesn't look promising. But we realize that this is a very impoverished area, and this man is too far away from Prester John's proper realm to represent anybody. Also, I think God is testing my resolve to reach Prester John.

Our captain meets with Bahr Nagach on a carpet on the beach, and that would have been a normal event if it hadn't been for the arrival of seven emaciated monks. They come from the monastery of Bizan and have broken their fast to meet their Christian brothers from the faraway land.

Now we truly rejoice. Yes, I am not exaggerating to say that we cry over this long sought-after reunion of Portugal and Ethiopia. Here is the proof and justification of our mission. These monks have been expecting us!

Back on the ship in the night, we see a brilliant cross on the dark sky westward over the land of Prester John. Everybody on the ships falls onto their knees. We are deeply grateful. Here is the sign: God is showing us the way.

Fortified in the belief of our mission, we finally start our trip towards Prester John on the 30th of April, 1520, under the leadership of Dom Rodrigo. Our climb up the dusty paths is arduous, and our thirst makes us drink up the brackish water from our cowhides. We had underestimated the amount of water needed for the uphill trek under the scorching sun.

It doesn't help either that our obstinate Matthew insists on making a great detour from the direct path to go by the monastery of Bizan, where he has stored all his belongings. But I guess God was not with him in this, for he fell ill and died on the way. I feel sorry for him: such a long journey he has taken to Portugal and back, and now he doesn't even get to relate the story to his master.

Finally, on the 10th of October, we sight the tents of Prester John.

We now learn that the fabled Prester John is a twenty-year-old nomadic king by the name of Lebna Dengel Dawit. (He is not called Prester John but Dawit in his own country.) He has been considered the savior of Abyssinia since the age of seventeen, when he defeated the terror of his country, the Muslim Emir Mahfuz, on the plains of Zeila. Dawit had returned victorious, with his opponent's head as a trophy. Everybody believes Dawit is favored by God.

We are provided with tents and food and treated royally by the King's attendants. Prester John himself we do not see.

He is invisible.

But he communicates with us through his messengers and asks for the magnificent gifts, which have long been rumored to be on their way to Abyssinia. Our explanation about the destruction of the gifts is not satisfactory to the King. It is hard to quash his high expectations.

The King remains invisible in his royal tent. He communicates with us visiting Portuguese through interpreters, who scurry back and forth between the two parties. Many a night the King summons us emissaries, and we scramble to dress our best and wait in the biting cold night for words from Prester John.

While we are standing out there in the cold wind on the top of the mountain, Prester John poses questions through his messengers. How many wives does Dom Manuel have? How many children? When did he ascend his throne? How many wars against the Moors has he conducted? Are the Portuguese afraid of the Moors? (The latter is an insolent question.) Then come religious queries. On and on, information is passed back and forth through the canvas of the tent.

But words are not enough, and Dawit is not satisfied till we have proven our fencing skills, performed our art of dancing and demonstrated the beauty of our singing. This is when I come in useful, as Father Alvares had predicted. This was my one chance to impress the hero of my life, so I sing from the innermost depths of my soul. And I must admit I don't think I ever sang more beautifully than on that cold night with the wind biting my nose.

All this time we never see the King, who peeks at us through a chink in his tent. I guess he is as curious about us as we about him. But in the end, his curiosity must have been satisfied, for the next day again, in the middle of the cold night on that high mountain, we are summoned. (The King seems to stay up at night.) I must admit I had to rub my eyes very hard and pour cold water onto my face several times to wake up.

As we approach the royal tent we realize that this is a special occasion. A row of arches, swathed alternately in white and purple cloth, leads up to the royal tent. Two squadrons of one thousand men are lined up on each side. In front of them, four mounted guards sit dressed in silk brocade.

Each holds onto a chained lion.

We are beckoned forward and proceed under the arches towards the royal tent, where the front curtains are drawn apart. There, on a platform six steps high, sits Prester John in all his glory, with a golden crown on his youthful head. In his hands, he holds a silver cross, and he is dressed in a brocade robe and silk shirt. A cloth of gold is draped over his knees.

Two servants hold a blue taffeta veil in front of his face, concealing it up to the nose. I feel as if my heart has stopped beating. This is the fabled King I have heard stories about and dreamed about as long as I can remember.

This is my dream come true.

The two servants lower the blue veil, and the King's entire face is revealed before the veil is raised again. I see the face of him. I see the purity of his forehead, the nobility of his high-bridged nose, the firm expression of his mouth.

But it is the eyes that captivate me. They mystify me and make me love him. I cannot find the words to describe them. But they are innocently powerful. They are knowing, yet questioning.

They seem ready to conquer the world.

III. The Nightmare

It is a marvel to encounter your dream in real life: whatever I experience after that seems dreamlike.

After the sighting of the King, we make deep obeisance, touching the ground with our right hand. Dom Rodrigo delivers the Governor's letter. The letter from the King of Portugal has been lost. This was another serious blemish in our presentation, but the King gracefully ignores our shortcoming, and we exchange the customary compliments.

We continue our conversation through the interpreters, and the King proceeds to encourage us Portuguese to build a fortress in Massawa to help keep the Mussulmen at bay. Also, we are welcome to conquer Zaila, down the Abyssinian coast from the Mussulmen. Dom Rodrigo thinks the latter will be an easy thing to do. We are all keen to make big promises, especially after we have failed so miserably with our gifts.

All we have to do now is to wait for Prester John and his wise counselors to formulate the reply to the Portuguese King.

Such undertakings proceed slowly in Abyssinia. Besides, the King is not sure he will even allow us to leave for our homeland.

Finally, the triple linguistic effort is completed, and the letter in its Amharic, Portuguese and Arabic versions are tied up, each in a separate brocaded bag, which are then packed into a leather-lined basket. By then, our delegation has missed a couple of the yearly Portuguese boats in Massawa. But now the benevolent King has allowed us to return to our home country, with the exception of some carpenters and painters, who are deemed indispensable in Abyssinia.

Finally, the delegation leaves from Massawa on the 28th of April, 1526.

All this doesn't concern me, as I have decided to link my fortunes to those of the King.

In my new life, I follow in the train of the nomadic King with hundreds, if not thousands, on the move. If you were a bird, you would see the great lords who accompany the King, each with an army of servants in charge of tents and goods and chattels. The poor families on foot carry their few belongings themselves. People, horses, donkeys, camels fan out in open spaces and narrow down into a line, to file through the narrow passes and gorges.

Up in the front, in the center, Prester John rides his mule, concealed by a canopy held up around him by servants on foot. Ahead of him, guards are leading his chained lions. Behind him, carriers are laden with raisin wine and baskets of loaves to be distributed on the way to the deserving and thankful subjects. After the King come his thirteen consecrated tents, surrounded by eight priests in charge of each tent. Two acolytes walk with the cross upheld and censers swinging. Continuously, they ring a bell so anybody in their path can stand still with bowed head till the moving Ethiopian church has passed.

I feel elated in these processions, and sometimes it makes me break into singing the praises of God's nature. Here I am, in that enchanted land! It also contributes to the marvel of the journey that Prester John has arranged for a beautiful Abyssinian woman to look after me. She isn't the woman I have described to my two friends on that happy ship in the past. I well remember how Jorge mocked me for my high ideals. (I still don't see what's wrong with high ideals.)

My Abyssinian wife already carries the secret beginning of our first child.

History is like watching a magic lantern where the colorful images flow across a whitewashed wall. There I watch Lebna Dengel Dawit celebrating his victory over Emir Mahfuz every year, and the Emir's shriveled head is becoming worn, with all the display and merry making. But the picture moves on to Ahmed-ibn-Ibrahim el Ghazi, the late Emir's son-in-law, who comes forward to avenge Mahfuz. And avenge he does, with his left hand, which gives him the name of Granyé—the Left-handed one.

I tell you, Lebna Dengel Dawit is a braver warrior than any of the Mussulmen, but they have superior armaments and manpower. Slowly but surely, Prester John's kingdom shrinks, and with his waning luck, his vassals change sides. I follow the King throughout those unfavorable years. I do not fight in the forefront, but serve in the reserves in the back. Now Prester John loses one son in battle and one to captivity. His beautiful wife, Sabla Wangel, has to seek secluded security on one of the impenetrable mountaintops. Granyé would have liked to add her to his harem.

The Moors kill and burn the churches and villages. The countryside is laid waste. That's when we learn that outer splendor is nothing compared to inner conviction and faith in our Lord, the Savior. The more we lose, the stronger we become. Faith is impervious to sword and fire. I understand that I have been mistaken and too impressed with the outer magnificence of Prester John. I no longer look for the earthly glory of my King; I have discovered the invincibility of true belief.

The pictures from the magic lantern may be less colorful—more white and black—but they are purer.

But then it happens, what I could not have imagined: Prester John dies in the year of 1540. With his death, something ceases in me too. I am not sure his son and successor, Galawdewos, can become the new Prester John to me.

Also, I am beginning to get tired of roaming around, of the constant back-and-forth fighting with the Mussulmen. It seems to be going nowhere, with no decisive victory. My wife and two children are still traveling with me. Should I end this wandering life and return to Portugal? Should I bring my growing family? Should I travel back to my childhood home and settle down? Or should I stay, like old Pêro da Covilhã, whom I have finally met?

How does it all fit with my dream of yore?

Looking for guidance I decide to travel to Massawa to meet with Dom Estevão da Gama, son of the famous Vasco da Gama. Estevão da Gama is the new governor of India, who arrived in the Red Sea in 1541 to chastise the Mussulmen in the area. Maybe da Gama can show me the way? He is Portuguese.

I decide to go back to Massawa, but the morning, when I step out of the door to mount the donkey my wife has prepared for me, she suddenly holds on to my sleeve and begs me to stay. She has never done anything like that before. I am annoyed. I must mention that my wife has proven capable and caring, even though she has been more strong-minded than is becoming for her gender. She isn't the woman I had dreamed about. I tell her to be reasonable and set on my way.

I turn around before I start the descent down the mountain path and she remains standing there, waving her shawl.

It turns out that it was not a good decision to return to Massawa. Da Gama is away, busy fighting the Mussulmen along the Red Sea coast. The captain in charge of the remaining fleet is a cruel man, whom the sailors hate, and desertions become common. To make a long story short, on the beach I run right into a group of deserters, at the same time as a man who has just offered to guide them back to Prester John. Although the young man seems very sympathetic, he appears too innocent and inexperienced to be a guide.

That's when I get the unfortunate idea that my knowledge of the place and the language can be of help to my countrymen. Rather than rotting away in that hot town waiting for da Gama, I can make myself useful and bring those men to Prester John.

We waste no time and immediately start up the scorched, hot mountain path, carrying our muskets and swords. We even have a fife and drum to cheer us while we struggle up the rough and rocky mountainside. But one thing we have not thought of bringing in our impatience to get going: sufficient water.

Life has a way of repeating itself!

As we proceeded through the burning hot night, we develop a craving thirst. But there is not a drop of water to be found in this desert landscape and soon we can think of nothing but water. I tell the guide in Amharic that he must show us a source of water as soon as possible. Our accommodating guide seems to know where water is to be found in a nearby valley.

He courteously promises that we will soon get our fill.

With dry mouths, and breathing heavily, we force our way through the vegetation towards the camp of the local king.

There I see him, the imposing chieftain holding a string of beads with a cross attached. He extends his cross towards us and tells us how he uses the beads for his prayers. That is very obvious.

I look curiously at the face of this formidable leader and ponder who he is. His imperious face has a haughty and sly expression, but it is his eyes that catch my attention.

There is a pain and a fatigue in them. As if he has seen too much and it has left him dreamless. Then I recognize him, and I turn petrified with fear.

He is the dark rider of my fantasies. I am not fooled any longer.

Now large gourds of water are brought, and the sailors drink to their hearts' content. Water runs down their faces. They loosen their weapons or put them down to better hold the gourds. They drink and drink, oblivious of everything else. In the meantime, their hosts smile and express pleasantries while they discreetly remove the weapons they can reach. I notice it all and pull a little back under the cedar tree next to me.

At a nod from their seated leader, the Mussulmen attack the Portuguese. In a flash. Too late, everybody understands that we are faced by none other than the feared Granyé himself.

Those who have weapons fight back bravely, but many are simply slaughtered. Blood splashes all over, like the water that just poured down. A lance pierces my hand, and I receive a blow on my head. It doesn't get me too hard, as it also partially hits the tree. I fall down, with my face in the blood of my fallen comrades.

"Surrender," shouts Granyé, "and your lives will be spared!" Even though the situation is hopeless, fourteen of us fight on.

"Unfortunate men!" they shout to us. "Why surrender to traitors? Die like men, for they will kill you cruelly."

And so, they died like men.

The sailors who surrender are stripped of their clothes and pushed into a sheep pen. The Mussulmen tie up the door with a rope from the outside and leave on their horses to some place in the shade to rest through the worst heat of the day.

Well, so I, lying under a dead compatriot, act dead like my fallen comrades. That is when I am struck by the most intense longing for my home back in Portugal. It's as if the image of my dear childhood home with my mother and siblings and my dog Caro, under my pine tree, pierces me with arrows.

By then I succumb to my fatigue and fall into a daze.

Towards evening, I am awoken by the noise of approaching horses. The Mussulmen line up on their horses, with Granyé in the center on an imposing black stallion. One man moves towards the pen and unties the rope on the door.

From my position on the ground, I can watch the whole scene from the corner of my eye.

The first prisoner to come out squints his eyes in the light after the darkness of the pen. The Mussulman guard loosens the ropes of the prisoner standing in the flaming red light of the setting sun.

Granyé orders him to come forward towards where he is sitting on his horse.

As the prisoner advances towards the mounted rider, he thrusts his lance through the legs of the man. He staggers but he doesn't fall, and the other riders have their turn at shooting their arrows at him. More arrows pierce his legs and lower body, until one through his neck strangles him.

It is like Sebastian—the St. Sebastian my mother had told me about. I can see the man's face turned towards the setting sun.

Is he looking towards Portugal?

After the first prisoner is finished off, the next one is called forth, and the slow killing game continues, till no one else remains in the sheep pen. The last one has to be dragged out from the farthest corner and killed without his ropes loosened because of his resistance. When all the men are lying in a large lifeless heap, there is no more fun to be sought for the cruel Mussulmen, and they turn their horses away in the dusk.

I have not moved. I know the slightest movement would doom me, but to tell the truth, I am paralyzed with fear. I cannot think. I cannot feel. This is worse than death.

But then why had God left me out? Why had he not chosen me to become a martyr? St. Sebastian?

I must have dozed off again, for I awaken to a wild dog licking the wound on my hand. I start up. Is it Caro? Where am I? How have I come here? I do not know if I can move, or if this all has just been a terrible dream. But the dog makes me move my hands. Then my toes and legs. My arms. Slowly, I get up. I hear dogs and hyenas howling and snarling. They will have a feast now. But I can move. I am alive.

In the now pitch-dark, overcast night, my fear of the dogs makes me crawl away as fast I can from the dead bodies. Towards the east. Towards Massawa and friendly Portuguese. The recent nightmare gives me superhuman strength. I crawl and run and crawl to get back to my Christian brothers down on the ships and somehow, I make it to the beach, where some sailors take me out to the ship of the Portuguese captain in the rays of the rising morning sun.

IV. The Old Man

I survived. I have a deep scar on my hand where the lance pierced it, but my wounds heal. They heal on the outside.

People notice that I have become very quiet. I don't sing anymore. Fortunately, people's attention is soon caught by big, new events. The magic lantern throws the colorful images on the wall again. The victorious da Gama returns to Massawa, and everybody celebrates his victories over the hated Turks. But the celebrations are cut short when the King's old faithful vassal, Bahr Nagach, tells the Portuguese of the plight of the Prester John and entreats them for help.

The Citadel of African Christianity stands in danger of sinking into the Muslim Sea.

The newly arrived Portuguese are sympathetic to the cause of Prester John, and the soldiers are eager to revenge the treacherous slaughter of their comrades, so Dom Estevão da Gama selects four hundred men for the mission. His eager younger brother, Don Christóvão, becomes their leader.

The young hopefuls set off up the well-worn steep paths towards the threatened Christian highland. I ride with them. I shake my head at these hopelessly naïve daredevils, but I have to admire their courage and to admit to myself how the fountain of youth renews itself.

I am not planning to do any more fighting. I am only traveling with Christóvão da Gama and his four hundred men, till I can take my own route to my family. My oldest daughter must have given birth to her third child by now. I long to see my grandchildren.

But before I go my own way, I see the foolhardy Cristóvão and his companions in action. Maybe Cristóvão is the new St. George? But I am not going to witness any more fighting, so I bid farewell to the heroes and set upon my course towards my Abyssinian home.

I have hardly reached home when the news of a victorious battle by Cristóvão with the Granyé himself arrives. And a short time after, while I am hoeing my vegetable garden, I again receive the joyful news of a victorious battle fought by Cristóvão and his men. This makes for a happy celebration with my dear wife and children.

Soon after, on 28th August, in the Lord's year of 1542, comes the bad news that Don Cristóvão has been defeated by the immense army of the Granyé. I try to hear no more, but evil news cannot be kept at bay. People tell how Cristóvão has been tortured. The tweezers he had sent as a taunt to Granyé to pick his feminine eyebrows are now used against him before he is killed.

Strange, but as I see it, Cristóvão was a happy man. Yes, he paid with his life, but he lived and died with his dreams intact.

Ten years pass. To me it is like the magic lantern turns faster and faster, sweeping history's images by me on the wall. I feel like my life moves past me in the reflection of those pictures.

Galawdewos is back on the scene. Then it is Granyë's turn to lose his head. Many of the Portuguese now leave the country that they have served so well. The King regrets that he doesn't have gifts to give them, but they had once been in the same predicament, and they declare that they have not come for riches, but for the honor of defending the Christian realm.

I tend to my garden and my family. Our favorite times are when we tell fairy-tales and talk about old Portugal. Then I relive my old life back in Portugal—like a faint echo. At times, my longing grows intense, and I see my parents' cabin, the pine trees, with Caro wagging his tail in the needles below.

I am losing my interest in the events in Abyssinia, but my neighbors will tell us how it becomes Galawdewos' turn after all. The Muslim chief, Nur-ibn-Mudi-Ali-Guazil, defeats Galawdewos and departs with his head.

Adamas, his brother and successor, has no patience with the Catholics, and we Portuguese fall out of favor. Thus, the wave turns over into a new wave, and I stay outside of it all. I don't think the Christians and the Muslims are so different any more. War is war.

Also, we hear news from travelers from Portugal, how times have changed there too. The Portuguese are no longer interested in conquering foreign lands. While the Muslim power grows along the coasts of the Red Sea and the Indian Ocean, the Portuguese have become busy saving their souls. The young people no longer know Prester John, and the clergy calls him a heretic.

My most recent pleasure is teaching my grandchildren Portuguese. The oldest, Pero, who will soon be sixteen, resembles me. Well, he is black-haired, as I was, but not as thin, and his skin color is darker than mine was. Also, he is a strong worker, who enjoys cultivating the lands we have gradually acquired. But he says he wants to return to Portugal to take over the land of our ancestors, to grow olives and oranges.

He wonders if he will be considered Portuguese, with his Abyssinian mother and Abyssinian looks.

For some time, Pero has been asking me about my life and why I came here to Abyssinia and what happened. He's very sharp, that boy. So that is why I have been telling him about the events in my life. It has been quite emotional for me to relive my many experiences while relating them to Pero. Sometimes I do wonder why I came here.

Finally, yesterday, my grandson made me tell him about my fearsome encounter with the dark rider. (I had never told that whole story to my family.) So I told them how I was wounded and was lying there pretending to be dead, while my comrades were tied up in the pen and the Mussulmen had ridden away.

I was deeply moved by the memories, when Pero interrupts me, "But why didn't you release the prisoners when the bad Mussulmen left? The door was only tied with a rope." I look into his open, innocent face—his big questioning eyes.

Strange, I had never thought of that. I just remember how at that very moment, I had wished I were back in Portugal.

Also, I guess, I was afraid. As I said, I was not really a fighter. Or did I tell?

That was the end of our conversation, except that I asked Pero to plant a pine that I had just received from the Abyssinian King in front of our house. It won't grow big in my time, but for the grandchildren....

Oh, yes, it was a beautiful sunset, so I was sitting humming to myself. Then I told Pero to go get his grandmother to come out and watch the sunset with me.

The lower sky was flaming red, and a pile of clouds flowing perpendicular from the horizon looked like the rising phoenix.

I saw it clearly and pointed it out to my wife.

Epilogue:

This novella builds upon the legend of Prester John, who ruled a mysterious Christian empire somewhere beyond the boundaries of the known world. Originally it was believed to be in "the Indies"—a vague geographical location in the Middle Ages. In the fourteenth century, the country, which was surrounded by "Mussulmen," or Muslims, was thought to be located in Africa. That became Ethiopia, or Abyssinia, as the country was then called.

An important source for the myth about Prester John and his kingdom was a widely circulated letter in 1165 purporting to come from Prester John himself. It was addressed to the Pope and various European kings. The letter is a clever fabrication by an unknown author. In the letter, Prester John claims to rule over the three Indies; he gives a colorful description of his magical kingdom and declares his intention to defeat the enemies of Christ.

The first extensive description of Ethiopia by a European is *The Prester John of the Indies*, written by the great Portuguese traveler Father Francisco, who spent six years in Ethiopia in the 1520s. Through Francisco's description, Prester John became identified as the Ethiopian King Lebna Dengel Dawit. The Ethiopians themselves did not refer to their King as Prester John.

The character of the dreamer is a fictional Portuguese by the name of Pero, who travels to Abyssinia at the time of Prester John.

Sources:

The Prester John of the Indies: *A True Relation of the Lands of the Prester John*, being the narrative of the Portuguese Embassy to Ethiopia in 1520 written by Father Francisco Alvares. Eds. C.F. Beckingham and G.W.B. Huntingford. Vol. I-II. Cambridge: The Hakluyt Society, Cambridge University Press, 1961.

Igor de Rachewiltz, *Prester John and Europe's Discovery of East Asia*. The thirty-second George Ernest Morrison lecture in ethnology, 1971. Canberra: Australian National University Press, 1972.

Elaine Sanceau, *The Land of Prester John. A Chronicle of Portuguese Exploration*. New York, Alfred A. Knopf, 1944.

Vsevolod Slessarev, *Prester John, The Letter and the Legend*. Minneapolis: University of Minnesota Press, 1959. This book contains a translation of the original letter.

Quotes:

"Surrender," cried the King, "and your lives will be spared." "Unfortunate men!" they shouted to their comrades. "Why surrender to traitors? Die like men, for they will kill you cruelly!" Sanceau, p. 115.

Vocabulary and names:

Adamas ◉ Vehemently anti-foreigner and anti-Catholic. Killed in a battle against rebels and Muslims in 1562.

Afonso ◉ Afonso de Albuquerque was governor of India whose mission was to build an empire for Portugal. Brilliant but lacking funds and means. Died of illness in 1515.

Afonso de Paiva ◉ Also sent off to find Prester John. It is not known whether he reached Ethiopia.

Ahmed, Ahmed-ibn-Ibrahim el Ghazi (Granyé) ◉ Attacked the Christian Kingdom in 1529. Defeated Christóvão da Gama in 1541. Defeated by Galawdewos in 1543.

amba ◉ Mountain with a flat plateau on top.

Bahr Nagach ◉ The governor who ruled the lands by the sea coast for Prester John.

Bartolomeu Dias ◉ Rounded the Cape of Good Hope in 1486.

Diogo Lopes ◉ Diogo Lopes de Sequeira took Matthew and his party to Massawa in 1520.

Don Christóvão ◉ Elected by his brother to lead the mission to fight the Muslims in Abyssinia. Skillful fighter who won several battles before he was beaten by the overwhelming numbers in Ahmed Granyé's army in 1542.

Dom Henrique (1394-1460) ◉ Son of King João. Instigator of the search for Prester John. Scientist and explorer.

Dom Rodrigo ◉ Dom Rodrigo de Lima took over for Duarte Galvão on the inland mission to Prester John.

Duarte Galvão ◉ Appointed Ambassador to Prester John by Dom Manuel. Experienced ambassador who led the expedition to Prester John in 1515, although he was seventy years old.

Emir Mahfuz ◉ Emir of Harar, who invaded the highlands in 1516.

Estevão da Gama ◉ Governor of India, who went to the Red Sea to fight the Mussulmen.

Father Alvares ◉ Padre Francisco, chaplain on the trip to Prester John. The first European to write a book on   Abyssinia, *The Prester John of the Indies: A True Relation of the Lands of the Prester John.* Arrived in Ethiopia in 1520.

Galawdewos ◉ King of Ethiopia 1540–1559.

João Gomes ◉ Explorer who reached Ethiopia.

João Sanches ◉ Traveled with João Gomes. There is no record of where he ended.

Jorge de Abreu ◉ Became second-in-command on that mission.

Lebna Dengel Dawit ◉ King of Abyssinia 1508–1540.

Lopo de Vilalobos ◉ The secretary on Galvão's mission.

Lopo Soares ◉ Lopo Soares de Albergaria was in command of the abortive trip to Ethiopia in 1517, and is described as incompetent and malicious.

Lourenço de Cosmo ◉ In charge of the ill-fated present from the Portuguese King.

Manuel da Gama ◉ Relative of Estevão, left in charge of the fleet while Estevão was fighting along the coasts of the Red Sea.

Matthew ◉ Queen Helena's emissary to Portugal. King Dom Manuel of Portugal sent Ambassador Matthew back to Prester John in 1515, with Duarte Galvão's mission.

Nur-ibn-Mudi ◉ Nur-ibn-Mudi-Ali-Guazil. Successor to Ahmed, who defeated Galawdewos in 1559.

Pêro da Covilhã ◉ Linguist and experienced Ambassador for João II of Portugal. Was instructed to find Prester John. Never returned.

Prester John ◉ Mythical figure: ruler of a Christian kingdom dating back to the twelfth century. First thought to be from the Indies, but from the fourteenth century, believed to be African in a land surrounded by Muslim countries. At the time of this story, he turns out to be Lebna Dengel Dawit, the Abyssinian king.

Queen Wangel ◉ Beautiful queen of Lebna Dengel Dawit.

Vasco da Gama ◉ Sailed round the Cape of Good Hope in 1497 to Calicut in India. The Portuguese became the rulers of the Indian Ocean.

The King

27 March 1868

WE HAVE NOW BEEN PRISONERS HERE on Magdala for over twenty-one months. And if we had known, when they put those abominable chains on our legs on that fateful day of July 16, 1866, that we would still be in chains in March of 1868, we would surely have despaired. We have lingered as captives of the Ethiopian King through two rainy seasons and two Christmases and New Years.

When I think back at the long months of inactivity and boredom; the discomfort of our chains; the recurring fear of the next unpredictable move by the mad King Tewodros; the indignity of our captivity and treatment; the lack of food and comfort, I don't know what has been the most unendurable. Yes, I do know. The most unbearable has been our humiliation as prisoners in a backward country, where we have been at the mercy of the whims and tricks from the King to the lowest prison guard.

Only our pride as British subjects has made us endure the insults. Our never-failing hope that Britain would come to our aid has kept us going from day to day. And now they are coming, the gallant British, with guns and artillery, to show Ethiopia and the world that you don't maltreat a British subject with impunity.

Our prayers have been answered, and God has shown mercy and justice.

This is the first entry in my new notebook. The old one was full, and Rassam kindly gave me this unused diary. He himself thought it too compromising to keep a diary, and warned me to be careful.

28 March

It was just in time that I hid the diary under my *shama*. Imagine, we're forced to live in such a fearful and humiliating manner that a diary could be sufficient pretext for any cruelty.

How naïve I was that time in Aden almost two years ago, when I asked Mr. Rassam if I could accompany him into the unknown Ethiopia on his mission to free the European captives. I had heard so much about that strange land and was full of curiosity and desire for adventure. And my joy when handsome Lieutenant Prideaux of her Majesty's Bombay Staff Corps joined us in Massawa. His role was to add his military status to our group. We were all enthusiasm. Little did we know what was in store for us.

But my interest in the conditions of health in that isolated country has been fully rewarded. I have had ample opportunity to study the diseases prevalent in the parts of the country I have been able to observe. The following are some of my observations: smallpox epidemics are quite common. And cholera. Of course, much illness occurs because people are starved or undernourished. For example, we saw lands ravaged by swarms of locusts, where starvation followed. Such populations are susceptible to cholera. However, the greatest mortality happens with childbirth. I don't know all the reasons for that.

I have seen all stages of syphilitic cases, leprosy, elephantiasis, epilepsy, scrofula and the after-effects of the cruel mutilations of men by the Gallas. Malaria, dysentery and diarrhea I can treat with great success. I have reduced swollen spleens with local application of iodine, plus small doses of quinine and iodine of potassium. Chronic diarrhea responds positively to some doses of castor oil, followed by opium and tannic acid.

The problem is that once I have success with the treatments, there is no end to the crowds of people who come to seek a cure for their ailments. They are so ignorant and superstitious and believe I have magic medicines for everything. I would hear the continuous cries of *"Abeit, abeit; medanite, medanite"* (master, master, medicine, medicine). Here on Magdala, I treat only those who have been permitted to see me by Samuel, the *baldereba*, our go-between with the king.

29 March

Today, King Tewodros returned to Magdala after his latest campaigns to plunder, burn and kill his own people. The King is in a foul mood, after fighting his increasingly resistant subjects. He must know that he is moving towards the end of his reign.

The change in the King since we first met him is unbelievable. Then, he appeared polite and generous. Gradually, we noticed his mood swings and proclivity towards passion. But it wasn't till he made his unwarranted attack on Stern and the missionaries, then on Rassam, Prideaux and myself, that I came to fully understand the extent of his unpredictability, morbid suspicion and willingness to inflict suffering upon his victims.

I see his familiar red tent at a short distance. Like a glowing spark in the ashes.

30 March

Yesterday, after the King arrived, we were suddenly ordered to sleep together in the same hut, with our guards inside. The crowdedness. It was unbearable and a typical example of the sudden unreasonable decisions made by our captors. I barely closed an eye, and my left ankle was pressed against the iron ring till it was throbbing with pain. It made us all remember the great discomfort we suffered at the beginning of our stay here on Magdala, crowded together with our guards.

Only gradually have we managed to improve upon our conditions. Tightening the roof against leaks, building a small bed to get off the wet ground. As a prisoner in conditions of hardship, you learn to be grateful for small improvements.

The greatest progress came when Prideaux and I were given a hut to ourselves; we even had it completely rebuilt after the rainy season. Not only did we gain much desired privacy, but the company of such an excellent individual as Prideaux has been a source of great pleasure and consolation for me.

31 March

Good news—if it is indeed good? The King met with Rassam yesterday afternoon. The King calls him his friend. Rassam has been incredible. Whichever way the King humiliates us, he always accepts, in the most obsequious way. *Everything is right if it pleases his Majesty.* Rassam's self-effacing and humble manner has ingratiated him with the vainglorious King. Maybe Rassam can do this because he is not European? It surely goes against the character of the British. On the other hand, we can probably thank Rassam that we are still alive.

So the King met with *his friend* Rassam and immediately declared that there was no reason for his chains. The good man then appealed for me and Prideaux and Consul Cameron and said that he would vouch for us. Reluctantly, the King then gave the permission for us to also have our chains removed.

The reason I question whether this is a good thing is because we have observed that benevolence on the King's part is usually followed by the opposite. He eases the burden on his victim, only to suddenly pounce back on the unsuspecting creature.

It was a painful and complicated affair to take off those rings. First, an iron wedge was hammered in where the rings were joined, then three or four loops of strong leather rope were passed inside the irons, which were then pulled apart by six men, with all their strength. Slowly the rings gave way, causing much pain and discomfort on our sore shanks and ankles. (It took at least half an hour to take off my rings.) Afterwards, we could hardly walk. We kept lifting our legs up too high in the air. My legs have turned very thin, and it is almost like having to learn to walk all over again.

But maybe this improvement of our lot is a mere act of diversion?

1 April

Food is becoming scarce. As the King has laid his own surrounding country bare, there is no more grain, no more livestock. Nothing. The chicken we had for lunch must have been old and starved. There was no meat on it, so we mainly were licking the pepper-sauce off the scraggly bones. Fortunately, we still have a few vegetables from our gardens. I don't know what we should have done if our countrymen hadn't sent us seeds to grow a few fresh vegetables. We must ration them extremely, for example sharing one tomato between the three of us. But I believe just that minimum of greenery has saved our health.

I didn't mention that Prideaux had an acute case of dysentery, which I treated with ipecacuanha, followed by astringents. He recovered fast—not surprisingly considering his general strong constitution. There are times as a doctor where I feel great satisfaction to be able to help. This time was especially gratifying to me.

The King is in a wicked mood and often sits brooding on his favorite stone, facing the valleys below. He is looking for the arrival of the British. I wonder what thoughts go through his head?

2 April

We were told to dress as we used to dress and present ourselves to the King. Full of foreboding, we put on our uniforms; there was nothing else we could do. Rassam and Cameron appeared from their huts and we all hurried down the hill after the unusually taciturn Samuel, until one of Tewodros' chiefs took over and Samuel went back up.

It was with great difficulty that we could keep up the pace, on our wobbly legs. We were amazed how big Magdala is. In our long confinement to our huts and the space just around them, we had forgotten how big the place was. It was a pleasure to walk without chains—even if we thought this might be the end.

I will describe the following scene in some detail, because it gives a picture of the King at his best.

So, tiptoeing downhill, we suddenly perceived the King standing farther down, on the open space on the saddle of Islamgee. He had his back to us and was looking down the hill.

The King is a thin, wiry man of medium height. His dark hair, with a few gray strands, is braided in three plaits down the back of his head and the sides. He is wearing his simple cotton shirt and loose local trousers, with a cotton belt with a pistol stuck in one side and a sword in the other. He is, as always, barefoot.

As we came closer, the King turned around and to our great surprise, his dark face was smiling. He waved us forward in a friendly manner. Hesitantly, we stepped closer and looked down the hillside of the vast massif. And what a sight!

There on the middle of the slope was the great mortar, Sebastopol, which the Gaffat missionaries had managed to melt and mold under the direction of the King. The giant sixteen-thousand-pound iron cannon was resting on a fragile-looking wooden structure, which was pulled by five to six hundred workers by long ropes of cowhide fastened to the structure and the cannon. Workers were pushing uphill and inserting rocks behind the wooden sledge to prevent it from rolling backwards.

It was an incredible sight: the pulling by pure human power of this heavy cannon, with barely a road, up the steep mountainside.

Tewodros was directing the work, shouting orders to the supervisors, who were in turn commanding the workmen. This was Tewodros at his best. The natural leader flourishing in his effort. Doing the impossible. A deed that only Tewodros' iron willpower can accomplish. If he could? The cannon rocked dangerously. Some of the cowhide thongs snapped. The whole thing could turn over or roll downhill, escaping the hundreds of arms pulling against gravity.

We were watching with beating hearts and silent prayers. As wonderful as this feat seemed, it might turn into a disaster. We prisoners, standing right next to the daring King, would bear the brunt of his wrath if the cannon suddenly took its independent course down the hill. A tremendous thunder that would be!

The King was beaming with pride over his accomplishment, and we all expressed our deep admiration over this success. Of course, Rassam praised the cannon more loudly than anyone else, and the King nodded. We all congratulated the King, and we worried more about the cannon reaching the plateau than about what kind of damage it might later cause the advancing British troops below.

The King now talked about the British troops. (The British are clearly on his mind all the time.) How many they are and how they are equipped? To Rassam's answer that he thought there were about five to six thousand men, the King curled his thin lips into a disdainful smile. That was all that was needed to defeat the formerly mighty Ethiopian King?

The cannon had reached the plateau, and the King offered *tejj* to his little select group to celebrate the event. He was all friendliness and smiles. But he no longer talked much. We could feel that he was striving to hide his excitement.

It was still morning, where the King is usually at his best. But he was already taking his drink, which would surely increase his volatility. But soon he dismissed his obsequious audience, and we bowed reverently before being led back up to our huts by the King's chiefs.

My legs were painful and I had developed a throbbing headache in the suspense of the situation and glare of the sun. My mouth was dried out from the *tejj*, and I was thirsting for water—but grateful to be still alive.

3 April

We were summoned to the King again today and were seated on a carpet next to him. This humility on his side made us uneasy. What would come next?

Tewodros spoke calmly (although the calm seemed forced) about our security. If the attack by the British endangered us, he would move us to a different spot. We refrained from commenting on this sudden solicitousness from a King who had kept us imprisoned for so many months. But then, of course, Rassam thanked him for his concern.

The King, who normally wears the simple white cottons of the ordinary Ethiopians, today wore a gaudy brocade robe.

4 April

The days are passed in this anxious waiting, where we alternately fall into despair of surviving this ordeal and the hope that we will indeed be liberated and live to return to our dear homeland. From our huts, we can see over to the King's tents, and as he mostly stays outdoors we often catch a glimpse of him *fakering* (play-acting) with his soldiers or conferring with his chiefs and advisers.

It is impossible to concentrate on anything. McCulloch's *Commercial Dictionary*, which I have of course read more than once already, cannot keep my attention any more. Gadsby's *Appendix* I know by heart. All our activities have submerged into that one big preoccupation, of waiting for the arrival of the British.

My one outlet of diversion is my medical profession. Unfortunately, my latest inoculation program for smallpox came to an abrupt halt today. I had received vaccine lymph in small tubes from General William Merewether and had great success vaccinating children against the feared *koufing* (smallpox).

When I ran out of vaccine, I took it from children with a mild case. Now one of our ill-natured guards has spread the rumor that the child from which the lymph is taken would die. Nobody dared offer their child after that, and my successful experiment came to a frustrating end. In this case, I had convinced the parents of the blessing of this pro-phylactic—not an easy thing to do with these ignorant and supersti-tious people. But it takes just one wicked person to undo the progress.

5 April

We all ask ourselves the question: What is going on in the head of the King? Nobody knows. All we know is that the Devil possesses him more and more frequently. Then it is crucial to stay out of sight, or else! After his rages, we can watch him pacing up and down in front of his tent.

Sitting on his stone in the fading light, waiting for the British to come.

I feel the need to put down what happened to Lij Kassa and his glorious dreams, as we (Prideaux and I) have been told by Cameron through our long hours of forced inactivity. How did the young hope-ful King turn into the cruel tyrant of today? I have recorded bits and pieces in my earlier diary, but I would like to put it down as a continu-ing story—and I may not have much time left to do so.

So, there we sat, warming our cold feet by the little fire in the middle of our hut, while Cameron related the story, all the way back to the King's modest childhood. His mother had been a poor woman forced to sell *kosso* to make ends meet. (A fact that cost Stern the shackles because he had mentioned it in his book.)

Lij Kassa had gone to the convent of Tchankar. There he had been taught by the strict monks. He had revered the holy books with their torn pages and colorful pictures of saints and religious events. He had become a strong believer in the Christian tradition. The Ethiopian, Christian tradition. Christ and the Saints. All the noble and brave heroes: St. George, St. Michael. He had thought that he would become like one of them. (But he hasn't killed the dragon—he has killed his own people.)

Then the opportunity suddenly arrived one night, when the marauders attacked the convent; they had killed and pillaged and set it on fire. The assault became Kassa's chance to act, to be brave, to distinguish himself. And he had escaped out of a back window, along the secret path in the forest around the convent.

If this attack hadn't taken place, Lij Kassa might have ended as a *daftera*, a kind of church scribe. Maybe he would have become an affectionate husband and devoted father?

But everything had turned out well for Kassa in the beginning. Everything he touched succeeded. Even against great odds. His years as a rebel. His daring marauding and plundering. He took great risks, and he had always prevailed. He had taken from the rich and given to the poor. A kind of Robin Hood. Even then, the treasures had piled up in his hideout. And the young Ethiopians had joined him. They all wanted to take part in his luck. Everybody sided with the winner, so when he beat a chief, the followers of the latter switched sides to him.

Yes, the King had been under a lucky star, and that star became his first beloved wife, Tawavitch (*she is beautiful*). His luck was so great that even his enemy Ras Ali had had to give him his daughter. Tawavitch, the beautiful. She had rallied her husband to go even against her own kin to avenge an insult.

With her as his muse and inspiration, he could do no wrong. The battle of Djisella. The battle of Deraskie. He had been unconquerable. He even tamed the feisty Gallas. His goals had grown vaster and vaster. First, he conquered the surrounding provinces. Then he aspired to claim the whole of Ethiopia. He would recreate the Ethiopian Empire. He was crowned King of Kings over Ethiopia by the *Abouna* himself in 1855.

Intoxicated by his success, he dreamed he would go all the way to Jerusalem. Beat the Sudanese, the Egyptians, the Turks. He was the enemy of the Musulman. He would liberate Jerusalem. The world.

But then God had taken Tawavitch from him.

Before that, there was a British man by the name of John Bell. He had been in the service of Tawavitch's father, Ras Ali, but had switched to Lij Kassa after meeting him and admiring the young military leader. They became close friends, and Johannes (as Kassa called him) became like an Ethiopian. He lived and dressed and ate like an Ethiopian. Married an Ethiopian. Went with Tewodros everywhere.

John Bell was the only one ever to share Tewodros' dishes on the *messob*. He slept in front of Tewodros' door every night—the King loved him almost as much as his wife. And after Tawavitch died, Johannes had taken her place as the person closest to Tewodros.

During those rainy, cold nights, Cameron described (and Samuel told the same) how Johannes and Tewodros had talked together for hours. Johannes would also tell Tewodros about the life and customs of that faraway country. Their civilized customs with servants of the state, who held a salary. Disciplined soldiers. They had been paid; they didn't have to plunder to get food. Kassa had let Bell train some of his best warriors. But it turned out to be impossible. His men were too wild and unruly. They were not civilized. (He envied the British their disciplined troops.)

Tewodros would also agree with Johannes that he would do away with the slavery and slave trade. How he would take away the power of the feudal lords and create a centralized system with paid officials. He would modernize his country. Develop it. So, what had happened?

King Tewodros never got beyond the state of military campaigns. He never obtained the peace to develop and build up the country. There was always fighting to be done. He would subdue one rebel and another would rise in a different region. He had had to become more tough and cruel to his vanquished enemies. No more gallant clemency.

Bell had been the only one who had been able to persuade Tewodros to leniency. Speak to his better angels. But then it pleased God to take away his last friend, as Samuel put it. King Tewodros and Bell had set out on the campaign to avenge the murder of the British consul, Walter Plowden. There they had run into the murderer, Tewodros's own cousin Gared. Unhesitatingly, Bell had shot Gared to revenge his friend and compatriot, but then he had thrown himself in front of the King as a shield against the bullet from Gared's brother.

Bell had saved his life. Johannes, his beloved brother.

Tewodros exacted a terrible revenge for Bell's death. He had killed and mutilated over a thousand of Gared's followers. And Gared was even his kin. But what did it help? All his rage could not bring back his friend and companion.

He had mourned.

6 April

It is amazing. After writing down the King's history and love stories, I had a strong and vivid dream last night. I don't know if I should really put this down, but it was such a compelling dream that I will do it anyway. I dreamt that Tewodros and Johannes were resting languidly on stuffed cushions caressed by the soft breeze from outside, while they talked and talked. The sunny patches moved over their heads as they planned the future of Ethiopia. Johannes also told Tewodros about that great British poet. Tewodros's favorite scene was the mad King Lear on the moorland. (But how could he let his daughters reduce him to that state?)

During that long balmy siesta, there was only Tewodros and Johannes. The King would listen to the sonorous voice of Johannes, till it blended with the song of the cicadas and lulled them both to sleep next to each other in the warm afternoon. It was at this very moment that I reached out to touch the arm of Tewodros. That's when I woke up and realized that I had stretched out my arm towards the sleeping Prideaux.

I sat up with a jerk. Who had touched whom? Right after the dream, I felt as if I was those two men—or one of them. It was very strange, and I didn't understand it, apart from the fact that I had been moved by my rendering of Cameron's description of the young King's relationship with his British friend.

The place is full of rumors. Samuel tells us about the growing rebellion against the King. Samuel has been very helpful to us. He is a clever man. He bargains that a good relationship with us will help him if the King falls. So, in the meantime, he is balancing his chances between the two parties.

Like us, he tries to anticipate what the King's next move will be. Right now, Tewodros seems to deal with the many prisoners on the *amba*. Some are pardoned. Right afterwards, some are executed. He seems to want to finish off his large prison population in anticipation of the British.

Where will we fit into this pattern?

7 April

But I must finish the story about the King. I feel that time is running out.

The life story of King Tewodros did not continue to be a happy one. It became clear that God no longer favored Tewodros, as Samuel also expressed it. He was running out of luck.

King Tewodros now met the woman who was going to be his second wife. Although he was smitten when he perceived the chaste young Terunish praying in church, the marriage did not turn out well. The pristine Terunish (*thou art pure*) did not return the King's feelings. (This time, he had to free her father, Dejatch Oulie, from his fetters before Terunish accepted the marriage.) But there was no luck in that marriage. She did not love him. Maybe she hated him?

Terunish took away his love. She replaced it with pride; she thought she was better than him. She did not see him as the promised King but as a parvenu, and she sat in her Queen's white tent mumbling with her saints.

One day, Tewodros entered the Queen's tent and she had pretended not to notice him. When he had asked after her health, she did not answer and kept reading. When he requested an answer, she had replied coolly, without lifting her eyes from the pages of a book of psalms, "Because I am conversing with a greater and better man than you—the pious King David." It was an insult to the King, but it was as if he didn't have the strength to deal with her.

His luck had turned.

Tewodros's wife disdained him, and he became very particular about his lineage, all the way back to King Solomon. The chiefs around the country rebelled, and he turned cruel. A certain treacherous Negussie, who evaded the pursuing King several times, became the victim of the King's furious revenge. Now was not the time for gallant clemency. Now was the time to settle scores and to set an example for other chiefs, who might contemplate following Negussie's example. Tewodros had the rebel's hands cut and twisted off. And his feet. And left to die. No water. Nobody dared ease Negussie's sufferings with a single drop of water.

But the rebellions did not abate. They had spread to Gojjam, Walhait, Shoa and Tigre. Tewodros's formerly pampered soldiers were emaciated and dressed in rags. Where they went to plunder they found nothing. Everything had already been robbed and burnt. The peasants hid in the forests and in the remote mountains. Tewodros had destroyed his country himself, and soon nothing was left.

Tewodros sent Terunish away to Magdala and took consolation with a fat Galla widow, Waizero Tamagno. No more high-flying hopes and ideals. No more love. Just the carnal desires: the flesh and the blood. Had God willed it so?

Terunish is still residing here on the *amba* with their young son, Alemayehu—the King's only legitimate son and heir. So now they are all together here on this massif in the middle of nowhere, with a crowd of white prisoners.

9 April

The horror. The horror of it!

I cannot put it into words. The sight. The drunk and mad King screaming to the guards to let out the prisoners. The first old man, who stumbles out into the light. The King chops off his head in one swipe. Then an old woman. Or was she old? Meagre. He hewed his sword into her shoulder. Maybe he meant to cut off her head and hit her wrong in his fury. The sword hit her bone. Her shoulder bone. There was no meat to soften the blow. He swung and cut at the emaciated body lying on the ground.

Then a child appeared in the sunlight. The King hesitated but still he lunged at the child and shouted to the guards to throw him over the precipice. The guards shot the flailing target in the air.

Was it the child's parents whom the King had killed at first? Or his grandparents? Was it just his parents aged prematurely, like so many in this hard country?

We had been taking a little walk to strengthen our legs and were near the square in front of the prison. That's how we happened to see this horrible scene. We quickly turned around and proceeded back to our huts. Luckily, the King hadn't noticed us—or it could have been the end of us. But screams and shouting and shots followed us back into the hut.

Later, Samuel told us how the King had been in a benevolent mood that morning and released some prisoners. Encouraged by this temporary leniency, other prisoners had started chanting *Abeit. Abeit.* The King had heard it and asked what they meant, and the guards told him that the prisoners were asking for food.

By now, the King had been drinking heavily, and he flew into a fury. "I will teach them to ask for food, when my faithful soldiers are starving." Then he had stormed to the prison door and demanded that the prisoners come out.

Three hundred and seven prisoners had been put to death. (Ninety-one were left for later decisions.)

I close my eyes and I see it: the sword into the woman's shoulder. The dirty rag. The bone. The cracking bone. The sword glinting in the sun.

I must sleep with open eyes tonight. I don't know how—but I must.

10th April—just after midnight of the ninth.

I feel too sick to sleep after the latest horrible events. We can see the King dimly sitting there on the mountaintop, in flashes of moonlight between increasing clouds. There he sits, surrounded by hateful enemies, ready to kill him. He is trapped here on this mountain.

He is as trapped as his prisoners.

So, there he sat, on his favorite stone.

King Tewodros looks up. Somebody is making sounds behind him. His stalwart Prime Minister Engedda is bowing deeply behind him, holding the long looking glass in his hand. (A present from Queen Victoria over which he had pretended displeasure.) A faint light is unveiling the contours of the mountains to the east.

"Milord, we see and hear some movement in the distance from Dalanta towards Bechelo. The avant-garde of the British troops is approaching. You must rest a little while we watch. And you must take some food. Today may be a great battle, where we will beat the enemy."

"You fool. We'll not beat the British. You don't know the guns and weapons they have. They'll kill you before you even get near them."

"We're not afraid. With God's help, we'll persevere."

"You speak like a donkey. What do you know? Our only hope is to settle with them. Prepare some breakfast for me."

The King waves Engedda away with an impatient sweep of his arm.

These chiefs of his. They were maybe brave and faithful (a few of them) but they had no imagination. They could not fancy anything being different. They could not even imagine the inventions of the British. They always thought of things according to the old ways. How it used to be. And how could he even explain that he had the desire to settle with the British, so he could get their help to combat the rebels in his own country? He wanted their craftsmen and modern tools and weapons to develop his country (as he had discussed with his dear Johannes.) He wanted his country to be like that of the British. (Except that they were ruled by a woman!) His *ferengi* prisoners could help him towards that goal. Rassam was to settle matters with his smooth tongue. Or he would kill him and the others for bringing the British into his country.

He hears thunder approaching.

They could hear thunder in the distance. It was after midnight of the ninth of April. After that horrible day of the massacre. The *baldereba* Samuel warns Blanc and Prideaux in a low voice to stay quiet and unnoticed by the King, because he is in a very dangerous mood right now.

Superfluous words. They know about the danger and prepare to go to bed while the guards settle on the ground outside their hut. They don't talk, Blanc and Prideaux—the horrible scenes they have recently witnessed leave them mute. They stretch out on their little homemade platforms and pull the threadbare *shamas* up over their heads. But behind their eyelids, emaciated bodies, some with just a small dirty loincloth, are moving back and forth. Skinny arms raised pleadingly to the sky. The terrible sword gashing into their bodies. Cutting into their bones. There was hardly any flesh to soften the blow. Bones cracked or split asunder.

Blanc tries to keep his eyes open, looking at the rafters of the hut. But he grows tired, and the eyes force him to close them. He squeezes them together in pain and attempts to make other images appear. He would think of the British troops sent to Ethiopia to rescue the prisoners from the savage King.

He sees before him the able Sir Robert Napier, leading the disciplined red-coated young British men. How they progress in orderly columns. Donkeys loaded with provisions. Blankets, food, cartridges for their guns. Elephants carrying guns and mortars. The sound of the bugle. The English voices.

Up the winding paths they come. Then they stop, because the forest before them is impassable. They cut it down and proceed. They carve a road into the cliffs and slowly, slowly, they approach the stronghold of the feared King Tewodros. They cannot hurry through this impenetrable land. Blanc and the others would have to be patient. They have been patient while the British columns wound their way forward down the cliffs, over the valleys, up the next escarpments. Through gorges, over muddy rivers. Thirsting. Relieved by the muddy water. But forward, forward. Driven and enthusiastic about their rescue mission. The brave British.

The image of the child, appearing behind the killed man and woman, intrudes on Blanc's eyelids. The child had stretched his arm imploringly towards the fallen woman. He squeezes his eyes again. Back to the British and their cheerful coats and sounds.

Up and on they climb and crawl. They meet natives but are not attacked and are even helped and fed *doro wat*, and entertained by occasional chiefs. They are in the enemy land of Tewodros. The Tigrinians are pleased. God is helping them; the British would deliver them of the tyrant. And then God would help them get rid of the British afterwards.

But first, the British soldiers would come to the rescue of the British prisoners. Blanc keeps repeating this mantra to himself, to ward off the horrifying images.

Maybe they would get killed, but at least they would be revenged and the honor of the British restored. Every humiliation that Tewodros had imposed upon them would be wiped out. Like the degrading fetters that had made their legs so weak. Was it because the British showed their power that they had been removed? And now they would teach Tewodros that he couldn't get away with impunity with his misdeeds against his visitors from the British Empire. There was justice. And God would help.

The thunder is roaring right over the hut when Blanc thinks he hears another sound. He pulls his *shama* back from his face and listens. Is it echoes of the thunder, or is it…? Could it be? Yes, as the thunder abates, Blanc feels sure it is the volleys of guns and rifles being fired, and which are now rolling up the hill to them from the valley below.

Prideaux, who always sleeps very soundly, wakes up with a start. He looks at Dr. Blanc. They both break into big smiles. They jump up and listen. They embrace each other. What a happy sound! Their rescuers are near. The hour of liberation after their long months of suffering and humiliation and uncertainty is finally approaching. They may still be killed, but the burden of defeat will be lifted from their shoulders whether they were dead or not. Embarrassed, they break off their embrace.

It's not like them to show their emotions like that.

Too excited to sleep, Blanc and Prideaux sit up, each on his primitive cot, and talk in low voices. It is impossible to even pretend to be sleeping under the circumstances. They tell each other about their friends and family at home, how they look forward to seeing them again. Mr. Blanc tells Prideaux that he is thinking of getting married if he makes it back to England. He is not sure to whom, but he invites Prideaux to attend.

"Isn't one supposed to get married?" he laughs.

The shooting and noises outside seem to abate, and the two tired companions finally doze off to an uneasy sleep in their cots close to one another. Just before surrendering to sleep, Blanc realizes that there is no other place in the world he would rather be than right there next to Prideaux.

An eerie quietness has descended on the *amba*. But the peace is short-lived. Samuel soon sticks his head in the doorway. "Quickly, get dressed. The King wants to see you all."

Samuel's brusque tone is hiding something, Blanc realizes. But nothing can be done about it. He and Prideaux tumble out of their beds and put on their uniforms. At least they can dress quickly now they have no chains to contend with. They would dress their best. It was important to look one's best. Dressed in their uniforms, they stop in front of each other. They briefly clasp their hands and look into each other's eyes. In silence. They both know this might be the end, but somehow that is not so important anymore. Then they step out into the daylight.

There is no more time. They have to hurry.

Outside their hut, they meet with Rassam and Cameron and are told to report to Mr. Rassam's hut. The King has sent messengers to the British prisoners to inform them about the battle of Fahla the previous night. In Rassam's hut, the messengers tell how the King's chiefs had been watching a train of baggage through their field glasses and had begged the King for permission to do battle and hopefully conquer great spoils. It looked as if there were only a few British soldiers, by the baggage donkeys and elephants.

The King could not say no, and he had rallied his warriors with a great *fakering* scene abusing the British and exhorting his own past glorious deeds. Then they had fired the mighty Sebastopol, but it burst, because, in their zeal, they had put two cannonballs in it. This was a bad omen for the superstitious King, but the enthusiastic chiefs could no longer be held back, and they had galloped down the mountainside, their colorful silk robes flowing after them.

The British riflemen had been just out of sight right behind the baggage train, and as the brave horsemen approached the British, they had fired their new, effective rifles. Scores of Ethiopians fell. And thus it continued till the few remaining survivors had turned back up the hill. They couldn't even get near the British soldiers (just as Tewodros had warned) and the British had not lost a single man, as far as they knew. As one of the chiefs cried out indignantly: "Of what use is it fighting against your people? When we fight with our countrymen each side has its turn; with you, it is always your turn."

Now the King had acknowledged that he had been defeated by the foreign army and he had sent an imperial message, "I thought that the people that are now coming were women; I now find that they are men. I have been conquered by the advance guard alone. All my musketeers are dead. Reconcile me with your people."

Blanc and the other British felt great happiness and pride swell in their chests, but they were also acutely aware that they were now in greater danger than ever.

Rassam advised the King, through his chiefs, to make peace with the British and obey the demand of Napier to set the prisoners free. The King should send the brave Lieutenant Prideaux and one of the Europeans he trusted—like Mr. Flad or somebody else—with one of his own chiefs to make a settlement.

After Lieutenant Prideaux and Mr. Flad had departed for the British outpost, the other *ferengis* settle down to an anxious wait in their huts. They talk little, and pace up and down in their small space. Would there be a settlement? What would be the next move of the unpredictable King? Should they write a last note to their dear ones? Mr. Blanc thinks of Lieutenant Prideaux in the British camp. What will be King Tewodros's reaction to him and Mr. Flad when they return?

Samuel joins them and tells them about the events of the previous night. How the King had waited for the return of his chiefs. He had called for his closest chief and friend, the brave Fitawrari Gebre. No answer. He called for the next chief. No answer. No answer. They were almost all dead. Dead and gone. Only a few climbed back the long way up the mountain. Upon seeing them, the King had broken down and cried, with his face in his hands.

Engedda had told him to stop acting like a woman.

Finally, Prideaux and Flad returned to the King, who was still seated on his stone, drinking heavily. They hand him the message from Napier that called for the immediate release and safe passage of the prisoners, as well as the surrender of the King. In return, he would be offered honorable treatment. They have to repeat the wording several times to Tewodros. He was thinking for a little and then asked, "What does honorable treatment mean? Does it mean that the English will help me to subdue my enemies, or does it mean honorable treatment as a prisoner?"

Prideaux cannot answer the King's question, but assures him that General Napier is only interested in rescuing the prisoners and has no other motives for being there. As soon as conditions have been met, he will withdraw the British troops.

The King makes no reply, but the *ferengis* perceive that his emotions are in turmoil. He is drinking continually and now turns to his scribe to continue his rambling, rebellious letter to Napier, which is sent back to the General, folded up in Napier's own letter. The *ferengis* are dismissed.

After Lieutenant Prideaux and Mr. Flad had left, the King went into his tent to consult with his remaining chiefs. Samuel later tells Rassam and the others how the chiefs had counseled the King to kill his prisoners and do battle with the British. He should shoot them or better guard the entrance to their huts, put dry wood around them and set fire to them. Burn them alive, as he had done with so many of his Ethiopian opponents.

The proud Engedda was not in doubt as to what course to take, and the chiefs were in accord. But the King had told them that they were fools. He had already killed enough in recent days, and he would only invite the British to make a bloodbath of them all. That might be so, but the chiefs preferred that to womanly behavior. He had jumped up and put one of his revolvers into his mouth, but the shot did not go off, and his chiefs had wrestled him to the ground. And he had calmed down a bit and said that it was God's will he should live.

Now Tewodros returns to his stone in a somber mood, when he suddenly orders Bitwaddad Hassenie and Ras Bissawur to go to Rassam, Blanc and Prideaux to tell them and the others, "Go at once to your people: You will send for your property tomorrow." The King looks ominous, and Hassenie and Bissawur appear downcast.

The prisoners, who know well how to read the faces of their jailers, have their fearful thoughts. But as there is nothing to be done, they quickly change into their uniforms. Their servants bid them farewell with tearful eyes. Samuel looks troubled and says in an excited voice that it is extremely important to stall the King at this moment, to give him time to calm down a bit.

A messenger is sent to the King to ask for a chance for the *ferengis* to bid him farewell before leaving. After some anxious waiting time, the messenger returns and reports that the King is no longer in his tent but down the hill. Another chief arrives to escort Rassam along a different route, because the King wants to say goodbye to his friend. The others are to take a path a little below Rassam's.

The *ferengis* start to ride down the path, headed by Blanc. Blanc turns around to see Prideaux, who is some way behind him. He has to steer his reluctant donkey, and it is not an opportune moment to say anything. The path is very steep, with narrow turns. On the one side, the cliffs rise straight up into the sky, on the other, the escarpment disappears into the empty abyss.

The path is utterly lonely and wild.

As Blanc rounds a sharp curve, he suddenly finds himself face to face with Tewodros. The King's body movements reveal that he is in a great passion. He has turned back, looking over his shoulder, to take a musket handed to him by a warrior behind him. A whole row of the King's riflemen is lined up behind him on a small platform of the narrow cliff. Beyond the cliff is the empty space above the precipice.

King Tewodros directs his fierce, fiery eyes towards Blanc, but at that very instant seems to perceive that it is him. Blanc. Or somebody else?

His eyes soften, and his entire bearing changes into a sorrowful posture. He drops his arm. The King looks right into Blanc's face, as if he is remembering something. Then he asks him, in a low voice, "How are you, my brother? It is my wish that you and the others go back to your people. God be with you."

And he turns his horse around.

Epilogue:

On their way down the hill, Blanc and Prideaux and the other Europeans had been ordered to stop by some of Tewodros' soldiers. For a moment, they thought they were lost, after all. But then they saw one of the King's servants come running towards them, with the swords that had been taken from Prideaux and Blanc some twenty-one months earlier.

Soon after, they had celebrated their joyous reunion with the British, sipping the champagne that Napier had had brought all the arduous way from Massawa to Magdala to mark their liberation. (Blanc and Prideaux clinked their champagne glasses gently together.)

There was no feasting in Tewodros' camp.

The following day, Tewodros had sent a letter of apology for his previous rebellious message. He also sent a new letter, with a gift of a thousand cows, as a peace offering and to celebrate Easter Sunday. When the King learned that his peace offering had not been accepted, he had tried to leave the *amba*, on the side away from the British, with a few faithful followers. But as the King and his party had begun their descent, they noticed the Gallas advancing on all sides. He knew what kind of reception he could expect from those enemies and decided it was better to retreat back to Magdala.

There he rallied with a few remaining chiefs, galloping in circles waving their guns and spears, the wind billowing in their colorful, silken robes.

Meanwhile, his people were streaming down the hill, away from their defeated King. The refugees passed the British troops on their way up to capture the fort. The British did not encounter much resistance, and as they entered the King's compound, King Tewodros shot himself.

His pistol was a present from Queen Victoria, with the inscription *To Theodorus, Emperor of Abyssinia, as a slight token of her gratitude for his kindness to her servant Plowden, 1864.*

Sources:

Acta Ætiopica Vol. II. Tewodros and his Contemporaries 1855–1868. Ed. Sven Rubenson. Lund University Press, 1994.

Percy Arnold. *Prelude to Magdala. Emperor Theodore of Ethiopia and British Diplomacy.* Ed. Richard Pankhurst. Bellew Publishing: London, 1991.

Henry Blanc, *A Narrative of Captivity in Abyssinia.* London, 1868. Reprinted by Frank Cass & Co. Ltd.: London, 1970.

G.A. Henty, *The March to Magdala.* Tinsley Brothers: London, 1868.

Paul B. Henze, *Layers of Time: A History of Ethiopia.* Hurst and Co: London, 2000.

Clemens R. Markham, A *History of the Abyssinian Expedition.* Macmillan and Co.: London, 1869.

Sven Rubenson, *King of Kings.* Oxford University Press: England, 1966.

Quotes: All quotes except for the last one are from Blanc, *A Narrative*:

"I'll teach them to ask for food when my faithful soldiers are starving," p. 388.

"Because I am conversing with a greater and better man than you—the pious King David," p. 20.

"Of what use is it," they said, "fighting against your people ... always your turn?" p. 399.

"I thought that the people ... Reconcile me with your people," p. 392–393.

"What does honorable treatment ... honorable treatment as a prisoner?" p. 397.

"Go at once to your people: You will send for your property tomorrow," p. 400.

"To Theodorus, Emperor of Abyssinia, as a slight token of her gratitude for his kindness to her servant, Plowden, 1864," p. 142, Henze.

Vocabulary and names:

Abeit ◉ This word can be used in two different contexts. It can mean "master" to get the attention of somebody. But it can also be used in distress or sorrow as "alas, alas," or "woe, woe."

Abouna ◉ The head of the Ethiopian Church.

amba ◉ Flat-topped mountain.

baldereba ◉ Intermediary appointed for relations with persons of high rank. They may function as translators as well as spies.

Bell ◉ John Bell (called Johannes by Tewodros) entered Ethiopia in 1842—good friends with Consul Walter Plowden.

Blanc ◉ Henry Blanc, M.D., Staff Assistant-Surgeon in Her Majesty's Bombay Army, published *A Narrative of Captivity in Abyssinia* in England in 1868.

Cameron ◉ Captain Charles Duncan Cameron, appointed consul after Plowden. Reached Massawa February 1862. Mistrusted by King Tewodros after his visit to the Sudan. Also blamed for Queen Victoria failing to answer King Tewodros' letter to her.

daftera ◉ Scribe (not an ordained member of the clergy).

doro wat ◉ Traditional, spicy Ethiopian chicken stew.

faker ◉ Pretend, enact.

Mr. Flad and Mrs. Flad ◉ Belonging to the Djenda Mission, Mr. Flad entered Ethiopia for the first time in 1855.

kosso ◉ Leaves of an Ethiopian tree used as an anthelmintic medicine to treat tapeworms.

messob ◉ *T*all basket used for storing food.

Plowden ◉ Walter Plowden, Britain's first consul in Ethiopia. Well liked in Ethiopia but feared by Tewodros.

Prideaux ◉ Lieutenant W.F. Prideaux of Her Majesty's Bombay Staff Corps.

Rassam ◉ Hormuzd Rassam, first secretary of the British Indian Agency in Aden.

Samuel ◉ Special servant to Dr. Blanc and Lieutenant Prideaux, and go-between the prisoners and the King.

shama ◉ Ethiopian toga-like garment.

Stern ◉ The Reverend Henry Stern arrived in Ethiopia in 1860. Published *Wanderings amongst the Falashas of Abyssinia* while back in England. After returning to Ethiopia, Stern was severely beaten and maltreated by King Tewodros in 1863 for comments about him in Stern's book.

King Tewodros ◉ 1855–1868.

waizero ◉ Mrs., Madame.

tejj ◉ Mead, honey wine.

The Diplomat

WHAT A FANTASTIC OPPORTUNITY FOR A young man! He agreed with his uncle. This was his great chance to see another world, and it would ensure his future career as a diplomat. Pietro's uncle, the highly esteemed Count Pietro Antonelli (after whom Pietro had been named), had just asked Pietro if he would join him on his next mission to Ethiopia. Pietro could be a kind of unofficial escort to his uncle.

If he would join him? Pietro shook with delight as he stretched out in his big mahogany bed and put his hands behind his head. He was too excited to sleep, and lay there dreaming, caressed by the soft air under the rotating fan. Africa! He saw the rugged mountains and the Christian churches carved out of the solid rock. He saw himself galloping on horseback in the wide valleys of that faraway, legendary land—passing women who lowered their gaze bashfully to the ground.

If Pietro would join his uncle? Surely, the uncle had not been in doubt that he would. This was a perfect way to end his stint in the army and learn the ropes of diplomacy from a professional, who happened to be his relative. Pietro thought of his friends Giovanni and Marco, who were studying medicine and law. Not to forget Antonio, who was already amassing his fortune as a businessman. Now Pietro would make something of himself too. He smiled in the dark.

He imagined himself returning to Italy as a well-known diplomat.

Yes, Pietro would join his uncle's mission. Now he could be right where things were happening, where history was being written at this very moment. Pietro could become part of it. He would learn quickly, and maybe there was a role for him to play?

All that was needed was clever diplomacy.

A streak of light came through the heavy curtains from the street lamps.

Lucia would be proud of him. But what about Lucia? He would have to leave her behind, and worse, they would have to postpone their wedding. Depending on how long he stayed out there. If only Lucia was not too upset. His sweet Lucia, she would support him. She always did. She would wait for him, and then they would have a splendid marriage.

But for now, Pietro would have to sacrifice his personal happiness for the importance of his career.

The next day Antonelli informed his nephew and his brother's family that he would be leaving in two days, on the first of February, 1889, as he would have to reach Wuchale in Ethiopia by early May for the signing of the important Wuchale treaty. They would be sailing from Naples through the Suez Canal and the Red Sea to the port of Massawa. From there they would be going inland by donkey.

Things happened so fast that Pietro barely had time to think. And that was how he wanted it. He got busy packing his clothes and saying goodbye to his friends and family. His fiancée, Contessa Lucia, came for the goodbye-dinner, and after the meal they sat out on the family balcony, hand in hand, discussing their future to the monotonous stridulating of the Roman cicadas. Lucia sat with a sweet smile on her pale face, framed by her dark wavy hair. She looked like an angel, and she had accepted Pietro's decision, just as he had expected. She would wait for him.

"Eternally," she added with a dreamy smile.

Sitting on his deck chair on the steamer on its way towards the Suez Canal, Pietro had lots of time to think of the balmy Roman nights he had spent on their balcony in the company of his uncle, Antonelli. How he used to sit with Lucia's hand in his, secretly under the tablecloth, while his uncle and father discussed world politics, puffing on their after-dinner pipes, and his mother gave orders to their maid, who was serving coffee.

Antonelli had told his raptured listeners about Ethiopia, how it really consisted of autonomous states that were competing for power. The two main rivals were Yohannes in the north, who was considered King of Ethiopia, and Menelik to the south, in the state of Shewa. Italy was putting its bets on Menelik. Antonelli had been to Shewa several times and explained how he had worked on trade relations between Italy and Shewa. He had signed an important trading treaty already, on 21 May in 1883. Italy had sold a lot of guns to Menelik. Those rifles made the Ethiopians very keen to please the Italians.

Pietro remembered that he had asked whether the King had not paid for the guns. He had, the uncle confirmed, but as a diplomat, you tried to wrest as much advantage as possible out of the situation. Worth paying attention to. Pietro had nodded and caressed Lucia's soft hand under the tablecloth.

But Antonelli's diplomatic career had had its ups and downs. It had been difficult for him when Italy veered from the diplomatic route he had envisioned. Just after he had been named the head of a mission from King Menelik to Rome (a mission where he felt he could obtain a lot of advantages for Italy), the Italians proceeded to occupy Massawa on the Red Sea Coast. Incensed, the Ethiopians had canceled the mission, and Antonelli and the other Italians had had a hard time convincing the Ethiopians of the good intentions of Italy.

When the Italians had gone further inland with their troops, the Ethiopian Emperor, King Yohannes, had demanded that Menelik expel his Italian visitors from Shewa. But Antonelli had persuaded Menelik to make an exception for him because of his long and ardent service to the Shewan king since he first arrived in 1878.

Thanks to his superior diplomatic skills, he had managed to stay. He had nodded to Pietro.

But more entertaining than trade were all the stories about the people and the life there in Shewa. Pietro and his family especially liked to hear about the royal couple, King Menelik and his Queen, Taitu. Antonelli himself was fascinated by the Queen. It was not until his third trip to Shewa that he met the Queen for the first time in Boru Meda.

On that occasion Antonelli had presented Taitu with some Italian hair tonic. The attractive Queen had been pleased to replace the Ethiopian rancid butter with this pleasant-smelling and luxurious foreign water. Taitu had asked about King Umberto's wife, Marguerita. He had told her how Marguerita was pious and charitable, neglecting, diplomatically, to say that she was also bigoted, xenophobic and despotic.

Pietro and his mother had laughed.

They already seemed so unreal, those Roman nights on the balcony when Pietro had learned the outlines of Italian diplomacy in Ethiopia. Antonelli had explained how Menelik aspired to become the King of King—the sole ruler of Ethiopia—and how he needed Italian support for this endeavor. The King would give concessions to the Italians if they would keep Yohannes busy in the north while he expanded his kingdom in the east (Harar was his immediate goal) and the south. The land bordering on the Red Sea was of less immediate concern to him, and he couldn't confront both Yohannes and the Italians till he had consolidated his own power.

King Menelik understood *Divide et impera*, his uncle said with a laugh.

But the Italian military was not patient enough to wait for Antonelli's diplomatic machinations, going on to occupy the town of Adwa. Uncle Antonelli went on to explain the complicated events between the Italians and the Ethiopians: attacks, counterattacks, hostage-taking and finally the infamous massacre at Dogali, where Ras Alula had killed 550 Italian soldiers. Emperor Yohannes had called the incident *the work of the devil*, but no Italian could be in doubt as to how the Ethiopians felt. Antonelli knew; he had been there when the Ethiopians feasted and celebrated the Italian defeat. Antonelli shuddered at the memory.

Yes, it was not always easy to be a diplomat.

The balcony evenings usually ended with Pietro's father and Antonelli having a small goodnight glass of *grappa*. The very last night, Pietro had some too and felt quite tipsy when Antonelli had raised his glass to congratulate Pietro on his decision to join him on his return to Ethiopia, at such short notice. The houses across from the balcony were swaying, blurrily, as he listened to his uncle declaring that his nephew wouldn't regret their joint venture, to their common benefit and that of Italy.

Pietro celebrated his twenty-fourth birthday in Massawa, although he didn't feel there was much to celebrate in that *infernal cauldron* of heat, as he wrote in the diary he had begun for lack of better things to do. He already did regret it.

The morning of the second day in Massawa, they also learned the latest news from the country of their destination. Yohannes had been mortally wounded in a fight against the intruding Mahdists from Sudan. He had died the next day, after proclaiming his son, Mengesha Yohannes, his successor.

This was indeed great news, and Antonelli didn't take long to expound upon the new perspectives opening up for King Menelik (and the Italians). The road would now be clear for Menelik to become emperor over the entire land, if he played his cards well. The young Mengesha Yohannes would not be strong enough to oppose him. And the Italians would help Menelik in return for other favors. Antonelli nodded, portentously.

Tossing and turning in his hot berth, after a day of such diplomacy talk, Pietro would re-experience the droning of his uncle's voice. Diplomacy, as his uncle had explained it, was the skill of explaining one's views (or those of one's country) in such a manner that your opponent ended by believing that those views were their own original views—or at least preferable to their own original views—or views that....

Pietro had finally fallen asleep.

Finally, they left the cauldron, on their heavily packed donkeys. After some weeks of traveling, first up the steep, dusty paths and then through rocky gorges and the highlands, the travelers spotted King Menelik's camp of tents at the village of Wuchale. Already, the next day, they were led to meet the King himself. The many cases of rifles had been unloaded from the donkeys and were now presented to the King.

Pietro watched his busybody uncle scurry around the rather bulky King, showing him this rifle and that. Pietro later described his uncle as *slight* next to the stout King, for whom Pietro felt an immediate sympathy.

The next day, Menelik signed the treaty of Wuchale as *King of Kings of Ethiopia*, even though he had not yet been crowned. In this treaty, the land between the coast and Asmara, which for the first time was designated Eritrea, was turned over to Italy. Pietro was surprised when the full extent of the treaty dawned on him. But as Antonelli explained, Menilik could not control these northern areas on his own, so it was better that Italy help him. In return, he could now become the Emperor of the rest of Ethiopia.

Pietro felt a little nonplussed, but he was proud on behalf of Italy. Now his country was a world power to be reckoned with, he confided to his diary.

The busy Antonelli had to return to Italy shortly, and it was agreed that Pietro would stay with the Italian compatriots, who had made their homes in the country. He also had the possibility of living with a Swiss engineer by name of Alfred Ilg, whom Pietro had taken a liking to.

The day before he left, Antonelli and Pietro were sitting on their little verandah under the flowering bougainvillea. A house servant had just served their coffee when Pietro saw Antonelli's Ethiopian mistress for the first time. Pietro had just asked his uncle what this story about Article XVII in the Wuchale treaty was really all about. The uncle had explained how there was a translation problem, where the Amharic version said, "Ethiopia may use the good offices of Italy in foreign affairs." However, the Italian version stated, "Ethiopia consents to use Italy as its representative with foreign Governments." It really was just a question of words, the uncle concluded.

"Why don't you just change the Italian word to fit with the Amharic one?" The uncle threw a surprised glance at his nephew.

"But you do understand, we want Ethiopia to become a protectorate of ours? They will resist if we put this in Amharic. But if we can make them sign the Italian one, they will not be aware of what they signed."

The uncle paused, "When they learn, it will be a *fait accompli*, and then it is too late to protest. Then, hopefully, they will acquiesce."

"But that's outright treacherous!" Pietro exclaimed.

"Treacherous, traitor. Those are just words. In diplomacy, you play the diplomatic game. You need to outwit your opponent to win."

"I honestly don't understand."

"I know, you don't. But I think you'll learn."

That was the moment Desela entered through the low gateway, holding two little girls by the hand. She was tall, and the most strikingly beautiful woman Pietro had ever seen. She appeared both slender and voluptuous, youthful and mature, mistress and mother at the same time. She seemed everything—not just angelic, like Lucia. Her presence overwhelmed Pietro.

He looked down. But as she came closer, he saw how young she really was and he realized that she might even be younger than he was. (How could she *belong* to Antonelli, who was in his forties? Pietro later wondered in his diary.) He had jumped up, so his little stool turned over, spilling his coffee into the dusty ground. Antonelli got up too, and walked towards the young woman with open arms. The two little girls hid behind their mother and poked their little heads out, to peek shyly at their father. Desela looked down, with a faint smile. A small braid fell over her olive face.

At that first meeting, Pietro vowed to himself to learn Desela's language faster than he had learnt his own mother tongue. Pietro had seen many pretty women in Rome, but this beauty was different. She seemed so real. Her physical presence so overpowered Pietro that he could no longer look at her, but sat staring down at the cobbled stones under her sandaled feet and listened to her exchanging commonplaces with his uncle. Pietro would have remained perfectly satisfied in this state had not the uncle suggested that Pietro take the two little girls to their grandparents, while Desela stayed with him. The girls knew their way home.

Pietro felt he had just been delivered the sentence of death. Reluctantly, he rose and left with the girls, without looking at Desela.

Shortly after this meeting, Antonelli left, and Pietro preferred to stay in his hut rather than with the other Italians. Only the Swiss engineer,

Alfred Ilg, could entice him to a visit. He had a charming house with a real wooden floor and two lively sons. Ilg worked for King Menelik and had built a wooden bridge over the Awash river for the King's troops to cross on their way to conquer Harar. Ilg was full of plans and projects. He was working on a railway plan from Djibouti to Addis, telegraph lines, and water pipes in the King's palace. His bridge had later collapsed but it was going to be rebuilt in iron. Maybe Pietro could help with that and other projects?

Pietro spent more and more time with the handsome fair-bearded Ilg, who helped Pietro learn Amharic and whose competence and energy inspired him. He was the *ferengi* most favored by the King. Ever since Ilg had asked the King why he had allowed the Italians to enter the door of his house at Asmara, the King had trusted Ilg.

Ilg wasn't just talk—he was about real things, like technical innovations. Pietro found Ilg a lot more interesting than his uncle. Ilg had recently brought a telephone to show to King Menelik, who was very fond of technical gadgets. But then the priests had mumbled that it was *unnatural*. It was even worse when he showed the King the lightning rod he had brought back from Switzerland. That was the pure *work of the devil*, according to the superstitious clergymen. Ilg had had to remove it quickly, as if the lightning had already struck. And he had roared with laughter.

Ilg's lively company helped distract Pietro from what was becoming an obsessive passion after that fatal meeting with Desela. He could not believe that this gorgeous young woman had simply been given to Antonelli for his pleasure while he was in the country, as he wrote in his diary. He kept pondering over the arrangement, but as he wrote, it was his impression that this beautiful daughter of poor parents probably counted herself lucky to be the mistress of such a prominent *ferengi*. Pietro knew this was a customary matter, but he didn't like the thought.

He was writing and he was writing. If only he could show them. Yes, what could he show them? That was the problem, he admitted.

Ilg had introduced Pietro to some ladies for pleasure and Pietro had not turned them down. He had eased his physical needs in the same manner in Rome. He had not felt guilty towards Lucia—that didn't interfere with his feelings for his angelic Lucia. But with Desela it felt wrong. It became clear to him that it was Desela, he desired, and not the other women—however attractive. He would try to get some advice from Ilg about it at some opportune moment.

Ilg also had a mistress and two sons.

The Conquering Lion of the Tribe of Judah, Menelik II, elect of God, King of Kings of Ethiopia, informed the heads of states of his recent coronation: "By the will of God, through the love of the people, the celebration of my coronation was accomplished on 3 November 1889. I hope by the grace of God and with the assistance of my friends to defeat my enemies and, in uniting Ethiopia, to make it a strong nation."

The big coronation of the King and the Queen was like a fairy-tale turned into real life. Pietro watched the King on his official dais after the coronation inside the Entoto Church. He was literally radiant as his slippers, sword, scepter and crown made of gold reflected the strong rays of the sun. There he sat, lavishly distributing gifts to his grateful subjects. Then the clerics had danced their swinging, elegant slow dance round and round to the sound of the tambourine and sistrum. Spectators prostrated themselves, canons were fired and torches flared in the night. Thousands of heads of cattle and sheep were slaughtered to feed over ten thousand guests, who were treated in the big tents with long tables and benches.

Pietro was there and experienced it all. It was history, but history played out in real life with real people. They felt like his new family. To Pietro, it was almost as if Menelik and Taitu were father and mother to him. He watched them wheel and deal with the diplomats and their own subjects. He observed Menelik's many mistresses, he listened to Taitu's down-to-earth handling of her subjects. Her strong voice threatening them, encouraging them—whatever the situation demanded. Pietro admitted to his diary how he admired the strong woman.

Ever since that fatal meeting with Desela, life had become very intense for Pietro: the rain felt icy cold, and the sun burning hot, and the smell of the jasmine intoxicating. But most of all he was longing to stroke his hands down the smooth skin of Desela's back. He would dig in his hands, his face, into that beautiful body of hers. He imagined it was Desela, when he made love to the occasional mistress—with his eyes closed.

One weekend Pietro went with another Italian diplomat, Salimbeni, to visit a Dr. Traversi in his charming farm, Let-Marefia. There on the farm, surrounded by greenery and yellow fields, the two lively Italians cultivated their Ethiopian mistresses.

Both Salimbeni and Traversi had Ethiopian mistresses and children. Those *ferengis* seemed to live a second life here in Ethiopia, completely separate from their existence in Italy, where they all also had wives and children. Pietro later enumerated those Italian-Ethiopian children in his diary: "Ilg has two sons, Dr. Traversi a daughter, Antoine Bremont a son, Dubois eight sons—that's not mentioning Antonelli's two daughters (which Pietro would rather not). The country was teeming with foreign bastards, while Taitu could not produce an heir. Life wasn't always what you wished for. Pietro was more aware of that now.

So for the moment Pietro was just watching those men, so happy and free with their Ethiopian women and children, when Desela entered with her two girls. She had been invited by Salimbeni and greeted the two men and their wives and children with what seemed to Pietro very natural and subdued manners. She appeared familiar and comfortable with them all.

Pietro experienced an acute shortness of breath till he realized that he should just keep breathing. It was still too overwhelming to look directly at Desela, so he decided to address himself to her two young daughters instead. They giggled a little, but he succeeded in enticing them over to him and engaging them in some conversation. He pulled out his drawing pad and began to draw for them. Horses. Elephants. St. George and the dragon. Angels.

He felt how Desela threw a quick glance at him. It seemed to be the first time she had perceived his presence. A little later, when he moved further away in the room with her girls, he felt her dark eyes resting on him. It felt like a caress to him.

Later on, he wrote in his diary: how "He knew. Yes, but what did he know? Everything. But what could he do?"

Then Antonelli came back.

Pietro traveled to meet Antonelli at Meqelle, where his uncle had returned with the Mekonen delegation from Rome to report to the King. Article XVII was not being discussed publicly. But the questions of the border issues were very much on everybody's mind. Ethiopians had fought and bled to keep their borders, and now Mekonen and others were giving away their land to the Italians. As people said, the negotiators must have been paid to betray their country after "stuffing themselves with rich food and good wine."

But Menelik was satisfied. He enjoyed the submissions of the Tigrayan leaders on 23 February, 1890, and was told that Megesha Yohannes' would follow in twenty days.

Pietro was present at the audiences, and thanks to his Amharic lessons with Ilg, he could understand much of the conversation between the King and the returning delegation. The King's trusted nephew, Mekonen, who had led the delegation to Rome, was just explaining how he had signed an additional treaty to the Wuchale one. It stipulated that the borders of the Italian territory were to be fixed as of their de facto position on that day. The Italians were simply quietly in the process of invading Ethiopian territory. Pietro now saw the Italian policies clearly: their two-pronged drives. One was to expand the Eritrean border as much as possible; the other was to turn the rest of Ethiopia into a protectorate. Weren't the Italians a little greedy?

Pietro noticed how uncomfortable Antonelli appeared. His uncle later whispered to Pietro about the recent advances of the Italians, which the signatories had been unaware of. Fortunately, Menelik didn't seem to be paying much attention at this very moment. He had had a long day. He had relished his submissions—a sign of his growing power as emperor—and was now enjoying himself drinking *tejj* and eyeing a new bedmate for the night.

Both Antonelli and Pietro were tired after a long day and their recent travels. They were just sitting, making small talk, pretending to drink more of the *tejj* and waiting for the moment they could leave for bed without offending anybody. (A couple of letters from Lucia and his father were burning in Pietro's coat pockets.)

Just as Antonelli was rising to sneak out, with a glance to Pietro, Mekonen came towards Antonelli and sat down next to him. Mekonen told Antonelli that an Ethiopian who was studying in Rome, by the name of Afewerq Gebre Iyesus, had come up to him and told him about something, he had read in an Italian newspaper. The newspaper article had claimed that Ethiopia had become a protectorate of Italy.

"Had Antonelli heard any such thing?"

"Why hadn't he told him about this before?" Mekonen did not answer; he just sat there with a worried expression.

"What nonsense!" By the way, Antonelli had met this young man. "Not very proficient in Italian. He was just a troublemaker. Trying to seem important interfering in political issues. He hadn't understood. He had just misread the situation. It was just a problem of translation." He threw a glance at Pietro. Mekonen should not pay attention to such an ignorant, meddling person.

By now, Pietro pretended not to be listening. He felt too embarrassed to want to seem part of these ongoing insinuations. This so-called diplomacy.

Antonelli had traveled back to Addis, but Pietro stayed behind to help Dr. Traversi treat the many patients. Menelik's soldiers were starved and emaciated after their campaign in Tigray. The poor, barren Tigray could not sustain an army, and the soldiers were now catching all kinds of diseases and dying like flies. This was the first time Pietro saw human suffering that was not just the headlines in a newspaper. He tried to put food into the mouths of emaciated children too weak to swallow. He dressed the wounds on oozing open sores. He carried the skeletons of the dead out of the hospital tent to be buried. Pietro touched and smelled the suffering people and when he was stricken with diarrhea himself, he became one of them.

But with his strong constitution, Pietro soon overcame his illness, and he accompanied Dr. Traversi to Taitu's camp in Desse. There, the nursing of the sick and dying continued till Taitu decided that enough was enough and now it was time to celebrate the many submissions to Menelik. There was death and suffering in Ethiopia, but in honor of life, there should also be extravagant banquets and celebrations.

No effort was spared in preparing the banquet, and before anybody knew, the dinner was in full progress. The plates were heaped, the *tejj* was flowing, and the music played. The Emperor and Empress looked splendid in their imported silks. Taitu looked every bit the match for her royal husband. Her round face was illuminated by her intelligent gaze and the resolute expression round her mouth spoke of a person of action. She was not just for ornament.

They were laughing over a joke by Taitu's brother, Wele, describing her resolute handling of the danger that his family had been in while he was away with Menelik, when an Ethiopian man came running into the tent. He ran right past the guards. He took them completely by surprise. (It was something they would pay for later.)

"Stop that man!" a guest near the door shouted.

"Stop that man!" the other guests shouted.

"How dare you enter with shoes on?"

The guards had now caught up with him and grabbed him. He prostrated himself.

"His Highness, Emperor Menelik, I have something important to tell you."

Menelik stopped chewing a big mouthful that he had just put in his mouth with his right hand.

"Take that man out," he said crossly.

"Wait," said Taitu, getting up as she wiped her mouth. "I will hear what that man has to say. It must be important if he dared enter our tent like that."

The man was led to the doorway, with the guards still holding on to him, and Taitu came up close to him. To Pietro, it was just like a river of words. She stood attentively and listened. Then she turned around.

"Will all the men of Tigray and Gondar rise—we are going to fight the Italians." Men around the tables began to stand up, but her brother, Wele, was still sitting. (Maybe he was thinking that Taitu had acted too much like a man?)

Then Taitu addressed him: "Here, you take my skirt, and I will wear your trousers."

Pietro had watched the whole scene with mouth agape. He so forgot himself that he had almost stood up with the other men, but in the stillness after Taitu's words, he had taken his side.

Pietro returned to Addis, where he became busy working on the plans for water pipes in the royal palace with his friend Ilg. When not working, Pietro sought an opportunity to talk seriously to his uncle, even though he doubted that talking would change anything. Antonelli was clearly stressed. He had told Pietro about Prime Minister Crispi's speech, delivered in Torino on 18 November, 1890. "Italy," he had said, "needed land on which to settle her excess population, and soldiers must go to protect these people." How much more blunt than that could it become?

Although Antonelli agreed with the reality of this statement, it did not fit with his diplomacy. Pietro began to feel sorry for his uncle. He was caught in these contradictions between words and reality. Pietro had less and less faith in diplomacy, as he wrote in his diary. In fact, he had almost given up keeping a diary. His entries became fewer and shorter. "Why doesn't my uncle?" What could he say?" "Saw Desela the other day." What else to say? Words were powerless.

This was not so at the Ethiopian court, where the wording of Article XVII was to be played out with great effect. The Italian version had reached the ears of other European sovereigns, as demonstrated by a letter Antonelli had just handed to Menelik and which had made Menelik laugh because of its flowers and ornaments. (Typical of a woman!) Well, the contents were not flowers to the Emperor's ears, when Queen Victoria referred—eloquently—to the new status of Ethiopia as a protectorate of Italy.

Menelik blew up.

Taitu lost her temper.

What had long been a suspicion had come out in the open. The world had been given to understand that Ethiopia was a protectorate of Italy.

No mere translation error but a political fact, although Antonelli kept blaming Yosef Neguse for *the mistranslation*. The imperial couple didn't buy that. What interest could the competent and experienced Yosef have in such a mistake?

Antonelli's part in this only Antonelli knew, but Menelik and Taitu were not in doubt about his complicity. And Pietro could do nothing but keep quiet.

The letter from King Umberto to Menelik wasn't too convincing either. The King claimed that it was only because Menelik had failed to secure Tigray that the Italians had had to guarantee the peace of the land. Concerning Article XVII, Mekonen supposedly had agreed to the necessity of Italy upholding Ethiopian rights in Europe. The letter ended with, "Have a little faith in us."

Exactly what the Ethiopians did not have.

So, the wrangling over Article XVII and the borders continued. Patient talk was interrupted by angry shouting. Menelik vacillated between his hard attitude (abolish Article XVII) to a mediating stance (no other country would be allowed to protect Ethiopia) to the weakest position (keep the wording of the two versions without change for the next five years.)

Taitu became exasperated, calling Menelik weak and stupid, warning him about the reputation he would leave for history. "What will history say of you?" When Menelik answered her, she sometimes grew even angrier, and once resorted to turning her fleshiest part towards him in contempt. (This extreme behavior was also prompted by the intrusion of pretty maids in the already explosive domestic sphere.)

Ilg repeated to Pietro that these treaties meant nothing. The Ethiopians would tear them to pieces any time it suited them. So why all the hullabaloo? But the impasse went on and on, with Antonelli caught in the middle. Sympathies, which tended to develop through social evenings with food and drinking and games, were undermined at the negotiation table the following morning. Everybody's wits were challenged to their utmost; everybody's mental state was stretched to the breaking point.

Taitu, as usual, summed up the core of the problem. "You want other countries to see Ethiopia as your protégé, but that will never be. *Imshi.*"

During this turbulent period, Pietro finally succeeded in having Antonelli to himself in their hut after dinner one night. He brought his uncle his favorite pipe and sat down in front of him.

"So, what do you think of the Italian position, uncle? Really."

"What exactly do you mean, Pietro?"

"What is Italy's aim? Not about the wording of Article XVII. But Italy's goals behind all the words and maneuvers."

"Well, I really can't tell you. With General Orero at Adwa, I am not sure. I believed we would have Eritrea, but maybe we are going for more?"

"But don't you think that is wrong? Italy is simply robbing the land from Ethiopia." (And its prettiest women, he thought to himself). Pietro's voice was tense.

"Well, Pietro, that's the realities of the world: the stronger takes from the weaker. If you want something, you've got to take it. You're not going to get it for the sake of your pretty brown eyes."

"But can you personally agree to this policy is what I am asking, I guess."

"Well, Italy is my country. If Italy wins, I win with it."

"But in this case, it will come to a break between our countries. What will you do then? You will have to leave Ethiopia." Pietro's voice sounded uncertain.

"Yes, sadly, I will."

"How exactly do you mean?"

"Pietro, to tell you the truth…. We have been together for so long now that I feel I can do so." Antonelli placed his pipe on the ashtray.

"I love it here in Ethiopia. Except for that damned Article XVII. I feel a peace here, a tranquility I cannot have in Italy. And you have met Desela and my two daughters. Isn't she a magnificent young woman?

Between the two of us, I prefer her to my wife's company." Antonelli was almost whispering now. Pietro had to lean forward to hear him.

Then he seemed to try to distance himself from this intimate revelation, and he continued in a stronger voice, "There is nothing I would rather do than buy a big plot of land and settle with my Ethiopian family. Cultivate my land, write a few books. Give up diplomacy."

He sighed. "That damned Article XVII."

Pietro looked down. He sat quietly for a while, "But could you not take Desela back to Italy?"

"That is out of the question. That would create a scandal—I have my Italian family. My children, as you know are grown up, but my wife is alone. And can you imagine what the rest of the family will say?"

"I guess you have to make a choice in life," Pietro said hesitatingly.

"Well, till now, I could have two lives, but that may be over with soon. It looks like it could be over soon."

"But what about Desela?" Pietro couldn't help asking.

The uncle threw a quick glance at his nephew, "I will secure her as best I can."

He straightened up, "but I do worry about them…. Enough of that. You'll surely be going home soon, whatever happens with Ethiopia. I know somebody who will be very happy to have you back." He patted Pietro on the back.

Pietro looked at his folded hands. "Of course," he said quietly. He would have liked to say more, but he didn't know how to, and his uncle seemed ready to retire.

Pietro was no longer writing his diary. He was tired of moaning about Desela to himself. He no longer believed in all those words. Life was concrete: it happened through action. He was through with being a diplomat, even if he had not succeeded in telling his uncle. He felt very content working with Ilg on the water pipes and the railroad plans. These were things that would make a difference in Ethiopia—not all that talk and talk. As Ilg had said, the Ethiopians would just tear those documents to pieces.

The Italians' diplomacy was on a fast downward-spiraling course. Antonelli made a last, half-hearted attempt, with two final letters to the Emperor and the Empress not to break the peace after they had all worked so hard for it. His concluding reasoning for Italy's actions was that they didn't want Ethiopia to fall into the hands of France and England. He also finally submitted Italy's recall of Salimbeni to the imperial couple. And while he was at it, he added his own resignation to that of Salimbeni's, with his complaint that the Emperor had shown no confidence in him.

However, the Emperor shared the disappointment of the two *ferengis*. He also thought that much work and effort would go to naught. He also felt the impending loss of the friendships that had grown behind their respective official roles. After some hesitation, Menelik therefore offered to accept the last proposals from Antonelli. The Ethiopians would write up the treaty again.

On this sudden reversal, the Italians withdrew their letters of recall and Antonelli finally set down to draft a host of letters.

Everybody was cheered by this unexpected but welcome turn of events. Everybody wanted a happy outcome. After all, these matters were not only personal (Antonelli even made up with Yosef); they were international questions that could lead to cooperation or enmity—peace or war between two nations.

Antonelli signed the document, and the Empress smiled benevolently.

All that needed to be done at this point was to make a translation of Menelik's agreement, which till now only existed in Amharic.

Two days passed, and the new translator, Gabriel Gobena, hadn't turned up to do the job. Nobody knew why. Was he sick? Salimbeni and Pietro decided to go ahead, and sat down to work, placing an assortment of dictionaries in front of them.

Peace reigned in the little room.

Antonelli was smoking his pipe in his Turkish chair.

"What is this word?" Salimbeni wrinkled his brow as he puffed on his pipe. Pietro turned the leaves in the dictionary. "There it is, *cassare*. *Cassare* it means."

Salimbeni jumped up. "Death and damnation! What the devil? They have tricked us. And you have signed."

He looked down at Antonelli, who had dropped his pipe.

"But they only did what you...." Pietro could not finish his sentence before his uncle jumped up with a snarl, throwing him a swift glance of anger.

Salimbeni and Antonelli rushed towards the throne room, where they knew a banquet was taking place. Pietro followed them not because he was asked to and not because he shared their emotions. In fact, he couldn't help smiling to himself. He knew Antonelli wouldn't see that smile as he stormed ahead of him.

They sent a messenger in with a note of urgency to Ras Makonen. They were told to wait till the meal was over. They could join the dinner party at the coffee ceremony. As if they were in the mood to attend a coffee ceremony. The audacity! One thing was that the Italians had tried to trick the Ethiopians—but that the Ethiopians dared....

No more ceremonies with them.

Finally, they were shown inside, and Count Antonelli rushed up in front of the Emperor. Ras Mekonen told Antonelli to show the treaty to the Emperor. Antonelli lifted the paper into the air and in a dramatic gesture, tore off his signature.

Ras Mekonen watched, horrified, as this caused the Emperor's seal to fall off. Antonelli shouted that he had been tricked.

The Emperor maintained that he had put what they had agreed upon.

The Empress smiled and held out the Amharic version of the Treaty of Wuchale. She asked Antonelli in her sweetest voice to point out the words that said that Ethiopia was under Italian protection. As it was the Amharic version she was waving in front of Antonelli, he would have to consider her inquiry a purely rhetorical question.

Pietro looked at his uncle as he stood there, facing the glum Emperor and the smiling Empress.

He could see how waves of anger at having been tricked shot through his impeccably dressed body. Pietro feared the worst, as he knew how hot-tempered his uncle could be. Pietro could read the expressions of his uncle, how he tried to calm down, before his anger got the better of him. Pietro had the feeling his uncle was going to regret what he couldn't help himself from saying.

Antonelli straightened his slender body, put on a most diplomatic expression and spoke eloquently about the customs of civilized countries, where certain rules and conventions were upheld. He began to speak faster and faster and ended with "Italy would not make any concessions in financial matters. On the contrary." (There goes my uncle's long years of diplomatic work, Pietro thought); " … and Italy will remain at the Mereb river…." (There goes his friendship with these feisty, wonderful people). His uncle topped off his jeremiad with the final threat that "the Italians would uphold Article XVII…." (and there goes Desela and his two daughters—his future and happiness in Ethiopia).

"*Gidyelem* (so be it)," said the Emperor.

Pietro felt sorry for his uncle. It was as if he had watched the end of a Greek drama.

Strange, but he felt relieved.

Two days later, early in the morning, Antonelli came out to the two, saddled donkeys. He was going to meet with his nephew to begin their long trip back to Djibouti. At that moment, Dr. Traversi and Salimbeni, who were to travel with them, came around the corner on their mules. Traversi had three letters in his hand, which he handed to Antonelli.

"Pietro is not joining us. I was informed by his servant this very morning. He has already left on an elephant hunt with Ilg." Traversi handed the three letters to Antonelli, who was too shocked to say a word. One letter was addressed to Pietro's father and one to Contessa Lucia. Both were sealed. The third one was for Antonelli. He tore it open with shaking hands and read:

My dear uncle,

I am sorry to have to disappoint you and I do want to thank you for all that you have done for me. But as you may have already discerned, I no longer believe in diplomacy or the diplomatic career. I have been struggling with this matter for a long time. It was your little 'speech' to the imperial couple that suddenly made it clear to me what I did not want to be—what I did not want to miss.

My life is what is important to me. And I want only one—not two.

I will stay in Ethiopia. I have already signed some private contracts with Alfred Ilg. He will furthermore get permission from Emperor Mene-lik for me to stay in this beautiful country.

As for Desela and her daughters, remain assured....

"Death and damnation!" Antonelli crumpled the letter in a fit of rage and threw it on the dirt road.

"The traitor!" he shouted.

Epilogue:

The failure of the negotiations between Italy and Ethiopia finally led to open war between the two powers in 1896, and the famous (or infamous—depending on the viewpoint) battle of Adwa, where the Italians were defeated and routed by the Ethiopians.

Sources:

Paul B. Henze, *Layers of Time*. Hurst & Company: London, 2000.

Harold G. Marcus, *The Life and Times of Menelik II: Ethiopia 1844–1913*. Clarendon Press: Oxford, 1975.

Chris Prouty, *Empress Taytu and Menelik II. Ethiopia 1883–1910*. Ravens Educational & Development Services: London, 1986.

Sven Rubenson, *The Survival of Ethiopian Independence*. Heinemann: London, 1976.

Quotes:

"By the will ... strong nation" p. 117, Marcus.

" ... stuffing themselves ... wine" p. 71, Prouty.

"Will all the men ... Italians" and "here, you ... trousers" p. 71, Prouty.

"Italy ... people" p. 87, Prouty.

"You want ... never be" p. 92, Prouty.

"He topped that with the ultimatum that Italy would remain at the Mereb river, defend Article 17 and make no concessions in financial matters. 'Gidyelem (so be it),' said the emperor," p. 96, Prouty.

Vocabulary and names:

cassare ◉ Italian for break, cancel or abrogate.

enjera ◉ Pancake-like sourdough bread.

Dogali ◉ The place where Ras Alula ambushed and massacred a 550-man column of Italians in 1887.

filweha ◉ Boiling water from the hot springs in Finfine.

Imshi ◉ It will never be.

messob ◉ Tall basket to put food on.

Massala ◉ Red Sea town.

Mekonen ◉ Diplomat and relative of Menelik.

Salimbeni ◉ Ambassador of Italy.

sistrum ◉ Old stringed instrument.

tejj ◉ A kind of mead.

The Emperor

When one rules over men in righteousness,
when he rules in the fear of God,
he is like the light of morning at sunrise
on a cloudless morning,
like the brightness after rain
that brings the grass from the earth
     —2 Samuel 23

THE CONSTANT DOWNPOUR STOPPED A FEW days ago. Momentarily, the sun peeks through a little blue hole between the massive layers of cloud formations. Then it doesn't rain for a whole day, and the sun glances through bigger and bigger holes in the gray and white sky. The spaces grow larger between the dissolving clouds, which finally fade into the horizon. Meeting no further opposition, the hot African sun is again the undisputed ruler.

On the ground, the overflowing rivers shrink into their normal beds. The roads, torrents of muddy water and rolling stones, turn into soft mud, kneaded into patterns by human feet and by donkeys' hooves. The patterns are baked hard and finally pressed flat by daily usage. The roads, primitive though they are, can be traveled again. Ethiopia's natural protector, the big rains, have left the scene, and the country lies open, once again vulnerable to foreign invasions. Much as the Ethiopians dislike the pummeling rain, which wets their feet and confines them to their dripping huts, it is that same solid rain that waters their fields and shields them from scheming invaders.

The Emperor, Haile Selassie, is acutely aware of this fact. His brow furrows as he is driven up the hill to his Sunday service. Day and night, awake or asleep, he is preoccupied by his diplomatic battle in the League of Nations against Italy's plans to invade Ethiopia. It has been a race against time ever since the Wal Wal incident in November last year. If only he could delay the Italian invasion until the onset of the next rainy season.

On the short walk from his imperial Rolls-Royce to the steps of St. George's Cathedral, Haile Selassie finally notices the glorious spring day. Today is the celebration of Mascal, commemorating the discovery of the True Cross as well as the end of the rainy season.

Haile Selassie looks up at the Italian Renaissance facade of the Ethiopian octagonal church. The architecture of the church, built by Italian prisoners-of-war for Menelik II, reflects the history of the two cultures. It is strange that St. George happens to be a favorite saint in both Ethiopia and Italy.

God's ways are indeed mysterious.

An hour later, it is a transformed Emperor who steps out from the Mass in the cool cathedral into the glaring sun of this magnificent day of 27 September 1935. His face now radiates the spirituality of the Orthodox ceremony. He has been inspired by the Old Testament and David's long struggle against the Philistines. Like David, he will follow God's advice, and God will lead him to victory.

Standing there on the steps, Haile Selassie looks larger than life. Although he is small in stature and finely built, his dignified posture and movements are those of a natural leader. His penetrating gaze and fine-featured face radiate the confidence of divine right. Isn't he the Lion of Judah, a descendant of Solomon? His mission lies in perpetuating the legacy of the people he knows so well from the Old Testament.

But there is an ethereal look about him. From a distance, on the square, he looks like some celestial bird, with his robe spreading like wings in the gentle wind.

Haile Selassie has to be shielded by his guards from the closely packed throngs of people on the square. The Emperor's private guards open a path to a small construction, with a gilded dais. A low railing is covered in colorful silks, with embroideries of the royal Lion of Judah. An enormous parasol, in resplendent silk and with gold tassels, is attached to the railing.

As Haile Selassie proceeds, in a slow and dignified manner, to his temporary throne, the people around him dance, holding long poles dangling with yellow daisies. It is the Ethiopian flower of spring, because the cessation of the rains at the end of September signifies the beginning of a new season. The celebrants are beating on their drums, and trigger-happy men are shooting into the air. The Ethiopians are celebrating and see no reason to save their gunpowder.

The Emperor nods to his subjects, to this side and that. His solemn face lights up in a sudden fleeting, imperceptible smile, in response to the antics of his people. But mostly his mien is impassive, beyond the hustle-bustle of the throngs around him. His countenance is befitting of the dignity of the role that he plays for his people. He personifies the proud Ethiopian traditions, a living symbol for which his subjects will gladly sacrifice their lives.

But now is the time for feasting, and so the Emperor momentarily permits this flicker of a smile.

The impassive face also serves as a mask that hides the leader's passionate thoughts, a shield of apparent calmness behind which Haile Selassie can speculate, anticipate, scheme, plan, guess, and hope, in a pell-mell of contradictory emotions about how to save his country from obliteration.

There really isn't time for celebration, but the religious ceremonies and traditional customs give his people the opportunity to live the moment and connect with history. Who would they be without it? How can they be Ethiopians if they don't have Ethiopian traditions to tell them who they are? Mascal is important, the Emperor reminds himself, with the hint of a smile toward his people.

The crowds are pushed back with sticks (and whips when needed) to make room for the impending traditional military parade. Soon the chiefs of the country begin to march in front of the Emperor, with their private retinues and soldiers. Fierce-looking chiefs sport their ancient rifles, surrounded by motley groups of warriors. Many wear animal hides, and the chiefs favor lion skins and fanciful head ornaments and feathers. Proud and vain, these fighters invest their whole personality—body and soul—into their patriotic profession.

They are prepared to die for their country.

Mascal offers the exceptional privilege for the chiefs to air their advice for the benefit of the Emperor. One aged warrior, a veteran of the battle of Adwa in 1896, raises his ancient rifle in the air, shouting that they need new rifles, and asking: "What can I kill with this useless stick?" He smashes his rifle into the ground, where it breaks into two. Now he will be reduced to using a spear, for the Emperor has no more rifles to provide. The few weapons that Haile Selassie obtains in spite of the sanctions must be given to his own imperial troops. The destruction of a rifle is a waste of limited resources but effective histrionics.

The Emperor maintains his impassive expression, but his sorrowful eyes reveal how painfully he is aware of the pitiful state of his army and armaments. And he knows well the frustration of his soldiers over his refusal to mobilize, because his only hope, as he sees it, is to abide by the charter of the League of Nations. As long as the partners are negotiating, he is not supposed to mobilize (despite the fact that the Italians have for long, and openly, been doing just that.)

Haile Selassie sticks to the rules. Only the laws as stipulated by the League of Nations can secure international law and order. What else can protect the weaker countries? That's why he has also made sure that his armies are far from any border. Nobody shall be able to say that he has broken any agreements.

While his barefoot warlords parade past him with their retinues, the Emperor undertakes his own inner review of his diplomatic moves, from the hopeful start to the final impasse of the Committee of Five. Has he been too naïve to believe in using the diplomatic route? Should he have known that his case was hopeless, right from the start, when he was presented with the insolent demand to pay reparations and apologize to Italy after Wal Wal?

The British and French seemed to condone this humiliating proposal, because they are afraid of alienating Italy with the renewed German threat under Hitler. And furthermore, Italy is European. An African country has no standing, no rights, compared to a white country. That was a foregone conclusion of the powers that be. (The Emperor's face remains rigidly immobile.)

Haile Selassie recalls how he has argued for neutral arbitration, referred to past pacts of friendship, how one ineffective commission after the other has been established, from three members to five to ten to eighteen. Whatever it was! They were formed to stall the arbitration that, as everybody in the League knew, Italy opposed absolutely.

Eloquent statements, further investigations to make sure the facts were correct; endless lofty discussions of procedure led to the proposal of the disastrous and ultimately insolent Hoare-Laval plan. Large parts were carved out for Italy, leaving a small center under Italian or international mandate. Aggression rewarded. The impertinence! (The Emperor's face turns to stone.)

He should have known that the colonial powers could not be expected to be impartial and neutral. How could they condemn Italy for what they had already done themselves? What did it help that the British foreign affairs official, Anthony Eden, who was sent to negotiate a deal, seemed sympathetic to the Ethiopian cause? Was it just a case of European feelings of guilt?

However, all things considered, Haile Selassie feels he has taken the only avenue open to him. How could he hope to fight an advanced industrialized nation like Italy? His only chance lay in *collective security*, where stronger powers provide the protection. If he had failed so far, it was because of the underlying threat of Hitler. It has been beyond his power. The rest is up to God!

He is interrupted in his thoughts by the appearance of his principal chief, Mulugeta. His belligerent old war minister, who at one point, frustrated by the Emperor's humiliating appeasement strategy, had issued an order to mobilize. The proud old man couldn't get it into his war-scarred head why his country didn't just attack the aggressors and throw them out of the country. Hadn't they beaten the Italians at Adwa? Couldn't they do it again? They are not afraid, and they are surely better fighters than the soft Italians. He swings his silver-tipped spear vigorously in the air, surrounded by his wild-looking warriors.

The old man shows surprising virility as he stages a mock fight with an imagined enemy who comes to a hapless end. He caps his lifelike enactment by pretending to cut the head off his adversary and presenting it triumphantly to the impassive monarch. He takes a threatening step closer towards the Emperor (causing Haile Selassie's guards to tighten their grip on their spears) and shouts, "You should not meddle any more in the affairs of the outside world, but look after your own country!" He takes one more step, declaring, "This is what we do to our enemies," extending the imaginary head close to the Emperor.

The Emperor catches a whiff of *tejj* and manages not to wrinkle his sensitive nose.

The guards gently push the old man past the Emperor, and he dances on, swinging his spear. Now the Imperial Guard marches by Haile Selassie. their regular lines a sharp contrast to Mulugeta's disorderly band. In lockstep, they present their new rifles at precisely controlled angles. Some wear regular boots. The Emperor can relax a little. There are fewer surprises to fear as his disciplined soldiers parade past.

He can sink into his thoughts again. Yes, how should Mulugeta and men like him understand the situation? They can only react in the old way. There has not been the time to educate them. As much as he has tried, it takes time to change attitudes, a generation or more, and the clergy has been a tremendous reactionary force that he can turn around only little by little. He knows the church has no reason for modernizing. That is not in its interest.

Only the young can be educated and absorb new, fresh attitudes. That's why he has concentrated his efforts on them, even beyond his own means. But the educated ones are only a drop in the bucket.

The whole feudal system will have to be dismantled. This Imperial Guard is a small beginning. They swear allegiance to him and the country, unlike the chief's soldiers, who follow only their own chieftain, if they follow anyone at all.

The Italian threat has arrived before the Emperor has had time to modernize his country. Now, he is trapped. His chiefs will follow their traditional ways, and he cannot defend his country without them. All his plans for modernization and development will have to be put on hold while they fight the invader. And the Italians claim they came to develop and modernize. To *civilize*! That is the incredible arrogance of the colonizers. As if they don't come to serve their own interests!

The Imperial Guard has passed and is followed by a hodgepodge of military cadets, Boy Scouts, liberated slaves and a motley group of volunteers.

The Emperor stares straight ahead.

That night, Haile Selassie has a conversation with Mussolini.

As usual, the Emperor tosses and turns in his wide mahogany bed, trying to find some rest after his strenuous day. He must have fallen asleep, for it all began as a dream, where Mussolini appears before him speaking to the Italian masses below his little balcony on the Palazzo Venezia. *Il Duce* is standing dark and solid against the lit facade of the old palazzo, next to a giant symbol of the Roman fasces—a tall bundle of rods tied around an erect ax on a long shaft, with its threatening blade sticking out of the top. His devout audience intones hypnotically, "*Duce, Duce, Duce.*"

Mussolini lifts his arm majestically in the Fascist salute, and the crowd falls into a hushed quiet. The abrupt silence is accentuated by the loud, steady buzzing of the Roman cicadas.

This is his chance, Haile Selassie's, to speak up. In that moment of silence, he hears himself clearly saying (maybe not so clearly, but so it seems to him in the dream), "Your Majesty (he uses the honorific), "Why do you invade my country? We are equal members of the League of Nations."

"League of Nations, *me ne frego* (I don't give a damn)." Mussolini makes a grimace. "Everybody knows that the League of Nations is just *papier-mâché* facade; every leader takes care of the interests of his own country. The British think of the British, the French of the French. I protect Italy." (He lifts his little hand in a threatening gesture.)

"But you have no right to take the land from my people," Haile Selassie responds vehemently.

"You have more land than you control, and you have failed to develop it. The great power of Italy has not only a goal, but a duty to develop and improve a poor African state. In short, we are on a *civilizing mission*."

There it came, the word, making the Emperor sit up and turn on his light. His *valet de chambre* comes running, and the Emperor asks for a sip of fresh water. He inquires about the time, although he can clearly see it on the Louis XVI clock on the Empire dresser across from his bed. "Bring in my dogs."

The Emperor doesn't have to ask. His dogs always come running into his bedroom. Three cocker Spaniels and a Pekingese race towards the big mahogany bed and gracefully leap onto it.

"Did you dream last night, little Lion?" (His favorite, the Pekingese, is known as Lion because of his fierceness, in spite of his size.)

All lights are lit in the Palace. The Emperor's day has begun.

It is already two weeks since the Emperor made his new headquarters in the town of Dessie, closer to the areas of the fighting in the north. He is now settled in the former Italian Council or commercial agency. (Although Italy has no commerce with Dessie, it has established a council there, as the Italians have done all over Ethiopia, as part of their nationwide network for spying and for bribing Ethiopian officials.) The council building is the finest building in town, and therefore best suited to be the Emperor's new headquarters. Even in his private quarters, the Emperor seems destined to be reminded of Italy.

Haile Selassie has reduced his staff somewhat but he feels it important to keep up his imperial persona even in these temporary palaces. Always aware of his symbolic role, the Emperor insists on observing the etiquette of his palaces in Addis Ababa. He still entertains his visitors with four-course European dinners, with imported French wines, in addition to the usual Ethiopian dishes. Although the location is different and the scope somewhat diminished, the trappings and activities are similar.

Here are also the usual throngs of Ethiopians outside the fences and gates, waiting to catch a glimpse of the father of their nation or the opportunity to present a petition to their supreme leader. Haile Selassie likes to meet the common man; this sometimes provides him information that differs markedly from his official sources'.

The Emperor's life, even in the new location, exhibits the usual intense activity from before dawn to the late-night office work. Talking to his chiefs, developing war strategies, communicating with his commanders in the north, keeping supplies moving. The Emperor believes it necessary to supervise all the aspects of running his country personally, especially now that it is at war with a formidable enemy.

Most important, under the present circumstances, are his war councils and his consultations with his advisers, like Colonel Feodor Konovalov and his trusted adviser, the American, Everett Colson. Nobody could claim that the Emperor doesn't trust *ferengis*. Many of his closest advisers are foreigners, who are useful in these international negotiations. They are more familiar with the foreign politicians; they can explain their strange ways of thinking and even stranger ways of expressing themselves. The Emperor would listen and learn.

Soon he would know more than them.

The reports from the theatre of war become increasingly disturbing. The bombing is bad enough; now there is clear evidence that the Italians are using mustard gas against the Ethiopians. In session after session, Haile Selassie is informed about the calamitous events of the Italian invasion.

The hesitant General Emilio De Bono has been exchanged for the brutal General Pietro Badoglio. And Badoglio means business. How could he otherwise, with Mussolini constantly pressing him for decisive victories?

The Italian people at home are running out of patience. (They never have been too enthusiastic about the war.) And past Italian military disasters rattle on in Badoglio's mind. Better to exaggerate than to fall short. If it means killing a fly with a hammer, so be it! After some initial Ethiopian victories, the Italians are taking no chances. Once

a contingent of the soldier's of Ras Imru, the Emperor's cousin, surprised the Italian troops in Dembeguina Pass and chased them out of
the garrison at Selaclaca. And there was the time when Ras Seyoum,
after prolonged fighting, managed to rout the Italians and take over
the town of Abiy Addi.

There is the danger that the Ethiopians may discover the Italians
aren't as motivated as the Ethiopians. They aren't willing to pay as
high a price as the Ethiopians and most of all, they aren't invincible.
Therefore, all measures have to be considered.

Mustard gas becomes the solution. Ras Imru is the first Ethiopian
leader to experience this new kind of extermination, sent from the
blue skies by the Italian Regia Aeronautica. Two of its keenest pilots,
Vittorio and Bruno, are sons of Mussolini. The war is a family business,
so to speak.

Ras Imru becomes one of the first serious targets for this new warfare of gassing. He has followed the Emperor's call for guerrilla-style
warfare, with damaging raids on Italians. He has also obtained caches
of weapons that enabled him to equip his army and has thus become
a thorn in the eye of the Italians.

Ras Imru has now succeeded in stationing himself, with Ayelu Birru,
in a position to attack Axum and Adwa, or even to circumvent the
not yet ready Italian troops. This way, they could invade Eritrea. That
could be very embarrassing, not to say dangerous, for the Italians.
The Italian generals and Mussolini understand the potential threat to
their hinterland; and the Italians are ready to use gas. It contravenes
international agreements, of course, and is therefore only to be used
in particularly aggravating circumstances. A *defensive-counteroffensive
aim* is the phrase used.

This is clearly such a case, now that Ras Imru has maneuvered himself into a position where he can threaten the Italian colony. Wasn't that
the danger the Dictator pointed out in many of his speeches in the first
place? That the Ethiopians are threatening their colony?

On 23 December, as Ras Imru and his troops reach the north bank of the Tekezé River, near Mai Timchet, Italian planes come diving out of the sky. The Ras and his men run for shelter, as they always do. But these bombs are different. They are containers that burst open upon contact, releasing colorless liquid. The men hit by the liquid scream in agony and run towards the river. But the river water is also contaminated, and the men soon fall over in convulsions. They try to drink to cool their burning lungs, but that only exacerbates their suffering.

The injured men writhe in agony for hours, through the night, till death finally releases them. Ras Imru and his men are no longer thinking of approaching Eritrea. Badoglio's foresight in using mustard gas has defused a dangerous situation. *A counteroffensive measure.* This is Mussolini's favorite phrase; it could also be called a pre-emptive strike.

Slowly but surely, the Italian troops have positioned themselves in overwhelming numbers to attack the main Rases and their armies. First comes Ras Kassa, a conservative commander more interested in church matters than military pursuits. Ras Kassa and his men fight bravely. After many days of fierce battle, where the situation looked grave in certain locations for the Italians, a stalemate is reached.

In his office in Dessie, Haile Selassie knows that Badoglio will finally be ready to attack Mulugeta, his army chief, with his thirty thousand men. It is with a heavy heart that Haile Selassie finally turns into his bedroom to retire for the long night. How can he sleep, with his people being killed and gassed all around him?

So, sure enough, he has to continue his conversations with Mussolini, once he enters the shadow land in his mahogany bed. As usual, it begins with Haile Selassie having to listen to Mussolini speaking from his favorite balcony on the Palazzo Venezia. The Dictator lowers his jaw slightly, his forehead wearing a worried frown, as he begins to talk in a low voice about his concern over Italy's colony in East Africa, how it is threatened by the aggression of a neighboring country. He needn't mention the name of this aggressive country. Everybody knows he is referring to Ethiopia.

Then he talks about how Italy has been cheated at Versailles. Had the Italians spilled their precious blood on the side of England and France in vain? Italy had been promised equitable compensation. But what had they been offered? Some worthless desert. As he had mentioned, he was not a collector of deserts. If Italy wasn't compensated, they would help themselves. Why shouldn't they have a place in the sun, too?

Carried away by the sound of his own words and reassured by his threats against the enemy, he goes on and on. Again, Haile Selassie has to interrupt the dictator mid-sentence.

"Why are you using mustard gas against my people? You also signed the 1925 International Protocol against the use of poison gases."

"As I told you the other night, we're a militaristic state and proud of it. If you want the goals, you must be willing to use the means. This is not the time for weakness. This is not the time for the effeminate. To tell you the truth (and I don't intend to), I personally find the Italians too soft—they need to be hardened."

"You need not harden my proud people; they are used to deprivation and hardship. You're just cowards who are killing with gas from the safety of the air. You Italians are the dastardly cowards who dare not fight us in equal combat." Haile Selassie is shocked to hear his own language—he who always speaks in measured tones. Here, in the depth of the night, he can't help but speak from his raw emotions. "You're just a plain murderer."

Mussolini smiles. The conversation is finally to his liking, abandoning all this orotund League nonsense. "You have to be willing to sacrifice others to reach your own greatness. We may have to sacrifice Ethiopia for the greatness of Italy."

"You are just a common criminal. You talk about civilizing, but you are just a proletarian from the dregs of society."

"Aha, what do you know about the poor? You were pampered with silks and fine food while I went barefoot and hungry. And that's what I want to change: to make the poor and downtrodden rich and powerful."

"You, you … rogue. You, you … impostor." The Emperor knows it is beneath his dignity to engage in a conversation with the Dictator, but it is so hard not to in his dreams.

Of course, the Dictator doesn't even listen to him. He loves to hear his own voice, and continues in a melodramatic tone, "It is the war of the poor, disinherited, proletarian Italian people. Against us are arrayed the forces of reaction, of selfishness and hypocrisy. We have embraced a hard struggle against this front. We shall continue this struggle to the end. It will take time, but once the struggle is begun, it is not time that counts, but victory." He ends emphatically, "We will stay the course."

Indignant, Haile Selassie is finally about to speak, when the Dictator is approached by a servant balancing a big silver platter with a large cake on it. The cake is made in the shape of Ethiopia and covered with little people. The Dictator gleefully takes the platter, grabs the cake and takes a big mouthful. Some children fall off as he takes a bite. He quickly sweeps them up and stuffs them into his mouth.

The Emperor wakes with a cry, and turns on the light. His dogs, who now sleep with him in the bedroom, stretch their relaxed limbs, and Lion licks the Emperor's hand.

The *valet de chambre* comes running.

Whether asleep or awake, nobody listens to Haile Selassie, so the war continues on its doomed course.

Mulugeta and his men are ensconced on the great mountain mass of Amba Aradam, but the constant bombing and gassing have kept him and his troops in their hideouts. Every time they are about to emerge from their caves, a new bombardment begins, and they retreat further into their protective crevices.

What kind of war is this? They can't even get out into the open land to fight a proper battle. They are hiding like rabbits in their holes while the bombs rain down on them. They are all so deafened by the noise from the planes and bombs that they don't notice the enemy crawling up the mountainside. When the bombing stops, the attack is already upon them, and the dazed commanders pull their swords and the hornblowers sound the alarm while they are already being slaughtered.

Mulugeta and his men defend themselves as best they can. If it were not for the merciful dark, which finally descends over them, they could have been finished off right then and there. If the prudent Betwoded Makonnen from Wollega had not fought to keep an escape path open south of the mountain, Mulugeta would have been trapped right there. Now they escape in the darkness of the night and begin the retreat south towards Haile Selassie's camp at Quoram.

Haile Selassie has been moving northward stepwise, from one temporal palace in the caves to the next. His household has constantly shrunk, his staff reduced to mere necessities: cooks, dog keeper, pillow bearer (to put pillows under his feet when he cannot reach the floor from his seat), wine taster and *valet de chambre*, to mention a few.

Haile Selassie has let go of his two lion cubs and some of the dogs. (The lion cubs were a gift from Mussolini when the Emperor and his wife, Menen Asfaw, visited Rome in happier days.) Now, the animals are on their way back to safety in Addis Ababa, where they will join his beloved lions, the ant eater and the zebras. (Apart from his children and wife, he misses them more than anyone else in his palaces.) Now, Haile Selassie only keeps his favorite Lion in the bottom of his bed, while his nights continue with the usual shift between sleeping to waking, with the *claire-obscure* in between. By now, Haile Selassie resists talking to Mussolini any more. It is beneath his dignity. But he cannot ward off his dreams completely.

The Emperor has been fortifying himself with readings from the Old Testament, so it is not so strange that he should dream of David and Goliath. Mussolini becomes Goliath, of course. A giant with copper armor on his chest and legs. He has advanced the rows of the Philistine warriors, beating his hand on his armor and defying the Israelites to send a single combatant against him. *What a pack of cowards they were, the Israelites.*

So Haile Selassie steps forward, even though he is small and knows he shouldn't do this (and even in the dream he thinks that) and declares he will fight Goliath. It's good that he has read the Bible to know what to do. So he pulls this stone out of his pocket (for lack of a weapon) and puts it against the string on his sling. He shoots it off before Goliath can get to him, and lo and behold, the giant is knocked unconscious.

Again, he knows what to do, thanks to his knowledge of the Old Testament. So he runs up to Goliath, unsheaths the giant's sword, and plunges it into the slit between the armor. Then he grabs the giant's head by the hair and cuts it off.

This is what we do to our enemies!

The Emperor has a long, deep sleep after this satisfying deed.

Unfortunately, there are no happy endings in the present war against Italy. Mulugeta lost some six thousand men in battle, but that is nothing compared to what will take place during the retreat. Now the slaughter begins in earnest, with gassing by the Italian birds of prey from above and raids by the Galla tribes on the flanks. (The Gallas have been well-paid by the invading enemy.)

The gas proves very successful, and another fifteen thousand of Mulugeta's army are annihilated. (The gassing has also become much more efficient, as the technique has been improved. Sprayers have been attached under the planes, which fly side by side. In this fashion, a large area can be covered, as compared with the very limited effect of the initial barrels.)

The old Ras reaches Amba Alagi, where he tries half-heartedly to gather his army for a last stand. But he has lost his authority and his men no longer obey him. In a single night, the most feared commander in Ethiopia has turned into a weak old man. The unbowed warrior has been reduced to a trembling refugee. The former commander has been rendered obsolete, and all that is left to him is to die.

Ras Mulugeta continues his final journey towards the man he has served so proudly and to whom he is no longer of any use. Another five dangerous days of walking, and he reaches Maychew. Numbed by the constant air attacks and raids by the Azebu Gallas, Mulugeta thinks nothing worse could happen than his own death.

On the last morning, when Mulugeta and his son and a large party of refugees have halted near the beautiful Lake Ashangi, they are once again bombed by the Italians and attacked by the Gallas. Mulugeta is a little ahead of his son, Major Tadessa Mulugeta, when his son is killed by a bomb dropped by Vittorio Mussolini. (From son to son, so to speak.) Mulugeta promptly turns back to see if his son has been struck. This is the last affliction, which he had not had the imagination to fear.

As the grieving father leans over the dead body of his son, a bullet mercifully finishes him off.

After the annihilation of Mulugeta's vast army, Badoglio and his commanders can finish with Kassa and Seyoum, whose combined forces have been severely reduced by desertion. Outflanked and outnumbered, the Ethiopians are totally defeated in a few scant days. About three weeks later, Kassa and Seyoum arrive back to temporary security in Haile Selassie's camp. The commanders, shorn of their armies, prostrate themselves before the Emperor to ask for his forgiveness.

"We have failed you," they profess.

The last of the Emperor's commanders, Ras Imru, is next. He was the commander who best understood the concept of guerrilla warfare, and his army fought bravely when it was attacked at the beginning of March. Ras Imru's soldiers show a complete contempt for death as they advance and are often cut in two by the Italian machine guns. The retreating soldiers are then gassed by Vittorio and his brother Bruno as they try to cross the Tekezé River. The defeated soldiers massed at the congested crossing places provide excellent targets for the proud pilots of the Regia Aeronautica.

Three major Ethiopian armies have thus been annihilated. The Dictator can be pleased, and he can feel quite reassured that the next battle against the Emperor himself will have a similarly satisfying outcome.

Haile Selassie has been on the move northward again.

His army is now the last to stand in the way of the Italian advance towards the capital. The days have been long, with frequent bombardments and gassings. As the Emperor and his party trudge northward, they pass the solid stream of surviving soldiers and refugees coming back from the north, hollow-eyed and skinny in their dirty rags. Even though he had anticipated this, it makes the Emperor cry to see the soldiers who had marched so proudly in front of him at Mascal, in this utterly destitute state.

They have now reached the season of the little rains. The dirt paths have again turned into soft mud imprinted by bare feet and animals' hooves. But the benevolent clouds dissipate and disappear like a thin veil of gauze. The Italian armies would reach the houses of Addis Ababa before the big rains could stop them.

Haile Selassie's last cave residence is on Mount Aia. This will be the final temporary palace before the Emperor will meet his enemy. But as usual, his staff tries—and succeeds—to make the imperial residence as comfortable and stylish as possible. Even a cave can be made fit for an emperor with precious Persian carpets, pictures and silk embroidered wall hangings, plus a white silk curtain to shield the abode from the sun and the tumultuous outer world.

There is an atmosphere of order and serenity here. Visitors are greeted courteously and served fruit and French wine. The Emperor is dressed impeccably in his white Ethiopian cotton pants and velvet jacket. His speech and manners are every whit impeccable and dignified. (Nobody knows of his coarse sleep talk but his trusted *valet de chambre.*)

Only the Emperor's eyes cannot hide the sorrow and the hurt.

For stolen moments, he sits with a melancholy expression on his little throne, with Lion curled up on his lap. Images from his arduous journey from cave to cave pass before him. The rugged scenery, the steep paths. The flow of refugees going the opposite direction, away from the horrible war. The wounded. Even though he tries to suppress them, the sights of the gassed people overpower all the others.

One scene has been particularly horrifying. He and his guard reach a plateau where a few persistent Red Cross workers are treating gas victims. Hundreds of them. They are crowded around a bucket of yellow picric acid solution, which they apply to the burns before the bandages are rolled over the burned limbs. But there is not enough. Most of the people cannot be treated.

One old man is sitting near the path along which the Emperor is traveling. The man sits rocking to and fro, under the shade of a small juniper. He opens his cape to show his wounds to the passers-by. His body looks as if someone has tried to skin him alive. Raw, oozing, red meat on his chest, arms and legs. He closes his cloak again. He says nothing and sits down to resume his rocking.

The Emperor gently strokes Lion's back.

An attendant brings the Emperor a telegram. He unfolds it and reads it twice before he lowers it into his lap. The League of Nations' Committee of Thirteen has now made a recommendation, similar to an earlier one, "to get in touch with the two parties and to take such steps as may be called for in order that the Committee may be able, as soon as possible, to bring the two parties together and, within the framework of the League of Nations and in the spirit of the Covenant, to bring about the prompt cessation of hostilities."

Haile Selassie looks at one of the pictures nailed to the wall of his cave dwelling, depicting St. George and the dragon. (It is a reproduction of the big painting inside St. George's Cathedral.) Surely, the dragon he was fighting was the murderous Italian war machine. He pauses to ponder, "Who was the dragon to the Italians?" Was it the black people of Africa?

Is that also why the powerful states cannot agree on proper sanctions against the aggressor? Sanctions that did not exclude all the items, like oil, necessary for conducting a war? And why the British don't close the Suez Canal? It could be so simple. Maybe they don't feel so differently, the European dictators and the democratic leaders?

Haile Selassie now looks towards the opening of his cave. His attendants are bringing in more stools and lifting up the white curtain for more light and room. It's March 30. The Emperor's top commanders and their retinues are entering and bowing before him, before taking their allotted seats. Kassa and Seyoum, his armyless chiefs, sit on lower stools on either side of him. Other commanders sit to the side. The cave and the space in front of it become quite crowded.

Then the war council begins, with one commander speaking after the other. Many claim they are not ready for the battle planned the very next day (even though they have forced the Emperor to postpone the battle several times already) and they disagree on tactics. Haile Selassie notices their hesitation and bewilderment. And these were his brave commanders, the proud victors of Adwa!

He announces that the next morning, early, they will begin the battle against the Italians.

Now, the commanders all speak up. There is no waiting for turns. Wild arguments erupt among them, even resulting in blows. The Emperor has to silence them by raising his arm. In the meantime, he thinks of how they have wasted valuable time. They should have made a surprise attack before the Italians had prepared for the battle. They should have embarked on guerrilla warfare. Attacked everywhere, while remaining nowhere to be found. They knew the country. They could have delayed the Italian advance into the next rainy season, when the Italians would have been completely bogged down. The big rains could have beaten the Italian army. But it was too late for that now. Or was it?

The Emperor also knows that his commanders would never agree to this. It goes against their honorable ways. They will only accept a big, pitched frontal battle in the middle of the plain. From daybreak till nightfall. Well, they would have it their way. And they would be massacred by the Italian machine guns and armored tanks and airplanes. They would die with their spears and outmoded rifles and bare feet.

"My decision has been made," the Emperor says, firmly silencing the cacophony. He nods to his attendants, who bring forth the *messobs* for the traditional warriors' meal.

The attendants stream in with big dishes piled high with small pieces of raw meat and glass containers of *tejj*. At the prospect of food and drink, the hungry men calm down and reach for the fresh meat, which they pack into their mouths and rinse down with *tejj*. The torrent of words turns into the chomping of food and smacking of lips. The Ethiopian late afternoon meal merges lunch and dinner into one frugal meal. The Last Supper, the Emperor thinks, the body and blood of Christ.

He is ready to die with his men.

After the meal, the men scatter to nap. The Emperor, who needs almost no sleep, goes outside the cave. The sun is getting low on the sky, bathing the green, grassy plains in a mellow light. Eucalyptus and juniper dot the gently rising foothills below the mountains, providing some shade for the crowds that are always camped below the Emperor's cave. Lower down, the cactus-like euphorbia trees curve their arms gracefully upwards, like a plea for more of this momentary peace.

The Emperor knows that the Italians will soon resume their bombing. They always do in the late afternoon (probably after their own afternoon naps, he thinks, with a hint of a bitter smile.) He had better hurry and write to his wife, Menen. Tomorrow may be his last day.

He writes to her that he and his men are well, thanks to God, and ready for the great battle the next day. He leaves out all the troubling news and suffering around him and focuses on his resolve and the help of God. He encourages her and tells her to leave all in God's hands. He mentions that Lion will be brought back should he not return from the battlefield. He asks her to take good care of him. What else can he write to his respected wife?

He must have fallen asleep right there, sitting on the chair in the filtered sun. To his amazement, he is back with David and Goliath. He is David again, and Goliath is standing there in front of the Philistines. Ready for combat. He is larger than ever and completely covered by his copper armor. He looks like one enormous metal statue.

"But I thought I killed you?" the astonished Emperor shouts.

"You sure did. But I always come back." And the metal mouth opens in a roaring laughter, "Har, har, har."

"Ta, ta ta." It is the metallic keening of the bombing machines. The bombing from the Regia Aeronautica planes, which have appeared over the mountains. Soon afterwards, explosions and the thunder of guns and the screams of the people lower down rise in a crescendo towards the abruptly awoken Emperor.

He rushes down the path to the plateau below, where he has his anti-aircraft positioned. He tears off the cover, dons his helmet and begins to shoot, while turning around to aim at the planes. From a distance, his people can see the birdlike creature aiming at the vultures hovering in the sky. Then people are screaming in agony not very far from him. The hostile birds are spraying a rain of deadly dust.

The small figure breaks off from his shooting, while watching a group of people lower down who have been drenched in gas. Soldiers, women and children. Because the soldiers are often accompanied by their wives and children, the families share the fate of their men. The chaos and agony reach a crescendo, and the Emperor hurries back up the path towards his cave.

The planes have already left looking for new prey. It doesn't take long for them to do their damage.

The sky turns eerily silent as the birds of prey disappear in the horizon.

It becomes almost quiet. But what is this?

A strange high-pitched sound emerges, an uncanny chantlike plaint from afar. Like the stridulating cicadas. It rises and sinks in a persistent rhythm. Like a mourning ritual.

The Emperor hears it and recognizes it. "*Abeit, abeit, abeit,*" the word of the beggars asking for alms. The words of any miserable Ethiopian asking for help. Attention. Or just expressing their misery. Words the Emperor knows only too well.

He is also aware that they are not addressed to God or any of his fine commanders. They are addressed to him. The father and protector of the people. Isn't the father supposed to help his children?

They have turned to him. Who else should they turn to? They vocalize their suffering through him. Through him and up into the big, empty sky.

However, as the monotony of the chant indicates, the miserable victims do not expect any reply. They are merely chanting, like a mournful

Greek chorus. A chant that will never end, even if it dies down, because it is not answered.

There is no response to their suffering. They are left alone. Their injustices will never be addressed. They can be heard, but they will not be answered before they die.

They are the victims.

The chorus chants its sorrowful tune. On and on it goes. "Why? Help. Relieve me of this pain." On and on.

It will never end.

The Emperor, who has not been able to protect his people, paces up and down in front of his cave. His eyes are burning in his impassive face. Then he loses his composure and puts his hands over his face. For a little while. After a moment or so he takes them down again.

He has his battle to fight early the next morning.

Epilogue:

As expected, the Emperor's troops met with a fate similar to his vanquished commanders. Like his defeated chiefs, the Emperor's army suffered by far the greatest casualties on its retreat, when they were attacked by the Gallas on the ground and bombed and gassed by Vittorio and his cohorts from the air.

In spite of the danger of being caught, the brave Emperor spent two days fasting and praying in the churches in Lalibela. Finally, edified by this spiritual retreat, the Emperor emerged ready to continue the uphill fight for his country.

At the beginning of May, the imperial family fled the country, and the Italians entered Addis Ababa. The Emperor would continue his resistance against the occupying power from his base in England.

The colonial occupation brought some of the usual colonial advantages, in the shape of roads and hospitals and more efficient civil administration. That was development. It also brought much cruelty and repeated atrocities against the conquered people. Was that the *civilizing mission*?

The Ethiopians were defeated but not vanquished, and Haile Selassie encouraged the resistance from his exile in Britain. The Italian grip on the country was limited geographically, and the proud, freedom-loving Ethiopians were just waiting for their chance.

On June 30, 1936, the Emperor addressed the cause of his country in the League of Nations, in an eloquent and moving speech. It would survive as a commemorative token of a victimized people and nation. As he pointed out, the League's failure to provide collective security opened the way for the next cataclysmic war.

"It is us today; it will be you tomorrow!" he is reported to have muttered, as he stepped down from the rostrum. His prophesy was proved correct, as World War II spread like wildfire all over the world.

When Mussolini joined Germany in the war, Britain finally came to the help of the Ethiopians. In cooperation with the Ethiopian resistance movement, British troops liberated Ethiopia in April of 1941, and in May, the rightful Emperor returned to his country. He was again the undisputed ruler of Ethiopia. Addressing his people on his return, he called on them to act magnanimously towards the defeated occupier.

Which they did.

David had defeated Goliath after all.

Sources:

George W. Baer, *The Coming of the Italian-Ethiopian War*. Harvard University Press: Cambridge, 1967.

A.J. Barker, *The Civilizing Mission*. Cassell & Company Ltd.: London, 1968.

Thomas M. Coffey, *Lion by the Tail. The Story of the Italian-Ethiopian War*. Hamish Hamilton: London, 1974.

Ryszard Kapuscinski, *The Emperor. Downfall of an Autocrat*. Tr. William R. Brand and Katarzyna Mroczkowska-Brand. Harcourt Brace Jovanovich, Publishers: London, 1983.

James Dugan and Laurence Lafore, *Days of Emperor and Clown. The Italo-Ethiopian War 1935–1936*. Doubleday & Company, Inc.: New York, 1973.

Harold G. Marcus, *Haile Selassie I, The Formative Years, 1892–1936*. University of California Press: Berkeley, 1987.

Harold G. Marcus (ed.), *Haile Selassie I. King of Kings of Ethiopia. Volume Two*. Michigan State University Press: East Lansing, 1994.

Peter Neville, *Mussolini*. Routledge: London and New York, 2004.

Peter Schwab, *Haile Selassie I. Ethiopia's Lion of Judah*. Nelson Hall: Chicago, 1979.

Quotes:

He "should not meddle any more in the affairs of the outside world, but look after his own country." p. 149, Coffey.

"It is the war of the poor, disinherited, proletarian Italian people … it is not time that counts, but victory." p. 250, Coffey.

" … to get in touch with the two parties … to bring about the prompt cessation of hostilities." p. 314, Coffey.

"It is us today; it will be you tomorrow!" p. 275, Barker.

Vocabulary:

Ras ◉ In the Amharic language, the word Ras, literally means "head," the Ethiopian title equivalent of prince or chief.

Wal Wal ◉ An obscure cluster of wells about 60 miles inside the Ogaden border. In December 1934, an Ethiopian patrol clashed with a party of Italian troops defending this illegal Italian outpost on Ethiopian territory. In spite of the fact that the Ethiopians suffered great casualties, Mussolini demanded apologies and reparations.

The Ideologue

A Modern Folk Tale

Plus ça change, plus c'est la même chose.

ONCE UPON A TIME, NOT SO long ago, a weather-beaten bus was rumbling down a road full of potholes. It was crowded with people bumping up and down in delayed action with the movements of the laboring vehicle. A colorful knitted beanie stood out as it moved sideways in the bobbing sea of dark heads. It belonged to a student, who seemed to be trying to make himself more comfortable in his seat. The seat was worn down, and something was poking him in his back.

Tesfaye figures he had better make the best of it, as long as he has the chance to sit down in the crowded bus. His turn will be up in an hour or so. Well, this isn't a trip for comfort. This is a trip for ideals. Revolutionary goals. He is on a mission to educate and enlighten the Ethiopian peasant. He has done it before—but this is big time. This time, the ideas of their young revolution are finally about to be carried out: words put into action.

He looks at all the peasants around him, men, old and young, women and children. They come from the famine-stricken areas in Wello and Tigray. He himself joined the bus here in Addis, and now they are on their way to Wellegga in the south-eastern part of Ethiopia. Resettlement and communal farming—core ideas of the revolution.

Not the city but the countryside is where the battle will take place. The battle for the new Ethiopia.

A feeling of contented excitement goes through Tesfaye. He is to be part of the historic resettlement effort. In fact, he is one of its organizers. With his experience from the *zemecha* and smaller resettlement schemes, he has been asked by the Relief and Rehabilitationon Commission and Government people to help organize the illiteracy program, as well as the general ideological campaign. He can't wait to teach his Ethiopian brothers and sisters. He knows his doctrines inside out—he is ready.

Tesfaye settles back in the uncomfortable seat and gives himself over to recent events, while his limber body is jolted up and down on the bumpy road. The glorious day at Siddist Kilo in Addis. All the chanting and jubilating students, in procession past the man. The man who made it all possible—the man who had adopted the phrase of the radical students: "scientific socialism." Not some homegrown ideas, but the true Marxist-Leninist ones. No more *Ethiopia Tikdem* (Ethiopia First) but international ideas. Universal.

He remembers Mengistu standing there next to the head of the Military Council, Teferi Banti. But it wasn't Teferi the students looked at, but Mengistu. Their new leader, who would lead them to victory. "Viva Mengistu! Mengistu is a revolutionary! Viva Mengistu! We want Mengistu!" Shining in the sun, their new leader saluted with his clenched fist. Tesfaye's eyes tear up just at the memory. The euphoria. That was the happiest moment of his life.

Outside, the landscape is turning into twilight. Tesfaye discovers himself in the glass of the window on the other side of the crowded bus. It is like seeing himself from outside. How others see him. A young revolutionary with a knitted cap of the Ethiopian colors: the green for the fertility of the earth; the yellow for the new hope of the Ethiopian people and the red for the martyrs' blood.

Yes, blood there would be. You cannot make a revolution without spilling blood. Mengistu had showed he was willing to pay the price, and had executed lots of people. Enemies of the revolution. Even Haile Selassie had had to be sacrificed. Tesfaye thinks of how the feeble old man had been suffocated with a pillow in his prison, on the order of Mengistu. It was brutal, but it had to be. Haile Selassie was the symbol of the old oppressive feudal system. You had to clear the old to make way for the new.

Many others had had to go, like Amman, Habte, Nadew, Teferi, Alemayehu and Mogus. They were in Mengistu's way—they slowed him down—slowed the revolution down. *The Red Terror.* Yes, the issues became murkier. But you don't change an old, feudal state into a modern communist country without resistance and momentary chaos. Wasn't that how it had been in Russia?

But many students had been killed. And there was Telahun, his best friend in law school. He had been for reform, not revolution. He really had been a reactionary. There just wasn't room for people like him in the new Ethiopia. Where was he now?

No, better forget about the killings. Now they were all equal in the communal effort. This was the new beginning of a society based on modern science and technology. A promising future guided by progressive, international ideas. No more religion and old customs and superstition. No miracles, just plain hard work.

Tesfaye's glance falls on the hands of the peasant next to him. Old, wrinkled hands with dirt under the nails. A hand for digging the soil. A hand that never held a pen, never wrote a word.

This will be the challenge, to change and transform these people. To make them understand their own good. Now with all land nationalized, a new dawn has burst upon the Ethiopian man and woman.

Tesfaye looks enthusiastically at his fellow passengers, and his own image in the mirror catches his attention again. With the growing darkness outside, his face has become quite clear. He cannot take his eyes away from it. Yes, the revolution. It is necessary to stay focused. Not to weaken or get distracted from the goal. His eyes take on a determined look. He, Tesfaye, has a role to play in Ethiopian history. He will be somebody. Doesn't he look like an Ethiopian Che Guevara?

But at this very moment, the light goes out and deep darkness swallows up the passengers and reflections.

The light has just come back on, but dimmer than before. It makes him think of the dusk creeping up from the valleys below. The chirping birds settling in for the night. The smoke rising from the embers of his wife's coffee making.

His daughters would appear up the slope with their jugs of water on their backs. Bent over. They would pour some for the little ones playing in the dust amongst the chicken.

Why then, did God take them all away from him?

The land had betrayed him. There was not much to say. That's how it was. It was *the quarrel of the sky* that had made him powerless. He had no longer been able to protect his wife and children. They now rested under the soil of their ancestral home. And without his kin, he was not alive.

They were the lucky ones; they got to stay at home. He had been forced to go.

Everything they had tried. They had borrowed grain to sow again, but if God would not help, how could people do it alone?

They had sold their goats and slaughtered their cow. Finally, they had let go of their starving oxen for a pittance. They knew that was the last straw. *Their stomachs had turned cruel.* Unless you give it food, it won't let you sleep.

He sees his two oxen for him. His trusted animals. Walking behind them steering the wooden plough that turned the soil, he had had faith for tomorrow and hope for a successful harvest. Following his oxen, he had been filled with love. Love for the soil, his fields, his home, his family. But the oxen had become thinner and thinner until their sorrowful brown eyes had asked for rest from work. Rest from life.

The pain. The shame.

No longer a farmer, he had looked for work, but so had thousands of others. When their baby had died, they had walked the long way to the feeding center. Two more children were lost on the way, and in the center, the food was so scarce that his wife and another child had fallen ill before they also died.

It was too hard in Tigray. Without his family, he had no reason to stay, and he had signed up for the resettlement project. Like so many others. Half a year later, they had put him on this bus. His life was no longer in his own hands. He had become a stranger in his own country.

In the falling dusk Seyoum perceives the contours of his round peasant face in the window panes of the bus. He closes his eyes.

What can one say? No words can express it. The whole country was going to pieces. It began after they lost their father, Haile Selassie. The father of them all, Haile Selassie, had been cruelly murdered. Their father could no longer take care of them.

And who is this Mengistu? Surely couldn't be any good, the way he killed his way to power. And all those new slogans and nonsense about revolution.

What did they need a revolution for?

They had their proud history and their cherished traditions. They had their religion and churches. Rumor had it they wouldn't even be allowed their religious practices anymore.

Surely nothing good would come of that. Maybe that was why God kept punishing them?

Seyoum looks up and down the bus—like cattle locked up in a pen. Seyoum's head is now clearly reflected among unfamiliar faces in the window on the other side of the bus. It's a stranger next to him. Not his own son.

Seyoum notices the hands of the youth. They sure look like the young man had never worked a field. What good could they do?

Maybe he was a man of the church?

But not with that ridiculous hat. He looks more like an actor. One of those men, who puts up a stage and jumps around and makes you all laugh with silly gestures and funny speeches.

The faint light again begins to flicker before it goes out altogether. It is not good for security, but on the other hand, most of the passengers (even those standing or sitting on the middle aisle) seem to have fallen asleep, dulled into a slumber by the monotonous sound of the engine and the vibration of the old bus. He can relax. The situation is under control for now.

He is not happy with this assignment escorting these miserable peasants to their resettlement, but they can't escape as long as the bus is moving. Nothing doing. Orders are orders, and maybe this will be an easier assignment than keeping peace in the capital. Not to mention having to fight the terrible Somali war.

He would miss his nightly visits to the bars and brothels, but then this resettlement assignment might offer new opportunities and advancement.

Dawit points to a young student and a peasant sitting to the side of him. Time to change and to give the seat to the young woman right in front of him in the aisle. He will take the other seat himself. Soldier or not, he cannot stand all the way.

That's what you could say about a revolution. It shook up things and created opportunities. Changes could happen faster now. And Mengistu would pave the way for courageous and loyal soldiers. If you were clever enough, you could advance.

But for now, this dreadfully boring bus ride. Dawit looks at the pretty young woman who has just sat down next to him. She keeps her eyes lowered. Dainty, feminine hands. With these peasants, you don't have to ask. You just make them. (Zeritu last night. She was wonderful. Such a sexy broad.) In the mirror of the dark window, the soldier and the maiden already look like a couple. Just a question of timing. Dawit smiles, and the image smiles back to him.

Dawit leans back and closes his eyes. The revolution had been good for him. Just as it had been a blessing in disguise when his uncle had made him join the army when he was a troubled teenager back in Gojjam. True, he also had problems adjusting in the Moleta training camp, and it wasn't till he joined PMAC, the Provisional Military Administrative Committee, that he was sent on to the Derg. He had finally found his place, and now Mengistu had sent him to this resettlement camp, where he would be right in the center of a major historical development. Dawit wasn't sure if this was a banishment or a promotion. He would find out and choose sides accordingly.

But he was a daring man, this Mengistu. Didn't back away from any obstacle, ever since he began his ascent with the strangling of the old man. Good riddance. Even though Haile Selassie had been like a father for the military, there had not been enough opportunity for a low-rank soldier like himself. Everything remained the same under the Emperor. Revolution was better. Now things would happen!

Despite his duty as guard, Dawit had finally fallen asleep when the bus came to a screeching halt. The front door is torn open by a soldier outside, who screams at the passengers to move fast, out into the pouring rain. The startled Dawit throws a glance at his wristwatch, which shows it is five o'clock in the morning. He must have been asleep for hours!

Outside, the rain is streaming down, and the drowsy passengers are slow to move. The soldier gets busy and pokes the peasant and the student in front of him with his gun.

"Get moving. This is not a Sunday fair."

"What's the hurry?" the peasant mutters, as he proceeds slowly down the aisle.

The student turns angrily towards the soldier "Don't you see we can't move any faster than the people in front of us?"

"Obey orders, you troublemaker." He gives the student an extra poke with his rifle.

They stay in the transit shelter for over a month in the pouring rain. There is a shortage of buses, and many break down. Revolution doesn't provide new buses, they learn. There are no facilities apart from the leaking tent. They have to relieve themselves wherever they can, outside the tent in the constant downpour. Many die and are buried out there in nowhere land—Muslims and Christians together. There are no separate facilities. Transitory difficulties, Tesfaye is confident.

The survivors of this monsoon ordeal drive on and finally reach their settlement location in a region called Wellega or "The end of the world," according to some of the Tigrayans. The rains have finally stopped, as it is September in God's year of 1985. Again, there are no facilities waiting for them, just this forested hilltop, which slopes into dense, semi-tropical foliage full of hair-raising sounds of wild animals. Seyoum remarks dryly, "I thought we were going to settle on land, but this is the wilderness." They are told that the slope ends in a river teeming with crocodiles. It looks like an enormous task to clear such land. "And what will be the point of reaching those crocodiles?" Seyoum asks.

It so happens that the teacher, the soldier and the peasant end up in huts near each other. They are among the early arrivers, who come to function as part of the local resettlement leadership. They sorely need literate workers, sharpshooters and most of all, farmers. As Seyoum soon notices, the Government people from Addis sure don't know much about farming.

Tesfaye is impatient to begin his assigned tasks as an educator, but in the beginning, far more basic concerns than literacy and ideology have to be taken care of. Survival comes first, and Tesfaye has to roll up his sleeves to slash and burn and dig like everybody else. Dawit provides security and makes sure the settlers get out of their beds at six in the morning. Apart from shooting a prowling lion, Dawit's job increasingly consists in trying to stop disgruntled settlers from escaping from the camp. Seyoum, who displays the independent farmer's natural authority and who has experience as a local leader back home, is elected to be team leader. But most importantly, he is a farmer, and it is thanks to people like him that anything edible is produced in the camp.

Days and months pass in a hazy agony of cutting down brush and the backbreaking pain of putting seeds into the dry earth under the scorching sun. The settlers sow the seeds for sorghum and maize. These are not the crops the Tigrayans are used to from home, and they miss their habitual *teff*. To make up for the bland taste of the sorghum, they add chili pepper, which they sneak back from a local market in exchange for canned donation food. Tigray now seems a world away, but at least they can reminisce through their tastebuds. And when nobody overhears, they pray to God to take them back to their rocky *teff*-growing Tigray. But God seems busy with the revolution or whatever, so they are left to their own devices.

Time proceeds in spite of it all. The next rainy season, *disease again sweeps like a broomstick*. The burials pick up all over. Tesfaye helps carry the dead ones on stretchers from the big tents to the nearby hill, which is soon named the Hill of Death. There is a constant line of people carrying the dead to the graves. They form a moving silhouette against the horizon. It looks like a *danse macabre*. People get so fed up with burying that it becomes hard to find anybody to do the job. Dawit has to find them. The faster it goes, the more slipshod the job. Some corpses are put down so quickly that their toes still stick up afterwards. Then the hyenas take over at nighttime.

In the meantime, busload after busload of new settlers increase their numbers, in spite of the deaths. With tremendous collective effort, the settlers persevere in their battle against nature. Guided and misguided by the cadres of Government leaders, they succeed in clearing the land, building the villages and digging the latrines and graves.

The first year and a half of settlement has been an eye-opener for Tesfaye. He had had no idea that the settlers would suffer such hardships, but he accepts it as part of the revolutionary struggle. Rome was not built in one day. He understands that the Government has been badly prepared for such big projects, but he feels that a revolution by definition has to be an experiment. Just like the cooperatives in Russia had been experiments! So Tesfaye tries to keep his revolutionary spirit intact by reading *The Communist Manifesto* when he goes to bed at night. Whether it is the *Manifesto* itself or due to the day's hard work, Tesfaye falls asleep quickly.

But Tesfaye also hears rumors from the capital, which unsettle him. A student friend from Addis, who joins him as a teacher in his hut, tells him that Telahun has been imprisoned and maybe killed. Although Tesfaye has foreseen this might happen, he feels bad about Telahun. He has to remind himself of the greater cause. And Telahun's fate is just a drop in the bucket in these turbulent years of revolution. *Ethiopia Tikdem*, Tesfaye repeats to himself, forgetting that this phrase is already outmoded.

Some years pass, routine has set in. Chaos has been organized, so to speak. Everybody is assigned their role: the leaders hold meetings and supervise; the guards guard; and the peasants till the soil.

The leaders tell the settlers to grow crops they do not care to eat. They are informed that Tigrayan crops will not grow there, although they seem to grow just fine in their little private plots. But however great the effort, the output fails to get anywhere near the projected goals, and the settlement continues to rely heavily on subsidies. The donated canned food, pasta and rice are liked even less, so an intrepid trade develops on the local market.

The settlement people have hardly any free time (the new point system keeps them on their toes) but the little they grant themselves, they use to walk the long way to the market to trade. Seyoum invites Tesfaye to join him to the market. There they exchange canned goods for some chili peppers and maybe a few smuggled grains of *teff*. What a liberating feeling the act of trading is! Seyoum can haggle about the price, exchange some gossip and share a few gulps of illegal liquor. In this manner, the canned goods make their way back to the capital, where they came from, and where, hopefully, some more appreciative soul will pay the extra birrs to cover the long journey back and forth.

Tesfaye and the settlement administration have finally succeeded in getting regular literacy classes going. The settlers are divided into classes and assigned a schedule of twice-weekly meetings. Due to the large number of illiterates, classes have to run both in spare time and work time. The latter is by far the most popular, and those classes are well attended.

The evening classes suffer from absenteeism, and students present often fall asleep. Slowly, they learn the letters and the first simple words. But Tesfaye is at his wits' end thinking up learning situations in which the peasants can stay awake. It helps when he starts making funny sentences with the words. "Peasant," and he will act like a peasant working with a hoe. "Soldier," and he will copy a soldier shooting an enemy. "Student," and he will impersonate a person reading a book. There will be alert smiles. But in need of variations to keep the students awake, he will let the peasant grow his secret plot, while the soldier pursues escapees and the student falls asleep. There are giggles and laughter. The words take on a meaning of their own.

In constant search of entertainment, Tesfaye's teaching develops into little plays around settlement life. Laughter indicates where their sympathies lie, and the busybody cadre people, who visit the camp three times in the year, become a popular target. This earns Tesfaye a serious reprimand from the powers that be. He is not serving the spirit of the revolution—the revolution is no joking matter—and this could have *consequences* for him, Dawit informs him, on behalf of the management. Tesfaye tries to explain, but Dawit cuts him short. "Orders are orders. Are you for them, or are you against them?" He tones down his humor (*consequences* do not sound desirable) until he is carried away again. It is hard to resist the laughter of the students.

Seyoum takes Tesfaye's classes like everybody else. He mostly sleeps, because he works hard throughout the day. But a special relationship has developed between Seyoum and Tesfaye, ever since they walked off that bus into the cold rain on that first night. They seem to stick together, and when Seyoum discovers that Tesfaye has been on a *zemecha* and speaks Tigrinian, the two begin to talk to each other. They have opposite views with regard to the revolution and everything else they talk about, but somehow, they seem comfortable in each other's company. When it comes to practical matters, they end by helping each other, Seyoum getting the job done in his taciturn way, while Tesfaye slows down his work in order to explain the theoretical implications.

Like everybody else, they have their bouts of diarrhea and influenza, but one night, Seyoum falls seriously ill. He is delirious with fever and is shaking so much his teeth clatter in his mouth. As usual, the hospital is out of all medicine, and the health unit leaves him to his own devices, which consist in fasting and putting an amulet under his shirt and praying as long as his strength allows. Having thus exhausted his own means, Seyoum lies in a stupor, and that's how Tesfaye finds him, emaciated and soaking with sweat in his little draughty hut.

Tesfaye guesses Seyoum has contracted malaria from the mosquitoes by the river and explains he has the medicine that can help him survive. Seyoum is not a believer in modern medicine. Didn't his wife die in spite of it?

He believes he is going to die, and asks Tesfaye to find him a priest to give him his last rites. Tesfaye explains there is no priest and that after the revolution, people have to rely on science. Seyoum is not strong enough to argue at this point, so Tesfaye manages to get him to take his quinine pills on the condition that Tesfaye will read from the secret Bible Seyoum has hidden in his tattered bag of skin.

"Where do you have this Bible from?" Tesfaye asks as he opens the torn, dirty book.

"From a *ferengi*."

"I thought you didn't like *ferengis*."

"Well, this was a Christian man, and he gave it to my father's father, who gave it to my father, who gave it to me."

"But you cannot read. Neither could your father or your father's father."

"Yes, but I know my Bible. Now you read for me."

Tesfaye realizes that Seyoum doesn't have the strength to talk anymore, so he opens the Bible and reads where his eyes fall, "If I speak in the tongues of men and of angels, but have not love, I am only a resounding gong or a clanging cymbal." He gets drawn in by the words and the resonance of his own voice. He has always liked reading aloud, to listen to the sound of well-formed phrases. It doesn't really matter what it is, if it sounds good. Suddenly, he remembers that he is reading the Bible—that's what Seyoum has brought him to. He looks over at the bedridden man and discovers that he is fast asleep and breathing calmly.

Slowly, Seyoum gets better, but his recuperation is sluggish, so the administration allows him to take some more days off from work without losing too many points. Energized from his bed rest, he begins to take up discussions when Tesfaye returns to check on his friend after a long day's labor.

Seyoum's idleness seems to have given him the opportunity to think about life in general and the revolution in particular. He lowers his voice as he gives vent to his disdain for the revolutionary ideas. The one that gets him the most excited is "abolition of private property." How would a farmer want to farm if it wasn't his own soil? When Tesfaye tries to explain about "the inevitable victory of socialism," he merely calls it nonsense. Or "Proletarians of the world unite." Who are the proletarians? If they are the peasants, why doesn't he say so? And what should they unite about? They are busy enough cultivating their fields, taking care of their cattle and feeding their families.

Tesfaye thinks he finally has a strong card in hand, now that Seyoum is getting better, and he spends a great deal of effort on explaining "scientific socialism." How their society will be based on science and knowledge rather than belief and superstition. But Seyoum merely answers that you can't know why something happened. His own cure most likely was caused by God. Or put differently, simply a miracle. And what does "scientific socialism" have to do with Ethiopia anyway?

"Sounds like one of those *ferengi* ideas to me."

"Well, they come from Russia. People like Lenin and Marx."

"I don't know where they come from. They sure don't sound Ethiopian. How can they be fit for Ethiopia?"

After a couple of weeks, Seyoum is deemed well enough to work the next day. Their unit is going to sow the plowed field, but Seyoum gets very excited when he hears that there are no oxen available for the sowing, as the cadre has been promising. He complains to Tesfaye about the uselessness of *the ox machine*.

"What do you mean?"

"Yeah, it's broken down."

"Oh, the tractor. Yes, it's broken down, but that doesn't mean it's not good just because it is broken down."

Silence. "Yes, because it's broken down."

"See, this is typical. It's broken down now, but that doesn't mean that it is not good in theory."

"I don't know what is theory. Maybe it's in your books? All I know is that it is broken down."

Silence. "Then it would be better with a live ox."

"I will grant you that. But only as long as it is broken down."

"Ah, so it will be repaired?"

"Well, that won't happen right now."

"So, it's better with a live oxen."

"Oh, you peasants are so obstinate!"

"Maybe. All I know is that I would like a live ox—not a broken machine—so I can plough my field."

Tesfaye cannot help himself, he has to argue with Seyoum. It is in his blood: the exchange of words through the logical conclusion. Apart from the fact that this is his job—his assignment—as the educator in charge of ideological indoctrination. However, a slight feeling of exasperation begins to sneak into him, even when he feels he has won the arguments with Seyoum. One thing is words. Another is the reality. Almost imperceptibly, there seems to be a growing distance between theory and practice. He, Tesfaye, is right that in theory, the tractor is to be preferred to the ox. But the reality is that the tractors they have from Russia are all broken down. So now they have in fact nothing but their bare hands. Some weathered hands they are going to be.

Tesfaye is thinking these thoughts one day as he is walking through the bright morning sun for the biannual Peasant Association (PA) meeting. The sunlight fails to cheer him up. He is getting tired of all those meetings. Do they serve any purpose but to underscore the discrepancy between the goals of the revolution and the poor reality surrounding him? Seyoum joins him from the direction of the river, where he has been tending his little private plot in the early hours of Sunday. Although he is the team leader, Seyoum really is an incurable anti-revolutionary, with his enthusiasm for his own little plot. This issue is exactly what is on the agenda for the day's meeting.

They greet Dawit, who has become a member of PA and is in keen discussion with one of the government representatives from Addis. There are people from the Ministries of Agriculture, Health and Education, people from trade and industries, from the Domestic Distribution

Corporation and the Small Industries Development Agency. Whoever they are, they are Mengistu's men, who come from the city. They don't know much about cultivating the land, and most of all, they have their orders from above and their quotas to meet. The agricultural report from the village leaders does not please them, as production lags far behind the goals. The leadership complains about the poor results; the settlers complain about the poor support in grains to sow, tools and machinery. The *ox machine* discussion is biting its tail all over again, until suddenly, the PA foreman asks its new member, Comrade Dawit, to explain the issue of the mushrooming of small private plots.

Dawit, who has pretended not to notice the plots and who has neglected to report their existence, embarks upon an elaborate rhetorical exercise to explain their existence, in contradiction with the communal ideas of the glorious revolution. His flow of rhetoric is abruptly arrested by Comrade Legesse's order, "Dismantle them today."

Tesfaye now speaks up in favor of the plots, as a transitory phenomenon till the communal efforts function better. The settlers are often hungry, and these plots play a major role in ameliorating the poor nutrition of the settlers. Legesse's face turns to stone.

"We are not here to enter all sorts of arguments. We have to stay focused on the ideas of the Revolution. If we start all kinds of counter-measures, our direction will be diverted. Do as I say."

"But we cannot improve our harvest without even some oxen," Tesfaye hears himself say.

"You will get new tractors shortly. The orders have been accepted in Russia. As a modern nation, we use tractors, and here the oxen suffer from rinderpest. Just have a little patience, and you will be on the right track."

"In the meantime, the settlers starve and their children are malnourished," Tesfaye fires back. "You talk about orders from Russia, but we try to live today, tomorrow. We cannot eat promises." Tesfaye recalls "the resounding gong" he read about for Seyoum. "All you give us is words, words, words."

"You are becoming a nuisance, Comrade Tesfaye." The word "comrade" is pronounced icily, with a slightly ironical tone.

Tesfaye doesn't miss it. "Comrade"—same word, different tone. Legesse nods to Dawit, who gets up and escorts Tesfaye outside the meeting room. For a moment, Tesfaye panics. Has Dawit been ordered to shoot him? But out on the steps, Dawit pats Tesfaye calmly on his back and returns inside. Tesfaye sucks in the still fresh morning air, with a deep breath.

Death can be just words away.

But first, the everyday sets in again. The cadre people leave, after the private plots have been razed to the ground. Seyoum keeps quiet, but soon after resumes his secret, or not so secret, work on his plot down by the river. Sunny days follow rainy ones. Tesfaye marries Tariq, with whom he has lived for a long time already, it seems. No big deal in a time of revolution, except that Tesfaye feels that his marriage has sealed his fate with this settlement. By marrying a peasant girl, he has made the commitment to stay with the whole experiment. And Tariq is expecting a baby in three months.

It is now half a year later, in the year of 1989, and Tesfaye has a lovely young son, Attalel. He had seemed weak right after the birth, but he picked up with the plentiful nursing from his mother. And Tesfaye made sure that Tariq eats as many of Seyoum's vegetables as possible and receives lots of boiled water. The rains have ended and Mescal is going to be celebrated before the Government people arrive. They do not appreciate Mescal celebrations.

In between looking after his young baby, Tesfaye has a sense of foreboding. The harvest does not look promising, and many settlers have absconded, hotly or not so hotly pursued by Dawit and his men. Some are caught and ordered to be executed as a warning to the others. Tesfaye wonders if Dawit just follows orders or what? Is he still truly on their side? Rumors of summary executions come from the neighboring camps. But in spite of this, or because of this, the whole settlement seems in the grip of anti-revolutionary feelings.

The private plots have yielded precious vegetables, but now, the more apparent ones are destroyed or camouflaged to hide them from the visitors from the city. Seyoum seems quite oblivious to the lurking danger and is happily absorbed with his little plot. He has gained a not-so-secret reputation for his hot peppers, which he sells at a high profit. Some chili has even found its way to the higher-ups.

Seyoum also has met a woman from the next settlement whom he is going to marry shortly. He seems immersed in his own life, in disregard of the goings-on around him. With his natural authority, he has remained a popular team leader, but he does not seem interested in politics, and now he spends most of his free time with his new love in the next resettlement village.

Tesfaye and Tariq have settled into married life, and they have employed a middle-aged widow to look after their son while they are working. They pay her in kind, mainly from Seyoum's vegetable garden.

Tesfaye enjoys his married life, with its little ups and downs. Marriage makes his life ordinary—normal. It sometimes makes him forget the constant stress of the ongoing revolution. But it is never far away, the ongoing struggle, the violence.

One day, Tesfaye is taking a walk with his son and the twenty-five-year-old widow, thinking over the upcoming meeting the next day with the Government people. He takes his son out of the nanny's arms and strolls down towards the river, where he admires the colorful hot peppers in Seyoum's little plot. Seyoum is crazy about Tesfaye's little baby, whom he thinks of as one of his lost sons. He has named his little garden after him: Attalel. May he trick death, it means. Tesfaye has just turned around to stroll back, when he thinks he hears some shots in the direction of the neighboring village.

What could it be? Wild animals? Warning shots? Villagers absconding? He had better get home with his little Attalel; he has to write down his report for the next day anyway.

He has just started uphill when he hears heavy panting behind him. He turns around and sees Seyoum, his face white, sweating heavily.

"Come, come. Give Attalel to your nanny. You'll be next. They are executing counter-revolutionaries, and Dawit warned me that it would be your turn when they get to our village." Seyoum grabs the baby and passes him to the widow.

"Follow me if you want to live." Tesfaye runs after the heavy-set but agile peasant into the forest next to the village, while he hears his son set into a full scream. Up the hill they run, and down the other side towards one of the local Oromo villages. In between the houses, around the corner into a grove of cedar trees, where Seyoum bends down and lifts a lid off a hidden well.

"Down you go. There's some water. Don't move till I come and whistle like this." He whistles hoarsely. "It will be night time and the signal that you can continue your escape."

"But, what about...?" Tesfaye cannot finish his sentence before he is pushed into the little shallow well, and the lid set back on top. Some rustling of branches that are moved to cover up the lid, and he hears Seyoum walk away from his hideout, talking in Oromo to some locals.

They must have done this before, is all he can think. And I didn't know about it.

He sits down in the shallow well, with a little pond of water next to him. He cups his hand and swallows a few mouthfuls. It tastes of soil and trees, but it is cool and feels good in his burning throat. What else does he not know about? And Seyoum, who always walks around as if he does not notice what is going on. Has he just been pretending, behind his taciturn façade? And Tesfaye himself, with all his clever words, has he just been naïve, if not outright stupid?

He feels a growing anger as he sits there. He becomes burning hot in the cool well and gets up to try to lift off the lid, but it doesn't budge. What is the use, anyway? He will just get himself shot. That would do no good. But he feels so angry: this was *his* revolution. Here he sits hiding in a well, while *his* revolution has been stolen from him. And from the people. People like him: students, peasants, women and children. What about Tariq? His little boy? Here they were supposed to work together in equality. Here they were supposed to have done away with oppressor and oppressed. Mengistu's regime hadn't changed any of that. They have just become different oppressors and different oppressed. How has he, Tesfaye, taken so long to understand that?

Now the military and the new bureaucracy rules and if you are not with them, you are considered the enemy and eliminated. It was too late for this revolution. He would have to go to the north and join the TPLF. He has heard many good things about them and their new leader, Meles Zenawi. They were supposed to live in true equality that even included women fighters. He wouldn't like Tariq to be a fighter. But it was true: what were words of equality if you didn't live it in action? That had been the problem with his revolution, where everything was merely slogans. Empty air, "the clanging cymbal." If he survived, he would go north and join the true freedom fighters.

But what if that revolution was going to be the same thing all over? New oppressors, new oppressed?

One thing Tesfaye does not understand is how Dawit, who served the Mengistu regime, had had him warned. Dawit had saved him, with Seyoum's help. Why? Tesfaye thinks and thinks, but it does not make sense. Dawit had said, "Are you for or are you against them?"

Tesfaye has plenty of time to ponder this question, for Seyoum doesn't seem to return. Sometimes he hears people running and shouting above him. He also hears shots fired. What is going on?

Now he is sitting here, and can do nothing but feel hungry. Maybe they will never come for him? Maybe Seyoum got killed and nobody knows about Tesfaye? He thinks about Seyoum and how he had believed that he was going to die. How Seyoum wanted his last rites and how he had calmed down when Tesfaye had read to him from the Bible. He wishes he had somebody to read for him now—even if it had to be from the Bible.

Tesfaye has fallen asleep and woken up so many times that he cannot remember any more. He feels disoriented and *his stomach is cruel to him*. He remembers Seyoum's expression. He has tried to lift the lid to no avail, and now he feels that he will run out of strength before he succeeds. There is nothing to do but to hope. Have faith that somebody will rescue him.

He comes close to praying. It was tempting.

He keeps up his courage thinking of his little son, Attalel, and what kind of a life he might have. He tries to feel optimistic about him. Tesfaye continues thinking good thoughts about Attalel, about how he loves him, until he dozes off. This is the only way to endure his loneliness and misery.

He is lying dozing, when he suddenly hears noises from far away in his dream corridor. Instantly, the lid is pushed partially aside, as someone whistles the note that was agreed upon.

But it is not Seyoum that Tesfaye hears. He only sees the dark contours of a person against the bright stars in the sky. He is blinded after the total darkness of the well.

Then he recognizes Kasa, his next-door neighbor.

"Where's Seyoum?" are his first, hoarse words. Kasa puts his fingers to his lips to keep him quiet, and helps him out of the well.

"Don't ask a lot of questions, it's very dangerous for me to be here with you. Seyoum is fine, I believe," Kasa whispers. "He disappeared.

Camp leaders got the idea that he had helped you escape. Yes, you know, there is the death penalty for that. I think Dawit warned him which direction the wind was blowing. Anyway, he already knew what the leadership thought about him. That he was an anti-revolutionary. Plots and all. He took Tariq and Attalel with him. I don't know how he managed to. I guess he figured it wouldn't be good for them here now. He left me a note with a message to get you out and to head north to meet him, you would know where. And you would all join the revolution for the liberation of Tigray."

"Here," Kasa hands Tesfaye a dirty bag of hide.

Tesfaye quickly peeps into it and sees some *enjera* wrapped in crumpled paper. Inside it lies Seyoum's old Bible.

"I thought you should take it along," Kasa says apologetically. "We have no use for it here."

Tesfaye stands speechless. The wily peasant. Revolutionary or not, he was Seyoum Egziabher and one thing for sure, he had been right about that *ox machine*.

"Now you must run. They have stopped looking so intensely for you tonight, but you must take advantage of the dark."

They embrace quickly, and Tesfaye turns to leave. Now words come to him. "See you when we and TPLF have liberated the country." He smiles and heads into the darkness of the forest, clutching the tattered Bible to his chest.

Millions of thoughts race through his confused brain. He tries to stop them and keeps repeating: north first to Addis and then on to Tigray. North first to Addis and then on to Tigray. Half-running along the starlit forest path, he keeps mumbling his new mantra, when suddenly the image of his friend Telahun comes to him. Dear old Telahun. He must try to find out about him on the way. Maybe he is still alive somewhere?

Miracles happen.

Epilogue:

While Meles and his compatriots were fighting Mengistu's dwindling followers and approaching Addis Ababa, Mengistu fled to his friend, President Robert Mugabe, in Zimbabwe. Mengistu still lives there. Meles succeeded in liberating Ethiopia from its cruel dictator and has been in power since. It is now his turn to be tested on his commitment to democracy. A new student movement, which has risen against those in power, is now being suppressed. They are fighting for change.

Sources:

Dawit Wolde Giorgis, *Red Tears: War, Famine and Revolution in Ethiopia*. Trenton, New Jersey: Red Sea Press, 1989.

Alula Pankhurst, *Resettlement and Famine in Ethiopia: The Villagers' Experience*. Manchester: Manchester University Press, 1992.

Jenny Hammond, *Fire from the Ashes. A Chronicle of the Revolution in Tigray, Ethiopia, 1975–1991*. New Jersey: The Red Sea Press, 1999.

Paul B. Henze, *Layers of Time. A History of Ethiopia*. London: Hurst & Company, 2000.

Quotes:

"Mengistu. We want Mengistu!" p. 23, Giorgis.

Figures of speech from Pankhurst:

"The quarrel of the sky"

"Stomach turned cruel"

"Ox machine"

"Disease sweeps like a broomstick"

Pankhurst also quotes the saying:

"Plus ça change, plus c'est la même chose (the more things change, the more they stay the same),* " p. 10.

Vocabulary and names:

Historical figures.

Amman ⊚ General Amman, who had been elected head of the Military Council as a compromise candidate, committed suicide when arrested by Mengistu's army.

Alemayehu ⊚ Major Alemayehu Haile, leader of the police force. He and Mogus and Teferi were gunned down by Mengistu and his henchmen during a regular meeting of the Steering Committee of the Military Council in the Palace of Menelik.

Habte ⊚ Major Sisay Habte, popular Chairman of the Foreign Affairs Committee, was arrested and executed with 18 officers and civilians.

Meles ⊚ Meles Zenawi was prime minister of Ethiopia from 1995 until he died in 2012.

Mengistu ⊚ Major Mengistu Haile Mariam became the Chairman of the Military Council after a ruthless and bloody power struggle in 1977. He remained the Leader of the State until he fled the country in 1991.

Mogus ⊚ Captain Mogus Wolde, head of the nation's economy.

Nadew ⊚ General Getachew Nadew, the Govenor of Eritrea, executed when asserting his authority.

Teferi ⊚ Teferi Banti, Chairman of the Military Council.

Fictional characters.

Attalel ⦿ Means "May (s)he trick (death)."

Kasa ⦿ Means "compensation."

Seyoum Egziabher ⦿ Means "gift of God." He is a person who has to live up to a promise.

Telahun ⦿ Means "Be an umbrella, insurance, shade."

Tesfaye ⦿ Means "my hope."

Political acronyms.

Derg ⦿ Popular term for the military government of Ethiopia. Amharic for "committee."

PA ⦿ Peasant Association.

PMAC ⦿ Provisional Military Administrative Committee.

RRC ⦿ Relief and Rehabilitation Commission.

TPLF ⦿ Tigrinian People's Liberation Front.

Ethiopian words.

Ethiopia Tikdem ⦿ Ethiopia first.

enjera ⦿ Round, spongy and lightly fermented, pancakelike bread.

teff ⦿ Grain crop preferred for *enjera*.

ferengi ⦿ Foreigner.

zemecha ⦿ Campaign to teach literacy and help the farmers establish peasant associations. In March 1975, 50,000 students were dispatched to the countryside.

The Beggar

It became a kind of a game—like playing *Catch me if you can.*

Every morning on her way to work in her silver-gray Pajero, the *ferengi* passed by the traffic light next to Urael Church. If the light was green, she zoomed by and turned left in the intersection. But if the light was red or turned yellow, her Pajero came to a squeaking halt, and all her beggar friends came running to the driver's side. Strongest ones first, then the fingerless ones, who often dropped the coin onto the street. Last came the legless ones who pushed their little homemade wooden carts close to the hot asphalt.

If the light turned green before the distribution was over and the drivers behind the Pajero began to honk, the *ferengi* threw a handful of coins out the window before rushing on into the turn. The beggars would scuffle all over the street and the pavement.

Their routine meetings at this intersection made beggars and *ferengi* driver feel like friends, or at least old acquaintances. The beggars called her *Mama*, and once, when her husband came by driving in her car, one of them exclaimed, "But where is *Mama*?"

Mama was on home leave in Europe. When she came back she seemed pleased to resume her daily interaction at the intersection.

"Hello, how are you today?"

"Fine, how are you?"

"It's a little cold," or, "A little hot."

"Why are there so many people today?"

"It's St. Urael's day."

Sometimes a policeman chased the beggars away. He might be new on the job or a zealot carrying out recent instructions from police quarters. However, sooner or later, affairs would return to normal and familiar faces greet each other again.

"How are you, Mama?"

"Fine, except I forgot it rains this much in Addis in July."

"Yes, the summer is cold here in Addis." The beggar tightened the plastic sheet around his shoulders.

The *ferengi* lady, whose real name was Mrs. Brown, watched the beggars in the pouring rain and wondered how they kept warm and dry? How they survived? Mrs. Brown had already spent a year-and a half working in reproductive health in the World Health Organization. She was fond of her job and pleased to be able to help, especially the women in this poor country. She felt it truly satisfying to be able to make a difference in some people's lives. But sometimes when she drove her Pajero around town, she felt overwhelmed by the number of beggars; she never could get used to all those destitutes. She had brought up the issue at meetings, and some projects had been started to help especially the younger women in the streets. But the number of beggars never seemed to decrease, and the problem appeared beyond any short-term repair.

What troubled Mrs. Brown the most were her own bewildered and sometimes negative feelings, whenever she approached those beggars around town. *Oh, not again.* Or, *Not just now.* Then she couldn't help blaming them for their annoying presence, even if she knew they were the victims of poverty. She caught herself wanting them rounded up and deported elsewhere, out of her sight. Or she would harden herself and watch them as if they were some kind of foreign species—not human beings like herself. Then she would keep her windows closed till the lights turned green.

But Mrs. Brown's growing familiarity with the beggars at the crossing near her house gradually made her feel differently towards them. As she had come to recognize the faces of this toothless old woman; that old, bent-over man; those cute, dirty children, she started to wonder who they were. Where did they come from? What were they doing? Their faces popped up in her thoughts as she sat home in her little garden reading a book with a cup of tea. Imagine if *she* could never sit in her own little private space with a cup of tea?

She felt especially attracted to that polite, nice-looking young man with half a leg missing. What could his story be? Who was he?

After some time, she thought that she might talk to one of the beggars. She could bring her housekeeper along; Mabrat could act as her interpreter. In fact, she felt an urgency to help that young man. And it occurred to her that she didn't know how long she would have the opportunity to do something.

So, one day the *ferengi* happened to have her housekeeper in the car when the traffic signal turned red, she asked Mabrat to roll down her window to talk to that young man on crutches.

Mabrat wasn't happy with this unexpected task, and protested, "I can't talk to a beggar whom I don't even know."

"I understand this is a little unusual, but I shall explain to you later."

"I don't feel comfortable about this." Mabrat felt she was within her rights to resist what she perceived as an impulsive whim by her *ferengi* mistress.

Mrs. Brown was just going to say something, when the cars behind her started to honk. The light had turned green. "Idiots," she sneered at the drivers behind her, and turned her car abruptly next to the curb. She opened her door and took a step towards the young beggar, who was watching in surprise. Reluctantly, Mabrat also stepped out of the car to translate for her lady.

It turned out the beggar understood Mrs. Brown's English very well, and they arranged a meeting at a nearby outdoor café. This whole little street event seemed to be of great entertainment value for the gaping onlookers, and it occurred to Mrs. Brown that she might have appeared slightly ridiculous to the locals. All the more reason for her not to give up on this idea, she thought to herself.

The next day when they entered the café, smartly dressed Ethiopians glanced quizzically as the *ferengi* pulled out a chair at one of the little tables for the beggar. They recognized the beggar and quickly determined that the *ferengi* was accompanied by her maid. These *ferengis*, they were crazy; they *felt sorry* for the poor and thought they could *do good* with little gestures and handouts. And when they had had enough, they would run back to their own, rich country feeling oh, so virtuous.

The Ethiopians returned to their own business, smiling disdainfully.

"What would you like to have?" "Coffee? Or something else?"

"Umm, I would like a Coke, or no, maybe a coffee with milk."

"And would you like some pastry too?"

"Yes, anything you like," the beggar was struggling to place his crutches on the ground next to his chair.

The *ferengi* lady leaned keenly towards the beggar on the other side of the table, "As my housekeeper, Mabrat, told you when we met, I will ask you some questions about your life, and she will translate for you and then back to me whenever needed."

"That's OK. Madam, anything you want to know."

"But your English is quite good, how did you learn it?"

"Well, some in school, some in the Army and then just what you pick up talking with the *ferengis*."

"You were in the army? Why don't you tell me the whole story? Where do you come from?"

"I come from the countryside near Debra Zeit. My family was poor, also we were many children. Ten, two died. I'm the fifth. I have two older sisters and three older brothers (one older brother died from, what do you call it, um, smallpox; one became blind from it). My father worked for other farmers and my mother helped with cooking on different holidays. The older kids looked after the younger ones. Some of us went to school, the village school, but I was the only one who stayed all the way through and went to secondary school in Debra Zeit. I used to do well in school, and some people helped pay for my school uniform and books."

"What's your name?"

"I was called Tekka after my uncle—what do you call it, the brother of my grandfather?"

"You mean great-uncle?"

"Yeah, great-uncle, who died fighting the Italians. That's one of the reasons why I wanted to join the army."

And Tekka went on telling about his life, with Mabrat helping him out with a word now and then. How he used to look after his siblings, how they would be hungry and cold and wet in the rainy season, how the younger ones learned to beg from the older ones. They would sing a little song and they would receive some dry bread or *enjera* or some brown bananas. Begging was not new to Tekka.

School was the high point of his life, and he began to dream of leaving the poverty of his family behind him. He received his diploma with distinction but decided to join the army, when Mengistu was in power, rather than go to high school.

"But wouldn't it have been better to stay in school and get some good education?" Mrs. Brown interrupted Tekka's story.

"I know you think so," Tekka answered with a smile. "What you don't understand is our situation. To us, it is very important to get better condition quickly."

"Yes, but...."

"Also, the army recruiters had already approached me. It was too late to say no."

"You mean they would force you?"

"Naturally. Me they asked, but often they just come to the villages, where they, what do you say, *catch* the young men for the army in the middle of the night."

"But *you*. You couldn't say no."

"Yes. I mean no," Tekka laughed. "Couldn't say no."

Tekka told how he received more education and was doing well in the army, but he was sent north to fight, before he became an officer, because Mengistu needed men to fight the Ethiopian People's Liberation Front. Up near Dessie, he had been sent on reconnaissance, when he and his comrades ran into a Tigrinian ambush. Several of his army comrades were shot just around him. Their unit, led by a young, inexperienced officer, retreated towards where they came from as fast as their legs could carry them. They got separated from each other in the dark, and then.... This was difficult to tell, and Tekka paused.

Mrs. Brown took a sip of her strong coffee. She looked around at the people at the other tables. They were all talking together, but she suddenly got the feeling that they were also listening to Tekka's story.

Tekka lifted his head after a long silence. The *ferengi* looked at him with pity in her eyes. "I can't tell this. I lost my foot and part of my leg. I just lost half a leg."

"I'm sorry," Mrs. Brown muttered. She kept twisting her coffee cup on its saucer, while Tekka continued quickly, in a toneless voice, how he had wrapped his shirt around the torn-up end to slow down the bleeding; how he had waited for help while the sun rose mercilessly; how he could hear the moaning of other mortally wounded comrades.

Then he told how he had finally heard the sound of a horse cart on the gravel road a little below him, and had managed to stand up on his one leg and called for help. He couldn't hear any sound from his mouth himself, but the farmer looked up and saw him.

Through many ordeals, he finally reached a military hospital, where his leg was amputated at the knee.

"But doesn't your country do something for the veterans?"

"Well, I got some crutches, some training—what do you call it?"

"Rehabilitation."

"Rehabilitation, yes, and 500 birr. This is not America, where the soldiers are provided for the rest of their lives."

"I don't know about that," Mrs. Brown wrinkled her forehead. "But why don't you just continue?"

"Sure. Here, if you are an invalid, you must become a beggar."

Mrs. Brown asked some more questions and was made to understand that Tekka had resigned himself to life in the street but also that his desire for life was unabated. There was always some little hope there, around the corner of the dusty street. So, if the *ferengi* would help him get a job, he would be very grateful. He looked optimistic.

Mrs. Brown promised she would find him something, but although her decision made her feel better, she also sat with a nagging feeling of … she couldn't find the word for it. What was it? Here she appeared so all-powerful, and what could she really do? How much was she willing to do? How far beyond her immediate feelings did her commitment go?

"Anything. I am willing to do anything. And you know where to find me," Tekka added wryly.

It was getting to be rush hour, and the traffic was dense. That was both good and bad: good because there were more cars but bad because the drivers got irritated. But it was more good than bad, and Tekka concentrated on his task surveying the cars for potential donors.

He knew who they were: *ferengis*—especially middle-aged ladies driving the car alone—they tended to give. Some *ferengi* men would donate, but some would be particularly nasty and even try to run him over. That was the hazard of the trade. It took all Tekka's concentration looking for the best cars, like a car with a sticker, *Jesus is Lord*, a UN car, a car with children. But even those were tricky, and he always had to be ready to beat a retreat. Also, putting on that cheerful smile could be exhausting in the long run, but Tekka had learned that a smiling face and polite manners brought more profit. A miserable face or too provocative manners or the opposite, self-effacing demeanor, were counterproductive. The trick was to not make the potential giver feel uncomfortable.

After a couple of hours and half a pocketful of coins, Tekka called it quits. His friend Telahun had joined him for the last hour, and they decided to go away from the big streets to their little alley, where they could buy some cheap *enjera*, with a little vegetable and bean *wat*. They walked down the road past Urael Church, where women, covered in the traditional white cotton *shammas*, thronged before the gates to the sound of prayers over the loudspeakers.

They greeted a couple of familiar beggars and passed a coin to a raggedy newcomer from the countryside. He was old and sick-looking, and hadn't managed to do any begging yet. "Thanks to almighty God," he mumbled repeatedly, and bowed deeply.

"God provides," one of the onlookers joined in.

Tekka and Telahun turned down the little dirt alley with crooked dung houses under corrugated iron roofs. Tekka had no trouble keeping up with Telahun's pace; his crutches had become a natural part of him.

A young, heavily made-up prostitute in short black, silky pants and high heels came towards them.

"Heading for work," Telahun smiled to her.

"Yeah, we can't all go to work at the same time. It would get too crowded," Zeritu laughed back, revealing a sparkling set of teeth behind the full red lips.

Tekka had looked down when Zeritu flashed her smile. He had not said anything.

The two men continued down the road till they bent their backs and turned into the opening of one of the cow-dung huts. It was dark in there, and smoke-filled from the charcoal fire. They sat down at a rickety wooden table, and a thin young woman put two plates in front of them. A couple of children were crawling on a dirty mattress in the semi-darkness by the other wall.

"So how are you today, Ababa?" Tekka asked.

"Nothing to talk about, and Sophie has gotten the flu. And I can't afford to go to the doctor or get any medicine."

"Just keep her warm and give her enough to drink. Those doctors don't do anything but order medicine, and that usually doesn't help anyway. So why bother? She's better off right here," Tekka tried to cheer her up.

"And how about some *tejj*, of your best?" he added. "Time to celebrate; I was invited to a café yesterday by a *ferengi* lady."

"What did she want?" Ababa asked.

"Who knows? But maybe she can get me a job."

"They all promise that. Don't get your hopes up. But she must have had some purpose." Ababa grimaced.

"She wanted to hear about my life. Maybe she was some kind of writer. She seemed kind enough, and her maid whispered to me that she was a good lady."

"What's that supposed to mean? Ababa slammed two cups of *tejj* in front of her customers. "You can pay for this?"

"We're rich today, and the lady gave me 10 birr," Tekka turned out the lining of his torn pants, and some coins rolled onto the table.

"I must be careful with that hole in the pocket, I could lose half my fortune," he laughed. "Here's one for Sophie and an extra one for good health. Cheers!"

Tekka and Telahun woke up with heavy heads the next morning, and Tekka quickly felt for the 10 birr he had stuck in his secret pocket. They were still there. They had slept over at Ababa's and paid her a couple of coins.

Now Tekka remembered how he had been thinking of what he told the foreign lady about his accident just before falling asleep. Of course, he couldn't tell a white, *ferengi* lady how he had really felt. How in just one second his life had been annihilated. She wouldn't understand. Then he had fallen asleep and the whole experience had returned to him in a dream. Only it was as if it was real, the pain that dark, cold night when he had stepped on a land mine. The explosion that tore through his eardrums, the sudden light that blinded him. And the hot, wet pain. The pain, which was at first pure pain. But that was the easy part, the pure pain.

After some time, his brain insisted on registering what was going on in the dark, in the pain. It insisted on interpreting the chaos. It centered his pain in his upper leg and made him look in the first faint daylight. Look at his leg. At his missing foot and bloody lower leg. The foot was not there.

He tore off his jacket and shirt and wrapped the shirt tightly around the stump of his leg as they had learned in their training, while his thoughts raced on.

Where was it? His foot. Blown to little particles? Maybe it would fertilize the field he was lying on?

He was prostrate on an ordinary field of early spring grass. Maybe it would be good for the grain? But his brain wouldn't stop there. It went on and on. Where was his foot? He wanted his foot back. What would he do without his foot? What would happen to him?

What he also didn't tell the kind lady was all the thoughts that had raced through his head, bitter thoughts of how nobody seemed to care about the dying soldiers. Why didn't anybody come to help? The villagers had heard the shootings. The army, didn't they come to the assistance of the wounded soldiers? He had prayed to God repeatedly, even if he hadn't thought he would suddenly help him. Was there a God? Would he become an invalid? Would he end up as a beggar, like all the beggars in Addis?

The horror of it had been too much and as the sun rose, he had lost consciousness. Maybe God had had mercy on him, after all?

A ray of sun through the thatched roof had brought him back to Ababa's dwelling. Yes, he had survived to experience the pain and agony of it all. How he had wished it was all over. How he had hoped he was dead, but he had been alive.

They had drunk too much last night, maybe that's why the old experience had come back to him so vividly. Now Sophie was screaming, and the sound pierced his fragile head. The same seemed to be the case for Telahun, so they decided to go elsewhere for a little coffee.

Bending their heads, they left Ababa's house through the doorway and headed farther up the lane to a public tap installed by the Ethiopian Red Cross. They waited in line and could finally splash their heads in nice cool water. They cupped their hands to drink from the cold, clear fluid. They agreed they could use a bath one of these days, and decided they would go down to the river at a good spot they knew. It sure would be neither clean nor warm water, but it was better than nothing.

. Refreshed, they proceeded to a *tukul* at the top of the winding road. They entered for their cup of coffee. The barkeeper gave them some bread from the previous day to go with the coffee.

"She's sure a pretty broad, that Zeritu," Telahun chewed dreamily.

"She's too expensive for us," Tekka interrupted him curtly. "Then you better try Ababa. There may be a chance, if you can get her to drink a little *tejj* to soften her up."

"But the kids. They are all over."

"Yeah, you may have to get them all a little drunk. Or you can pay the older one a little to keep the younger away. I once did that."

"You did? You screwed Ababa? I always thought she was such a prude. Fancy that," Telahun said, a little after.

"How was it?" he added after emptying his cup.

"You think I will tell you all my secrets. Find out for yourself."

"But it would be more exciting with Zeritu."

"Fucking exciting AIDS and all," Tekka said angrily. He got up and brushed crumbs off his pants, "time for the midday traffic at Urael. What saint's day is it today? We may have to go to the other side, if they close the road."

Noon clouds darkened the midday sun, and Tekka and Telahun took up their position at opposite sides of the road. Tekka waved to the silver-gray Pajero as it zoomed by for green light. The *ferengi* lady smiled broadly and waved.

In truth, she felt awfully ashamed. She had asked a couple of friends if they could use a guard or gardener. But when they learned that he was on crutches, they were not interested. She had also asked some NGOs for some kind of accountant job, but no luck. She had then decided she would take him as her own guard, and find another job for her old guard. She hadn't succeeded yet, and anyway, most of her time had been spent on the fundraising gala for the Women's Association.

For sure, she would get something done right away, she thought, as Tekka disappeared in her rear-view mirror.

"I guess it's funny," Tekka mumbled to himself.

He kept his eyes on the traffic. There was that black Mercedes AA 2144; that driver sometimes gave. But the light changed to yellow. The car crossed the intersection. Now the policeman on the other side waved for it to stop. Those policemen knew exactly how the cars couldn't make it if they crossed for yellow. He also took his little extra. See. He put his ticket pad back in the pocket. There, he threw a quick glance over his shoulder and grabbed some paper money, which he quickly pocketed, waving off the Mercedes.

A sudden gust of wind raised the dust across the street. Tekka realized it was going to rain. He didn't want to stay out here any longer. Here it came, the rain. Tekka had to run for shelter under an awning. Hopefully, the shopkeeper, Abraham, would be in a good mood and not chase him away. There came Ababa, with a torn umbrella, holding one kid by her hand and with another on her back. She was shopping. Too bad she had all those kids. A poor Ethiopian woman: yesterday pretty, today old, tomorrow dead. At least Zeritu has some style.

Now the rain was really coming down. The drainage didn't work. Look at the gutter, it was filling up. People were running—jumping over the pools of water, holding onto the plastic bags over their hair. Waving their umbrellas. One umbrella turned inside out. The spikes looked like the ribcage of a carcass.

The big hole with the sewage pipes on the other side was filling up. The workers were huddling under the protruding roof of the house. The sidewalk quickly turned into one big mudslide. There one old woman slid down right in the mud. A sewage worker was helping her up. Abraham was grumbling that the pedestrians (especially the beggars) were blocking the way.

"Fuck him!" Tekka squeezed closer to the wall of the building.

Maybe he would go to the church, Tekka thought. Where did Telahun disappear? Well, the sun seemed to be coming back. These were just the small rains. They do stop sometimes. Tekka decided to go and sit on the church steps even if they were still wet. There was Ibrahim, that old beggar crook. What was he up to? Tekka settled down onto the steps in front of the church. He stretched his tired limbs and decided to think things over.

That *ferengi* lady was good news. Something always happened unexpectedly (in the middle of the daily boredom); mostly something bad, like car accidents; poor people and their stories and troubles; funerals. But sometimes something good: a wedding, if that was good? And then this lady. One thing for sure, the *ferengis* were his best chance. That would be some good luck.

If only he could get a job, that would be great. With the money he had already saved up, maybe he could afford to set up a little store. Didn't need much: a little corrugated iron, an open spot, a few goods.

Good he had never told anybody about his secret stash of money, buried down in the cemetery. He had better go check it was still there. He praised himself on resisting telling anything to Telahun. No saying if he wouldn't be tempted to find it, the rascal. But it was tempting to tell about money when one stood about so much. Nothing much to talk about. That was something to talk about. It sure kept him going through the long day, thinking about his hidden money. (Apart from women.) And imagine that UN guy the other day. Tekka couldn't believe his luck. Did that guy mean to give him a 100 birr, or did he think it was only 10? One never knew. Sometimes those *ferengis* got those attacks of acute guilt feelings about being so dirty rich. Who knows?

He sure hoped that *ferengi* lady would stop at a red light soon. Or just stop.

Tekka was heading back towards the steps in front of Urael Church when he saw Zeritu walking towards him. Not in her shorts.

"What the hell are you doing out at this hour? Must be early morning for you," he said with a laugh, his heart pounding.

"It's no joke, and I need to talk to you. Can we go somewhere?"

"We can go sit by the river. I know a good spot, if you want to talk in peace. I see, you don't have your high heels on today."

"OK. I guess the river is as good as anything." Zeritu was not smiling

They headed down the road as the clouds disappeared on the horizon. It was chilly after the rain, and Zeritu shivered. Tekka offered her his beat-up jacket and placed it over her shoulder. They proceeded down the embankment and seated themselves on some big boulders. Tekka placed his crutches on the ground next to him.

A little downriver, two men had stripped and were washing themselves with brisk movements in the cold air.

"You better look the other way," Tekka laughed.

"As if that was any news, and I told you, I'm not in the mood for joking."

"Well, what brings me the honor?" Tekka bowed his head reverently.

"If you're not going to be serious, forget about it." Zeritu looked pained.

"OK. What's the story? Spit it out."

"I need some money."

"You have sure come to the right man," Tekka's tone was sarcastic but pleased.

"You told me you had some money some night at Ababa's. Some night we had a couple of glasses of homebrewed beer. I guess you lost some of your caution. You started mumbling about some money hidden away. You wanted to start a store or something."

"Did I? I'll be darned. Anyway, I could hardly earn as much as you do?" Tekka watched her pretty, pained face. No sparkling teeth today. "But what's the trouble?"

Zeritu looked around to ensure nobody was near them. Then she told in a low voice how her period had stayed away. She had gone to a doctor to be checked. The good news was that she was HIV negative; the bad news was that she was pregnant. She wanted an abortion, but she had spent a lot of money on clothes, and the rest she had given to her poor parents and her unmarried sister with her three kids. "And don't forget, half my salary goes to my pimp."

"Who's your pimp?"

"Never mind who. But you do understand that I need a convenient room, clothes and other things for my *work*." She added ironic emphasis to the last word. "The thing is, I need the money right away. I need to have the abortion as fast as possible. I am already in my third month."

"How about having the baby?"

"You know that would be the end of me. Just look at Ababa."

"Why don't we join our rags? I can look after the kid," Tekka looked earnestly at Zeritu. "Seriously."

"I don't do rags," Zeritu got up from the boulder and took some hurried steps along the river. "Come on. I have my profession. Be realistic."

She stopped in front of Tekka. "But thanks, anyways." Bent forward, she embraced him quickly and gave him a light kiss on his cheek.

Zeritu sat down on the boulder again next to Tekka. He could feel the warmth of her body on his arm.

"Well, if you continue in your profession, AIDS will be the end of you. You have been lucky so far."

"I know. Especially all those bastards who refuse to use condoms."

The sun was setting behind the clouds in the horizon, turning the sky into a palette of orange, red and purple. The boulders by the river turned rosy. "See, that bloody sky is a bad omen," Zeritu exclaimed, looking up at the sky.

"That's just old superstition. I thought you were smarter than that."

The two sat in silence and watched the bathing men get dressed. All kinds of thoughts raced through Tekka's head. He sure didn't want to give up his hard-earned money, but he did want to help Zeritu, and maybe it wasn't a coincidence that the *ferengi* lady had just promised him help? With a job, he could soon be back on his feet. But he didn't want Zeritu to return to her profession. He didn't want her with those sex-hungry men. They had no right, and they didn't care a damn about her; she was just a piece of flesh to them. Tekka didn't want to pursue the thought any further.

Suddenly he straightened up with a big smile on his face. "I will help you, but on the condition that you take up some other profession. I will even help you with some education, some computer course or the like. With your good looks, you will be able to get a job."

Zeritu sat in silence as the last splatter of red turned dark. Stars appeared on the sky. "I guess if you'll help me, I have no choice. And one profession can be as good as another as long as I don't have a child."

"That's a deal. Give me your hand," They got up from the cold stone and solemnly shook hands as darkness blurred the landscape. Zeritu bent forward and placed a soft, warm kiss on Tekka's lips.

The next day, a tired Tekka was back on the job. Last night, he had walked on his one leg to the churchyard to ensure his money was still there. His armpits were sore from the crutches. But he had counted one thousand three hundred sixty-eight birr and 25 cents. He had put most of it in a bag he was now carrying under his shirt. Just as he was wondering how to proceed with the money, the grey Pajero glided by and turned for the green light. He just had time to wave to the lady.

"Third time is the charm," he mumbled to himself.

Zeritu got her money and Tekka started on afresh, so to speak. Business was up and down, and it was very hard in the rainy season when the drivers didn't want to roll down their windows and let in the rain. He was ready to take a break for some weeks till the rainy season was over, but he wouldn't risk missing the silver Pajero.

Zeritu had had her abortion, and she had moved into a small place with a sister of hers to begin her new life. She had enrolled in a computer course and had gotten a part-time job in a small fancy apparel shop. As Tekka had predicted: her good looks made her an attractive applicant for many a job.

Tekka beamed over this happy turn in Zeritu's life. He knew he shouldn't get up any *unrealistic* hopes, but he dreamed away as he stood the long hours by the traffic signal. Every so often, his thoughts returned to that recent encounter. And he would think for the millionth time of *the kiss* there by the river. It was very different from that other time long back.

Now he just needed the job from the white *ferengi* woman.

A week later, the grey Pajero finally appeared, the light turned yellow, and the big car stopped. With a pounding heart, Tekka ran to the driver's dewed-up window and knocked on it. It was rolled down, and a man turned his head towards him.

"But where is Mama?" Tekka exclaimed.

"My wife got sick and had to be evacuated. She won't come back."

Perturbed, Tekka placed his hand on the window rim, "But…."

"I'm leaving too. If you don't mind, I will close the window. I have a cold."

The man in the car handed Tekka ten birr. The light turned green, and the Pajero escaped into the silvery rain.

The Pretty Maid

THE DRIVER SHIFTED DOWN AND THEY began the descent towards the town by the lake.

It brought to mind how excited she had been when she came to Awassa the first time. How beautiful she had found the lush greenery along the lake, full of colorful kingfishers and white egrets. Reflected in the water loomed the mountains which could change from clear to hazy in a matter of seconds. The sudden transformation from quiet sunshine to tropical storm, where torrents of rain would perforate the mirror of the lake.

And the rainbows. Never had she seen such magnificent rainbows as here in Awassa. They stretched from the mountains in the horizon to the palm trees in the town like a bridge from nature to human dwellings.

She hoped to see the rainbow again.

She looked through the dusty windows of the Land Rover, and her body tingled with memories of her visit here ten years ago when she was still new in the field. So here she was again. She recognized the simple town with the one main road going down to the lake. How young and naïve she had been those days, with her fixed ideas about development and justice. She had believed poverty and illness could be eradicated; the world could be changed just like that. Well, she knew better now—after years with UNICEF and NGOs. Disillusioned would be too strong a word, but she had certainly become pragmatic.

She stretched to peek down the wide road to the lake before the driver turned left towards her hotel. Some of them had gone on the lake, bird watching. So *romantic* she had been, falling in love with John, her colleague in the health sector. Yesterday, she had mustered the courage to ask the present head of the health sector if he knew anything about John Fellows. To her great surprise, he had told her that John had settled in Awassa after he left UNICEF. "As far as I know, he's still there, Mrs. Greene." He had given her John's old address. Did she dare see him again?

The old boat on the lake. She had gotten red paint on her pants when she sat down on the seat. The owner of the rickety boat had just given it a touch-up, a tourist façade. It reminded her how reluctant she had been to see the poverty—the naked destitution behind the idyllic village front. Even the horses that pulled the tourist carts had oozing sores under their harnesses; after noticing that, she found it frivolous using them.

The driver turned the Land Rover onto the crunching gravel in front of the Pena Hotel. The same hotel she had stayed in the last time. She looked forward to sitting on the balcony, sipping mango juice, while looking over the palm trees down to the people and animals in the street.

It came back to her in a flash, the sight from the balcony ten years ago, the peasant who kept beating his collapsed horse till some vendors took pity on the dying animal and restrained him. She could see it again, the protruding ribs of the prostrate horse, the look of despair in its bursting eyes. She had tried not to notice that part, because she had wanted a happy experience in Ethiopia.

What would it be like to see John again?

Her driver came to a stop between the flagpole and Hotel Pena. The green, yellow and red stripes of the Ethiopian flag were waving in the wind. The flag reminded Mrs. Greene of the pretty maid at the hotel. She had had many a conversation with that maid, who wanted to practice her English and meet the *ferengi*. Medina was her name. She was so cheerful, and her English was good. She had told her how she was first in her class and that she had wanted to become a doctor, but there was no money for it and she had decided to work as a maid. Temporarily.

Medina had told her about the significance of the colors of the Ethiopian flag. The green was for the fertility of the earth, yellow for hope and red for the blood of the martyrs.

Imagine, she had forgotten about Medina. Mrs. Greene looked at the flag flapping against the pole in the gentle wind.

Mrs. Greene had her bags carried upstairs and settled in. She would rest a little, before the dinner on the balcony. She wondered if Medina and her girlfriend were still there. Hardly. Ten years was a long time. And Medina had said *temporarily*—she was only working as a maid temporarily. Ten years was a long time, especially for women in that country. Medina was probably happily married with a flock of children. Maybe she had managed to become a nurse? Maybe she was still in this town? Mrs. Greene would try to find out.

She lay down on her bed, and the whole room turned a little. It had been a long day and a bumpy ride to Awassa. She inhaled the faint smell of the newly lacquered furniture, mixed with a touch of the *berbere* from the *doro wat* cooking in the kitchen below, and a generous splash of mosquito repellent. Funny, how each country had its particular smells. These were typical smells of Ethiopia—they made her feel at home.

But it was an eerie feeling, she felt sure she was in the same room as ten years ago. Now she remembered how, when she left, she had given Medina and her friend a hundred birr each in that very same room. The girlfriend had been so grateful that she had kissed the hem of Mrs. Greene's skirt. She had been so embarrassed over such extreme gratitude. She even flushed at the memory—as if the ten years had been instantaneously erased.

She closed her eyes. She had been another person then. She hadn't been Mrs. Greene. She had been Susan Jones. How did all that time pass so quickly? Her marriage to Bill. Their long struggle to become pregnant. Their terrible loss. But they had gotten over it and had a happy marriage anyway—or because of it? They had had their interesting work, exciting travels, their beautiful home and many common interests. Their lives were full—they couldn't possibly ask for more. Mrs. Greene dozed off.

She had woken up with a jolt and rushed to get to her dinner. Fortunately, people ate late here, so nine o'clock was no problem. After a delicious meal under a full moon in solitude and more memories—waiting for John, being with John—Mrs. Greene descended the stairs to pay her bill at the cashier downstairs. She kept looking at the woman in the cashier's box. Was it? She did look like Neguisse, Medina's girlfriend. In an aged and robust version. Her name, long forgotten, resurfaced just like that.

"Are you by any chance Neguisse, Medina's girlfriend?" Mrs. Greene asked.

The woman looked puzzled, but then her eyes focused on the speaker.

"And you are Mrs. Jones, who gave us a hundred birr each." Neguisse got up from her chair, grabbed the hands of the *ferengi* and shook them. "How nice to see you. It's a long time," and her face seemed to take on a pained expression. Or was Mrs. Greene just imagining?

"How is Medina? Is she around here?"

"She is no longer here," Neguisse hesitated. "A lot has happened. Something tragic. I will tell you but I have to work now. There are customers."

"Well, when can we meet? I am only here for three days, and we're on field trips to visit villages. And I may visit an old friend. That is, if I can find him," she added a little afterwards.

"How about tomorrow night? Then I will be off at seven o'clock."

"Very well, I shall meet you right here at seven o'clock. And I would like to pay my dinner bill," she said with a smile, and handed Neguisse a hundred birr.

During the day, Mrs. Greene had revisited some of the same villages from ten years' back. They were much like then, idyllic from a distance, nestled between palm trees in the mountains. It was only when you got closer that you noticed the poverty: the smoke-filled huts, the toothless old women, the barefoot youths. And the flies. They seemed to have gotten worse. They were sitting in the faces of all the villagers. Some kids had thick cakes of flies around their eyes.

Mrs. Greene kept busy waving them away from her own face. She would jerk away every time one managed to settle on her skin. The kids were amused by this. To them, it was some kind of eccentric behavior. They started to imitate the *ferengi* lady waving away flies, with big exaggerated gestures and little jumps. Mrs. Greene had had to laugh.

At seven o'clock that night, Neguisse showed Mrs. Greene the way to her house nearby, where she lived with her husband and a whole crowd of children. Mrs. Greene asked her how many and she had answered, "Five, no, actually six."

Neguisse told how she and her husband had been blessed with the many children, but that now she wished for no more *blessings*. One more was on its way, though. She patted her stomach. But now she was thanking God, and telling him that they wanted no more. They had trouble making ends meet.

The two women bent their heads to enter a low door in a modest clay house. One young girl caught Mrs. Greene's attention while Neguisse was speaking. She was very pretty and watched them with big serious eyes. Mrs. Greene felt as if she had met the little girl before.

The gentle-mannered husband was put in charge of the children, and Neguisse sat down on a stool in one corner of the sparse room, where she started brewing some coffee. She would search for words and stop for intervals, but her English was much improved. Thanks to Medina, she had learned English to be able to speak to the *ferengis* and the customers in the hotel. She paused.

"You asked about Medina. I will tell you her story," Neguisse leaned forward on her stool and placed her metal pan with the green coffee beans on a small stove with embers on it. She blew on the embers and shook the pan with the green beans.

Neguisse told how Medina had been born under a lucky rainbow. On May ninth, there had been a full rainbow. From the horizon to the town, with the green, yellow and red colors of the Ethiopian flag clearly visible. After a pause, she added, "It was fertility all right, but alas, the red should prove true also. But we didn't know then."

Medina had stood out among all her siblings. Like the rainbow she was colorful and radiant in a kind of hazy way. Her parents treated her like a little princess with dresses with … frills. (Mrs. Greene had supplied the word, when Neguisse hesitated.)

"Yes, frills, and lacquered shoes. When she started walking, she would tiptoe around the muddy pools from the rain. When the other kids would splash through the water and throw mud at each other, Medina would stay away from them. Like she was from a finer world. The villagers began to call her *the pretty maid*.

"In school, she was the top of our class. She could always remember everything. That was good. Then the teacher didn't have to hit her with the, what you call the stick for making lines?"

"The ruler."

"Hit her with the ruler. Or she might have thrown a temper tantrum. There was a devil inside of that little angel—if I may say so. She was very proud behind her angelic smile. If she felt slighted by any of the other kids, she would punish them by ignoring them. She expected everybody to be faithful … um … to serve her."

Neguisse poured the black roasted beans into a wooden grinder. She looked up again and smiled.

"The teachers said she could become a nurse—even a doctor. She could do anything. We stayed in school till twelfth grade. We had to take a bus to town for that. Our family and the villagers gave money to help us with books and uniforms. That's what I mean, I was lucky to be her friend. All our brothers and sisters only went to at most fifth grade. The boys. The girls only to third grade. Then they had to help at home, and some girls were married."

"They were married that young? But you have laws against it."

"Maybe now. But that doesn't make a big difference. Villagers do what is their tradition. It is also to protect the girls. Some girls are kidnapped and raped on their way to school or to fetch water. Then they have to stay with the man who raped them. When we went to school, a brother would accompany us all the time, or we risked getting abducted. So, it was a great sacrifice for the family.

But in the end, it was impossible anyway. How could we continue with an education? How could we get the money? So, my family forced me to marry. But I was lucky. I got a nice husband, even if we are poor," Neguisse smiled in the direction of her husband, who was busy putting some of the younger ones to bed at the other end of the room. He didn't understand his wife's English, but he nodded back.

The pretty young girl with the big, serious eyes sat on a stool nearby. She didn't take her eyes off the *ferengi* lady.

"As I told you, Medina finished first in our class, and we began to look for a job to help our families. I have to tell you that my husband is Medina's cousin, and that her family first put pressure on Medina to marry him. But she wasn't interested. He couldn't give her, I don't know … give her what she wanted. She was used to getting her way with her parents, so she won that battle. That's when my parents took the chance and put pressure on me to marry Simret. I couldn't oppose my parents' wishes, like Medina. Maybe that was my luck." Neguisse sent another smile in her husband's direction.

"So then we got those jobs as hotel maids, and they thought it was good that we could speak some English with the *ferengis*. We could communicate with the *ferengis*—especially Medina—but then the hotel manager (what's the word?) reproached or reprimanded us for talking too much with the *ferengis*.

"But that was not the worst," Neguisse raised her voice over the sound of grinding. "Medina was also talking with the Ethiopians—especially the Ethiopian men. They paid her a lot of attention. She was pretty and charming and not shy."

Neguisse turned silent and she concentrated on her coffee making. She put a kettle of water on to boil.

Mrs. Greene was aware of the little big-eyed girl watching them intensely. As if she could understand everything that was said. Mrs. Greene asked the girl's name.

"Little Medina," Neguisse said almost in a whisper. "We never found another name for her. I will tell you about that."

She spoke to the girl in Amharic, and the girl got up reluctantly, curtseyed for the *ferengi* and walked slowly towards her father at the other end of the room.

"Where were we? Yes. This is difficult to tell. It is hard to say exactly how it happened. As I told you, Medina was very … um … open with both Ethiopian and *ferengi* men. It could be misunderstood. I tried to tell her. I don't know. It was like she didn't believe me. Everybody had always treated her like a princess.

"So one day, Medina was making up the bed for an Ethiopian man who came here regularly. She had talked to him many times. This is very difficult to tell," Neguisse hesitated.

"Anyway, so it happened that he came back to the room to pick up something, he had forgotten there. Then he saw Medina. Then he locked the door from inside. Then he raped her.

"Crying, she told me afterwards. I told her to tell the manager. But she wouldn't. She begged me as her only friend not to say anything. We were afraid of her losing her job. It was terrible. She was crying so much, and I was so worried about her. What could I do? What should I have done? I still ask myself that question," Neguisse looked up at the rafters of the ceiling.

"Then she began to change. I could feel she was different." Neguisse wasn't sure what to say. "She was no longer herself," she said emphatically. "And I must tell you. She was never a strong believer. Like she didn't have to be. Now it seemed she lost her faith completely," Neguisse mumbled. "I knew that was very bad, and I became afraid for her.

"So, to continue the story, Medina stopped crying and started to use makeup. Now that Ethiopian man came more frequently and she showed me some jewelry she had received from him. Later, there were other men too, also white *ferengi* men, who visited the hotel or stayed there for a long time. And she took money, which she hid in my house. She was not so sweet anymore. And proud. Sometimes she would switch to her old self when we were together on a day off. We would lie under the shade of a tree and laugh and joke. Then I felt so happy. Maybe there was still hope?"

Neguisse fell silent again. She was in the process of pouring the boiling water on the ground coffee. She took a deep breath.

"Now came the first disaster. As you may have guessed, Medina became pregnant. Those were terrible days. We went crazy. What to do? Her Ethiopian man, whom I also knew by now and had talked to, offered to pay for an abortion. But she was afraid of that. She was afraid of hospitals. (And she had wanted to become a doctor!)

"Anyway, nobody could force Medina to do anything she didn't want. When it started to show, she got a vacation from the hotel and went to live with a relative in Addis Ababa, where she gave birth to Little Medina. Soon after she brought her baby daughter and settled in our house. So it was no secret anymore."

Neguisse boiled up the coffee. "Never was a secret."

"She wasn't fired from the hotel. It was incredible. But it must be because of the Ethiopian man. He is something in the Government. So maybe that's why? So after some time, Medina was back on her job. And everything continued like before.

"But she was *different*, and she was busy with her customers—if you understand. The hotel manager said nothing. Medina didn't talk much with me. I prayed to St. Mary and tried to take her with me to church. But she would not go to church, and she wouldn't talk with me.

"She was good to her daughter. She loved her and actually spoiled her. She treated her like she had been treated herself as a child. I told her not to spoil her daughter. But as you know by now, Medina didn't listen to anybody. She didn't care what people said. She didn't care about tradition. She didn't care about religion. I don't know what she cared about except her daughter. But she did save up a lot of money. She also paid me and Simret for our help with her baby. Even though I would have done it without pay. I would always do anything for Medina." Neguisse sighed.

Neguisse had poured the dark coffee into some little cups. "Do you take sugar?"

"No thanks, but a little milk if you have some."

"Simret," Neguisse said something in Amharic which included the word *ferengi* and Mrs. Greene was given a little milk in her small coffee cup.

"Then the next disaster happened.

"The man, I don't tell you his name, although I know him. He wanted to finish with Medina. He had trouble with his wife. Something about the wife's only brother had died in a car accident, and she had a breakdown. And she knew about her husband's affair and she insisted he no longer go to Awassa. So he was trying to please his wife." Neguisse fell silent.

"Or he got tired of Medina? You know the Ethiopian men! Maybe he wanted somebody new? Younger? You cannot imagine how Medina took it. She was so angry. Nobody ever let her down before, you know. She told me. I tried to calm her down and say that this was good. Now she could get out of it. This was her chance. She should go away. She could go to Addis or another town.

"But you know by now if she would listen. She just avoided me. She wouldn't talk to me. The only thing she said, 'I'm going to kill him. I'm going to kill him.' I was praying for her soul.

"Do you want more coffee?" Mrs. Greene said no thank you, or she wouldn't sleep. "I want to be fresh tomorrow."

The two ladies sat in silence for some time, listening to the subdued sound of some Ethiopian songs on the flickering TV in the background.

"You have a TV?"

"Yes, it is a gift from Medina. She would give gifts. She had so much money."

Neguisse cleared her throat, "One day, I was saying something to Medina. Trying to cheer her up. To tell her to change her life. But she got furious. She shouted at me and suddenly she yelled, 'I will kill him, and I will kill Little Medina. Then he will get what he deserves.'

"I was really scared. I knew she loved her daughter. I thought that she was going insane. And I became worried about Little Medina.

"Now I kept an extra eye on her. But I didn't really think that Medina would do these things. Just to take revenge—even if she was hateful towards that man. In the meantime, she had more new customers. And the hotel manager didn't say anything. Medina could do anything. Maybe he was involved too? What do I know? There were plenty rumors. So you couldn't even listen to them." Neguisse paused.

There was a murmuring voice in the TV in the background. Mrs. Greene looked at her watch, "It is getting late, and tomorrow I will try to find that friend of mine and in the evening, we have a dinner with the local government people."

"Yes, I have to get up early tomorrow; Sundays are usually busy. Just come over to my house when you come home from your field trips the day after tomorrow. That will be Monday night. Now you know where it is. I can make you some more coffee."

"Thanks. Maybe a soft drink would be fine. I'm afraid I drink too much coffee here in Ethiopia. And it's strong."

"Yes, Ethiopian coffee is the best coffee," Neguisse said proudly.

Back at the hotel on her way to her room, Mrs. Greene had run into one of the Government people, an old acquaintance from ten years back. Fighting back her bashfulness, she had asked if he knew about John Fellows. "Sure, everybody here knows John Fellows," he had answered laughingly. "Didn't you have some little … um … something with him at that time?"

She hadn't known what to say. And it hadn't been *a little something*: it had been her first and only serious love before she met Bill back in the United States. Not only did she feel embarrassed, but a rush of feelings suddenly overtook her. She didn't succeed in hiding her discomfiture and indignation, when the Government person cheerfully had added, "You weren't the only one, you know."

Maybe it would be unwise to revisit that old love of hers. After all, she was happily married now, and why stir up old emotions?

After the breakfast the next morning, Mrs. Greene debated with herself whether she should look up John Fellows or just forget it. But it was as if some outside power had gotten her to her feet and set them in motion in the direction of the address, which had been explained to her. It was a glorious morning with the dark mountains in sharp relief against the blue sky.

Quickly—too quickly—she found the cottage near the shore of the lake. Hesitantly, she knocked, and soon after, the door was opened. There he stood, looking at her in great surprise. "Lo and behold, isn't that Susan Jones? What a pleasant surprise! You look great, come on in," and he opened his arms to give her a hug.

John had gone native, and his formerly short curly hair was now braided in long strands—the Ethiopian way. He wore an Ethiopian-style shirt over some Levi's. His hair was streaked with silver gray, but he looked youthful. He looked the same as ten years ago—his features just slightly more chiseled. That was only becoming.

Susan at first felt awkward but began to relax while they had a cup of tea sitting looking over the blank, unbroken surface of Lake Awassa. They talked about their past ten years. She told him of her marriage, work and travels. (In between, she thought of their first passionate letters after they had parted and how his had seemed to lose their ardor very soon.) He gave her a brief account of how he had decided not to work in international development any more. He no longer believed in foreign aid. Instead he worked for the local Government—at a very low salary. (He had probably found somebody else soon after she left.)

In the early years, he had just lived at an annex to the Pena hotel, paying a low rent in return for staying there for so long. Then he found this cottage, which he rented. "You must admit I couldn't live in a more beautiful place." He waved his arm in the direction of the mountain-mirrored lake. "Here I go fishing, hunting and bird-watching."

He wasn't married, had never been. He preferred freedom and *free relationships.*

"What do you mean?" Susan was worried this was a rather silly question.

"After you left, I swore never to love just one woman again. So now I don't love one woman. I love all women—womankind," he winked teasingly. He clearly hadn't lost his charm.

Suddenly she had an unwelcome thought and before she could stop herself she had asked, "Did you know *the pretty maid*?"

"*The pretty maid*?"

"Oh, I call her that. I mean Medina. I met her when I stayed at the Pena that time."

"Maybe. Medina? I knew so many. I couldn't tell you. But it is possible," he smiled cheerfully at her.

After the tea, John went into the kitchen to make a couple of sandwiches for them. His housekeeper (his one *constant* woman, as he joked) had the Sunday off. While slicing some tomatoes, he suddenly exclaimed, "Why don't we go bird-watching in my boat and make it a picnic?"

Susan thought that was a great idea, and soon after, she stepped into John's little boat at the end of a homemade jetty of dirt and rocks. "Watch out for the paint," he joked as she sat down in the boat. She jumped up and sat down again with a laugh. So he remembered, too.

He had switched on the engine and they had gone almost all the way to the mountains on the other side of the lake. Then they would drift back along the shore to watch the birds. John had a pair of oars in the bottom of the boat so they could maneuver it without making any noise. They ate their sandwiches in between the bird-watching. They were both completely absorbed by their nature watch, and their only conversation was simple utterances, "Look at those sand plovers." "That's a water thicknee." "Pretty sure that's an African finfoot."

Forgetting time and place, they skimmed the water, eyeing African jacanas and egrets and hamerkop, and they searched the skies for the African fish eagle, great sparrow hawk and Egyptian goose. Finally, they had arrived at a big lagoon full of marabou storks, great cormorants and great white egrets. But Susan's favorites were still the kingfishers, the pied ones, but especially the malachite. Its colors were so sharp. Almost too bright for nature, she thought.

John rowed the boat in between the reeds, under the shady branches of the big trees on the shore. Their drifting boat had come to a standstill while they listened to the birds and the rustle in the leaves. In the quiet, they gradually perceived a distant rumbling of thunder. There was a sudden gust of wind, and when they looked up, they glimpsed big dark clouds moving briskly above the leaves of the trees. "Time to go home," John announced, and began to row the boat out of the reeds. Further out, he turned on the engine, but big drops of water were already falling and before they reached his little muddy jetty, the rain came pouring down and their clothes were drenched. Laughing, they tumbled out of the boat and ran into the house.

John closed the door to the glass veranda behind them. Then he locked it and turned towards Susan. Her muddy clothes were clinging to her like the scales of a fish. He stood looking at her in silence. She returned his look. "My pretty mermaid," he whispered and pulled her gently towards him. "You seduce me."

There was no resisting.

John had walked her back to the hotel late in the afternoon, but she had insisted he turn back before they were in sight of the hotel. She was wearing clothes she had borrowed from him. He would bring her dried clothes over the next day. But she had field trips all day and had promised to see Neguisse at night. She could see him Tuesday morning before leaving. Maybe she wanted to stay a little longer? he asked.

Susan felt both wonderful and terrible—she realized that she really wanted to stay more than anything else, but she also knew that she had to leave. She told John she would think about it. She squeezed his hand briefly but hard, before she turned away from him.

In a haze, she returned to the hotel and rushed up the steps to her room. Breathlessly, she changed her clothes. She didn't shower; she didn't want to lose her *fish scales*. She brushed her unruly hair and ran up to the dining room for the Government dinner.

Susan was exhausted that night when she finally went to bed. She fell asleep right away and didn't wake up till she heard the crowing cocks around five o'clock. She turned over in bed and let herself sink into the blissful feeling of having been loved and caressed. On the periphery of her consciousness was the big decision she had to make. But for now … just a few moments longer … she would merely dwell in her sensations of that completely pleasurable day with John.

But it soon was time to get up and face another day. She had to brace herself for the visits to the villages. There was not time for serious thinking, although it was as if John and Bill were right next to her—invisible—while she talked with officials, interacted with villagers and brushed the flies away.

After a rushed meal, she hurried over to Neguisse's home and bent her head as she entered the low door. The two ladies went right back to their chairs; they had no time to waste. There was a bottle of Coke and a Fanta between them.

Little Medina sat at a distance watching them. Neguisse said something to her. The child shook her head.

"I tell her to go and play, but she says she wants to stay here and listen to the *ferengi* lady."

"That's OK," Mrs. Greene assured Neguisse, "she doesn't disturb us." Neguisse said something to Little Medina, who cast a furtive smile at Mrs. Greene.

"To get back to the story. I also knew that Ethiopian man a bit. As I already said, he came so often and we talked together. He of course told another story than Medina. He said he didn't rape her that she had played up to it herself. But you know those men. They always say like that.

"And … and then there was this thing with his wife. So he stopped coming. Maybe he stayed somewhere else. I don't know. And Medina was very angry. She threw a fit, shouted and screamed and threw things around. And after that she carried on worse than before, as I told you.

"Till the next disaster struck.

"A sinful life like that, and you know there will be a punishment. Medina's period didn't come, so she went to a doctor and was found pregnant again. The um, fertility … of the flag, you remember. The worst thing was that they also tested her for HIV and found her positive. Here, we thought it was the end of the world when she got pregnant the first time. Yes, you never know how bad it can get. Now it was truly the end of the world," Neguisse said in a loud whisper.

Neguisse poured the soft drinks into the glasses, while she collected her thoughts. "This time, Medina reacted differently. She didn't throw a fit, like the other times she was unhappy. Instead she turned quiet, with this glow in her eyes. Like the smooth lake before a storm.

"I was very scared.

"I knew nothing good could come of it. I tried to get her to come to church. I tried to reach her, but it was impossible. She had closed her soul from God and the world. I prayed for her more than ever." Neguisse's eyes filled up.

"But my prayers didn't help and that Government man came to the hotel again. You should have seen Medina. I never saw her look more beautiful.

"She persuaded him?"

"No, you mean *seduced*."

"Yes, that's it. *Seduced* him. And it was like she used magic on him. She was like … the word from the old stories … *a sorceress*. You could see it on him that he was bewitched, and he also had that distant look in his eyes. He came very often now."

Mrs. Greene was staring at the floor, and didn't look up at Neguisse, who had paused to take a sip of her Coke. "It was like a dance of death. We knew it couldn't last, and soon her pregnancy would show again. Her man came to me to pay for a room we have for Medina. She was again on *vacation*. I gave her food and took care of her as best I could. The man would still come.

"One day, I made one great effort to communicate with Medina, and she finally said something. What she said made everything worse. But it was my own fault, I shouldn't have tried to talk to her." Neguisse's eyes welled up again. "I asked how she was feeling?

"And she says, 'I feel fine. I never felt better.'

"'Are you happy with … you know….'

"'Happy? I don't know if that is the right word.'

"And she pauses. Then she says clearly, 'Let's say satisfied. Yes, satisfied that I am getting revenge.'

"'Revenge? How do you mean?' I say.

"'Well, we have this wonderful sex. Lots of sex. Thorough—with no protection. It will do him good. His wife too. You understand now?' and she looked at me with those burning, fanatic eyes.

"I finally understood. So stupid I had been. But what could I do?

"I didn't even know that the worst was yet to come. God's punishment will come," Neguisse got up, went over to Little Medina and whispered something in her ear. Medina stood up slowly and began to walk away, throwing one last glance over her shoulder at her *ferengi* friend. Mrs. Greene smiled to her.

"I don't want Little Medina to be here any longer. Maybe she can't understand English. Still, I feel like she understands."

"Does she look like her mother?" Mrs. Greene asked. "Or her father?" she added abruptly.

Neguisse hesitated. "She doesn't really look like her mother or her father—also her skin is much lighter. He was handsome but very dark-skinned. But it's more her ways that resemble her mother. She seems so proud and independent. And … what's the word? … *persuasive* like her mother."

Mrs. Greene stared at Neguisse. "Are you all right?" Neguisse asked, and took Mrs. Greene's hand. "You look … so strange. Are you OK?"

"Yes, I'm OK. There have been so many impressions today. I think I'm tired." She looked at her watch, "I'd better go back soon."

"Yes, it won't be long now. I will make the last bit short.

"Now Medina grows bigger and bigger. The man still comes—sometimes. Finally, she has her baby. A little boy. The birth was easy and she nurses the boy. He was much darker-skinned than his sister. The father seemed very happy about the boy. He even told me that he only had daughters home in Addis.

"But it was to get even worse; I will make it short. One day, Medina comes into the room. It was a warm sunny afternoon, but she didn't look good. She asks for Little Medina, but Simret had taken her with him to the *souq*.

"She goes back to her room quickly.

"I sit for a little while. But I have this funny feeling; I was feeling uneasy. Suddenly, I get really scared and run outside and into her room.

"The sight. I can't tell you. She had killed her baby. She had cut his throat. Then she had killed herself. She had stabbed herself. She was smeared in blood. She was lying on her bed. The knife had fallen out of her hand and the blood was dripping from between her ribs down on the carpet. Red drops on the green and yellow stripes. (I had woven that carpet for her.)

"I just stood looking at that blood that goes drip, drip on that carpet. All I could think was the *green, the yellow and the blood of the martyrs.*

"But the worst was her eyes. They were not closed. Wide open—the look of despair." Neguisse gave a sob. "She couldn't hide it … in death."

The local and the foreign lady sat a long while not moving, their soft drinks barely touched. Finally, Mrs. Greene got up. Her voice was hoarse, "Like a Greek tragedy. It was fate. Nothing could be done. You did the best you could." She embraced Neguisse and held her for a long while.

"I will come and say goodbye to you tomorrow morning before I leave," she said softly.

"That would be good. I am off tomorrow," Neguisse answered.

Back at the hotel, Mrs. Greene ordered a beer to take up to her room. Maybe that would soothe her a little. And she was lucky, there was warm water in the shower. The hot streams of water massaged her skin into her human body again. She thought what had happened between her and John had been fated somehow. But it was as though Neguisse's unhappy story had made her miss Bill and their regular life together. Her life was with Bill, not here in Ethiopia. How long would it last if she stayed with John? No, she was not in doubt. But that didn't make her departure less painful.

She would write a note to John with the bundle of clothes she had put in a bag for him. She would just give it to him if he came by the hotel before she left. But she couldn't think of what to write: it sounded either *too big*—or *too small.* In the end she merely wrote, "Thanks forever, Susan."

Then she lay down in her bed and pulled her covers over her warm body.

But when she closed her eyes, she suddenly felt exposed to Little Medina's big watchful eyes. She dozed off and dreamt she was sleeping under the ceiling of Debre Birhan. The whole ceiling covered by big-eyed angels. Little girl's trusting eyes watching Mrs. Greene. They were imploring her. The same age as Maria, her infant, would have been. Then the faces were moving. Looking over their shoulder with a seductive smile. She heard a mischievous laughter. The little devils, she heard herself mumble.

Finally, the cocks were crowing, and light began to seep in between the dense curtains. Mrs. Greene got out of her crumpled bed with a heavy head. She took another shower to wake up. This time it was icy, and she dressed, shivering, in the cold morning air. She skipped breakfast and hurried over to Neguisse's house.

On the way, Mrs. Greene noticed how it was raining a little over the mountains behind the lake, while the morning sun threw its rays in through the dusty rain. The colors of a faint, hazy rainbow appeared. Her strained face relaxed a little.

Neguisse was sitting on a low stool in her courtyard, in front of a big plastic bucket bulging with washing clothes and surrounded by colorful buckets. She lifted her arm in greeting and waved away a lock of her hair from her forehead. Bubbles of soapsuds remained sparkling in the bright morning sun on her temple.

A couple of young children were playing in the dirt. Little Medina, in a bright yellow sweater was sitting nearby, washing her blonde doll. "A gift from her mother," Neguisse smiled.

Mrs. Greene sat down on an empty stool. "I have been thinking … thinking all night.…"

Mrs. Greene sounded out of breath. She slowed down and glanced around the washing scene in the sunny courtyard. She looked as if she was seeking strength from the idyllic domestic setting.

Then she heard her own voice, saying, "Maybe I could adopt Little Medina?" When she saw the incredulous expression on Neguisse's face, she repeated, "I am saying, maybe I could *adopt* Medina? I promise you she would have a nice home and loving parents. My husband would be a devoted father to her. And she could keep visiting you. And ... and she would get a good education. And ... and she could become a nurse, or even a doctor." She stopped abruptly.

She felt a ray of joy streaming through her body, just as she perceived the beginning of a heavy headache behind her temples.

Neguisse took her hands out of the washing tub. Again, she corrected the obstinate lock of hair on her temple. Again, her hand left soapsuds on her auburn hair. It matched some strands of gray already there.

Neguisse sat open-mouthed, without answering.

Little Medina picked up her doll and held her tightly in her thin arms.

"Well, what do you think? Should we try?"

The soapsuds melted away in the strong sunlight.

"Maybe Medina would have wanted it?" Susan said tentatively.

"Not a nurse. A doctor," Neguisse said firmly.

The Terrorist

THE STUDENTS LINGERED UNDER THE BRIGHT moon, savoring the mild evening. They slouched on the metal chairs in front of the cafés, stood chatting in clusters, strolled up and down the broad pavement of King George Street. It was Friday night, and they had oceans of time before Monday morning classes.

A drummer began tapping a beat for a group of female students, and the young, slender women began to click their fingers and sway to the music. The moon caressed the golden brown skin between their skimpy blouses and low-waisted pants. The drumbeat grew more intense, the bare midriffs coiled faster, and onlookers began to clap.

Anwar watched from a distance. Beautiful, silly women. His eyes fixated on the belly of one of them. The gyrating human flesh hypnotized him: *Come, come, come—if you dare.*

Hana would never have danced like that in public. His fiancée, who had won the immigrant lottery. Her father had applied as soon as she turned eighteen. Now she had further betrayed him with that coward in America. And Anwar couldn't go there—he was trapped in Ethiopia. You couldn't trust women.

Anwar just wanted to be left alone. Hopefully he wouldn't run into any of his old student friends—especially not Tesfaye. He started to walk towards his house in the direction of Arat Kilo, when a piece of paper was stuck into his hand. He looked around, but the kid who delivered the note was already darting away amongst the crowds. Was he already being contacted? He had barely finished his training. With beating heart, he turned into the courtyard of his aunt's apartment complex.

Anwar ascended the worn wooden stairs, where the stagnant air suffocated him. He fumbled with his key. The light was out on the landing as usual. He finally succeeded to unlock the rusty lock and entered the narrow, stuffy hallway. Thank God his aunt was visiting his mother these days. He wouldn't have to deal with her too. But his mother…? She would forgive him, was all he could think.

Anwar went straight to the kitchen sink to wash his hands before he read his note. The warm tap water came in a thin trickle, and he struggled to wash off the final soap suds.

Anwar switched on the bare lightbulb and read:

"*Bismillah.* Tomorrow morning at 10 p.m., take garbage truck parked at the university end of Freedom Street and drive it (keys will be in ignition) to No. 7. Turn right through blue gate, which will be opened. Proceed into building at the end of courtyard. Full speed into building.

Memorize and destroy this note immediately. *Bismillah ar-Rahman ar-Rahim.*

Anwar knew No. 7. The building housed offices belonging to various ministries. They were not official buildings, but it was where the Government people worked, Anwar knew from his volunteer work at the orphanage next door. What about the orphanage?" His stomach made some painful contractions, and he started to pace up and down. It was Saturday; maybe the children would not be there. He wondered who would be in the offices. He had often seen Americans there. The sheik had told him that for sure, they would hit the Americans. But he couldn't worry about that now. It was beyond him. At this point he was just following orders. *Allahu Akbar.*

Anwar went to the kitchen cupboard where he knew his aunt was hiding her cigarettes. He had given up smoking as part of his preparations for his mission, but now he told himself that he could be allowed his last cigarette or two in this life.

It would be atoned for.

He had tried to tell his aunt to refrain from smoking, but she had been completely unimpressed by any admonishment. We don't live in the Middle Ages, she had retorted.

He pushed open the peeling window frame, and a humming sound of voices and cars entered the room. He could still get out of it. The sheik wouldn't be pleased, but he had emphasized several times that his act should be one of free will. He was not coerced; he did it out of his pure heart. The smoke from his cigarette was sucked upwards. He stood listening to the ebb and flow of the cars, intermittent laughter, a raised voice. The world as he knew it. Pain and joy. But mainly pain. He couldn't imagine heaven, the garden of the flowing rivers. Flowing rivers with bathing virgins. Were there no bathing young men?

But he couldn't fathom that this could be the last night of his life on Earth. He could still refuse.

He stood indecisively as his dizziness from the smoking abated; then he abruptly walked to his aunt's cooler for a soft drink.

The phone rang. Anwar froze. Who could it be? Should he take it? It could be from them. He'd better take it.

"Hello … oh, it's you, auntie!"

"Yes, it's me. You sound so surprised."

"Oh … oh, no … of course not."

"I was just debating with myself if I should come back tomorrow or stay with your mother a few more days."

"Oh, do stay … I think you should stay."

"You sound like you have something up your sleeve—are you planning a party in my apartment? You know you're welcome—remember the beer is in a case in the back of the little pantry."

"You know I don't drink beer."

"At least your friends may."

"Oh, sure."

"Did you see about that suicide bomber in Baghdad? Wasn't it awful?"

"I didn't see TV."

"You know what I think it is?"

"No...."

"Just young men's glorified suicide."

"You there?"

"Oh, yes...."

"Well, I hope you're OK. It's a bad connection. I will run. So see you at the end of the week."

"See you. Bye."

Anwar stood with the receiver in his hand. Then he put it down and took a deep gulp of the sweet mango soda, after wiping off the mouthpiece meticulously with a paper towel. He was still shaking from the telephone call. His head was empty. He pulled out another cigarette and lit it. Mechanically, he walked over to the old TV and switched it on. It was news as usual. Anwar's attention was caught by the grainy images on the TV screen. Some swaggering American soldiers, who looked like aliens in their combat gear, were pointing their automatic rifles at a group of frightened women while their home was being searched.

Annoyed, Anwar switched to Al-Jazeera. He stiffened. He bent forward and looked in paralysis. It couldn't be true. He had heard the rumors about Abu Ghraib for months, but here it was, the nauseating images of Arab men sexually humiliated by the Americans. Naked Arab buttocks, female boots planted on the kneeling Iraqi. The dog on a leash.

The same thing. Sodom and Gomorrah. Enraged, he turned off the TV and stormed out of the apartment. He had to do it: the purification.

The scene hadn't changed outside, but the noise level had risen by a few notches. Anwar just needed to keep walking; his decision didn't bring the peace he had hoped for. He needed to move his agitated body, so he just kept putting one leg in front of the other. His thoughts went hither and thither. He couldn't focus. I will stick to my course, he mumbled in a conversation with his father. It may not be the cause we talked about. But it is a cause. I will show you that I can do it. You will be proud of me. Maybe not exactly of what I do. That I don't know. But that I can act for a just cause. Like a man.

Anwar turned left and headed up the broad pavement towards Sidist Kilo. The world is what it is, it never changes, Anwar muttered to himself and a passing girl looked questioningly at the tall handsome man with the short-cropped beard and somber look. Annoyed, Anwar looked down when she smiled at him. Couldn't they leave him alone?

The potholed pavement was lit by the moon. Anwar walked by the National Museum and headed towards the main gate of the University Campus. He knew that he risked running into a friend, but something seemed to make him turn into his old student haunts. Maybe he was saying his last goodbye.

A couple of street dogs were foraging in some food scraps on the ground. One lifted its legs against one of the dusty trees. He remembered the little puppy that he had pleaded with his father not to drown, when the father undertook his regular killing of unwanted street dog puppies. It was a small beige mixture of God-knows-what, with white paws—as if it had walked through a saucer of cream. It was on purpose that Anwar chose the smallest one. It was so defenseless and had keenly licked his nose. He remembered its particular breath—a smell of innocence.

His father had been stern but just. He had died so unexpectedly. Life could end that quickly. It was like yesterday Anwar had gone to his child home in Bahir Dar, where his father lay in state. The family was waiting a day with the burial, to give Anwar, the oldest living son, the chance to take leave of his father.

Anwar's mother had come out to meet him, wiping her eyes with a corner of her apron. She had looked aged. He had embraced her, and they stood a long time while he mumbled his condolences.

The father was lying in the parents' double bed, dressed in a white cotton robe, hands straight down by his side. His eyes were closed, the mouth a little ajar. His face was pale and peaceful; he had found the peace he always sought in life. He had been strong in his faith and had tried to draw Anwar into the world of the believers.

Anwar had sat down on a little stool next to the body. The father had lost his favorite first-born, Anwar's older brother. A precocious kid, he had been run over by a reversing garbage truck as a six-year-old. That's how Anwar, whose real name was Ashebir, gift of God, became the oldest son of the five children. Anwar, who had looked much less promising than his brother, had asked himself why he had survived. Even his father, who always accepted God's ways, seemed to have been asking the same question.

Anwar had moved closer; he wanted to touch him, to reach him. He took his father's hand and lifted the arm a little. It was as stiff as if it was made of wood. The hand was ice cold, and the fingers a little bluish. He had imagined his father's voice: "I'm waiting Anwar. I can't wait forever."

Too late to prove himself to his father.

That's when Anwar had decided to go to the Friday mosque.

Anwar was looking for a bench to sit down. He glanced at his watch; it was only a little after 10 o'clock. Exactly 12 hours left. There was no hurry. He leaned back on the broken bench and closed his eyes.

He had gone to the mosque, where he kneeled with all the other men. Self-conscious, but also drawn in by a sense of togetherness. He had not *believed in the unseen*, but now he felt it: some higher power, a feeling of community, of guidance. Were there things he didn't know that his father had known? As a student, Anwar had always tried to understand with his rational reasoning. When he chose to become an engineer, he and his student friends believed in science, not superstition. They wanted a new and different Ethiopia. They wanted to be proud of their country.

They wanted to be proud.

Maybe he had been wrong after all. How could he be right and millions of believers wrong? Maybe it was true that he had *sealed his heart* and *covered his eyes* to the voice of the tradition—the voice of Islam. *Submit. Submit*, the pillars in the mosque had whispered; they exuded peace. Strength.

His back started to ache, and he was disturbed by a rustle in the nearby bushes where a young couple had disappeared. With a frown, Anwar got up from the dilapidated bench. A campus light flickered and went out. Why does nothing work in Ethiopia? Anwar muttered to himself. Why is Ethiopia so poor? He straddled some straws scattered on his pathway and came to think of the papyrus *tankwas* in Lake Tana. Year 2004 and Ethiopians still went fishing in straw boats. How antiquated Ethiopia was. He had had many a heated discussion with his father about his country. Whenever Anwar complained about the backwardness of Ethiopia, his father would respond that Ethiopia was good. He was proud of his country.

"How can you be proud? What has this country achieved?"

"We beat the Italians at the battle of Adwa."

"Always the battle of Adwa. We can't live forever on the battle of Adwa. What can we show the world: a few fallen stelae in Axum, some rock churches in Lalibela?"

"It's all the will of God."

"But, dad, you're just willing to settle for anything."

When Anwar raised his voice, his father would turn his back and go into the other room.

His father's generation were fatalistic in their faith; that's why they had not progressed.

But what good did it do him, Anwar, to become an engineer when there was no job to be found and the whole system was corrupt?

There were no other options; he had to fight back.

Anwar had been circling around the campus but was slowly heading out. He was just under the ark of the entrance, when he came face to face with his old friend Tesfaye.

"*Tenastelin. Tenastelin.* Where have you been, man? I have been looking all over for you. Nobody knew where you were!"

Anwar hugged his pal with a *tenastelin*.

Tesfaye looked at him questioningly.

"Nowhere. Everywhere," Anwar mumbled.

"What's that for an answer?" Tesfaye laughed.

"Well, you know, time flies."

Tesfaye looked searchingly at his old friend, who looked down.

"I was also ill for a while."

"What was wrong?"

"It was just a little flu.... And some stomach trouble," Anwar added, feeling some painful contractions as he spoke.

"Well, you need to get back on your feet, man. Be careful of what you eat and take some yogurt every day. That has made a difference to me."

"Want to come to my place for a beer?"

"It's getting late. I had better head home."

"Well, you know it's Friday."

"Yes, but I have some things to do tomorrow."

"Can it be so important?" Tesfaye laughed.

"That depends how you look at it."

"OK, I won't press you. But where can I reach you?"

"I'm still at my aunt's place."

"Good, I will come by soon and then, I will have no excuses; we're having a beer together." They hugged, and Tesfaye lingered while Anwar walked quickly towards Arat Kilo.

That would never be. Tesfaye was a happy-go-lucky opportunist, Anwar told himself, as he dodged the couples who dallied on the broad sidewalk. Nothing seemed to faze Tesfaye. But their friendship had become strained after their big discussion about careers, when Tesfaye had told Anwar about his intentions to work in his uncle's firm. He wanted to make money. Big money. Start his own construction firm. That would enable him to go abroad; once you had a successful business, you could come and go as you liked. You would have a say.

Tesfaye wanted to establish business relations with America. That's when Anwar had become sarcastic.

"You didn't use to think so highly of your uncle's business."

"Why don't you stop trying to save the world and get a life?" Tesfaye had suddenly lashed out.

A great sadness had descended over Anwar.

Anwar turned into a small café. He badly needed a toilet. He had taken a suppository the same morning, and his bowels were screaming for release. He had suffered from debilitating constipation, but now the laxative joined forces with his mission fever. He barely made it to the little filthy hole in the ground behind the kitchen. There was shit all over the ground. He washed himself feverishly afterwards and kept wiping his hands, long after he had entered the café again. He felt as if he still had filth on his hands and decided against eating anything lest it should become contaminated.

He could use another cigarette, but he ordered a Coke.

There was no reason to hurry back to the hot apartment. Anwar let his thoughts flow. It wasn't strange that Tesfaye hadn't seen him for a long time. They no longer frequented the same places. Anwar had been meeting with the group of men daily in a room, where they recited the Koran. The least he could do was to get to know the Koran; or he wouldn't be in a position to question it. He worked hard with his Arabic, but mostly he liked the singsong of the recital. It emptied his mind of other thoughts and gave him a soothing kind of peace.

Afterwards, they would talk about what was *haram* and what not. This was what was great about Islam: it taught you everything you needed to know in the daily conduct of your life. It gave you rules in all the confusion. And it was a way of life, he could agree with, simple and pure. He felt he could trust those men with their unassuming and sincere ways. He had made friends with a young Somali called Muhammad—like everybody else. He had also dropped out of the University, disgusted with the treatment of the students after their demonstrations for freedom of the press on campus back in 2001. It was right there at Arat Kilo, the police had attacked the peaceful students. Students were beaten, and many killed. But that was nothing compared to the ensuing detentions and humiliations. Better not think of that.

There the new government of Meles had shown its true face. Christian guards humiliating Muslims. They were just the lackeys of America. His new friend Muhammad wouldn't forget. He would ramble on about *rivers of blood*.

They didn't share Tesfaye's phony optimism. They wanted revenge. Wasn't his name Ashebir?

Anwar took a sip of his Coke. He thought of his recent acceptance to make *the ultimate sacrifice*. He had been encouraged by the old Somali sheik. Anwar had told him about the detention, but he couldn't talk to the old man of the despicable and loathsome act in the basement. It hadn't been necessary; they connected in their hatred of the *infidels*.

But after his big decision, his old student days had seemed from a previous life. He had gone to a secret training camp in the countryside where they had also seen videos of suicide missions smuggled out of Afghanistan and Iraq. His training was hell, although the select group of suicide bombers were somewhat spared from the grueling exercises. Having opted for the ultimate sacrifice, they had already obtained an elevated status.

But it gave him a purpose that he, Anwar, would play his small role in the larger cause. His act would serve as a warning to the Ethiopian Government that the opposition to the Western infidels was right there in Addis Ababa. The Ethiopian Government should watch out before they chose sides. Not to forget that the Ethiopian population was over fifty percent Muslim—and growing.

But he missed Tesfaye.

Resolutely, Anwar got up from his chair. He had barely sipped his Coke. He looked down the almost deserted street and he began to walk slowly towards his aunt's apartment.

Was it right to kill for a just cause? Could he call himself a believer, if there were many things in the Koran he disbelieved? Everything became ambiguous if he thought too much. Only one thing consoled him, whatever doubts he had, would be eradicated by the act itself. The act of *ultimate sacrifice* would prove his sincerity to the whole world. And his self-sacrifice would erase all guilt. All shame. That was the whole point. That was all he needed to do. Nothing else.

The soda bottle felt lukewarm. Anwar took a gulp before he went to his trunk to pull out some clean clothes. They were all crinkled, and he looked for the iron in the kitchen cupboard and put a cloth on the table. Satisfied, he put the newly ironed clothes over the chair and the empty bottle in the trash can. He stripped off his clothes, found a washcloth and began to clean and scrub his body methodically from head to toe. He took extra care with his genital parts and his anus. This was the most important area to purify. His head was empty, and he concentrated on his body. Holding his penis, he hesitated; he felt a great pain radiating from his entire body. It was as if he was saying goodbye to his physical self.

Quickly, he wiped himself and put on his boxer shorts. He set his alarm clock for 5 a.m. In case he didn't hear the *muezzin* after taking a sleeping pill. The old Somali had given it to him. *Sometimes our martyrs falter*. He sat down on his springy sofa, and a rush of contradictory feelings flooded over him: his frustration with Ethiopia and anger with the rich world accelerated into his rage over the Christian guards in the detention center. But then his whirlpool outrage faded into sad visions of hikes with Tesfaye in the sunny eucalyptus hills around Addis. If only he could talk to Tesfaye. But that would be a betrayal.

Instead, he would be going to the Garden of Paradise. Maybe he should meet his father there. At least he would have done something; Anwar would have left his mark.

He finished the sickening drink and got up from his couch. He had better write a suicide note. He found a piece of paper and a pencil. It was strange, whatever he thought of writing; it didn't seem to make any sense. He couldn't think of anything meaningful to say.

Would Hana hear that he had died a martyr?

He tightened his fingers on the pencil and wrote that he wanted to be buried *next to good Muslims*; he was thinking of his father, but couldn't mention him. Then he had the thought that there would be nothing left to burry.

He wanted to write something to his aunt; she had always been good to him. But he imagined her disdain. She had her point. His hands felt paralyzed.

But his mother, he could write her. He saw her for him washing clothes in the tub in the backyard. Always working. She was always there for them. For him. *Mother*, he called out.

He could still fail to show up. Give up. Join Tesfaye and his ranks. He couldn't think any more; he was going crazy. He fell down in the couch.

His exhaustion and half a sleeping pill worked. Anwar descended into a dreamless sleep.

But his rest was short, and soon his chaotic life intruded again. He was fighting the Americans in the battle of Adwa. They were scared, but he and Tesfaye stormed against the Italians. But then he was locked up in Abu Ghraib by Meles' men, because he and Tesfaye didn't fight hard enough. The male officer entered with only an army shirt on. He was naked beneath. He was restraining a yelping dog on a leash. The long tongue hung out of his drooling mouth.

Anwar was roused.

His alarm went off at the same time as the call of the *muezzin* sounded. Anwar tumbled out of his couch and staggered to the kitchen sink where he turned the rusty water tap. Again, he cleaned himself in preparation for his final prayers. He scrubbed his genitals till he was burning. Afterwards, he stepped into his clean underpants and went for his white ironed shirt. Purified, he kneeled on the floor for his morning prayer. Praying was the tool. He stood up.

The first daylight was seeping in through the thin white curtains. Slowly the furniture took shape. The lilies emerged on the crimson Persian carpet. Outside were the first single cars, a man was yelling. Anwar could even hear the resigned swishing of the street sweeper just outside of his room. The new day was beginning all over. Just like every other day.

Anwar lay down gently, so as not to wrinkle his white shirt on top of his blanket. He put his hands under his head. There was nothing for him to do. Not till about 9 am. It was still a long time. Soon, he would be a *shahid*.

He fell asleep—the pill still worked. At eight o'clock he woke. Two hours left. He cleaned himself again and ironed the shirt all over. He prostrated himself for more prayers. But images intruded: Tesfaye, in the stern of the tugging rowing boat, turned his head and smiled to him. It felt so natural.

He stood up again and looked out on the hazy morning sky. The dark silhouette of a dove darted by his window. Suddenly he felt calm. He felt light-headed, but his stomach seemed to have calmed down. He felt pain-free.

Maybe I'm already in another world, he mumbled as he unlocked the door. But when he looked at the old worn handle of the door, it didn't seem so. He hesitated. Should he leave his door unlocked? Ajar? He closed it gently.

Unlocked.

He proceeded down the familiar worn steps. He didn't feel anything. He had already left this world.

Anwar turned the corner in the direction of Freedom Street, when he bumped right into Tesfaye.

"What are you doing here?" he said bluntly.

"I thought I would check in on you. You didn't seem your own self last night."

"Give me a break," Anwar brushed Tesfaye off. Then he put his hand on his shoulder.

Tesfaye looked questioningly at Anwar.

"What's up?"

"I'm on my way to pick up my aunt at the station. She is not so well."

"Listen, man, you have to get over what happened to us at the detention center. I know it was horrible and humiliating. Shit happens. But you have to get over it and move on with your life. Don't punish your-self—it was out of your control."

"She has terminal cancer." How easily the lie came to him. He lifted his hand gently from Tesfaye's shoulder.

Anwar immediately saw the effect of his words on Tesfaye; his expression had turned defensive.

"I have to help her with some things. She cannot manage herself any longer," he continued, in a monotone. It was too late now.

"Sorry, man."

They stood facing each other. Now Tesfaye put his hand gently on Anwar's shoulder.

"Why didn't you just tell me?"

"I can meet you at the café tomorrow night around eight." For a tempting second, Anwar almost believed his own lie.

"Sure. And say hello to your aunt from me." They hugged hesitantly and Anwar walked in the direction of the train station. He would have to turn right towards Freedom once Tesfaye was out of sight.

He looked over his shoulder and saw the back of Tesfaye, who was heading in the opposite direction. If only it didn't occur to Tesfaye to turn around, or Anwar might not be able to resist.

He reached the corner of Freedom Street where, true enough, the familiar garbage truck was parked in the right side of the street. As he climbed up the step, he thought he saw a glimpse of the old Somali in the rear mirror, *I am not alone. It may seem so, but I am not.* He sat up straight in the driver's seat. The air in the cab smelled strongly. Anwar thought he recognized ammonia and nitrate fertilizer in the pungent odors. The key was in the ignition, and Anwar brought the old engine to a roar.

He drove away from the curb and proceeded down Freedom. As he approached No. 7, he saw a garbage truck similar to the one he was driving, heading towards him from the other direction. That was strange, he wondered, That must be the real truck heading for the day's work. But doesn't he usually come from the other direction? Anwar had a vision of garbage trucks descending upon Freedom Street from all directions. The image made him smile sadly but he quickly suppressed his smile, in order to concentrate on the task at hand.

He was now close to the target building and tightened his grip on the driving wheel to turn right through the blue gate, which had just been opened by a person, who vanished down the street.

Was this one of the seven gates…?

He will cause you to die and again bring you to life, Anwar intoned as he turned the big truck in through the open gateway and pressed his foot hard on the accelerator.

Vocabulary:

Ashebir ◉ Terrorist.

Tenastelin ◉ Equivalent to "How are you?" (May God grant you health).

Shahid ◉ Witness, martyr.

The Guard

THAT'S FLYING, SUSAN THINKS. YOU LEAVE the quiet Cheviot Hills and the next moment you're in Addis Ababa, Ethiopia, bombarded by honking cars and the fumes of banged-up buses. Disoriented, Susan closes her eyes and feels the cool shade and the hot sun flicker as the car passes modern high-rises and low, corrugated hovels. In her dizzy, jet-lagged state, she feels like she's in a boat, bouncing out of control down a rushing river. A pungent smell forces her eyes open. The car has come to a stop next to two enormous, overflowing garbage bins; near the heaps of trash, two young Ethiopians guard a small herd of sheep that chew eagerly on discarded milk cartons.

Addis Ababa means *new flower*, John explains as he zigzags through the traffic and skirts the potholes. He has to slow the car for a cow crossing the road, and Susan cringes when a young man begins hitting the emaciated animal fiercely to stop it from heading for the green grass in the gutter. He uses his full power, his ebony torso twisting with each ferocious blow.

Susan averts her eyes while John continues telling her about King Menelik and Queen Taitu, who founded the town. Susan turns to look back at the young man one more time.

Glancing ahead again, Susan studies the new structures wedged among the old and thinks the new steel-and-glass buildings look as if they had dropped out of the clear blue sky and landed among the goat-and-trash-strewn village dwellings. The people in the streets mirror the buildings: fashionably dressed women and handsome men walk briskly among the poor, in their dirty rags. The well-clothed move with a clear purpose, checking their watches, talking and gesticulating with one hand, the other on their mobile phones.

The ragtags don't seem to be in a hurry to go anywhere. Susan watches some tattered beggars stretching out their hands for alms, then notices that they are sitting in front of a fancy boutique carrying exquisite ladies' apparel. Her eyes refocus on the shiny bras and luxurious thongs.

Now a traffic signal changes from green to red, skipping the yellow in between, and the Suzuki comes to a screeching halt. Immediately, beggars tap on the sides of the car. *"Abeit. Abeit."* A young man with half a leg missing holds out his hand with a cheerful smile.

After scrambling to find some coins, John and Susan cross for the green, leaving the beggars behind. Unsettled, Susan straightens up. It has always been her dream to do something for the poor. Not that she could become anything like her, but Mother Teresa was her ideal. Passing out bread and water and encouraging words. "Somebody should help those beggars get a life," she says.

"I thought you had lost your power of speech," John says, giving her a teasing smile. "I am reassured, now that you're talking again."

"Don't you think so?" Susan asks.

John shrugs slightly. "Poor people keep coming in from the countryside. We can only stop that if we improve conditions in the rural areas. But that's not done overnight, and Ethiopia has one of the highest birthrates in the world." John's voice sounds slightly tired. "You can't do just one thing," he adds, swerving past a stray cat. "It all hangs together."

"But it should be possible to do something about, say, just the beggars," Susan insists. "Soup kitchens and the like for the poorest. They can be paid to cook for themselves. It can be set up through the churches." She can easily imagine the whole thing.

"And the mosques. Don't forget that about half the population is Muslim," John says. "And if you start feeding them, more will just migrate to the city."

John crosses another treacherous intersection. "But it's a good idea if you try to do something on a small scale. I can help you," he says in an encouraging tone. Susan squeezes his hand on the wheel.

John turns the Suzuki into a residential street lined by tall hedges, stone walls and big metal gates with elaborate designs in smooth and shiny black and gold. The Ethiopian Cheviot Hills, Susan thinks. Between the villas, *Gurage* stores made of corrugated iron display Chinese-made house utensils, sacks of grain and cigarette advertisements with pinup girls. Maids in baggy T-shirts and scarves round their hair buy a few onions and soap, while chickens peck the sun-dried ground for a few grains.

They are almost there, and John announces, one more turn before they enter their residential road and first home in Africa.

The Suzuki comes to a halt in front of a big green and silver gate with spikes on its upper edge. John honks, and the gate is promptly opened by a handsome young guard in hand-me-down clothes. A Lakers T-shirt hugs his muscular torso. He deftly moves the hanging bougainvillea branches away from the one-gate door and closes the two sides by slamming down the vertical bar after the Suzuki has entered. The street noises are immediately muffled.

"Welcome to your new home," John says solemnly and kisses his radiant wife.

"And welcome to Muhamad, our new guard," he adds as he perceives the guard, who is standing right behind them, his face averted from the kissing couple. "He comes with the house, so to speak."

When John notices the puzzled look on his wife's pretty face, he quickly adds, "We can get rid of him, our landlady says. Any time. She said to do as we please. But you know what that would mean. He would then probably be in the street; jobs are few and far between and he won't qualify for employment with the *ferengis,* as he only speaks Amharic. Apart from Arabic, that is," John adds. "The advantage is that he knows the place well. And he should be honest."

"I would never want anybody to be in the street because of me," Susan declares without hesitation. "And he is good-looking," she says, sending Muhamad a bright, California smile. She turns her back to him and begins to survey her new house. The husky Muhamad busies himself with the voluminous luggage of his new mistress.

Before the Ikea furniture arrives, Susan spends her first month in an empty house. She places her little laptop computer on the floor in the bedroom.

"It sure beats staying at the Hilton," her husband says. Susan wouldn't go that far, but she is quite satisfied with the house's wood floors and marble fireplace. The small, neat garden is filled with every kind of flower, and apple and plum trees, and is surrounded by a tall green hedge. A little Eden behind her own gate, Susan thinks.

The Ikea boxes turn up and their new English-speaking housekeeper and cook, Mabrat, takes over the assembly work with the nuts and bolts, after Susan despairs over the directions. Muhamad carries the heavy pots of plants Susan has chosen in the nurseries. He shows her the way to the Leprosy Center, which produces Ethiopian cotton she will use for her curtains. Susan is pleased with her new helpers, except for the lack of privacy; on the other hand, she feels protected when, after observing him through the bedroom window, Muhamad catches one of the curtain tailors stealing money out of madam's handbag. Susan sends him one of her smiles, and he nods back seriously to his milk-skinned employer.

Driving around in her little white Suzuki, Susan becomes familiar with the city and gradually develops an everyday routine. When she wakes up in the morning and her husband rushes around to get ready to go to his office, she lies in her bed sipping her cup of tea, planning her day and her clothes.

After these morning meditations, she swings her suntanned legs out from her bed covers, gets dressed, and has her breakfast served by Mabrat. After breakfast—at about 10:30 a.m.—it is time for grocery shopping. Driving down the dirt lanes, she usually overtakes the guard, walking erect, with the trashcan. Once, she offers to take him along, but he declines politely but firmly.

Having finished with the groceries, she occasionally drives to some of the little smart shops and treats herself to a dress. Or she goes to the Internet café to check her e-mail. But mostly the computer is broken down. She enjoys driving around the sunbaked town with music tapes and air-conditioning on full blast. It is really a kind of joy ride, except for all the beggars lined up by the traffic lights. She has learned to avoid the traffic signals with the most beggars.

In the meantime, she has been going to the gatherings of the International Women's Club to meet some *ferengi* women and to become involved in their social work. She brings up her idea for a soup kitchen, and the women seem enthusiastic. Of course, many other possibilities are aired, and they all agree that an orphanage is one of the most deserving projects. With the growing number of HIV/AIDS victims, new orphans are added to the homeless daily. But the welfare work tends to be outshone by the social events, and Susan begins to feel impatient. *Rome wasn't built in one day,* John reminds her.

She enjoys her favorite pastime at the Hilton, (*Just take me to the Hilton*, the posters shout all over town), where she plays tennis with the young trainers (are all Ethiopian men so handsome?), swims in the pool, heated by natural hot springs, and works out, to loud pop music or the blast from CNN.

In this manner, she manages not to come home till her afternoon tea and something home-baked by Mabrat. That's when the day begins to feel rather long and a little lonely. She can't just pick up the phone for a chat with a girlfriend; can't just drive down Wilshire Boulevard on smooth asphalt between sparkling shop windows.

Susan is now focusing on the orphanage idea. She has been looking at possible sites but has not found anything yet. She has also discussed fund-raising events with the UN ladies. But everything has proven very difficult. There is the Ethiopian bureaucracy. John often talks to her about his frustrations at work. *It is as if they don't want to be helped*, she repeatedly hears—and sometimes repeats.

Maybe she could have a baby?

Most of the time the only man she sees around the house is that *perfect* guard. She wanders from room to room aimlessly, aware of the fact that the guard outside might notice her lack of purpose. She grimaces. If only he weren't so handsome.

Absentmindedly, she peruses her bookshelf. She has read the few books she brought, and has not been able to find any books of interest in the town. She has located only one bookstore with *clean* books, but hasn't found anything compelling. A friend in L.A. had convinced her to bring *Madame Bovary*. She had tried to read it, again and again, but found it boring—even if the subject sounded so interesting.

The last hours of the afternoon are the longest. Sometimes, when she runs out of things to do, she will take a nap to shorten the time. But the hot, quiet bedroom will stimulate her sexual fantasies and shamefully, she'll get up to make sure there is no gap in her closed curtains before she helps herself to a little secret, sexual climax.

Back in California, she had just wanted to please men; now she wants them to please her. This is what married life has done to her. Slender, muscular Ethiopian males. Were they different from American men?

Finally, at the end of the afternoon as dusk falls, she turns on some lights.

Outside, the guard does likewise.

At drink time, Mabrat is busy preparing dinner; Susan tries not to get in the way while pouring herself a glass of wine. Back in the living room, she settles down with some of the magazines—*People, Vanity Fair, Bazaar*—her father sends regularly from California. They keep her up to date on the latest gossip. But Hollywood seems so distant.

Why are Muslim men so handsome? It is disturbing that her very own guard happens to be so good-looking. Who is he? What does he think about? He is not very communicative, he keeps his distance. Yes, they don't speak a common language and she sometimes hears him speak with Mabrat. Those two seem to get on very well. Then Susan feels left out.

When she asks Mabrat what they have been talking about, it always seems such trivialities. The weather. The price of *enjera*. The people down the street. (Muhamad knows everybody. Everybody seems to trust him.) Street gossip. Muhamad has told Mabrat that he has a fiancée in Harar. It was arranged years ago, and they hadn't known each other except through hearsay.

The strange thing about Muhamad, Susan thinks, is that he never seems bored. Secretly, she sometimes watches him reading. Mainly the Koran. (In Arabic, of course.) Other times, she catches a glimpse of him through a crack in her curtains. She sees him merely sitting, looking at the apple tree as if he were perfectly content. At peace with himself. But he's a young man, for God's sake. What could he be thinking of?

How could he not be bored, stuck in this small, pleasant but, after all, stifling compound? Sweeping, gardening, washing the car. Walking away with the trash to those overflowing bins by the traffic signal and picking up some lunch. Talking to people passing by on the street. The monotony of his life! He had to be bored out of his mind.

But he truly doesn't seem to be. Susan rearranges the folds in the living room curtains. Is it because he is *a native*? Or what word to use? He just exists where he happens to be. He just follows his traditions and routines. He doesn't think about what he does. Maybe it hasn't occurred to him to think about it? He hasn't been any place else, so there is nothing to compare with. Nothing to raise his expectations. He is not happy or unhappy. He just is.

Susan moves further back in her living room so she can't be seen from the garden. She grabs an apple from the bowl on the sofa table. It is from the tree in front of her bedroom window. Absentmindedly, she takes a bite.

Or is it because he is poor? Poor people are not bored. They are happy if they get their food, and even happier if they receive money. At least she can feel good about that.

She has given Muhamad so much. A new mattress for his little room. Pants, raincoat, socks, shoes, umbrella, and now he wishes for a radio from her, when she returns from her planned trip to the United States. (There is never an end to what Ethiopians want from America.). She is always making an effort to do something for him. She has even insisted he take off two days instead of one.

Susan tries to forget about her guard and begins to read some old *New Yorkers* (John's favorite magazine), while she munches the apple. The jokes keep her entertained for a while, but then she lowers the journal.

Maybe that is it? He is a religious man. Everything is in God's hands. No reason to worry about anything. Allah will provide. Nothing to do but be satisfied with what he gives you.

Does Muhamad believe in an afterlife? Is he going to be rewarded with so many virgins? Why virgins? That would of course be something to look forward to. Susan smiles. Maybe that was his secret. You scratch the surface. Maybe he wasn't so different from her, after all. Now she could let go of her pressing questions.

Until she thinks about him again.

Susan's preoccupation with Muhamad is interrupted by the arrival of another Ethiopian man.

She begins studying Amharic, with a teacher recommended by one of her UN friends. Tewodros is not tall like Muhamad, and he is more slender, but he is handsome and charming and full of energy. It's as if a whirlwind enters the subdued little compound when Tewodros slides in through the gate. Now Susan can compare the two: the guard is always the same; her teacher seems versatile. He is less predictable, and therefore much more interesting.

Susan works very hard on her Amharic vocabulary and sentence structure. She is pleased when John notices, and is amazed over her industry. Now Susan almost feels sorry that she is leaving for America to visit her family for her father's sixtieth birthday. Well, she looks forward to it, but it will break up all that's going on in her present life.

Strange to say, but this is where her life is right now, behind the high green hedge and the spiked gate.

Preoccupied, Susan packs. She has her last, intense lesson with Tewodros and pronounces an emotional *See you before long*.

To the aloof Muhamad, she gives a curt goodbye as she steps into the Suzuki. He actually answers her in English, *Goodbye*. It sounds so funny. So unusual. Yes, he has begun to learn English. Susan has heard Mabrat teach him words. She will have to intensify her Amharic lessons, she thinks as John drives her through the wide-open gate.

John takes her along the usual chaotic roads to the airport, talking about his latest books and the trip they will take to Kenya when she comes back. Her thoughts are still in the compound, and the hope of soon being back again makes her smile encouragingly to John as she goes through security.

After three hectic weeks in California, Susan is picked up by John again.

A beaming Susan, in new California clothes. She is quite exuberant. She bombards John with questions about this person and that one. John thinks her vacation has done her good.

While John dodges around the potholes, Susan looks right and left, exclaiming how construction work has progressed in the few weeks, how this, how that. Most of all, the houses and sights, the cattle in the streets, the beggars seem so familiar. She has so much feeling for them.

It is like returning home.

The gates are opened, the obstinate bougainvillea branches are pushed back and the bar slammed down. She is careful to hide her excitement at seeing Muhamad again and can't wait to give him the radio, with earphones and all. (A possible diversion from the Koran?)

Muhamad looks the same. Susan is careful to hide her disappointment at his measured response to the gift. But what had she expected? That Muhamad would jump around for joy? This is how it is supposed to be. Susan smiles resignedly.

She makes love passionately with her husband that night.

For several days, Susan enjoys the excitement of her return and takes great pleasure in talking with her UN ladies, Mabrat and her merchants. She only has to say *California* and people get excited. The land of promise—it makes people dream. Everybody wants to go there, she knows.

Funny thing, she would rather be here.

It had been great seeing her family, especially her beloved papa (she is his only *darling girl*.) But her return definitely made her realize that she was on a temporary visit to her past; she is elsewhere now.

To tell the truth (which she didn't quite do), she had been a little disappointed in people back home. She felt they were not that interested in hearing about her life in Africa. After some initial exclamations, like *How interesting it must be to see that part of the world,* it seemed as if their eyes grew distant. Sometimes she would be in the middle of a story, when they suddenly interrupted her, "Have you heard that so and so…?" And it would be about somebody getting married, or divorced, or, even better, having an affair. They didn't notice that she hadn't finished *her* story. People were mostly interested in their own little worlds. Susan nods to herself: she knows what she knows.

There was just that one time when Samantha, her best friend from college, had shown real curiosity. That was when she had told her about her new Amharic teacher (she didn't say much about Muhamad), and how attracted she was to him. How virile and dynamic he was, in his foreign way. When she had perceived Samantha's interest (a real African man!), she had been tempted to insinuate more than had really happened. She had left Samantha in great suspense when she refused to tell her anything definitive.

Susan is happy to be back, except now the big rain has set in, in full force. It is a deluge from morning to night. Some days it doesn't let up at all, and she is more or less forced to stay indoors and keep the light on. Tewodros is away in the countryside; some relative had died. People always had a relative dying somewhere in this country.

Susan can't wait to resume her Amharic lessons, but she has to be patient (like everybody around her) and she tries to study her Amharic one to two hours every day. She finds it hard; it is so strange to her. There also is not much action in the International Women's Club; those foreigners who have the option flee Ethiopia in the rainy period.

Her old boredom sneaks back up on her. She fights it as best she can with books, music and finally, some daydreaming. Now that it rains so hard, she doesn't see Muhamad much. He is holed up in his tiny room and only emerges when he hears John honking the car outside the gate. Then he jumps out in his raincoat (given by her) and opens the gates, battling the wet bougainvillea branches.

Susan thinks of Muhamad and how uncomfortable he must be on these rain-filled days. But as always, he seems much more patient about the wet season than she is. He just hibernates and listens to his new radio. (Thanks to her.) She wonders again what he thinks about, whether he thinks about her. It is hard to imagine what goes on in the mind of a stranger. An African man.

But she has the time, and she curls up in her chair after adjusting the logs a little in the fireplace. The lustily dancing flames throw a rosy shimmer over the living room.

He must find her pretty, she thinks of Muhamad. Yes, very beautiful with her light skin and head of red hair. (Very different from his fiancée.) Does he find her attractive or does he suppress such notions completely? Does he disapprove of her? Her idle life? Not being a Muslim? He probably believes she will end up in eternally burning Hell, while he will go up to his virgins. Maybe he wants to beat her with his bamboo stick for being such a bad girl—beat her into submission.

The rain is beginning to seep in under the main entrance door. She will have to call Mabrat to wipe it up and to leave some rags there. No, she will do it herself and stay undisturbed. Susan puts some new logs on the fire and looks at her watch.

John will not be home for another couple of hours, so she may as well stay by her fire for now. She really couldn't be in any better place. And the nights with John were good. If only he weren't away such long days. What would it be like with another man? Somebody she didn't know. Somebody very different.

Enough. Back to the welfare. When the rains stop, she will jump-start her orphanage work, no matter what. Her husband is even trying to help her. He has assigned a UNICEF person to assist her in her endeavors; only that person didn't seem to take her seriously, and she feels too proud to complain about it.

She shudders and gets up to find a woolen shawl, which she drapes over her shoulders. Since she has nothing better to do right now, she might as well think of her Amharic teacher. She visualizes Tewodoros' face, his smooth skin and prominent white teeth. His enticing smile suddenly lighting up his volatile face. Before she can stop herself, she thinks of being his lover. What if they went off to Lungano Lake (which John has visited on many of his trips)? His slender body embracing her in the murky water. His arms and legs coiling tightly around her in the lake under the moon, which throws a shimmer on the dark water. The gentle, warm breeze from the hills around them.

She is abruptly brought back to her living room when the phone rings. It rings very seldom in the rainy season. It is always out of order. She gets out of her seat and runs to it, but she only hears rumbling, sloshing noises in the earphone. It sounds like a rushing river. After a couple of similar rings, she finally hears Tewodros' voice, calling to say that he is back in Addis and will come the next day.

The following morning, Susan wakes up to glorious sunshine and jumps out of bed immediately. John notices and says, "You seem full of energy."

"Yes, such beautiful sunshine. The rain was driving me crazy. Today I can get out of my house. My prison house." Then she says, casually, "By the way, I'll have my Amharic lesson this afternoon."

"Oh, good, so he's finally back." John was putting on his jacket. "Now I remember, I will be a little late today. We're invited for a cocktail hour with government people."

"Without wives?"

"Without wives."

"What else is new?" she says.

When Susan goes out in the kitchen a little later, Muhamad is talking with Mabrat. They fall silent as soon as Susan enters, and she just catches his last word, *Madam*.

He leaves quickly and Susan asks Mabrat what he has said. Susan knows it was something about her. Mabrat blushes a little and refuses to say anything. Finally, she reluctantly tells her, "Madam seems to be bored. She should have some children to keep her busy. Better than that Amharic teacher for Madam." Mabrat turns her head apologetically.

"Oh, so Mr. Muhamad has an opinion about me. I'm so honored to hear." Susan feels both angry and elated as she eats her breakfast. She avoids looking at Muhamad as she drives her Suzuki out of the compound to do her shopping.

Really, people are always so predictable.

Finally, it is afternoon, and Tewodros knocks vigorously on the gate. Muhamad opens it quickly. The two men greet each other with the traditional succession of Amharic expressions, while patting each other repeatedly on the shoulder. Susan closes the curtain to the living room, so she and Tewodros can't be spied upon.

Tewodros sits down, Mabrat brings tea and cookies. Susan and Tewodros talk for a long time in English. Amharic is so frustrating.

Her limited vocabulary constricts their conversation, even if they try to make it relevant to Susan's life. *My husband comes home late from work.* Or, *My guard, Muhamad, likes the apples from Madam's garden;* or, *The teacher is pleased to teach the ferengi Amharic.*

They take their time chatting about a million and one things in English. They talk about themselves and exchange observations on their differing cultures: religious holidays, food, family life. Finally, marriage. Even though Tewodros is for arranged marriages, he seems more liberal in his attitudes than Susan.

"Marriage is marriage. That doesn't mean you can't have an affair now and then."

"But you mean," Susan hesitates, "You mean just for the man?"

"Women too," Tewodros says quickly.

A long silence follows. Susan gets up to adjust the curtains. She sits down again. She remembers her Lungano fantasies the previous day and blushes a little. She hopes Teddy doesn't notice.

"I thought you Western women were more liberated," Teddy finally says, "but then maybe that isn't true about American women. I think the American culture is rather puritanical—just think of the president they elected." "Maybe," Susan says, thinking of her church-going parents, who never had an affair. But she decides against saying anything like that. For the life of her, she doesn't know what to say. In a timid voice, she insists they return to their Amharic lesson.

They get down to their sentences, *My husband does not come home late from work*; *My guard does not like apples*; and *The teacher is not pleased to teach the ferengi Amharic.* There is a short pause and Teddy continues, "He would rather … speak English." They both laugh. Susan begins to feel self-conscious and loses the thread of the grammar several times.

They shift to the alphabet. They bend over the Amharic letters, and then it happens. When they both point to the letter *z*, their fingers touch. Susan feels as if she has been bitten by a snake on the tip of her index finger. The shock goes through her whole body. She experiences that rushing river sensation in her head—her boat is out of control— when Tewodros doesn't move his finger away fast. Is he lingering? Or does she imagine it? The air seems charged between the two. Does he sense it too?

They end the lesson soon after and Susan walks Tewodros to the gate, which Muhamad opens. They chat for a while and Tewodros again encourages her to call him Teddy. (Sure, but Tewodros sounds more sexy, she thinks.) Susan feels Muhamad's disapproving glance on her back. It gives her a sensation of goosebumps under her shoulder blade.

She walks slowly back into the house and closes the door tightly behind her. Then she throws herself onto her bed. Is he playing up to her? Can it be possible? He is married. She thinks of how he has told about his wedding and marriage in a very matter-of-fact way. It was arranged by the families with everybody's agreement, including groom and bride. It was not *a love marriage* but they both seemed satisfied. Is her marriage with John a love marriage? If not, what else could it be?

Tewodros had even told her about being tested for HIV/AIDS. That is a common procedure before a marriage in Ethiopia nowadays. (Many a virgin was infected with AIDS soon after they had married their husband.) He was negative, by the way.

So he was negative!

She covers her face in her hands but is disturbed by a mumbling sound. She gets up and looks out the window. There is Muhamad, his face against the ground, praying under the apple tree. Ramadan has begun.

She thinks he will stop after a while, but he goes on and on. She starts to get irritated. It is as if Muhamad owns the lawn and the whole place. And not only that, it is as if he is doing this to reproach her, make her feel guilty.

She grabs a jacket and scarf and storms to the gate to get out of the compound. She will take a walk and not be afraid of the street dogs. She struggles with the crossbar. Finally, she gets it, but hurts her hand. She looks over her shoulder as she steps through the gate and out into the street.

She notices that Muhamad hasn't looked up. He hasn't moved. He's pretending not to notice.

The following weeks continue with more sunshine and Susan's daily routines of her UN activities, shopping, exercises and Amharic lessons. The International Women's Club has its fund-raising gala. It is a great success and raises more money than they'd expected. They agree to donate most of the proceeds to already existing orphanages. Susan's orphanage idea is lingering.

John is often gone to other parts of Ethiopia, and although Susan has not complained (she is busy with her life) they have discussed their vacation together. They will go on a safari in Kenya, which John finds more developed and comfortable than the primitive Ethiopia. John and she are now trying to get pregnant. Maybe she couldn't conceive? Now she really dreams about that baby. Has she done anything wrong? Maybe God didn't mean for her to have children?

The Amharic lessons continue in the new, electrified atmosphere. Weariness and boredom are banished by Susan's attraction to Tewodros. (Teddy had told her about Tewodros, the old Ethiopian King. How he had started out like a kind of Robin Hood but had turned into a very cruel man. Teddy described how Tewodros had killed and mutilated at the slightest provocation. Susan shuddered.)

As Susan's relationship with her teacher sweetens, her interaction with her guard grows tense. After Ramadan, she had given Muhamad a whole week off to celebrate *Eid*. He had promptly gone off to his hometown of Harar and married his fiancée. Upon his return, he had continued his job, as if nothing had changed. Susan is astounded: to go off and get married like that when they couldn't even be together?

The boredom in her little Eden has been diluted by a nervous energy. The omnipresence of Muhamad is challenged twice weekly by the knocking teacher—the *intruder* from the outside. Susan is beginning to feel as if she is stuck in a whirlpool, turning faster and faster. She's getting nowhere with her Amharic and her welfare work. To tell the truth, there isn't much progress with anything.

If only she could have her baby.

Teddy and Susan are speaking English in the kitchen. (It looks as if Muhamad will win their language competition.) They have made tea and some toast because Mabrat is at a family funeral.

Now they carry their tea and toast with some apples from the tree into the living room and proceed to do a little perfunctory Amharic. (*Husbands come home late from work. Guards guard apple trees. Teachers teach students.*) That done, they discuss computers (in English), as Teddy is very interested in purchasing one. The enterprising Teddy is always scheming and planning, filled with new ideas. Now he wants to start an Internet café—and Susan intends to help him.

Susan tells him about her excellent new laptop. Does he want to see it? He could see it. Maybe he could *inherit* it one day. Susan leads him from the living room through the marble-floored corridor to her bedroom to show him her new laptop. She feels a little self-conscious about entering the bedroom with her teacher, but then it is also her study. And what has he said about her? Prudish? Was that it?

She proceeds to her desk by the window and bends over the computer to press the start button in the back. Tewodros leans over her to watch the process. She can feel him right behind her—the heat of his body—and is brought back to that rushing-river feeling. She doesn't move, she is hardly breathing, when she hears a vigorous knocking on the windowpane.

It is Muhamad, with a bamboo broom raised to remove some spider webs in the corner above the window.

Susan stands up, grabs Teddy's arm tightly, and pulls him after her, dragging him by his sleeve back through the long corridor towards the main door, which she tears open. She is shaking.

"Please tell Muhamad that he is fired and that he must leave immediately," she says to Teddy.

"Are you sure?" Teddy asks in a low voice.

"Please."

Muhamad listens to Tewodros. He looks at Susan as if he were going to say something, but then thinks better of it. He walks over to his little guardhouse and picks up his few belongings. He turns towards the gate.

"Wait," says Susan. "Tell him I will pay him for the last month. And some more," she adds. "I will just go and get the money."

Muhamad seems to smile a little. Then he looks contemptuously at her and walks towards the gate. Tewodros says something to him and Muhamad waits with his hand on the gate bar.

"I told him I would leave with him," Teddy says apologetically and runs inside for his bag and jacket.

Tewodros and Muhamad walk out through the open gate. Susan notices a faint odor of sewage before she pushes the two sides of the gate towards each other. She thinks of the two overflowing garbage bins while she tries to lower the crossbar into the fork, but her hands shake so much that she barely succeeds. She returns through her garden to the house and pulls the main door closed till it clicks in the lock. She turns in front of the mirror but doesn't dare look at herself. She goes to the living room and sinks down in a chair.

The rumbling river sound subsides and is replaced by a gentle drizzle in the early evening dusk.

Some dogs are barking nearby.

She sits unmoving, frozen, for what seems an eternity. She starts to rub her cold toes, then her feet. She begins to caress her whole body, her breasts.

She straightens, thinking she hears a distinct, vigorous knocking on her gate.

Vocabulary:

Gurage stores ◉ Gurage people is an ethnic group with a reputation as
skilled traders.

The Girlfriend

BELOW HIM STRETCHED THE VAST FORBIDDING mountains, dotted with patches of cultivated land surrounding small straw huts. The huts glowed golden in the late afternoon sun.

Andy had spent two days in Addis Ababa, and was now flying to the Ethiopian town of Bahir Dar to visit Binyam Mekele, whom he knew from pharmacy school in Stockton, California. Binyam had not only been his closest friend during that time, but also the only foreigner Andy had ever known well. He had always meant to visit Binyam's country.

That must be the Nile, Andy thought, as the plane made a big circle over an extended gorge. He looked at his watch and realized they must be close to landing. As the plane continued to curve over a large expanse of water, he picked out the town of Bahir Dar nestled on the shore of Lake Tana, between palm trees and fields of green and yellow. Dark splotches of trees on the sparkling blue hid the islands with the ancient monasteries that Andy had just been reading about.

The plane was definitely descending now. Andy's excitement to be landing in the Ethiopian countryside was tempered by the pain of his aching back. He couldn't wait to leave the sterile, plastic-and-metal cabin and take a breath of fresh African air.

Andy was surprised to find Bahir Dar quite charming—almost like a resort town—as he rode along the main avenue leading to his hotel. It made him think that he should maybe have brought his wife, Anne, with him. She had never been to Africa, or any place remotely like it. But she probably wouldn't care for it. She didn't even like the beach, because she got sand between her toes—Andy was looking at some barefoot pedestrians. He leaned back on his hollowed seat and savored the balmy breeze that drifted through the open window. Plump palm trees lined the wide road, lending the town a holiday-like atmosphere.

True, if one looked closer, you noticed the shabby houses, the beggars, the skinny street dogs. Anne was supersensitive about dirt and poverty; she wouldn't hesitate to take off pieces of her own clothing or jewelry, her rings even, to give it to some poor mother with a pretty child. Ethiopia would be too much for her, but as for Andy himself, he was ready for his Africa experience.

"A message for you, Sir." The clerk at the Tana Hotel reception desk handed a handwritten note to Andy. He immediately recognized Binyam's large, hurried scrawl, welcoming him to Ethiopia and informing him that he would pick him up for an Eid celebration at a friend's house the next morning.

Expectantly, Andy folded the note into his pocket, and walked through the hotel out to the mown lawns sloping down to the lake. Trees and tables with chairs were silhouetted against the water in the dusk. The outlines of wooden boats rocked near the shore, and rustling birds settled in for the night among the bushes. In the distance, Andy heard the Muslim call for the sunset prayer. He decided to stay in the idyllic garden for a cup of real Ethiopian coffee before going to his room.

He sat down on one of the little iron chairs, which cut into his back and reminded him that he was in a Third World country. He beckoned to one of the waiters hanging around in his threadbare uniform. He looked bored, and his slow movements reminded Andy that he wasn't in any hurry either, even though he still glanced at his watch at regular intervals.

Finally, he walked back along the murky corridors, searching for his room number. *Ethiopian patina*, he thought as he jiggled the key to make it fit into the old lock. Inside, square, thickly lacquered furniture crowded the room, and the air smelled heavily of insecticide. The toilet was out of order, and the tap in the rusty sink was dripping. He rinsed his hands under the leaking faucet and wiped them on the worn towel, hard and scratchy from countless washings and dryings in the sharp African sun.

While he unpacked, Andy thought about his friendship with Binyam, and how he hadn't managed to visit him for twenty years. But he had had no time for visiting exotic places in Africa after he had finally married his high school sweetheart, had had two children and had been busy developing his pharmaceutical business. Now that he would be providing syringes and other medical equipment for UNICEF and other world health organizations, he had the chance to combine business with visits to foreign countries. He felt lucky to be able to bring some of civilization's blessings to the less developed parts of the world.

Finally, he would see him again, dear old Binyam, with whom he had spent some of his happiest times. Andy had been distressed when his friend had left America, but Binyam had been adamant about going home. He was one of the few foreign students who had sacrificed Western affluence in order to benefit his own country with his American education. Andy could only respect him for that.

Leaving his room, Andy struggled to close the door, which seemed to be of a different size and shape from the door frame. In the almost deserted dining room, he cautiously ordered pasta with tomato sauce. Better not risk anything on his first day.

Andy sank back into the upholstered chair and looked around: strange how this restaurant seemed so familiar, with its paper flowers and Muzak, its faded nature photographs on the walls, soft lampshades and checkered tablecloth. He could be anywhere in the world: Russia, Africa, America. *A Muzak place.* He felt comfortable—imagine, you could sit in a restaurant like that in Ethiopia!

He checked the time and allowed himself one more beer. One of the photos on the wall showed a line of tall, slender palm trees on a California beach. Now he almost had to remind himself that he was in Ethiopia. But he would see that tomorrow. There would be no Sunset Boulevard, no Santa Monica freeway. He didn't miss the bumper-to-bumper traffic.

The last beer arrived. He took a deep draft; he was getting slightly tipsy.

And Maryam, Binyam's cousin—what had happened to her? He could ask Binyam. He would.

Next morning, after a painful night of battling a couple of mosquitoes resistant to the insecticide, Andy couldn't get out of his room soon enough. He went to the lobby, where CNN kept repeating the week-old images of the tumbling Twin Towers in New York. What was once news had simply turned into virtual reality.

Andy tried to ignore the TV and stepped outside, into the bright morning. The birds were chirping in the dew-fresh hibiscus bushes when the sound was drowned by the engine of an old Land Rover, which came to an abrupt stop in a cloud of dust. The left front door swung open, and it was Binyam, in an American basketball cap he wore backwards.

Binyam got out of the car and embraced his American friend with some warm bear hugs. He had grown quite stout, but otherwise he looked just like the cheerful Binyam from their days in college.

"*Salaam aleikum.*"

"*Aleikum assalam*," Andy replied hesitantly, as he remembered their greeting from student days.

Binyam roared with laughter, "You almost forgot, old man." Andy was embraced in another bear hug, "You look like yourself, a little paler, a little thinner. White man." Andy received a couple of slaps from the bear paw. "Everything OK? How's your wife?"

"Anne, she's fine. That is, she just had a cold," Andy hesitated, "but that is not important."

"Great, old man. Sorry, my wife is out of town, she wanted to meet you so very much. Had heard so much about you. Yes, also from Maryam. But as you know, she decided to go to a wedding of a cousin in Harar. But step right in, it's air-conditioned," and Binyam swung the door open to the front seat.

Andy entered the air-conditioned car, and hardly had time to buckle up before Binyam drove off at breakneck speed through the wide lanes of Bahir Dar. He brushed by a cluster of bicyclists while he pointed out buildings and sights with his right hand. His left hand seemed barely to touch the steering wheel. Soon he turned on two wheels into some narrow lanes but had to slow down, as the alley was clogged by pedestrians winding their way between trash-eating sheep, skinny cattle and flapping chicken.

Andy noticed the transformation of the town around him. It was as if he had entered behind the postcard facade into the real town, where people and animals lived side by side. Young women were carrying their water pots on their heads; an old man was emptying a bucket of leftovers into the alley, and goats rushed over to eat the potato peels; a young man was beating a cow with a bamboo stick to make it move faster. Andy felt he was finally observing true Ethiopian life.

"Can't we open the windows and turn off the air-conditioning?" Andy suggested.

"It smells mighty strong in these alleys, and you used to always want the air-conditioning on back in Stockton."

"We're not in Stockton now."

"Right you are," Binyam grinned and turned off the air-conditioning at the same time as he pressed the button to open the windows. Hot air with a pungent smell of decay rolled in the windows. They were just passing the carcass of a dog, swarming with flies.

On the outskirts of the town, the Land Rover came to a squeaking halt in front of a big, blue gate in a tall wall. Binyam honked, and before the slow guard had finished opening the heavy gate, he raced the car into the courtyard, stirring up the fine dust. They were met by Binyam's friend Anwar, a handsome man, forty-something, with melancholy brown eyes.

Anwar walked towards them with his arms opened in a welcoming gesture. He was trailed by a succession of successively smaller children, dressed to the hilt in the sweltering sun. Long-sleeved shirts and vests and butterflies for the boys, layered ballroom dresses and silk bows in their full, curly hair for the girls.

Anwar smiled to his guests and showed them into a shady dining room with the same furniture as in the hotel room. In the center, a large table was overflowing, with dishes for the Eid celebrations. A big rack of lamb was surrounded by smaller dishes with lentils, rice, tabbouleh, red beet salad, boiled potatoes, carrot and cabbage, potato chips, lasagna and carrot salad with raisins. Mango juice, soft drinks, soda water and a bottle of whiskey were lined up on the adjoining buffet.

Anwar led his guests towards the buffet and offered them the whiskey. He poured a little for Andy before handing the bottle to Binyam. Binyam had acquired a taste for whiskey in his business circles. *The Westernized Muslim*, as Anwar had named him. Then he poured himself a small glass of fresh mango juice.

A pretty, small-boned woman with a scarf tied loosely over her head appeared in the doorway to what must be the kitchen. Anwar introduced his wife, who lowered her eyes towards the floor. Andy greeted the wife briefly as she approached the table with a big dish of chicken in a red sauce with halves of hard-boiled eggs embedded on top (the dish was called *duro wat,* Anwar explained). After the men helped the wife shift the dishes to make room for the last one, she left, closing the door to the kitchen gently. She did not reappear during the meal, where the men settled into men's talk, interrupted by the children wanting attention and their plates filled.

The conversation proceeded haltingly, in between encouragements to take more this or that, drink more, the kids wanting so and so. Binyam was the one who provided the entertainment, happily talking and laughing with his mouth full. Anwar was clearly a reserved man, but he asked Andy about his life in America ("California, I should say"). Did Americans really work as hard as they were rumored to and did they not take vacations?

Andy didn't really know what to say. Partly, he was struggling with a chicken bone from the *duro wat,* partly he didn't know if he should emphasize work or not or whether that would be a good thing or not. So he ended up with some in-between that Americans worked hard but also enjoyed their vacations. This prompted Binyam to tell about their hilarious expeditions water surfing. Andy struggled on with his bone and an unsatisfying feeling of having failed to provide the expected entertainment.

After many a refill, their host finally got up and showed them the way to an adjoining veranda, under the shade of a bougainvillea. Anwar's wife was already there on a stool, a little to the side, waving a small exercise book over the roasting coffee beans on a flat charcoal pan. Anwar now excused himself, as he had some driving to do for some Eid guests in the town. His three drivers were off because of the holidays, but to Anwar, it was important to keep up his *business as usual.*

"We also work in Ethiopia," he said jokingly, as he went down the steps.

"Anwar has struggled to get this business on its feet and going," Binyam explained to Andy as he settled down into the soft cushions of some old wicker chairs. He had a very hard time—to the point of starving—after Hana, his fiancé, had left for America and he couldn't find a job.

"But now he seems to be doing very well. There was certainly no shortage of food today," Andy remarked. "He also seems surrounded by a big loving family and devoted wife. He must be a happy man, despite the sad expression on his face."

"Well, in truth, it's a long story," Binyam mumbled, as he poured himself a glass of soda water on top of his remaining whiskey. "I guess I could relate it to you since we're sitting here waiting for the coffee.

At this point, the wife got up and waved the coffee fragrance towards the *ferengi* visitor. Binyam scooped up the coffee fumes, rotating his big hands in dramatic waves towards his own nose as well as that of his visitor. "This is what you're supposed to do."

Binyam settled back in the pillows of his bamboo chair, "It's actually a love story. And it relates to you and your country—are you interested?"

Andy answered in the affirmative.

Binyam emptied the last drops of whiskey in his glass before he began to relate about the young Anwar, who fell passionately in love with the slender, olive skinned beauty in his class.

"I never saw a boy so in love."

"Well, love sure is universal," Andy hazarded.

"Yes and no, for it makes a difference where you live. Love doesn't exist in a vacuum, as you know," Binyam added. He paused, "But there was a problem. She was a Christian from the Ethiopian Orthodox Church. Not that the parents were that religious, but her mother was dead against her dating, not to mention marrying a Muslim. She didn't have anything personal against Anwar, but Hana's mother was a traditional woman. And you know about tradition: like with faith, you cannot reason about it.

"Depite the parents' opposition (or maybe because of it) the girl fell violently in love with him too. They became inseparable. They even escaped in a friend's small boat to an almost deserted island in Lake Tana some afternoons. It was like a paradise of their own, apart from a few monks, who would meditate there in seclusion. Of course, that didn't last long. You cannot keep secrets in a small, traditional society."

Anwar's wife had gotten up and disappeared into the kitchen in the back of the house. "She went to grind the roasted beans," Binyam explained. They could hear the grinder through the muffled sound of the wind in the branches and the children's shouting in the courtyard.

They sat in silence for a little while, watching small clouds gathering on the sky. Anwar's wife returned with the traditional Ethiopian clay pot, which she put on the embers. "She is now boiling the ground coffee in water." Binyam explained the obvious.

"They were prohibited from seeing each other without the supervision of relatives. But because Anwar's family was respected, even though they were not well off, it looked like the fathers were going to reach an agreement. The fathers were *very* tolerant but I'm sure the mother kept praying fervently in secret. Her prayers were heard—it seems. The *solution*, so to speak, came from the rich world. Yes, from your country."

A dark cloud had stationed itself over the house, and it suddenly grew chilly. Anwar's wife poured some coffee from the clay pot into a tiny cup, shook it a little, and poured it back into the pot. She repeated this as if she was performing magic with the coffee, and then poured it into three of the little cups. She handed it to the *ferengi* and passed him the sugar cup and spoon.

"You take sugar like a *ferengi* or like an Ethiopian?" laughed Binyam.

"Like an American," Andy laughed back. "I have my little sweetening pills."

"Won't that ruin the coffee?" Binyam protested, and Anwar's wife looked horrified when Andy dropped three tiny pills into the black coffee.

Binyam continued to tell how the fathers had almost come to an agreement, when a letter from the American Embassy, addressed to Hana, announced that Hana's name had been drawn in the immigrant lottery and that she was requested for an interview at the U.S. Embassy in Addis. On her eighteenth birthday, her father had submitted her name in the lottery for immigration visas for the United States. And she had won right away.

All excited and dressed up, Hana had taken the bus to Addis with her father. She came back crying, because now she had realized that she couldn't go with Anwar. They were not married, and she would have to go alone—if she wanted to go. She declared that then she wouldn't go. She didn't want to be separated from Anwar.

It was then that her mother had stepped in, as if revitalized by God's hearing her prayers. She pretended she supported Anwar going to the United States with her daughter. After all, it was the land of *opportunities*. (Hana's mother had chanced upon a useful word.) If only one of them got to *the promised land*, there would be a million chances for the other to follow. In America, everything was possible.

Hana began to wipe her tears and listened to her mother, but her final change of mind was brought upon her by the noble Anwar. Anwar had done some serious introspection and come to the conclusion that he would not be showing Hana true love, or serve her true interests, if he tried to stop her from going to the new world. She would get a better life; there she could escape the poverty of Ethiopia. Anwar was also optimistic they would find a way for him to join Hana in America. And if not, Hana could even return. Separation wouldn't quench their love.

There was a sudden gust of wind, which stirred up a tornado-like dust column interrupting the men's conversation. Big rain drops started falling, and the party grabbed their coffee cups and pillows and ran inside, followed by the screaming kids. At the same time, the gate was opened by the raggedy guard, and Anwar appeared in his taxicab.

Anwar was satisfied to have completed his obligations, and the three men settled in for another round of the by now less strong Ethiopian coffee, while the rain poured down in the dusty courtyard. The fine dust was transformed into muddy puddles while the men exchanged small talk. Andy found Anwar a graceful host, but somewhat formal; Andy's first impression of Anwar's sadness was not dispelled. He surprised himself in feeling sorry for Anwar's loss.

When the sun broke through again, the guests got up and thanked their hosts for the lovely afternoon, and the wife came in to say goodbye.

Pacified by the food and drink and challenged by the muddy roads, Binyam drove a little more slowly back towards the hotel. Before he dropped off Andy, he invited him to visit him the next day. He would show him the *Tis Abay* waterfalls and then he would finish off Hana and Anwar's story after lunch. And whatever else they had to talk about. There was a lot to catch up on, Binyam nodded emphatically.

The next morning, the sun was shining again on the wet leaves of the hibiscus bush in front of the Tana Hotel, when Binyam arrived to pick up Andy. Andy was excited to visit the famous waterfalls. He had slept well, smeared in his mosquito repellent.

They had crossed the river in the traditional reed boat, the *tankwa*, and when the solid Binyam got up from his little boat, his bottom was soaking wet. Walking behind him, Andy fell into a fit of laughter as Binyam danced around, wiggling his wet behind. For a moment, they felt as if they were back in their happy California days.

The falls were bigger and more beautiful than Andy had imagined. The spray flew high and wide, and the penetrating rays of sun created the most magnificent rainbow. Andy marveled at the grandeur of this natural sight and how small it made him feel.

Tired and muddy from walking in the wet grass at the foot of the falls, they returned to Binyam's house, where a table had been set in the shade of some fig trees. Binyam's mother, who lived in her son's house, had cooked a grand lunch, similar to the one they had stuffed themselves with the previous day. Today, Andy's appetite was as big as Binyam's, and the two delved into the heaps of food.

After lunch, they settled down into their lounge chairs to finish off their mango juice and gin, while the mother (who didn't hesitate to share the gin) busied herself with the coffee ceremony.

"I heard your mother died," Binyam said. "How about the old man?"

"He finally passed away too," Andy said.

"He was a tough one with all his religious talk and admonishing. Did he really believe that he could convert me to his born-again Christianity?"

"He was pretty bad. But after his newfound religion helped him overcome his alcoholism, he couldn't help believing that others needed saving too."

"I guess that explains something, but it must have been hard with a father like that. I have thought about that," Binyam added.

"True. But I have put all that behind me. I never think about it anymore. The past is the past," Andy said.

"How about our love story? I was going to get the second part." Andy changed the subject.

"Oh, yeah, where were we?"

"Hana was going to America, and Anwar was not."

"Yes, Anwar was not," Binyam said thoughtfully. "So Hana went to Chicago and hated it. She found it cold and impersonal. She missed her Anwar terribly and her family and even the Ethiopian food. She sent tons of letters to Anwar and her family declaring that Chicago was no *promised land*—it was not nearly as beautiful as Bahir Dar. And the immigrant Ethiopians were different from people at home being mostly interested in making money, working and working. No time for coffee ceremonies.

"Anwar was equally unhappy back in Bahir Dar. He has gradually confided more about his love story to me: the island they sneaked off to and the *vows* they made to each other. They had made rings of straw and declared themselves married. They had made a little ceremony—Anwar had bent a straw into the shape of a ring. It was "till they could get real rings. He had put it on Hana's ring finger, and they had made their vows of eternal love. He couldn't get over his loss. Never did.

"The other thing was that now that Hana was in America, he saw Bahir Dar through her American glasses, so to speak. He became aware of the poverty and the hopelessness of all the young, unemployed men. Bit by bit, Anwar has told me about that time. As you may have sensed, he is a reserved man, but he told me.

"Once he told me," Binyam concentrated his thoughts, "how he began to work for the tourists. He drove for them, trying to save up the money to go to America. How he took them to *Tis Abay*, where we went today. He would carry their bags to the waterfalls, get them bottled water, chase away the beggars and the children. This gave him an idea."

At this point, Binyam's mother appeared and handed a small fragrant coffee cup to Andy and then to Binyam, and they went through the exclamations about the excellence of Ethiopian coffee.

"Maybe this is too lengthy for you?" Binyam asked.

"No, no," Andy protested vigorously.

"So Anwar got the idea of using a *ferengi* tourist to take him to America. So he started to *seduce* ladies. Ladies, who were maybe lonely and certainly rich, who might be willing to marry him and take him to America. He told about a German widow, whom he thought was interested. She was not exactly sexy, and he might have to go to Germany first. But if the lady could bring him out of Ethiopia, she could be ugly, old, uncharming. As long as she was rich … which all tourists were—by definition."

Binyam took a sip of his coffee. "Hana on the other hand, she got a job as a waitress and seemed a little more content in Chicago. Gradually, Anwar became a memory—a memory connected with Ethiopia. Now she became busy like everybody else. The weather got better in spring and she came to socialize with a group of Ethiopians. Through them she was introduced to an Ethiopian man, Theodore."

"Whom she married," Andy interjected.

"How would you know?" Binyam exclaimed.

"Isn't that what happens: true love and then comes marriage?"

"You sound disillusioned. Is that what happened to you?"

"No, well, I don't mean me. I mean so in general."

"Well, what's *general* supposed to mean?" Binyam laughed. "Things are one way or another. You can really only speak for yourself." Binyam drained his cup of the last cold coffee. "For myself, I was lucky, I was married to the love of my life. One knows those things." He sat quietly for a while.

"But anyway, Hana married this man, Teddy as she called him. He was quite a bit older than her and he could provide for her. She chose the comfortable solution. She was tired of working in McDonalds and Kentucky Fried Chicken. So she secured herself. A marriage of convenience, in other words."

Binyam paused. "Also, he was a Christian."

As on the previous day, the clouds were beginning to pile up around the blue sky above them. Binyam spoke quickly, to finish before the rain began, "Anwar became very angry after he overcame his serious depression at the news of her marriage. Her *betrayal*, he called it. Now he was talking about going to America to kill the guy—her husband.

He had grown a big beard—looked like a true terrorist as he would sit morosely in his neighborhood café. There the café owner's daughter is said to have looked after him. She served him coffee (without pay) and looked after him in little discreet ways."

"Aha," Andy smiled, "his present wife."

"You got it," Binyam laughed. Binyam looked up on the blackening clouds and the two men sat in silence till the first raindrops chased them inside.

Binyam's living room felt cozy to Andy, with its large upholstered sofas and traditional Ethiopian chairs. Hi-fi, TV and Ethiopian icons and family photos, a mixture of Ethiopian and Western furniture. Traditional rugs and colorful shawls draped over modern chairs. Posters from art exhibitions in New York and paintings by Ethiopian artists. Magazines and newspapers. A tennis racket slung on the sofa next to a camera and dirty socks. Binyam's room reflected an occupant of many interests and a mix of cultures. This was a place to relax and expand, Andy felt. He thought of his own living room; Anne was very tidy.

Andy looked around, and his eyes focused on a group of photos in frames on the large bookcase. He bent over them but averted his glance when he saw a big colored photo of Binyam with his arms around the shoulders of a beautiful Ethiopian woman. However, it was too late not to have seen it. It was Myriam. A more mature looking Myriam than he remembered. But as beautiful, with her striking, classical Ethiopian features. Andy felt his heart galloping and quickly went to another corner of the room, where he was studying an art poster intently when Binyam returned from the bathroom.

"There is something that I want to ask you about," Andy said hesitantly. Binyam looked at him. "How is Myriam?"

"Glad you asked. I have been waiting for that question."

"You have?"

"So, how is she?"

"Well, she is fine. Married to a well-to-do businessman. Started her own business. Running a little orphanage on the side. She is very effective—turns straw into gold."

"So there is nothing I can do for her now?"

"I don't think so."

"Well, if you will greet her from me." Andy hesitated and looked at Binyam's mother, who entered the room with refills of the coffee. "Just say, I wish her the best."

Binyam had an invitation to see some friends that night, and invited Andy to join him. But Andy threw a glance at the clock on the wall and suddenly felt tired. As he knew that he would have a round of meetings the next day, he suggested Binyam come for a cup of morning coffee before he went to the airport the following morning. Binyam thought that was a good idea and offered to take Andy to the airport.

"Have to send you off in style, white brother."

Andy had the same spaghetti dish with the tomato sauce that tasted as if it was right out of the Heinz bottle, with a couple of beers in the same little doll's room. He had one more beer, thinking it would help him sleep better. He left a generous tip, despite the lousy service, and glanced reflexively at his watch before he went for a little walk out on the lawn.

He listened to the distant barking of dogs and looked into the darkness over the lake. He thought of Anwar and Hana's love story and the paradisiacal island hidden away in the dark. Too romantic to be real. The image of Myriam also floated before him, and he decided he would talk to Binyam about her on the last morning. He hadn't thought about her for years. Strange how vivid his memories of her had become now. He hadn't really told Binyam about their romance, and he had stopped thinking about it many years ago. He would think about it more after the meetings tomorrow—now was time to focus on the plans for the next day. Having decided this, Andy returned to his room down the uneven pathway.

He brushed his teeth under the dripping faucet and checked for mosquitoes and killed one before he smeared the repellent on his face and hands. He lay down on the uneven mattress, pulled the cover all the way up to his face and folded his hands under the blanket, out of the reach of the little tormentors. Slowly, his body relaxed and he thought of the little waves on the sandy shore. They lulled him to sleep.

The contours of the island on the lake appeared for him. He saw them before him, the young couple, kissing under the jumping shadows of the oak tree. They whisper something. They laugh. Then they grow quiet, listening to the sounds in the stillness surrounding them. They blend into that little island under the drifting clouds. The gentle rattling of the leaves high up in the trees, the sudden chirp of some bird, the mechanical sound of a distant boat engine. Anwar pulls out a straw and begins to bend it in the shape of a ring. "Next time, I'll get us real rings. Expensive ones." Hana sticks out her ring finger, and Anwar pushes the ring onto her finger.

"Ouch, it hurts."

Anwar's consolation turns into lovemaking on the straw, in their little stone shelter belonging to a monk. It becomes violent and painful.

It is her face. It is Maryam. And it is him. Himself. There is no doubt. The pain increases, and he feels as if his head will explode.

Binyam is sitting by the shore laughing. He waves to them and shouts, "Well done, well done."

The sun comes through the clouds and the pain abates. Andy looks at his watch and says, "Oh, it's late. I must get back to Anne. Good the rain stopped. Anyway, it's only the small rains."

They get up, stretch and brush off stray straw. Myriam keeps the little straw ring in place, holding on to it with her right hand. Then she screams. (Such a real, heart rending scream.) The monk has come rushing up the hill and grabbed her. Andy feels paralyzed. He can't move as he watches the monk pulling Myriam down the hill, away from him. The monk turns his face. It is his father, in disguise. Yes. But Andy can't move. Now the monk-father pulls her into the boat. Andy is thrashing his legs on the spot. He moans.

"Who moaned?" Andy lay still and listened. The birds were chirping. The light streamed in through his curtains. He moved his hand to his forehead, where he had been stung by a mosquito. He was in his hotel. In Ethiopia.

But why did he feel so sad? This feeling of loss? The dream—now he remembered it. All this talk about love, it had gone to his head.

Slowly, he swung his pale legs out of the bed and began to stand up. A busy day of meetings was ahead of him.

The following morning, when Andy stepped out on the dew-fresh grass, the slow waiters were wiping off the garden chairs and placing them in groups in the center of the lawn. Andy moved two of the chairs next to a little table in a sunny spot, and sat down to wait for Binyam.

The chair was still a little wet and uncomfortable. He tried to make himself more at ease on the hard metal and shifted his back to make the chair cut less. The feeling of sadness was lingering with him, and he thought of the dream the previous night and what it meant. He could quickly see the connections to Binyam's story. But why did he dream like this?

Clearly, it was about Myriam and his feelings for her, which had been rekindled by his visit to her country and by Anwar and Hana's story. Did it resemble his? The passion. Had he felt such passion? But he had almost forgotten about her. He had put that love story behind him when he married Anne, after Myriam had left the country to go back to Ethiopia to take care of her sick mother. And he had completely forgotten. Maybe not forgotten—but for a long time he had not thought of it. It was as if it was forgotten.

So he, Andy, had had his love story, like most other people. He had left it behind him, as everybody does when they have to move on in their life. But why should he feel so sad now? He was happily married to his wife and had two wonderful children. Happy? Well, maybe content. What was happy? That word didn't really mean anything.

But now he remembered how his heart beat when he glanced at the photo of Myriam. For a moment, he had felt that intensity of feeling he had experienced with her. That complete merging with his sensations. Something he never experienced anymore. Maybe that was why he felt so low? But it was unrealistic to expect such feelings at his age. Could it have been different? He felt confused.

Fortunately, he was interrupted by the cheerful "*Tenastelin*" from Binyam, wearing his beloved baseball cap backwards on his smiling face.

"How is life?" he asked, as they used to say to each other in America.

"Not bad. Apart from this chair."

"Two coffees," he shouted in Tigrinian at the waiter, who was standing cleaning his finger nails with a fork, at a sunny spot between two trees.

Binyam took an envelope from his pocket and pulled a letter out with what looked like a little crude ring. "Anwar gave me this letter in which Hana returned their ring. He didn't want to keep it when he married Sara. He couldn't throw it away, either." Binyam held the brown straw up against the light. The ring had become undone and looked like a question mark against the pale sky.

"There is something I wanted to tell you about...." Andy hesitated. "But then your mother came into the room."

"Yes?"

"It's about Myriam ... she and I...."

"Yes.... Go ahead."

"She and I had a relationship."

"I know."

"But … it was not just a relationship … it was serious."

"I know. And my mother also found out. How couldn't she? Myriam was so distraught. But I didn't know it was that serious back in America, and that you were together when I was busy with my extra job." He paused. "She told me that you were her *big love*." Binyam smiled.

"Well, you could say it was similar to the story you happened to tell me yesterday."

"No," Binyam said firmly. "Anwar was trapped by circumstances. You could act freely. He lived in a poor, traditional country. You were an American, for God's sake. Myriam even told me that you had promised to come and bring her back to America when she had to leave so suddenly. And she didn't even hear from you. Why?"

Andy looked down and sat quietly for a long time. "Yes, we were in love. I guess it was real passion. Yes, I made those promises. But once she had left, I began to doubt. And there was my father. She had a different religion. She was from an African country. I was confused."

"You were no trailblazer," Binyam said matter-of-factly.

"Something like that," Andy admitted in a quiet voice. The chair was cutting into his back. "I guess I hesitated too long. I was really afraid."

"Like traditional people everywhere," Binyam added, with a sad smile. He put the straw ring back into the envelope.

"But why didn't you write her and explain? She waited for years."

"I'm not sure. I thought it was more clear-cut to do nothing. Not to give any false hopes."

Binyam took a deep draught of his cigarette.

Andy looked over the mysterious lake, where the morning fog was slowly dissolving. The rays of the sun fell on the surface of the lake until they were extinguished by the darkness of the deep waters. He still thought that his story with Myriam resembled the story of Anwar and Hana.

"When you greet her from me, tell her that I was wrong. Tell her … that I'm sorry."

The two men sat in silence for a while. Binyam hadn't said anything. He leaned forward and gave Andy a friendly pat on the leg. They got up and walked through the sunlit dining room and out through the lobby, with its small boutiques for tourists. Andy stopped in front of the jewelry shop, struck by a sudden idea. There in the window lay a ring of woven strands of gold. It looked a bit as if it was made of straw, but it was this rich-colored Ethiopian gold.

Andy couldn't remember when he had last bought something special for Anne.

The Immigrant

ALMOST NOON, THICK FOG STILL EMBRACING the windows, I keep patting my baby's back. Surely she is teething. I intensify the little taps. Finally, finally, I can tiptoe out of the room. At last, a little time to myself.

Or is there? "No," the kitchen and the living room scream in unison. They look as if a tornado has just passed through, leaving piles of dirty plates and cups and pans and children's clothes and toys and little booties all over. Just now a ray of sunshine breaks through the fog and illuminates a partially eaten peanut butter sandwich with the dry corners curved upwards.

Where to start—or can I be bothered at all? I pick up *Jasmine* by Mukherjee from the crinkled couch and drop it again. I stretch out an arm to grab a soiled Oshkosh overall on the Mission-style dresser and my glance falls on my image in the mirror? I freeze. Who is that Ethiopian woman looking back at me from under my civic lessons' clipping about "the pursuit of happiness" tucked in the corner of the mirror? That both distraught but also hopeful-looking young woman with olive skin and kinky hair combed away from her face. I try to smile, but it comes out like a grimace. I straighten my back and try again. Smiles are definitely overrated.

If I am pregnant again, I won't tell Teddy.

I drop into the couch. What would be so bad about a third child? My mother had seven. Yes, that exactly is my point, I don't want to repeat my mother's patient life of endless pregnancies and mothering. Fulfilling her lot in life. For God's sake, I'm in America. The country where "all men are created equal" and have the right to "life, liberty, and the pursuit of happiness."

I look around. My eyes graze the piles of dirty clothes, the scattered toys and crumbled pillows. I sink back again, brushing some children's books aside and pushing some onto the floor. "I'm not grateful enough," Teddy has said.

I need to think—more important than tidying up. Teddy will be upset about the mess, but at this point, I don't care. I put my legs up and close my eyes.

I think back on my first time in Chicago. How I had been scared of those concrete-and-glass skyscrapers reaching all the way into the cold, blue air. The cars gliding through at the foot of the towering buildings—like fish at the bottom of a water tank. On days off, I would walk along Lake Michigan sick with homesickness. Anwar's brown eyes would float in front of me. I left him behind when I won the immigrant lottery. I missed my parents, my siblings, the smells of the *souq*, the fresh breeze of Lake Tana.

My whole life I had left behind to begin all over in *the land of opportunity*. That's when I had developed a technique of talking to myself, Here you are, Hana, in the new world. Isn't it great! Now you make the best of it. You're going to be happy. And I was full of hope. I met other Ethiopian immigrants, I became a waitress at Denny's, and I began to drink American coffee. I had only one wish: to blend in and live a normal life like everybody around me. So what happened?

I was becoming one of them in *the melting pot*. But it took time. Only gradually did I learn to wake up without bad dreams and panic attacks, until finally, one morning, I suddenly realized that I had been dreaming in English. My life back in Ethiopia became more distant; I was less pained by Anwar's brown eyes, and when spring came, I took up jogging along the lake. I no longer imagined it was Lake Tana. It had become Lake Michigan.

That's when I was introduced to Tewodros Makonnen (Teddy, as I would call him) by my uncle. I remember him with his baseball cap and Yankees jacket. I thought it looked a little funny on him—as if he was rushing to become American. But I loved his enthusiasm.

He had offered to help me find a way to get Anwar over, and together, we talked to people and the immigration service. I was optimistic about our efforts but—slowly and imperceptibly—they turned into an empty ritual together with Teddy—something to do together. Oh, God, it occurs to me right now, Teddy never intended to get Anwar over here. How could I have been so naive? But thinking about it now, I admit to myself, It's no longer important.

What is important is how I feel towards Teddy now. It's not easy to say. He is my anchor. He is much older (in his early forties), a mature man to lean my head against.

Am I still in love with him...? Ye---s.... But our everyday life crushes my feelings for him. We're always so busy with the kids.

I guess he is right, I am no longer the same. America has done that to me.

Time is up—I hear Wossen.

After I have changed Wossen's diaper and have given her some mashed carrot from a fresh Gerber jar, I put her into the playpen. Then I will have between fifteen and twenty minutes to tidy up the apartment. I know exactly how long Wossen can entertain herself—a period I can prolong by about five minutes with small talk and little intermediate attentions.

I pounce into my work, wash the grease off the dishes with sponge and soap, and tidy up like a whirlwind. I even manage to do some pre-dinner chopping of vegetables. Teddy appreciates it if dinner is ready when he returns from work.

I put the chopped vegetables into a bowl with some plastic wrap over them, place it in the fridge and slam the door with a bang. I turn towards my daughter with a big smile, but honestly, all the time it is in the back of my head, What am I doing?

Tomorrow I will go for a quick pregnancy test at the clinic, I think, as I maneuver baby and carriage down the steps and through the front door. Then I will make my decision.

It feels good out in the fresh air. The sun's rays are pleasantly warm, and Wossen is babbling along. We pass a destitute-looking panhandler with a cup of coins in front of him. I give him a quarter. I always give, but for the life of me I cannot understand how anyone can be a beggar in this rich country.

Wossen and I continue as the man says *God bless* to my little girl, and at the end of the street I turn the carriage into the playground. The ground looks like a kaleidoscope of colors, with brightly dressed children crawling, swinging and sliding on the newly painted yellow, purple and green play structure under the bright afternoon sun. Wossen beams and wiggles free of her safety belt.

I eye my friend Amna, from Iran, with her two youngest (the three older ones are in pre-school and Kindergarten). Amna waves and laughs under her white scarf, and I steer Wossen towards them. Now Wossen recognizes her young friends and tears at the locking mechanism to undo the belt.

The children play, and we mothers make small talk, in between retrieving a stick from the mouth of one, and delivering an extra shovel to a couple fighting over one rake. I always feel attracted to the laughter-prone Amna. She seems so secure and satisfied in her role as a mother. She is not *discontent*. I wish I could be like her, and I think of confiding my situation to her. But just as I open my mouth, I relent, and simply comment on what a beautiful day it is. Amna wouldn't understand—after all she is a Muslim and lives a traditional life. To her, it makes no difference whether she lives in America or back in Iran. No, I realize I will try to talk to an American. I will see Mrs. Greene, a few houses down the street. I have talked with her now and then, and she is *one of them*.

Afterwards, Wossen and I pick up big sister Maria at the Co-Op Kindergarten and go to the laundromat, where my girls stare in fascination at the swirling clothes behind the glass door. Maria is now helping me look after Wossen, and sits with her in the playpen reading a little book to her (as her parents often do with her). I am keeping half an eye on them (that activity will not last for long—Wossen is already reaching out for an Ethiopian doll next to them), and another on my lamb chops, which I am marinating. I have to be very careful to get the right proportions of garlic, salt, *berberi,* oil and a tiny dab of sugar. Teddy is particular. He doesn't know about the sugar. That's my secret, but he always exclaims that it is so good, when I secretly add just a dab of sugar.

Tonight I will discuss with Teddy—calmly and rationally—how I want to get some more education and a job. I want to lay out the issues and make a clear plan with my husband. At this moment, I hear a key in the lock, and my heart skips a beat. I am not nearly ready, but at least, the girls are good and now Teddy can play with them. If he is not too tired. I receive a light kiss on the cheek. I feel Teddy's cold nose—the fog has rolled in again.

He places his briefcase on the usual spot next to the dresser, switches on the TV and sinks down in the upholstered chair, which I have fortunately managed to clear. As if synchronized, the two little girls turn their heads in the direction of the TV. Images of American tanks shooting in the direction of overturned cars and fighters with their faces covered by their headscarves.

"Bang, bang," Maria says.

"Is that necessary?" I hear how irritated my voice sounds. "You know, I don't like the kids...."

"You're sure in a good mood tonight," he answers lowering the sound a little.

"It's been a long day. I guess I feel a little tired." I feel my vocal cords tightened into a knot that changes my voice.

"You always seem tired these days." He looks at me with suppressed irritation.

"I never seem to have any time for myself," I whine, against my better inclinations, while I mix the salad dressing.

"All you have to do is look after two little girls. You don't even have a job." He is looking angrily at me and the TV the same time.

Teddy never says things directly, but what he implies is that I am not grateful. Here I am in this wonderful country and have everything. I don't even have to work. *Ungrateful.* I give up saying anything, and suddenly big tears are running down my cheeks.

He turns off the TV, comes over to me, and puts his arm around my shoulder.

"So, so, little girl. What's that?" And he embraces me, which only makes me cry the more. "You'll be OK. My little girl. It's probably hormonal. Now you've stopped nursing. Your body is going through a lot."

"It's not hormonal!" Now I find my voice through those tight vocal cords.

Wossen and Maria have their faces turned towards us. Wossen starts to cry.

"Hana, now you have upset the children." Teddy goes over to the playpen and picks up Wossen. That is the worst sin: to upset the children. "You should be more considerate."

"What about being considerate to me?" (Now I am talking and acting like a little girl—exactly what I don't want to be.)

"So what is it you want so badly?"

"Well, I.… I want some more education so I can get a well-paid job." The anger in my voice surprises me.

That's when the phone rings. Teddy hands Wossen to me with a significant glance and takes the phone. His voice is changed into that jovial Teddy voice. "Hello, *salaam*, Muhammad."

A joking and cheerful conversation continues, with a stern glance in the direction of me and my baby as Wossen starts to whimper again.

I go into the little room with my baby girl and close the door. Appearance is very important to Teddy. Here in America, we represent the perfect Ethiopian family, and that's that. Tewodros is a proud Ethiopian—becoming American hasn't changed that.

After the phone call, he peeks into the little room with Maria on his arm. "That was a bad start of an evening. Let's try again." He gives me a kiss and Maria does likewise. He attempts to maintain a normal, calm tone. I nod and return to the preparation of dinner, while Teddy sits with the two girls on the couch.

The TV is still turned off, and I give the salad dressing a tiny dab of sugar.

The girls have been put to bed and we are doing the dishes together. Teddy doesn't normally do that, but tonight takes a special effort. We had also had a glass of wine and had both placed half a glass on the sofa table. It is a little before ten o'clock, and I notice how Teddy is hurrying, throwing glances at the clock.

He wants to see the ten o'clock news. He asks if it is OK. I say I would rather talk and we compromise: he will watch only five minutes. I sit down on the sofa next to him after he has turned it off. Like a reward to him? I take a sip of the wine.

"We need to talk," I begin, and face him as I fold my legs up under me. (I know he doesn't like me doing that. He says it is unfeminine. Too late now.)

"What do you want to talk about?" he sounds quite normal, but of course, I sense that he is reluctant about it. (Teddy doesn't believe in talks. He doesn't think they serve any purpose.) I realize I'm maybe a little unfair—I have to give the man a chance. So I go, "I want to make some plans."

"Plans about what?"

"You see, I would like to get some education ... and a job."

"What's the rush? ... and I'm supporting us." I hesitate, I know how important it is to Teddy to be *supporting* us.

Then I hear myself say, "But I feel trapped. I take care of children. Maybe there will be another one. Then it will go on and on. For how long? Will I never be able to do something else? Just like my mother ...." I stop abruptly.

"What do you mean? You are in America! You have all the conveniences. Life is not nearly so hard as in Ethiopia. And we will not have so many children. We'll stop. Soon," he adds.

"What do you mean, soon? Isn't that my decision, too?"

"Sure. Of course. We agree on it."

"But we don't have a boy, that's what you want to say?"

"Of course, I would like to have a boy. But should I have only girls, that would be fine with me. God willing."

"What do you have to bring God into it for?"

"Don't be so sensitive. Let's have a good time." He reaches over and strokes my chin.

I am annoyed with myself. This was supposed to have been a rational conversation. I bend forward and kiss Teddy gently on his cheek. He moves closer to me and embraces me. I feel guilty: I failed.

Next morning when Teddy is leaving with Maria for her day care on way to his work, I almost cringe as he kisses me goodbye on the cheek. I quickly kiss Maria so he won't notice my angry blush. He had not taken any precautions last night, even though he had promised to do so. It all happened so fast ... but the point is, he wants a third child. The boy.

Passing Mrs. Greene weeding in her front yard, I manage to bring up my errand, and we agree to meet the following day.

So the next day I settle on the soft Persian carpet with Wossen and a bunch of toys in Mrs. Greene's cozy living room. There is a big stone fireplace and wooden walls and bookcases with books from floor to high ceiling. It is one of those homey looking wood-shingle Berkeley houses with high gables and a protruding roof. I remark how I like the house and wish I could have a house like that one day. Mrs. Greene doesn't think this is impossible, she and her husband had started with very little themselves.

Mrs. Greene had married Mr. Greene against the wishes of her family, and gone with him to *Barkeley*. (That's how she thought it should be pronounced, as she tells me with a laugh.) She was from Italy and her maiden name was Costello. "I am an immigrant just like you, although I hardly ever think of that anymore." I had always thought of her as an American, but I can see there is something Italian about her—she's a little more elegant than American women normally are.

Mrs. Greene offers tea and comes right to the point, as she knows that our time is limited to Wossen's benevolence. Then she tells me that she has had three children herself, but that one had died some years ago in a car accident.

I am shocked to hear this and express my sympathy as best I can. I had no idea. Mrs. Greene seemed so content to me, I could never have imagined that she had lived with such a great sorrow. Mrs. Greene admits that it has been very hard, but their love for each other in the family has gotten them through. The two other children are doing fine, and now there are three grandchildren—she beams when she says that.

Clearly, I do not want to talk about my little *problem* after hearing about the Greene tragedy, but Mrs. Greene insists that we now talk about me. So finally, I reluctantly tell about my feelings of "being stuck" and how I don't want any more children. When Mrs. Greene answers that that shouldn't be any problem, I have to be more precise and explain, "But I think that I'm pregnant again."

Mrs. Greene looks serious. Then she says, "So what do you want to do?"

"I don't know, I just don't want another baby," I almost start to cry. (I really have become such a crybaby lately.)

Mrs. Greene embraces me and pats me on my back to calm me down. "Well, first you take a test. Maybe you're not pregnant. But if you are, then we'll discuss it. You can have an abortion, you know."

"Teddy would never accept that," I shout involuntarily.

"So, so …."Mrs. Greene pats my back again. "Then you have your baby."

"Snow, snow, it's snowing," Maria screams excitedly. We have been driving in silence (both of us preoccupied with our thoughts), the girls lulled to sleep by the gentle vibrations of the car. Now they rub their eyes and we all look out through the windshield at the big soft flakes, which come sailing through the gray air.

Maria gets so excited that she presses her window button and sticks her arm out into the cold air till her father tells her to close the window. Her enthusiasm uncurbed, Maria keeps singing, and Wossen and I now join in, singing, "Snow, snow!" till we reach the top of the mountain before the long slow descent towards Lake Tahoe.

We reach the road to Carnelian Bay in a "swarm of bees" as Maria says. We turn and crawl inside the high walls of packed snow, while I direct from the little map open on my lap under the flashlight. We turn again and look for the number on our condo.

Yesterday, Teddy made the sudden decision that we all should spend a weekend in a condo by Lake Tahoe. He thought it would do his *discontented* wife good to have a family weekend together away from our daily routines. Normally, a condo would have sounded magical to me but this was not normal. My test has proved that I am, indeed, pregnant—a fact I have omitted to tell Teddy.

So we settle into our condo: kitchen bags into the kitchen, clothes into the bedrooms. We make a roaring fire in the living room after first filling the room with smoke, because the vent was closed. Teddy hangs an Ethiopian shawl across the large mirror over the sofa; it annoys him to see our reflection all the time.

I feed the children and put them to bed, while Teddy watches the news on our bedroom TV. (This is the place for him; no less than two TVs.) But he turns it off when I am through with the kids and come up the stairs to the living room, where I open the curtains and put the light on outside, so we can watch the falling flakes.

We put some Ethiopian music on the CD. The reggae rhythm of *Satta Massagana,* "There is a land, far far away," fills the room. Teddy pours some red wine of his favorite. In fact, the atmosphere is so idyllic that I become worried that this is not conducive to a serious talk. Nevertheless, I hesitantly bring up the by now familiar subject of my education. I had discussed this recently with Mrs. Greene (a frown on Teddy's tanned forehead) so I can now tell Teddy that I would like to go to a pharmacy school and later get a job as a pharmacist. Then I can help him support our family.

Teddy sits quietly sipping his wine. Then he goes to turn off the music. He looks neutral. When he sits down in the sofa again, he *commends* my idea of becoming a wage earner, but he can't quite see how I would be able to study with two children and a working husband.

He had taken it quite nicely I feel, so I begin to keenly outline how we might do it. We could get an apartment near the school. Maybe I could get my mother over? I could study at night and on the weekends. I am ready. I can do it—with Teddy's help.

He sips his wine, gets up to fix the logs in the fire and adds a new one. He doesn't say much, but he doesn't outright reject my ideas. He pours himself some more wine. (I stick to my one glass.) He puts the music back on. I lean back in his arms. He gives me a squeeze and begins to hum to the tunes of the Abyssinians.

He interrupts his humming, "See what a good life we can have here. How comfortable we can be. Your work is rewarded—unlike Ethiopia. It would be great if you could earn a salary too. If not as a pharmacist, as something else."

"But," I interject, "you know, now that I have thought about it, I specifically want to be a pharmacist."

"OK, that or something else."

"No, I really want to become a pharmacist."

"First, you don't know what you want to do, and then, bang, only a pharmacist!"

"I know, it may sound like that. Truth is, I didn't even dare think the thought. First, I just wanted a job. But I'm really interested in medicine. It would be very … fulfilling to me (big frown on Teddy's high forehead). And there are flexible work hours and plenty of jobs.

"Mrs. Greene says…."

"Mrs. Greene…." Teddy looks annoyed. "Must you always bring her into the discussion?"

"It's just that she is very supportive of me."

"So, and I am not?"

"Yes, you are … but, you're a man and you're…." I hesitate, "not American."

"So now it's a problem that I'm not American. Don't you see, it just doesn't make sense what you're saying. Actually … more and more I think being in America has had a negative effect on you. If we had a similar life in Ethiopia, you would be content, but because it is in America you're not."

"Well, but here it *is* different. Or here it *could* be different. My life here is not that different from that of my mother in Ethiopia except for a few machines and *gadgets*," (I was proud of that last word), "but here I am in the land of opportunity, where I can compare my situation to other women, who have jobs, drive their own cars, have their own bank accounts, who are…." I hesitate. "You know … the words: in *pursuit of happiness*."

I feel pleased over my own unexpected eloquence. Trying to still sound enthusiastic, I explain how I will take care of all the practical aspects. I would still make dinner for him—he would really be OK. I kiss him on his cheek.

He also wants to be accommodating. After all, that's why we had gone to Lake Tahoe. "My little pharmacist," he says teasingly, and embraces me. I stiffen, but force myself to relax. He had not said *no* to my suggestions after all. I would have to be patient and let him get used to my ideas. So I mumble "Mmmmm" in his ear and try not to think of anything.

There was so much more I wanted to explain. This is just the tip of the iceberg. Fortunately, we have the whole next day to ourselves out here in the sleeping nature.

The next morning, we wake up to a blinding brightness. The sun shines on the white layer of snow on the ground and on the pine trees, whose branches are bent down with the heavy load. The crystals sparkle so white, they radiate silver, purple and rose. White turned into color; I stand spellbound by the window.

We have never seen anything like it. We can't get out soon enough and tumble out, all bundled up. Teddy puts on dark sunglasses to protect his sensitive eyes from the reflection from the snow. We walk on our borrowed snowshoes and pull the girls on a little sledge. We make snowballs, throw them at each other and roll on the white, cold carpet. I sled down a little hill with Teddy, while Maria holds Wossen. We fall over and laugh so hard we have tears in our eyes. Teddy can be so funny, when he is in the mood. And he is while he is clowning around on one leg and falling into the snow for his three girls. In the middle of all the merriment, I suddenly think, "Shall I tell him?"

When the girls are put down for a nap, Teddy seems ready to cuddle up with me again, but this time I insist that I want to take a little walk alone. This is my chance to experience the magical snow scenery. Teddy looks a little sulky, but he gives up his resistance and laughingly replies, "My independent wife is taking a walk on her own. Do come back again." He kisses me and disappears into our bedroom, where he turns on the TV to watch the weekend sports.

In the meantime, I walk on the snowplowed path and turn into a bend, opening the vista to the undulating snow-fields of tiny sparkling diamonds. Water turned into ice crystals. I hold my breath; I have never seen anything so beautiful. Imagine that I should be twenty-six before I see a winter landscape.

I think of all this as I proceed out into the quiet fata morgana of snow and ice. So quiet it is. As if a white blanket had been pulled over the green grass, the pine trees and the chirping summer birds. Summer has been put to sleep till spring comes around again. In Ethiopia, the rainy season would be over. Recently, Teddy has mentioned we might go back to Ethiopia. (He has even made sure our passports are in order: our daughters' names in ours.) Is that a warning or what?

What if he insists we go back? I can't imagine it now that I have fought so hard to feel at home in my new country. Now I want to live a *modern* life, with a job and my own car. But how can I do that if I have another baby?

I stand still soaking up the snowy, serene landscape. But I've been gone for rather long. Time to return. The girls are probably awake by now, interrupting Teddy's TV. Teddy needs me to do what he likes. He would always do his own thing. His plans. They are, of course, his plans. Where was I in them? What is there for me? All I can see is helping him. His dreams.

My glance is caught by a lone skier. As the figure comes closer towards me, I see it's a woman. She looks so in control—so powerful—she seems at one with her skis. Suddenly, I'm overcome with a longing to be that woman, in harmony with the snowy landscape.

The female skier now passes me and greets me cheerfully. She looks happy—I can't help turning around to look after her. The distance between us grows quickly.

I turn back towards our cabin—I will go it alone. Teddy doesn't need to know.

Back in Berkeley, it looks like our little mountain retreat has done us good. We are very considerate to each other, but I'm wasting no time enrolling in a community college course to meet the requirements to enter the pharmaceutical school. My dream is possible, and as Mrs. Greene has pointed out, there is a shortage of pharmacists.

But first the greater obstacle has to be taken out of the way. After many a discussion with Mrs. Greene, we agree to go ahead with the abortion without telling Teddy. I just know there is no other way—he would never agree to an abortion. He would still want a son. True, Mrs. Greene has strongly discouraged me from going behind my husband's back, but as I explained, she has no idea what men from the Third World were like. So as she grew to understand how much this meant to me, she agreed and offered to pay as well as to house me for a night to recuperate. The latter I can't do, that would make Teddy suspicious.

In the meantime, I talk about my education plans with Teddy. He doesn't object, but he doesn't encourage me. He seems to be stalling me. So behind our peaceful façade, the tug-of-war continues. It is scary, but I know I have to make my own decisions and be responsible for them. I feel so much more cheerful now that I "have stepped into action," and I secretly sent my thanks to the lonely female skier by Lake Tahoe.

I go over to Mrs. Greene's house often now. Maria and I love the place, and it becomes a bit like a second home for us—Mrs. Greene has turned into the grandmother in residence. One day when I arrive at the house, Mrs. Greene's oldest son is there. He is my age, a handsome boy with a long blond ponytail, called Jonathan. He knows somebody who has studied pharmacy at the Stockton pharmaceutical school, and I get all excited, surrounded by the enthusiasm of the Greene family. My two daughters are laughing through the open doors to the next room. They are watching some old *Sesame Street* videos from Jonathan's time.

In the middle of the merry atmosphere, it suddenly strikes me how we miss that lightness of interaction in the Makonnen family (except for our time in the snow). We are always so heavy, so serious—*immigrant heaviness*. This Jonathan, a film animator, is so charming, sitting there explaining about a character in one of his films. I should have left half an hour ago, but I find it difficult to leave this comfortable atmosphere.

I have finally gotten up from the couch when the bell rings. It is Teddy, and he has been worried that I have not come home with the girls. He has even checked out the playground. He greets the Greene family briefly and goes straight to get his girls. I feel an anger rise inside me when I realize that I'm ashamed by my husband's heavy-handedness. Everybody feels the pleasant atmosphere come to an abrupt end. The girls don't want to leave their video when Jonathan says they can take it home with them—Teddy doesn't pretend to be pleased.

Outside, it has turned dark, and Teddy is carrying Maria, while I'm pushing Wossen in the stroller. "What's so wonderful about this old lady and that long-haired son that you're always hanging out there?" he asks.

"She's very nice to me ... us ... and she talks with me."

"Anyways, you should discuss private matters with me before you go to *ferengis*," he says, reproachfully.

"But she has so much experience. She even lost a child."

"I'm sorry to hear that, but it has nothing to do with us," Teddy grumbles. And that ends the discussion for now. Teddy has become suspicious—maybe he doesn't trust me anymore?

I arrange for Amna to take Wossen (I told her I needed a little female procedure) and Teddy will take off early and pick up Maria from her Kindergarten. Mrs. Greene brings me to the clinic in her weather-beaten Camry and promises to wait right there till the procedure is over. Honestly, I have lost some of my courage—maybe I have underestimated the whole undertaking?

I put on the hospital gown and am placed on my stretcher in a little space separated by curtains. Fortunately, it all goes fairly fast, with my blood pressure taken and the various other preparations. Finally, the anaesthetist sticks the needle in my vein, while talking calmly to me. I think of my daughters but soon I feel like I am falling, falling down through the narrow slip between the skyscrapers. Through the water, because it was really a giant aquarium. Bubbles of air rise up from me. I begin to suffocate, I gasp for air when finally, I just swallow and give up resisting. I am still sinking but now it feels pleasant—restful.

When I wake up, Mrs. Greene is right next to me—as promised. She whispers that the doctor has said everything went fine. Now I should just rest a bit, and then she will take me home. An hour later, I stand up on my wobbly legs. I feel weak—but I have a euphoric feeling of freedom. My life is full of possibilities again. Now I just have to deal with Teddy.

Not only has everything gone according to plan, I have even made sure I didn't leave the clinic without a diaphragm. I feel proud that I have thought of everything, and I'm sure that now, the future lies open. Maybe I will even be able to tell the whole story to Teddy one day?

But something happens—one of those little things that turn out to be just the tip of the famous iceberg. One evening, Teddy is tidying up the medicine cupboard in the bathroom (he is always tidying up), when he comes upon a brand-new plastic box with my diaphragm and asks what it is. I had forgotten to put it away in my private toilet bag. Maybe I had unconsciously wanted him to know that I use it.

He explodes about me going behind his back. He can't trust me anymore. (Like my visits to Mrs. Greene.) I have changed. America was doing this to me. It has made me selfish. Maybe we would be better off in Ethiopia. There, I wouldn't act up like this. *Education, independence, fulfilment*, Teddy grimaces. Maybe we had better go back.

After my initial surprise, I understand why he has exploded at this seemingly small issue. Now it is my turn to lose my temper, "You just wanted me to get pregnant," I shout. "But even if I did, I would end it."

"You would what?" Teddy looks at me in utter dismay.

"I would…," I hold my breath.

"You would turn into … a murderer," he whispers, with an expression of horrified suspicion. "That's what it has come to?"

I bravely hold his gaze, and he finally looks down before he turns into the girls' room, where Maria is crying. Just before opening the door, he turns and looks back at me. Incredulously.

When Teddy reenters the living room, I feel I can't bear to share my bed or even sleep under the same roof as Teddy. I say I will go sleep in Mr. and Mrs. Greene's house. As he knows, I have the key to the empty house while the Greene's are back in Italy. Teddy forbids me to go (now he has shown his true face by giving orders), but I can also see that he makes some sense. It is not a good idea to go when I am so excited. He is worried for me, after all. Maybe he really does love me? We agree that I will take a night and day to be on my own in the upcoming weekend.

Teddy looks very distant. He will sleep on the couch in the living room in the meantime.

The following Friday night, I put my girls to bed and kiss and cuddle them and tell Maria I will be back the next evening. "Don't go away, Mom," the little girl whispers. "I just have to do something. I will be right back," and I kiss my girl on her chubby, soft cheek. I also kiss an intensely reserved Teddy goodnight before I close the front door gently behind me.

I hurry down the road and lock myself into the dark house. I already miss my two little girls, and the Greenes' house is cold. Quickly, I turn on some lights. I have to fumble in the darkness to feel for the switches. I can hear the wind moan in the chimney and feel a little afraid in the creaking house. I decide to make a fire in the fireplace, and soon I am seated in front of the roaring flames with a cup of steaming herb tea. I already feel a little better—the room is cozy.

I already regret that I have been so angry with Teddy. I needed to calm down a bit, but my life has been such a roller coaster recently. It feels good here, in this calm house. Now I can think my situation through without disturbance. No children. No TV. No Teddy clearing his throat.

I must regain Teddy's trust. I know I can do it—only it will take some time. One thing for sure, I will need Teddy's help with the girls and the housekeeping and everything while I go to school and study at night. But we can do it, and Teddy will understand gradually. After all, he has also been influenced by living in America. He has also been exposed to new ideas every day, not to mention his dear TV.

I will have to be patient.

See how it does me good to be a little on my own. To be able to think things through in peace. I already feel much better. If only I have the chance, I will gain the courage and confidence I need! I smile and get up. I go over to the bookcase and browse through some books. So many books to read. One day, I would like to read more books. I would ask Mrs. Greene for suggestions.

The phone rings. It is Teddy asking how I am doing? I answer that I'm fine. There is a silence.

"Are you alone?"

"What do you mean: alone? Who could be here? I told you: Mr. and Mrs. Greene went to Italy."

"Well, but their children, their two children."

"Oh, Jonathan?"

Silence.

"That's ridiculous."

"So much is ridiculous. Anything seems possible."

"Well, I am alone—and enjoying it. Good night."

See, how Teddy ruins the atmosphere. I was just feeling such peace. But I won't think about it, I will just be myself. Where was I? Books. I turn back towards the bookcase.

I look at some family photos in simple wooden frames (Ikea guaranteed). Smiling parents in the sun under big straw hats. The young Mrs. Greene. Must be her. So young and lovely. The three kids spraying water on each other with a garden hose. Three teenagers: two boys holding their arms around their sister. I stare. The younger boy is no longer there. Who was it? I feel a pang of pain. That was the worst thing that could happen: to lose a child. Nothing compared to it. But I have had a child removed myself. But that was not a child—yet. That had not become a person yet. But had I done wrong?

I sit down with the picture in my lap and a surge of longing for my two little daughters rise in me. Little Hana sitting *reading* for Wossen.

Wossen trying to eat the book. She was teething. Maria explaining: *read* not *eat*. She was already a little mother. Well, I, Hana, was their mother, and I would never desert them. That was what I felt strongly now. Here in a foreign land (even though I know it quite well, it is still foreign) without my large family back in Ethiopia, my daughters become even more important to me. They are all I have. My love for them goes beyond anything else. Even beyond my education and job. But that is the point. There needn't be a contradiction. It can all be combined.

I go upstairs to the guest room to sleep. I crawl into the bed without brushing my teeth. I think of Teddy and reluctantly go out onto the cold floor and to the bathroom. With a clear conscience, I settle into the soft *duvet* (I haven't tried such soft covers before) and close my eyes to sleep. But it is as if I cannot cut off my thoughts. Maybe I doze a little, but it feels as though I'm awake and aware of missing my girls every minute the entire night.

It is a long night before the rays of daylight finally seep in through the thin cotton curtains. As I'm waking up, I have a panic attack, the way I used to in my early days in Chicago. The wall is the wrong place, the windows and the light are different. Where am I? I feel totally lost, till I remember that I'm in Mrs. Greene's house.

And then I have to fill a whole day, before I can return. Never had I thought that the time would seem so long.

I make myself some breakfast with the eggs and bread I packed for the purpose. I go and sit in the garden in a deck chair with my *Jasmine* and try to concentrate while I'm thinking of what my girls and Teddy are doing now. Jasmine was a very strong person: she left her old place to move on. She knew she would hurt others in the process. I nod.

I make Amna a phone call, to hear another voice, and water the plants as I had promised Mrs. Greene, while I think about my daughters. I sit with my hands in the soft water of the little fishpond. Content the little goldfishes—in their element, I think vaguely. Maybe they all had gone to the playground? Maybe they would meet Amna? She would be surprised that I was not there. I hadn't told her that I was at Mrs. Greene's. I went inside and put on *The Abyssinians*.

I look at the clock. It is only half past twelve. The time passes so slowly. Is it too early to make myself some lunch? I am not hungry, but it is something to do. I will make a risotto, like I learned from Mrs. Greene. The risotto would occupy some time.

An hour later, it is half past one o'clock. I go back to my book on the lounge chair in the garden. After reading without concentrating for about half an hour, I sit up with a jerk. Never mind. I will call it quits. Enough is enough. I am just wasting my time. I will surprise Teddy and the girls. They would be happy to see me. We still would have time for a lovely afternoon. I would cook them something good for dinner. How about some real Ethiopian food. I have some frozen *durowat*. I can still defrost it, as well as some *enjera*.

I jump out of my chair. Put it in the little wooden shed in the back of the garden. Tidy up and pack my things and remember to lock the door behind me. I hurry down the street and up the steps of my own house. The stroller next to the main door is gone. Then they are probably at the playground, I think, disappointed.

I turn the key in the lock and enter. The apartment has an empty feeling to it. I go from room to room. The beds are made, but something is missing. In the girls' cupboard clothes are missing. I rush into our bedroom. The suitcase on the top of the big dresser is gone. I feel like I am sinking. Has he…?

I run back to the living room. Teddy's briefcase is there. Has he forgotten it? I grab it and notice that some toys are missing. I rush into the darkish kitchen—the fog has engulfed the house again. Wossen's milk bottle and the rubber tops are not there. Where are my girls? Have they gone?

I return to the living room holding on to the briefcase and look on the dresser. Maybe there will be a note? I search. But there is just my own clipping, "In the pursuit … " next to my frightened eyes.

I stop and look at my face: is that me—alone in America? I drop the briefcase and grab the edge of the dresser.

I look back on that immobile frozen face.

The Rich Man

A Farce

HE HAD EATEN TOO MUCH. HE had stuffed himself. Again. He had fallen asleep the instant his head hit the pillow. One of those deep, unconscious, merciful states where one can forget about all one's troubles and pains. Refuge from the world of worries. Blissful oblivion. And then with a bang, instant full awareness.

Binyam sits up in his bed with a pounding heart, nausea down his throat and stinging pain in his stomach. He is intensely aware of the cold sweat on his body, the light snoring from his wife next to him, the barking dogs outside the garden wall. The moon's rays shine brightly through a crack in the curtains.

He glances at the fluorescent numbers on his bed clock. Three fifteen. He has slept for one hour. Damn it. He had drunk and eaten too much. In fact, he had stuffed himself. That leg of lamb. He can't even think of it now. The nausea. And the raw meat. "Oh, merciful God, let me forget. Let me fall asleep again and I promise—this time I will keep it. I promise not to transgress any more."

Holding up his pajama pants in his left hand, Binyam turns his heavy frame over the edge of the bed and tiptoes to the flowery curtain to shut out the bright moon. Hurrying over the cold tiles on his way back, he stubs his big toe against the leg of the bed. Suppressing an outburst of piercing pain, he crawls under his warm blankets and tries to make himself comfortable on his right side. Turned away from the snoring of his wife.

He tries to pretend he is perfectly comfortable. He is going to sleep. Nothing to stop him. And he doesn't need to go pee. It's only an hour since he went last. So he doesn't need to pee already again.

Damned dog. He will go and shoot it. And he doesn't have to go and pee, so he'll just forget about it and relax. Just forget about it. He doesn't need to. That clock ticks too loudly. Funny he didn't notice before. OK, maybe he had better go, so he won't have to think of it any more. There must be nothing to keep him from sleeping.

And if that dog doesn't stop, he will take his rifle and shoot it. He swears.

He curls up in the bed with his back to his wife. He just needs to empty his brain. Into a big blank page. But how can he when his chest burns and his stomach cramps? And the nausea. He shouldn't have continued with that whiskey so late into the night. He had felt so good and when he feels good, he forgets. It's like the devil takes over and makes him empty one glass after the other.

He gets carried away. Ephraim's jokes. The wonderful raw meat. The African music. The gorgeous women. Stephanie was there. Voluptuous. And now the punishment. Well, if he can't sleep completely, he can rest. He will just think nice thoughts. The store. Big order yesterday. Great profit. He will open those two new stores in Bahir Dar and Awassa. Everybody will buy their plastic buckets and plastic kitchen utensils from him. Images of shiny red buckets, blue tubs and green watering cans float past Binyam's closed eyes.

He thinks positive thoughts, how he really has a knack for selling. His intuition for the market. Unlike that nincompoop of a son. Young people nowadays. They are soft. Have no discipline. All they want to do is listen to that awful music and drink that sugary, expensive Coke. Not like in his youth, where one had to work and sacrifice to gain something.

Now, only good thoughts. He won't think of Binyam Jr. But what can he do with him? Stick him away in one of the stores. Binyam can't do too much harm that way. Especially if he puts somebody efficient in charge of running the store. Binyam only nominally the head. Then he can sit and play his cards with his companions in a back room.

People will talk. What can he do? Maybe he can send his son overseas. Others do that. To America? But there you are expected to work. Maybe Greece? But he doesn't want to go. Binyam doesn't want to think about it. And he also doesn't want to think about the car Binyam Jr. smashed up and the police fine for the fight in the restaurant. He will deal with all that in clear daytime. Rationally and wisely. There is a solution to all problems. "Just do your best, then take a rest," he says out loud. His wife turns over and mumbles something about shutting up. That's the thing with insomnia, it makes you feel lonely.

OK, so he can't stop thinking. Then he will just think of something pleasant. His good fortune. His business. And, oh, Tekka is asking for a big loan. He is not solvent. He will just lose it and what then? How can Binyam get out of it?

And those requests for support to these women's organizations. He will give them buckets. Red buckets for single mothers. Pay in kind. That's advertising. He'll make some posters about the donations and distribute them to his good customers and potential customers. That's it. Advertise where there is money to be gained.

And the Tigrinian Agricultural Association asked for sponsorship. Can't they leave him alone? People have no idea how difficult it is to be rich!

An hour later. Stephanie. She was great last night. That deep slit in her dress more than hinted at the wonderful breasts she possesses beneath. He will think of them. That will put me nicely to sleep. Wish they weren't on such a temperamental Greek lady. The sudden storm on the windless sea. That's her. But wonderful fuck. Then her storms are very arousing. Oh, there is that cramp again. "I'd better...," and Binyam tumbles out of bed into the bathroom, from where loud noises proceed.

It is now three forty. It's almost morning. At this point, Binyam will just relax a little. Then he will get up and go to the Hilton for a swim. He will even do the treadmill a little. Yes, he promises. He wonders if Mrs. Lark will be there? She will be leaving soon. What a story. What's his name? Anwar has definitely taken her on a lark. Ha, ha.

If only that burning in his chest would go away. But now he thinks it is a little better, and so is his nausea. He feels that distinctly. But the cramps are worse. Stephanie. Good thoughts. Wossen. How can she sleep like that when he is all awake? But better sleep and he won't have to listen to her complaints. No coffee tomorrow. Definitely no coffee tomorrow. Maybe never again. His stomach is churning. He has to....

Back in bed, he mumbles, enumerating his discomforts. His feet are cold and his stomach feels like a big rumbling hole. Not unlike in his days of starvation. Imagine, he actually starved. He remembers it as if it was yesterday. The sensation. The sensation he will never forget it. The physical pain and the agony of realizing that nobody was going to help him. He remembers how he walked in the hot, dusty road towards the souq. The pungent smell of trash. He had asked storekeepers for work. The intense sensation of his empty stomach then and now. It comes to him again. After another refusal, Binyam had sat down and thought about how incredible it was that nobody cared about him.

The young Binyam had thought people had religious feelings of brotherhood. And what was God sitting up there thinking? What was his plan? And why him? What had he done? Why did he have to be born in a poor village, to poor, ignorant peasants? One of a large group of siblings. God, he was not even sure how many brothers and sisters he had. Not that it made much difference. He couldn't help them anyway. Couldn't even manage himself. But why? He didn't get the point.

Except that it was unfair. Why wasn't he born a Rockefeller? It was ridiculous. It was absurd. It could make you cry and laugh. It was a farce. "It's a farce," Binyam moans, as he becomes acutely aware of his stomach again.

Back in bed from another visit to the toilet, he continues his memories in that half-awake state between sleep and consciousness. How towards the end of that particular memorable afternoon he started to feel the beginning of lethargy. Felt like a kind of peace or "I don't care anymore." Suddenly, he had become so angry that he had gotten up, and damning God, gone to the nearest greengrocer stall, taken a banana, peeled it and eaten it right in front of the storekeeper.

The store keeper was an Indian. He was gaping. Binyam chewed his banana methodically. The Indian had closed his mouth and said, "I have also been there. You can carry boxes for me and other work. I will pay you, and I will give you some food. You look like a resolute and strong guy." And Binyam continues his reminiscing, how he had managed to save up some money and begun selling "those lousy plastic buckets" till he got the idea of making better ones. Borrowed money from Wossen's father and started a little factory.

It's all history now. So is his marriage. "I have lost my desire for my wife." Binyam turns around and looks at the bulky woman snoring between her hair curlers. Why must she wear those hair curlers? Then he remembers that she has her ladies' luncheon today. He had better get out of here, the sooner the better.

The darkness is finally fading behind the curtains, and maybe the relief from the stress of trying to fall asleep finally relaxes Binyam into a slumber? Maybe because the street dogs seem to have reached the point of exhaustion from their barking. They were probably sound asleep by now. Or maybe it was that his stomach had quieted down a little? Or maybe some higher power took mercy on him at last? Binyam finally sinks into a big hole of floating red buckets, green watering cans and voluptuous breasts. Drifting in a bucket to the hypnotic beat of African drums. Bong, bong, bong.

Maybe God or somebody showed mercy. Not so his wife. "Wake up. It's eight o'clock. Are you going to sleep the whole day? I need you out of here; I have my ladies' luncheon today, which you surely forgot. And you promised to help Teddy with his car. It needs to be brought to a car repair shop. If you haven't forgotten."

Wossen is not in the best of moods. She rarely is in the morning. Today is no exception, and she had slept badly with Binyam running to the toilet all night. Her own stomach is rumbling quite a bit. She pulls down the pink lace of her nightie as she rolls out of bed and goes into the bathroom.

Who is that old hag looking at her from the mirror? "Who is she?" Wossen tilts her head. The head in the mirror tilts. But she cannot be her. She will have nothing to do with her. That double chin. Those narrow eyes hidden in puffy folds. That nose is looking like some kind of lump of clay. Her once so cute nose. She rubs it absentmindedly.

What is happening to her? She was once so cute. The roundish way, sure. Is that what life does to you? What has she done to deserve this?

It's all Binyam's fault. Giving her sleepless nights like that. He always does, with his women affairs. And now Stephanie Stephanopoulos. She is sure he has something going with her. The way he was eating her up with his eyes last night. It's disgusting. Revolting. Those *ferengis*. Think they can do what pleases them. Pick and choose among the Ethiopian men. As if they were something special. Little fat stuck-up Greek duck. Wossen will get back at him. "I will make friends with her," she says out loud and winks at her swollen eye before she sits down on the toilet with a thud.

Wossen is in the process of making the final restorative touch-ups on her waxen face. At least the hair she can do something about. She nods approvingly to herself as she backcombs her reddish hair. She proceeds to rummage in her overstuffed toilet bag and pulls out a gold lipstick. She pulls off the top and smears the brownish red lipstick on her lips, enlarging the Cupid's bow on her upper lip. She adds an extra line of lipstick just as the doorbell chimes down in the hallway.

"Get the door!" she shouts to the maid, as the bell rings a second time.

"Shit," her hand slips as she shouts.

"That damned maid." She quickly wipes off the lipstick, to the sound of the hysterical barking of her little Pekingese.

"Get that dog, Mabrat, for God's sake." She redoes the full curves as she listens to the resonance of the ladies' bright voices, with Luna's penetrating high pitch above them.

She throws a last encouraging glance to the made-up, middle-aged lady in the mirror and rushes down the stairs to greet her guests.

"How lovely you look, Luna. Nothing like traditional Guinean robes. You must show me how you wrap that turban. This one is especially impressive."

"Yeah, I thought I would go ethnic today. It looked like the sun was coming out. And just as I finish, the rain is back. Too late to change again. I could hardly get through the mud in my sandals."

"Well, you know Addis isn't made for high heels."

"But you get sick and tired of not being able to dress up here," Luna is wiping her stilettos in a paper towel. "Your road is also extra bad. When will they finish remaking it? It seems like it has been dug up for the last half-year now."

"That's Addis for you. Ethiopian efficiency. The Kebele people don't care. It's not their road, and they live in a muddy road elsewhere. Come in, come in. Mabrat has made a nice fire for us," Wossen waves her braceleted arms in the direction of flowered silk couches, arranged in a semicircle around the marble fireplace filled with family photos in big gilt frames. Snuffy, the Pekingese, jumps up in one of the chairs, as the colorful ladies spread out like a bouquet of flowers in the living room.

"Get down," Wossen tinkles her bracelets in the direction of Snuffy, who raises her offended face, not unlike that of her owner.

"Please sit down. Here is some homemade lemonade, made with our own lemons. Mabrat has finally learned how to do it. It's not the worst. But where is Stephanie? She is late, as usual."

"She may be busy running around for lottery donations, I talked with her on the phone last night," Heba from Cameroon interjects, adjusting her necklace with nervous hands. "She is overwhelmed and she needs you ladies to help more. She was quite upset."

"My maid had to go to a funeral, so I haven't had a moment free to help," Jeannette drawls in her Nigerian accent. Her silky green dress and turban glow in the light of the fire.

"You're always full of excuses," Luna snaps. "You ladies are full of talk, when it comes to action, you're suddenly *sooo* busy. How come you always have the time, when it is a paid luncheon?"

"You shouldn't talk…." Hakia is interrupted by the chiming of the front door bell. "Maybe that's Stephanie?" It occurs to Wossen that she may have sounded too eager. So she adds, "That lady is not too reliable."

"Hurry up Mabrat, what are you waiting for?" she adds in an irritated tone.

The double doors swing open and Stephanie enters, "Sorry, ladies. My maid ran away, so my house is in chaos, and I had to drive to the Embassy of Mali with some lottery tickets and to pick up some donations of wine, and my driver took the wrong turn. And the traffic was awful. And there was roadwork and beggars and churchgoers all over the place," she makes a dramatic gesture with her arms. She is a short, chubby lady in a tight white suit with golden buttons. Her auburn hair, made up in a soft wave, frames a cheerful face. Her teeth shine white between her bright red lipstick, and her eyes sparkle behind the heavy mascara.

"Those servants so unreliable," Wossen concurs, throwing a glance at Mabrat, as she serves some of her home-made lemonade to the latecomer.

"Not that I care," Stephanie laughs. "Good riddance. It's just that you have to start all over training them and all that. It always takes a while before you get them how you want them," she adds, sipping her lemonade with her little finger sticking out. "It's like with your men." The ladies join in hearty laughter.

"Yeah, I just went through all that," Wossen sighs and rolls her eyes. "My last maid began to have a boyfriend. She had the nerve to let him into the compound. I gave her a second chance and told her never to let him set foot inside our gate again. I also instructed our guard. But then I noticed that food was starting to disappear from the refrigerator. One day, the yogurt was low, then the bean salad, then the fruit salad. I know exactly what I have. I keep an eye on everything, every expense, every bag of rice. You can't be observant enough. You can't trust anybody. And sure enough, she was taking food for her boyfriend. The guard confessed to having seen it outside the gate when we threatened to fire him, if he didn't tell the truth. You have to keep them reined in."

"Well, whichever way works. The idea with servants is to make your life pleasant and convenient. Once you have trouble, it defeats the purpose," Stephanie smiles and makes herself comfortable in the pillow of the upholstered easy chair. She sticks her little foot out in the direction of the heat from the fireplace.

"We also had to hire and train a new maid once the old one became too lazy. She began to cut corners making up the beds, sweeping without going under the bed. That sort of thing."

Heba shakes her head approvingly. "She became spoiled," Stephanie concludes with an affirmative nod.

"The most important thing is to treat them correctly, then they know they have to behave correctly. " Hakia straightens the impeccable collar of her grey dress. "You have to be the role model. You can't expect them to know, considering where they come from. You are actually doing them a service that way. You're bringing them up."

"Whatever you say. You may disagree, but I have found the way that works. Maybe give them food, a room and clothes. But don't pay them a salary. Believe me. It works. My servants never ran anywhere. Start giving them money and they get ideas." Luna firmly puts an end to their philosophical discussion as Mabrat opens the double doors to a lavish table bathed in the lights of the Venetian candelabra.

The ladies now enter a lively discussion about the forthcoming fund-raising Gala at the Hilton. Much work still remains. They have to ask for donations for the lottery, check the music with the DJ, arrange about the food and tables, remind and encourage people to come. Details are discussed, and jobs delegated to the swallowing of steaming asparagus soup and to the munching of steamed Nile perch with saffron rice. Stephanie gets hectic red cheeks as she discusses her President's welcome address with the ladies and drowns her anxiety with some big gulps of Pinot Grigio. Various assortments of fruity and creamy cakes help appease excited nerves, and everybody agrees that this Gala will be the best ever and raise the most money.

Afterwards, the ladies enjoy the strong Ethiopian coffee back in front of the fireplace, while they discuss the latest gossip in town. The sun is already low before they gather their bags and shawls and head for the hallway.

Stephanie stays behind a little longer, because her driver is on an errand to the Greek Embassy. Long enough for her and Wossen to have a little girlfriends' tête-à-tête while Snuffy is snoring in little whiffs of dreams in one of the couches she had finally conquered. Her mistress is too occupied now to be consistent about house rules. She has just complimented Stephanie on her white suit. Jackie Kennedy style. Simple lines, jacket with big buttons, short tight skirt. Stephanie agrees that she is a Jackie fan, both for her fashions as well as a person. "Too bad she was married to such a womanizer." And the two ladies settle into more small talk. Judging from their serious faces, they are discussing important matters, and the ensuing laughter indicates that they have come to some kind of solution or agreement. When they embrace before the gate, it looks as if they are parting as the best of friends.

The front lobby of the Hilton is full of people in evening dresses in constant movement this way and that, but mostly towards the International Women's Association's tables, where the ticket committee members sit dressed to the hilt behind ornamental flowers.

"If you forgot your ticket, you have to buy a new one. How can I know if you have already bought a ticket?"

"But Madame Luna sold me two. My husband is coming later."

"Luna is not here now. So how can I know? This is not charity, we are here to raise money."

A Hilton man is standing discreetly clicking off the number of people entering. The Association is to pay for each. Hilton is not into charity either. The hotel did offer a complimentary glass of champagne in the next room, however. Nothing like a glass of wine to loosen the purse strings. The noise level from the conversation rises steadily, increased by some African drum music from a tape recorder. The DJ is late.

Association ladies are seen running around, setting up last-minute donations on the big tables along the wall. The President, in a gold evening dress, appears dragging a big model airplane onto a table, assisted by a Nigerian lady in shiny blue robes.

"Never in my life will I do this again. Next time we'll only accept posters. And they wouldn't let me take it out of the UN compound without special papers. But I had taken it in, and I even had diplomatic plates. They were not supposed to search my car. This monster! I would not exhibit such a decrepit old airplane, if I were Nigerian Airways. Who would fly in a plane like that? And where is Heba? She's supposed to be in charge of selling lottery tickets."

"Oh, hello, Mr. Ambassador. So pleased you could come." Stephanie puts on a charming smile. "How I spell Cameroon? Well, C-A-M.... You really want me to spell Cameroon?" Stephanie's smile is strained.

"Well, it is spelled completely wrong on the invitation, and it has your signature, so I thought you were responsible." The stout ambassador waves the paper in front of Stephanie's nose.

"Sure, I am responsible. In the rush—I must have done 50 invitations that day—and I was leaving for the summer holidays. I sincerely apologize. It was my oversight," Stephanie's mouth feels dry.

"Well, you know it is important that things are done correctly, especially when you are referring to a country. The honor of that country …." the indignant dignitary is interrupted by Luna's high voice, bidding the guests welcome.

The MC begins, "Your Excellencies, honorable guests, ladies and gentlemen. It is a great honor … and Luna proceeds to deliver the exact speech that Stephanie had prepared and discussed at the ladies' luncheon. The DJ has finally arrived, and his music momentarily interrupts Luna's address.

Soon, long lines are forming by the food tables, and Heba and her helpers are going from table to table selling lottery tickets. Heba has had a glass of whiskey behind a partition, and she is talking and joking while the guests pick their tickets. She is a little light-headed.

"Oh, I have forgotten a bunch," and she pulls a handful of tickets from her pocket, which she throws back into the basket. Two fall on the floor and she almost loses her balance picking them up from the dark floor under the table.

"This is too irregular!" An indignant guest wants his money back. "How can I know if tickets aren't missing? In fact, how can I know if this lottery isn't rigged?"

"Of course it is not rigged. We're here to raise money. I just forgot in the rush," Heba giggles hesitantly.

"I want my money back." The dignitary who feels strongly about honesty and transparency thinks he has found an issue. Didn't others continuously discover that same issue with him?

The President is informed about the irregularity just as she is in the process of calming down a disgruntled donor, who has at that very moment brought a couple of bottles of wine and offered a trip to Axum, and who wants to be recognized over the loudspeaker right away. The President discontinues the lottery for now and first thanks the donor profusely, then the other donors and everybody for their help.

Now the music starts up and the Ambassador of Lesotho asks the president for the first dance. He is being thanked and honored for his generous donations, and it pleases the elegantly dressed man to be in the limelight. He swings Stephanie around and whispers, "But you can dance."

The floor is now taken over by the festive guests, eager to loosen their bodies in the rhythm. The dance floor looks like a big kaleidoscope of rotating colors. The dancers rock and roll and twist and sway and shake, till everybody forgets their problems and misgivings.

Binyam has danced once with Wossen and has now succeeded accompanying Stephanie on to the floor. Maybe this is going to be one of the greatest Galas ever? The room is full. The Hilton banquet manager has also informed the President that there are 43 more guests than estimated. Could she immediately sign a check for the extra amount? One couldn't be sure if the entire Association wouldn't disappear and leave the country before working hours the next day!

But the dancing. The dancing is the mitigating factor. It smooths out antagonisms and differences; it makes people forget who is ambassador and who not. In fact everybody feels sympathy for everybody in that big mass atmosphere, where the individual can lose himself in a communal feeling of having fun and doing good simultaneously. A win-win situation.

Then the lottery can resume. And generous donors from the diplomatic corps and the business community are called up to the microphone to draw the winning tickets. People win exercise bicycles, fondue sets, Ethiopian crosses and wooden carvings, massage for three and dinners for two. People win plane tickets to Ethiopian destinations and abroad. More or less appreciated. One lady receives two plane tickets to the famous tourist attraction of Lalibela. She is none too pleased, and immediately returns her tickets for a redraw. "They have no decent hotels in Lalibela." She shakes her *permed* curls in disappointment.

The excitement is mounting for the grand prize, which turns out to be a weekend return trip to Nairobi with two overnights, at nothing less than the Norfolk Hotel. Courtesy of Kenyan Airways. For one. There is a catch: if you want to bring a guest like your wife or husband you will have to pay. The representative of UNICEF is to draw the winner, in recognition of all that UNICEF does for women and children in Africa. He stirs the tickets in the woven basket in long suspense until he suddenly picks out a folded piece of paper. Number six (he pronounces it "sex") and laughter ensues. The President takes the paper and reads out loud: Mr. Binyam Bedada, Manager of Ethiopian Plastic Inc. Mr. Bedada rises, to the boisterous applause of the guests, and walks up to Stephanie, who holds the envelope in her hands.

"Enjoy," she says and winks at him.

The next day, Binyam and Wossen agree that he will go alone. He needs a rest, and Wossen surprises him by insisting that he just think of himself for this once. He has worked so hard and been stressed out. And his stomach has given him trouble. A quiet weekend at the Norfolk would do him good. Besides, she was busy with her welfare work this weekend, she asserts with an enigmatic smile.

As the planned weekend approaches, Binyam feels unusually elated. He hasn't had a chance to talk to Stephanie, but he is sure she will be there. He feels extra elated because he has found Stephanie a little cooler recently, and she seemed awfully fond of that young swaggering Lesotho Ambassador at the Gala.

Life could really be sweet. Thank God for the good pleasures, in between the struggle to survive. Maybe there was a benevolent God, after all?

And now Binyam can't wait and has nightly and daily visions of their frolic and love-making. Would she wear his favorite transparent blue night dress, the one he had given her himself? He plans to spend two full nights and days lovemaking. Maybe they would never leave the room. Like John and Ono. Just have their food and champagne brought up?

If only his stomach does not give him any trouble. No raw meat or strong coffee.

"Just love and spring water," he mumbles to himself as the taxi takes him from the airport to the Norfolk Hotel.

"Just good old-fashioned copulation," he whispers to himself as he carries his bag to the reception at the Norfolk, where the receptionist tells him that his wife is already at his room. No need for the key, he smiles.

Binyam barely notices his surroundings. It's as if he is in a trance. He will finally have the opportunity to live out all his sexual fantasies and oh, boy, will he go for it, he mutters as he walks down the corridor, keyless. And he has a rousing feeling in his pants as he knocks on the door of the room.

The door opens and there stands … his wife. In that purple pink negligee. The color he dislikes intensely.

Binyam has a sudden cramp in the lower part of his stomach, as he listens to the words coming out of Wossen's painted mouth, "Stephanie and I agreed that I should give you a second chance."

Binyam has already turned away from his wife, but she grabs his sleeve and manages to pull him inside the doorway.

"But...."

"I know," she smiles, "you haven't had much fun with me lately. I talked about it all with Stephanie, and she gave me a lot of good advice."

"But ... I ... we...."

"Don't try to say anything. See. Here. Take that tie off. And off with your jacket. In fact, why don't you take off all your clothes, and I will give you a nice massage?" Wossen smiles sweetly at Binyam.

"Oh, no, no words," she puts her fingertips on his mouth. "Now is not time for words. I will take off my clothes too," and she pulls her little nightie off, baring her rounded, layered body.

The next morning, Binyam is woken from a long, deep sleep by the phone ringing. He reaches over to take the receiver and notices that he has never put on his pajamas. Through the receiver he hears the fresh, friendly voice of his son, Binyam Jr. He moves the receiver away from his ear and shakes it a little. Can this really be his son, sounding like that in the early morning? Well, it's almost noon, but still, before noon? Binyam looks at the clock on his night table.

"Morning, Pop. I heard from mom that you needed a couple of days off. Just thought I would let you know, I would like to look after our business in the meantime."

Binyam is too astounded to say anything.

"Just tell me. This single-mom welfare thing. Should I give them red buckets or green?"

Binyam is searching for his voice. "Red? Yes. No, make it green. What the heck, green for hope."

Vocabulary:

Farce ◉ From Latin *farcire* "to stuff." A humorous play having a highly improbable plot and exaggerated characters. And: a ludicrous, empty show; mockery.

kebele ◉ A local municipality.

The Tourists

YOU LOVED YOUR SISTER. YOU LOVED her like crazy, but you also got annoyed that she was always so perfect, always had her school-work done ahead of time; wrote thank you notes before your mother reminded you; always tried to see things from the good side. But you could never have wished for a better sister. That's what made it so bad, the Ethiopia trip.

Your sister would have preferred to go to Hawaii—a *clean* country as she would say—but you insisted on this silly blindfold game, where she happened to point to Ethiopia. You saw the bewilderment and disappointment in her face. But then you rattled off all the interesting things you could think of in Ethiopia: the famous runner Gebre Selassie; the Falasha Jews; Haile Selassie, who served caviar and champagne while his people starved; and the ace, the queen of Sheba. At which point, your sister declared that she had always wanted to go to Ethiopia.

That's when you were reminded of the Rastafarians and began to tell your sister about Bob Marley, the Back to Africa movement, its idolizing of Haile Selassie and most importantly, the reggae music.

You and your sister had inherited the estate of your aunt Susan, who had died childless from breast cancer. She had a lot of money from your uncle, who had died two years earlier. Your parents had helped you put the money into a savings account for your further education, but you had been allowed quite a sum for a trip to celebrate your graduation from Berkeley High and the fact that you had just turned 18. Your sister was 16 and she had just finished her sophomore year. It was supposed to be an educational trip, but your parents were not so enthusiastic about Ethiopia till you promised to *never let Anna out of sight*.

That's what kept haunting you afterwards: that you didn't live up to your promise. You are trapped by your own words, and you can't run away from them. Like the priest who was chosen to guard the tablets of the Ark inside that church in Axum, which he couldn't leave for the rest of his life. He tried to run away a couple of times, but he was brought back. You felt for that guy.

That's how, three weeks later at the end of the month of May, you found yourself lounging in the deck chairs of the Addis Ababa Hilton pool. It was a very nice pool, heated by the hot underground springs. Anna loved the comfort of the pool setting, in contrast to the *souq* visit the same morning. It had been very crowded, and dusty and filled with beggars and men, who tried to touch the fair-haired, light-skinned young woman. When a young, legless guy on some home-made cart had grabbed her skirt, she had overreacted and screamed. That's when you had to make it clear in no uncertain terms not to mess with your sister.

Now, in the peace and safety of the Hilton Garden, you could discuss your further plans. By this time, your sister had rejected your game of flipping coins about everything—a silly habit you had from your childhood of turning everything into a game or sport—so you agreed to visit the most famous places in the hope of running into the Rastafarians. While your sister lay in the sun (you agreed she could be alone for that), you went to retrieve a lot of cash. Your sister thought it was too much to carry around, but you claimed you couldn't be sure to get cash once you were outside Addis Ababa, and you wanted to have that extra money for donations to the poor. Reluctantly, your sister acquiesced, and you talked about how lucky you two were to have money (in contrast to those poor people in the *souq* today) and you discussed how you could give money to the poor. But who? Anna wanted to know. Just people you happen to run into, and whom you find sympathetic or deserving in some way, you had said. But what about robbers? Anna had worried, and you had to remind her of your karate chops. That should take care of it. You cringe in retrospect.

Back inside the hotel, Anna wanted to shop, and really fell in love with those typical Ethiopian silver crosses. That's all girls know how to do: shop, shop, shop. The compromise was not to do any shopping this soon—even gifts for your parents. It could be done at the very end of the trip; but Anna did throw a longing glance after those crosses.

You both were amazed the next day, after leaving Addis Ababa in a minivan taxi, to encounter the real Ethiopia. Here were no tourists, and the scenery was incredible, with rocky mountains rising above picturesque valleys, green from the recent rains. No billboards, no electric poles, no cars. Only cattle or people on foot and a rare wooden wagon under a sky with a rainbow. Anna said the scenery reminded her of one of her children's books about Adam and Eve in the Garden of Eden.

The slim, handsome, proud-looking Ethiopians seemed to appear right out of a story from the ancient lands. Barefoot and in tattered clothes, they looked as though they couldn't care less about material things or comfort.

In Gondar, an incredible priest was standing on the cold, bare stone floor, looking as if he was warming up the whole place with his enthusiasm. He had exactly the same expression as the frescoes of the big-eyed angels on the ceiling of the church, called Debre Birhan Selassie. He told us about Hell with a big smile, and pointed to some gruesome scenes from that hellish world. Even if you didn't believe in Hell, he seemed so cool, but when offered some money, he acted horrified. He encouraged a donation directly to the church; but the Ethiopian Orthodox is not like a person. So that didn't work out.

Everything was so strange and different in this country. So many hilarious experiences—like the banana story. In this case, the idea was to give some people, who were lined up for a church distribution of porridge, some bananas and figs in addition. Giving food instead of money seemed a good idea. So before Anna could protest, the banana cart had been bought, and you found you and your sister united at the front of the line, trying to hand bananas to poor Ethiopians. But wouldn't you know? They didn't seem to want them.

That is till suddenly, one couldn't tell how, the whole line dissolved and everybody was fighting for the bananas, on top of their benevolent donors. It became a mess of dust and mashed bananas. It was hilarious. The priests scolded, and Anna cried. So much for charity that day.

Then came Lalibela, with its rock-hewn churches. Yes, it was always churches. You flew there, and then you had to take one of those dilapidated taxis on wobbly wheels, with doors tied with a rope. But it did succeed in bringing you to the barebones hotel, where the lack of comfort was made up for with the most fantastic view over the wild mountains. The simple rooms opened up to a balcony running along the back of the hotel. Outside were craggy heights along the whole horizon.

Standing there taking in the view, that's when it happened. Unbelievable, but reggae music came floating through the open doors of the adjoining room. "*Live if you wanna live, Rastaman, vibration, yeah! Positive! That's what we got to give….*" And two Rastafarians emerged from their room, looking exactly as they were expected to look, with their orange, yellow and green striped hats on their bush of dreadlocks. They were making tea on a little burner. One was very tall, with sad-looking eyes, despite his big smile. The other had irregular features and narrow puffy eyes, which gave him a mischievous smile.

"Peace and love," the older and stouter of the two said.

"Hello," you replied, in chorus.

"Want to join us? We're just making tea."

"Sure. Sounds great." Everything seemed to have fallen into place.

Listening to the reggae songs in the background, Marley and Gerry told how they had come to Lalibela to attend the local Easter ceremony early Sunday morning. They planned to visit the Eastern and Western churches and some monastery already this afternoon. "Be our guests," they said. They told about the cool ceremonies and the role of the large golden cross, which had been returned to the church after it had been stolen. It was discovered in the possession of some art dealer by the customs in Belgium. As Marley said while he passed around the weathered teacups, "The West is the Babylon of greed and materialism."

When you concurred with that statement, your sister poked you in your side. Anna always has to remind you of something.

Now it was your turn to tell Marley and Gerry where you came from, what you were doing, your family and all that.

To which Marley answered, "Sure, we've heard of Berkeley. Bezerkeley. Rastafarian type of place, if you know what I mean." He chuckled.

Then he went on to tell about how they came from Kingston, Jamaica. The slums of Kingston. How they lived in all kinds of hardship, with lack of food and an abusive, alcoholic father. He went on to say how they had managed to raise the necessary money to go to Ethiopia with their reggae group. They were inspired by the stories of a new black leader for the blacks. That was Haile Selassie.

On and on the conversation went, while sipping the clove-spiced tea. Now Gerry and Marley told about their communal living in Shashamane. How they had come upon hard times, because Mengistu had taken away a lot of the land they had been given by Haile Selassie. How they were short of money; how they mainly existed on donations from outside. But that they had problems with robberies. Some local gangs would visit them and the police would do nothing. And they had no rights; they could not become citizens, in spite of having lived there since the nineteen sixties. Even the clergy were agitating against them. As if to underscore the troubles of the Rastafarians, big clouds were now beginning to gather on the horizon.

Then Marley wanted to know how you had happened to travel to Ethiopia. So Anna told them about the inheritance, which was maybe not such a good idea. Maybe she became aware of that, so she added, "We're just tourists. A kind of tourists."

To which Marley said, "Wow, an inheritance! Tourists. You must be rich."

It was like Marley was examining you. "You surely look like brother and sister. Bet you two had pampered lives. Everything served on a golden platter—so to speak." Again, his eternal laughter.

You had to answer something, something like, Guess you hadn't thought about that. But it really was as if your life suddenly looked totally different. You had always taken it for granted to have loving parents, food on the table, and having a good time with your friends, sports and all. You really couldn't give a good answer. It would just sort of fall down flat. You had never thought of your life like that. From Marley's perspective.

Fortunately, the conversation changed direction when Gerry asked if you would care to share some weed.

"Weed?" Anna had asked.

"Yes, our sacred herb."

Anna looked hesitant, and Marley had explained, "We smoke it every day to achieve and maintain a close relationship with God." Now he chuckled and continued, "You know, if you meditate and do good, the herb will develop that goodness within you."

It was clear that all kinds of alarm clocks had gone off in Anna's head, so you had to take over. "That would be cool." You meant it too, since you hadn't had any cannabis since you left Berkeley High. Gerry already had some small pipes out and was in the process of stuffing the leaves into the heads of the pipes. Like he hadn't really waited for the answer. He said this was their main source of income in Shashamane—apart from the donations, that is.

You tried to fit in, and you both inhaled to the background reggae beat, while Marley, who turned out to be a big talker, told about the Jamaican black nationalist Marcus Garvey, his Back to Africa movement, how he had predicted that a black king would be crowned as it happened with Ras Tafari, who was pronounced the King of Kings, Lord of Lords, and the Conquering Lion of the Tribe of Judah.

You were beginning to feel a bit light-headed as Marley droned on about Haile Selassie being the direct descendant of King David, the 225th ruler in an unbroken line of Ethiopian Kings from the time of Solomon and the Queen of Sheba.

At this point, Anna mumbled, "The Queen of Sheba." So she was still following.

Marley was beyond hearing now and continued with growing enthusiasm, "Here we are back to our roots, to our beloved Africa. This is where we find the freedom of Africa, freedom from slavery, and the freedom of spirit." He seemed to have forgotten about all the troubles he had just been describing. And you weren't going to remind him. In all honesty, you were beginning to share his feelings, you were beginning to feel a little religious yourself at this moment. You thought of the enthusiastic priest you had met. May be there was something to religion after all?

It was so euphoric cuddled up in blankets, watching the spacious scenery and marveling at the zigzagging lightning in front of you as you drew in the sweet herb, deep into your receptive lungs. Marley's words sounded so convincing, his message about slavery remaining a communal guilt on the exploiting part of the world. And that time had come to remedy the wrongs and repair the dignity of the black man.

"And woman," Anna whispered. You could never catch her not paying attention.

Marley's monologue came to an abrupt halt as the rain finally came crashing down and you had to run for shelter in your rooms. Disappearing in the doorway, rain dripping from his dreadlocks, Marley had asked that you come and visit them in Shashamane.

How could you not agree? This had been your wish all along, and right now, everything seemed so happy and promising.

The agreement was to get up at four a.m. and join the Rastafarians the next day at Easter Service. So, after a few hours of restless sleep, battling the mosquitoes and scratching your first fleabites, a hotel employee knocked on your door to the sound of cocks crowing from all corners of the dark.

You had scrambled into your clothes and joined Marley and Gerry down the road, along with Ethiopians in their white robes. The steps leading down to the Beth Maidan Church were thronged with beggars and churchgoers. The surrounding space was so filled with worshippers that you had to inch your way forward till you could see the priests singing monotonously in a swaying line. All four made it to the entry of the church, and you threw your fancy Adidas sneakers on top of a heap of thinly worn footwear, piled up next to the door.

Inside, the church was almost dark, the air thick with smells of human sweat and incense. Gradually, you perceived a priest in the center of the crowd; he was vigorously rubbing the famous golden cross on the back of some sick person. The cross glinted in the candlelight.

This was not silver but pure solid gold, right there in the middle of those poor people in their threadbare cottons. Everybody could feel the spell of the Cross, the faith and hope it inspired in the congregation. You also felt drawn towards it, as if pulled by the moving bodies. You wanted to touch it.

The chanting and swaying undulated through the thick air, on and on, while the priest went from one sick person to the next with his tool of healing. Everybody seemed in a mass hypnosis, and nobody paid attention to the *ferengis* in their midst. You were beginning to feel sick of the constant movement and lack of air—also from not eating and sleeping—so you looked at Anna to tell her that you wanted to go outside. But she seemed in a trance and oblivious of anybody, so you managed to squeeze yourself out into the fresh air. It was a beautiful cool morning with a faint watercolor blue creeping up behind the mountains.

You immediately felt better, at the same time as you realized that you had let Anna out of sight. You almost panicked and started to elbow your way back in, running right into Marley, who was leading Anna by her hand towards the entrance. Anna's face was white. "Where were you?" she gasped. "Suddenly, I couldn't see you, and if it weren't for Marley…." She started to cry.

You put your arm round your sister's shoulders and thanked Marley, who disappeared back into the crowd. Together you watched the light extinguishing the dark shadows of trees and hills.

"I suddenly thought I was in the Middle Ages," Anna mumbled. "It was so like another time—and I was back in it. And then I thought I was lost back in those times and that 2000 had not come yet."

You held Anna tighter, "It's OK." You admitted you sort of felt hypnotized too. That's why you went out for fresh air.

"But you promised never to let me out of your sight."

You promise you will never let it happen again. You have to admit you have failed your sister, like so many times in your childhood. You had broken your promises to your parents; not to do that, not to go there. All that. This had been like a test, to see if you could be trusted. But also, you had the feeling that anything was possible in this strange place—a kind of urgent danger.

You sure felt better the next day heading south in Marley and Gerry's old but solid-looking Land Rover. Like this crazy place was sort of normal, after all. Anna certainly seemed happy to be traveling with two locals. Four was more secure than two. So you were back to your happy-go-lucky mood and laughing at yourself for being so, what would be the word? Overwhelmed or powerless, like in that mass of swaying people.

You were in control again, and all had gone according to your plan. The night before, you had managed to call your mom and dad from the hotel. They seemed relieved to hear that all was well and reminded you to look after Anna—a reminder you no longer needed. You had met with Marley and Gerry to pick up their Land Rover at the service station right next to the Ras Hotel, where you had been staying. Now Marley was driving the Land Rover with his radio tape playing *"So much trouble in the world now…. The way earthly things are going. Anything can happen. You see men sailing on their ego trips, Blast off on their spaceships, Million miles from reality…."*

You were on the back seat, and Anna whispered to ask whether you thought the car was safe. Anna would always worry. But the car seemed fine, and you zoomed by rolling hills and villages, till you turned off for Lake Lungano. You had decided to visit for a swim, if ever so briefly, in the brown lake waters. Never know if there is water for washing at our compound, Marley had said.

Refreshed by the swim, you continued towards Shashamane. The talkative Marley alternated between singing and preaching and was in the middle of a long description of future plans for the Rastafarians when the car suddenly swerved abruptly to the side.

"Shit," you said. "It felt like a puncture on the right side."

"Let's take a look," and Marley was already outside by the front of the car.

"Sure enough," he said, "the tire has almost exploded."

Anna and you exchanged glances.

You said it was good that you had a spare in the back. As you had specifically asked at the service station.

You should be back on the road soon … before it got too dark, you had added.

Marley sauntered to the back of the car. "The extra tire is also flat," Marley now announced from the open trunk.

"But they said it was in working order!" you said, angrily.

"This is Ethiopia, man," Marley produced one of his deep chuckles. "You have to check everything yourself. Don't trust what anybody says."

"What do we do now?" Anna asked, and looked at the last rays of the setting sun.

"We need to get to a service station. It would be good if we could bring the extra tire. Especially if we pay a little extra," Marley said.

"That should be no problem," you said.

"Shall we all go?" Anna asked.

"It will be hard to get a ride for the four of us," Gerry interrupted. "Better just one of us."

"But who?" said Anna.

"We'll flip a coin," you said cheerfully.

"No, you need to stay with me, Carl," Anna said firmly. You had blundered again. But, of course, you wouldn't have left Anna behind.

"OK, I will go," our puffy-eyed Gerry said. "Do you have some money to give me?" He looked inquiringly at you.

You went to the back of the car and brought Gerry a bundle of birrs.

"Man, that should do," Gerry said with a laugh. "Never had so much money in my hands before."

"Just make sure you come back again," you said. Both you and Anna suppressed an unwelcome thought.

Gerry took a sip of water from their canteen, put his hat back on his dreadlocks and placed himself by the roadside facing the traffic. While some cars came by, Marley settled into the front seat, and you two tried as best you could to make yourselves comfortable on the springy back seat.

Finally, an old, rumbling truck stopped for Gerry with his wheel, and you other three, marooned, shouted to him to hurry back.

"Better lock your doors," Marley suggested, as darkness descended with lightning speed. "This area is known for gangs and robberies."

You locked your doors and settled in, sharing some apples Anna had thoughtfully brought for the trip. Then you adjusted your tired bodies for a nap. "*We the street people talking, we the street people struggling. Now they are sitting on a time bomb, Now I know the time has come, What goes up must come down, Goes around and comes around.*"

"Please turn off that tape, it's driving me crazy," Anna said crossly.

Marley turned off the sound, and again you tried to adjust yourselves to the worn, wobbly seats. You finally dozed to the accompaniment of Marley's regular snores, but after some time, Anna complained, "I have to go pee, but I dare not."

"No problem," you assured her, and you scrambled out and felt your way after your sister down the dark slope among the bushes.

"Turn around," Anna had said. "Stand with your back to me."

"Not that you can be seen." But you turned around and looked at the passing lights from the occasional car approaching and then swishing past on the road. You heard cracking twigs as Anna retreated a little into the bushes. To pass the time, you were trying to estimate the speed of the cars, when you heard Anna scream. "Help! Help!"

"Some snake?" you said with a laugh.

"Carl! Carl!" the sound was muffled but as you turned around, you felt a piercing pain in your side. A young man with curly hair and white teeth was poking a knife against your rib. "Give money. Give money or we take girl. One move and you're dead, man."

You could hear twigs breaking down the slope. "Help, Carl, help!"

"Leave my sister alone. Let go of her. There is money in the car."

You can't describe the awful feeling, but it was as if you had already experienced what was happening right now. The pain was intense and you pushed forward towards the car while your attacker climbed backwards, keeping the knife in your side. You turned your head to look over your shoulder for your sister and glimpsed some shady movements as you got a new poke from the knife. Walking forward, you looked back again and saw, in a flash, your sister being pulled towards some bushes. *Never let her out of sight. Never let her out of sight.* It echoed in your head. But you needed to get the money, so you almost crawled to the car door, which the robber opened before he stabbed you again. You were moaning. The pain. And you had failed to protect your sister. "Oh, God." This was Hell. Hell.

You kept saying, you would get the money. You would get the money, you said, like a mantra. The robber had let go of his knife so you could move inside the car. You could feel blood running down your side. You rummaged under the car seat and found a bundle of notes, while it occurred to you that you hadn't seen or heard Marley. Where was Marley? Had he run away? Or was he part of this? It was a terrible thought as you gave the money to the man.

"Now, give back my sister!" you screamed in his face as you got out of the car. But he pushed the door close and stuck the knife in you again.

"You promised!" you screamed, as his white teeth said, "Maybe you have more money?"

"First, my sister." It was as though your anger gave you strength and you knew you had to use your karate. Here you had taken it for so many years and never needed it, but you felt paralyzed. "God, oh God, please help!" you know you said. You admit. You could hear Anna's muffled screams and what sounded like a scuffle in the bushes. You knew it was life and death, so you had to concentrate. What were you supposed to do? You had to get back in that karate mode—take control. You know, it sounds crazy, but you pictured St. George, sword raised to kill the snake dragon, as you had seen it depicted in so many churches. It felt long, but maybe it was just a few seconds. You pushed off from the car door and kicked the man in the crotch full force, with your right foot.

The man lay crumpled on the ground, and you flew (that's how it felt) down the slope towards your sister and the man in the bushes. As you groped through the dark twigs towards the warmth of her body, you distinctly heard screeching of brakes and tires squeezing against the asphalt, followed by angry voices in heavy American accents.

"What the hell do you think you're doing? We could have run you over, stepping in the front of the car like that!"

As you grabbed the leg of your sister, you heard Marley's deep voice replying, "We're in trouble, man. Had to stop you. Cars just pass. Need help. Attacked by robbers with knife. Girl in trouble. Help!"

As you inched alongside your sister, doors were slammed, followed by men running towards you. Two Marines ran down the slope, waving a flashlight as you crouched down and reached towards Anna's face. One Marine waved his flashing light; you saw your sister's attacker fleeing down the slope. The light quivered back on the ground till it rested on Anna, with twigs and thorns in her long, tangled hair, her skirt torn off.

You put your arms around your sister and kept saying, "You're OK, you're safe now." Like a mantra to her, and maybe to yourself also.

"Can you speak?" you asked.

She kind of nodded, but didn't say anything. Maybe a faint sob.

"Thank God, thank God, you're alive."

One of the Marines now squatted down next to you. "You were darned lucky," he drawled in his Southern accent. "You young folks, so naïve. No sense of the real world. Think you can go anywhere. Do anything—without getting hurt."

"I want mom and dad," Anna whispered and she began to shiver and shake.

"Are you OK?" the Marine finally asked. Can you walk?"

You tore off your bloody shirt and tied it round Anna's waist, as the Marine helped her onto her feet.

"We'll take you along with the young man," the Marine said, ignoring Marley.

"You think you can walk, young lady? What's your name?"

"Anna," she whispered, while the Marine put his arms under hers to lift her up. "Easy does it," he said, while he supported Anna and shone the light on the ground in front of them. Step by step, Anna got back to the Suburban. As you helped Anna climb up into the tall car and Anna stepped into the light, you saw blood running down Anna's scratched legs.

You resumed your mantra, "Oh, God. You'll be OK. You'll be OK."

When Anna was placed safely on the seat, you told her you would be right back; you would just get your things from the Land Rover.

The Marine closed the door and you returned with the flashlight towards Marley, whom the Marine seemed to have ignored.

"Don't worry," Marley said, as if he could read your thoughts. "Gerry will be here shortly."

It was not until now you thought about your attacker, who must have succeeded in escaping.

"Thank you, Marley, you saved us."

"Don't mention it," Marley said modestly. "You seem to have done pretty well yourself." He looked at the wounds. "You better take care of those."

You retrieved your packs and hidden money, using your right hand, while you pressed your left against your wound. You handed all your extra money to Marley and said, "For a new well."

Marley backed up a little bit, "That's too much." But then he took it. "I want to say goodbye to your sister. Is that OK?" You said you thought so, and walked back with Marley to the Suburban and opened the door to Anna's side gently.

Anna sat wrapped in a blanket. One Marine was in the front, reporting into his crackling radio.

Anna wasn't shaking so much now, and she looked at Marley, who also told her she would be OK and that he had something for her.

He fumbled at a thin gold chain around his neck, and opened it, to pull off a small but solid gold cross he had been wearing. "I want you to have this," he said to Anna.

Anna looked at the golden cross. She reached out her hand and took it. It looked almost heavy in her delicate hand. She wound her fingers around it, and rubbed it gently.

I could see how smooth it felt in her hand.

The Lover

EVERYBODY THINKS I HAVE LOST IT. I can just hear them, *Menopause panic*. Anna was adjusting the monitor on her treadmill. The trim woman began to run at a slow pace. She felt a little sluggish, as her well-shaped legs settled into the rhythm of the music tape. The repetitive lines of "*Smooth operator, smooth operator.*" She made up the words to the hypnotizing beat of the tune, "*Desperado-old-wom'n —cloo-sing time rush.*" Her inner voice kept the tempo. He was clearly taking advantage of her to go to America, they said. He was just thinking of himself.

Trying to resist the pull of the tune, her thoughts carried her on. No, she was not in doubt what people thought about a middle-aged *ferengi* who wanted to marry a young Ethiopian man. Twenty years her junior. He could be her son—hardly older than her own daughters, Susan and Catherine. Anwar was thirty-four.

But she didn't feel old. She felt just right—no more obligations or considerations—she could finally follow her desires. No more well-meaning and sensible husband for her. Did you check the light and lock the door? What's for dinner? Anna had put domestic life behind her; she was ready for adventure and new experiences. And there was Anwar. He was her unexplored territory. She just wanted to follow that man, who turned his head and looked at her over his shoulders. That questioning and inviting look. Will you follow me? And her whole body like the roaring waterfall behind Anwar. Yes, she would walk with him right into that roaring turbulence on that moist, dark undergrowth of lianas and rubbery, iridescent flowers, wet mosses and bursting shafts of lights from up high.

Maybe people were right—maybe she was a bit crazy.

Anna pushed the button on the monitor board of her treadmill, and the number went from six to seven to eight. Determined, she adjusted her pace to the beat of "*Smooth Operator*."

Anna's treadmill was the middle one of three. On her right, a young Ethiopian woman was sprinting along. Anna guessed the athletic woman was in her mid-thirties. Like Anwar. The strong-legged woman ran with the natural abandon of youth. Her high-cheekboned face in profile, her feet barely touched the moving rubber band. In contrast to the older man on her left, who looked like he had lead in his shoes and whose eight-month-pregnancy-like stomach might tip him over. Changing his speed constantly and coming to frequent stops, he wiped his heavily perspiring forehead with a towel hanging over the front of the treadmill. Hopefully, the man wouldn't have a heart attack right then and there. A death in the gym. Could happen.

A whiff of strong smelling perspiration reached Anna. She was caught in the middle of this running trio. She was in between, not old—not young. "*Smooth maa-ture....*" Her mind tapped the beat into the rubber of the belt.

The floor-to-ceiling wall mirrors reflected people on stair climbers, stationary bicycles and treadmills. Padded benches below suspended handlebars, for pulling down or sideways or upwards, radiated out from the center of the room. An enormous weightlifting bench with a cross bar connecting millwheel-size weights on each side was silhouetted against the window light—a giant instrument of torture surrounded by weights of all imaginable sizes. For a moment, Anna felt trapped in this artificial indoor jungle of machines, with stretching and curving bodies in various positions: upright, vertical or upside-down. Was this a modern-day purgatory of no pain, no gain? "*No place for beginners or sensitive heart,*" as the hypnotic song claimed. Anna felt a slight tension in the back of her skull; she squeezed her eyes blurring the outlines of the inferno gym.

The mirrors were unforgivingly clear under the glaring fluorescent tubes. Veraciously, they replicated a lean Asian man switching his bamboo-like body up and down in elastic pull-ups, right in front of Anna. ("*No need to ask. He is a smooth operator….*"); they laid bare the difference between Anna and an obese, young girl dragging the heavy steps of the stair climber up and down—up and down in slow motion; and they outlined the ample behind of the German woman, pedaling laboriously on the spot. (No "*smooth operator*" there.) Anna had to smile at the unlikely panorama in the mirrors. She was one of them. Dreaming that the exercise demon would gradually transform the hopefuls into a Madonna or a Tom Cruise. Even the German woman imagined it. Anna laughed to herself.

She was all sweet expectations.

Through the aquarium-like window, Anna could see two gardeners in the process of digging some trenches for underground watering. Their digging missed the beat from the inside. The gardeners were cut off from her field of dreams behind the thick glass panes—they were just two ordinary laborers outside.

Anna had merged with that *smooth operation* pace, which carried her long, slender body and her thoughts past the first kilometer mark to her grown daughters in California. She had talked with her daughter Susan on the phone last night. "How are you, mom?" Should she tell Susan about being in love? Mom, aren't you a bit old for that? Would Susan understand that she was not too old? She was just right.

"I'm fine. Just superfine."

"What happened, you sound … almost excited?" That dumb Susan. You couldn't fool her.

"Just that I enjoy being here in Ethiopia. Away from it all." Silly thing to say. She felt like a daughter, trying to avoid saying anything to her mother. It was all inexplicable anyway. Especially to a super level-headed daughter—who actually resembled her dad. Which was all fine.

Anna felt a sudden acute pang of sorrow over her husband, John, who had died of cancer. Life was not fair. All John's healthy living and exercise and sensible life—all to no avail. In spite of aggressive treatments, the terrible colon cancer had spread to his liver and reduced his solid body to an emaciated shadow of its former shape. The deep hollows behind his ears had turned his head into the cranium of a living corpse.

Anna shuddered. She didn't want to think of that anymore. She did miss him. It had taken her a long time to get used to living without him. And she was glad she had taken this two-year contract with UNICEF. She had loved working here in Ethiopia, and it had done her good to get away from home and memories. Not to mention her sadness about John.

Her thoughts were drawn back into the centrifuge of her present being. Anwar. How she had met him in Bahir Dar. How she and Melinda had gone to the waterfalls near the source of the Blue Nile. They had crossed the river in the traditional *tankwa*, made of papyrus. Anwar became their guide. He had been so helpful and supported them so they wouldn't fall down the slippery bank, so they wouldn't get wet, so that, so that…. He had chased away the local children selling sodas by promising that the *ferengi* women would buy a drink from them on the way back, if they stayed out of sight. He carried her backpack and helped identify birds. He would point, "Yes, that's a malachite kingfisher. There is an African jacana. And that strange one is called an Abyssinian ground hornbill." (Anwar had learned the English names for the tourists.)

Little white fluffy clouds had passed overhead. The hot path descended into cool shade under the trees. They could hear the roar of the waterfall before they could see it. Anna followed Anwar around a wooded curve in the path. Suddenly, he stepped aside so she could see the fantastic sight: great masses of water falling over the precipice. Mist carrying a radiant rainbow. They proceeded down the gully—like a no man's land outside time and space—and Anwar held her hand down the steepest parts. The ground was covered by iridescent green grass, and the path was muddy.

Anwar had explained how the waterfalls were the best right after the big rains. (Melinda had retreated onto a big boulder and was talking with the other guide.) Here in the freshness of the mists, with the hot sun on her back and the explosive noise in her ears, Anna felt like she had had a glass of champagne on an empty stomach. Hypnotized by the falling masses of water, she was being drawn up, up, up. Irresistibly she was dissolving into that haze and soaring away, high into eternity.

At that moment, Anna had become aware of another presence. A big stillness behind her. She had moved around; there was the short-cropped outline of Anwar's dark head looking at the powerful water. Maybe he was spellbound too? He had turned his serious face towards her, and they had stood together in the silence of the roar.

When Anwar drove the two women back in the minivan, Melinda had been lulled to sleep by the movement of the driving. They had been up early that morning. Anna and Anwar felt they were still alone, and they retained that unspoken connection between the two of them. The moment of wordless unity by the rushing water lingered. (The monitor showed almost two kilometers.)

The next day, Anna had gone to visit some monasteries and churches alone with Anwar on Lake Tana, after Melinda left to return to Addis Ababa. She had convinced Anna that she could just go alone with their guide. Anna acted as though she had just been persuaded.

Anna and Anwar had sailed to the island monastery, Kidane Mihiret, on the peninsula of Zege, in a little boat on shiny blue waters. They had taken off their shoes and walked between the walls, round the sixteenth century murals of the walled-in church. The frescoes exuded the vitality of life. And St. George looked as if he was slaying the dragon for nobody but Anna herself. In the darkish corridor, it was as if he was returning her gaze, until she had to look away. Anwar put his arm round her and she closed her eyes and leaned her head against his solid shoulder. That's when Anna's world had turned so wonderfully inside out.

Anna increased her pace a little. Why shouldn't she follow her desires? Why should she listen to all those busybody people? Why exactly shouldn't she marry him? She had to leave the country, and she wanted him with her. He could only come with her, if they were married. When she had hinted to Haregewayne, her American-Ethiopian friend, about her relationship and that she wanted to bring Anwar to America, Haregewayne had shaken her head. She had said that she understood being in love, but why not settle for an affair here in Ethiopia? America would soon cure their romance, she had claimed. And you know Ethiopian men; they think of themselves! People were so cynical, and Anna felt she simply couldn't afford to listen to what people said. Now she had spent fifty-four years always considering other people's ideas. Her parents, her spouse, her children. Friends. She didn't have time for that anymore. Now, she would listen only to herself. And even if it shouldn't last? What's an uncertain *sometime in the future*? Now was real.

Who knew how much time she had left?

She looked up. There was CNN. News time. For the umpteenth time. Anna hated it when they turned off the music. And there was Bush hammering away on the TV screens, suspended on top of the jumble of gymnastic instruments. They will not get away with it. The responsible will be found and punished according to the rules of the civilized world. Osama Bin Laden may be elusive, but he is on the run nevertheless. And again, the picture of the towers going up in smoke and tumbling over.

The whole world was fixated on those images. A collective still life for the entertainment of the entire world population, those two towers. Phallic symbols of the powerful West. Click. The peaceful past before the fall. Click again. The slow-motion impact of the planes, the flames, the falling bodies. They were little specks against the empty sky. Then there were the crumbling towers. Collapsing like large, cancerous bones. Click, click. Did this really happen? In normal everyday life? The imagination of those terrorists. Spielberg couldn't have done it better. What is more incredible: real life events or imagined ones?

Anwar could have been one of those terrorists, Anna suddenly thought. She didn't know why. Yes, maybe if he became very frustrated in his life. Or if she didn't take him with her to America? Or because she did?

Two and a half kilometers. She had almost done half her distance. But it was easy when her thoughts and emotions carried her along— like an entertaining movie. Anna was interrupted by Haregewayne's cheerful voice. She was asking how much longer she needed her treadmill, as the two others had just been taken over by new occupants. Anna, who had noticed but not noticed the exchange of her running partners (so he hadn't died on the spot!) replied that she would be a little while, as she still had another three plus kilometers to go.

Haregewayne had answered, "Go ahead, you look like you're enjoying yourself."

Anna's thoughts slowed a little to settle on Haregewayne, who had had breast cancer. Anna had empathized so closely with her that she had felt as if she had lived through Haregewayne's cancer, from the first discovery of the lump in her breast till the mastectomy in the United States. Haregewayne had told her how she, who had always been so proud of her perfect body, now she would hide in the changing room. How precious your body was. One day you're fine, the next it turned against you. And you're so surprised. Anna looked over at Haregewayne, who was lifting weights in the light from the windows. Anna noticed the silhouette of her body. She was wearing a prosthesis—nobody could see that one breast had been removed.

Anna gradually slowed her jogging down a few notches. How would she handle it if she had metastasized breast cancer? What if the persistent little pain in the back of her head was a metastasized tumor from a hidden breast cancer? How would she deal with Anwar? How would he take it, suddenly having a relationship with a sick woman? Her age would stand out. Maybe their sex life would stop. Could she become a nuisance to him? An obstacle?

She could imagine him sitting by her hospital bed. Him on the one side, Susan on the other. Anwar and Susan might throw glances at each other over her bed—glances of compassion. Compassion for whom? What thoughts—what a wicked fantasy! But then it didn't matter: she would already be on another path—a path away from them.

The monitor showed three and a half kilometers. Over halfway. The gym attendant had not turned the music back on, so Anna continued in silence under the artificial daylight of the neon tubes. She ran and ran—right into her future.

What would their life be like in America? Anna thought Anwar would thrive, find a job and go back to school. He would be able to do all the things that a poor country like Ethiopia could not offer. He would no longer be an unemployed, frustrated Ethiopian. He would become his full self, and that would be good for their relationship. Just the opposite of what Haregewayne had suggested. And they would go bird watching in Marin County.

Her legs were beginning to feel a little heavy, and her whole body settled into a calm tiredness—as if she was wrapped in a warm blanket. They had had wonderful lovemaking last night, and afterwards they were both too awake to sleep. They had talked. First, they discussed *Snow Falling on Cedars*, the book Anna had just read and had now passed on to Anwar. But he had found it boring—he thought the characters weren't real people. Hatsue and Ishmael. Her guilt about sex with an American and all that cultural stuff. Japanese—American. He had grimaced. Then Anna had asked if it had made any difference to Anwar that she was American and he Ethiopian? He had answered that maybe he had been attracted to her because she was different, so milky white, and then he had loved her freckles. But Anna had wanted to turn the conversation in another direction, and suddenly she had asked him directly, "Did you seduce me in order to go to America with me?"

There had been a long silence. Then he had said, "Do you want to know the truth?"

"Yes, or I wouldn't ask you." The silence was very uncomfortable now.

"I did scheme to go with you to America." Anna had felt her heart stop. "*Smooth operator*" after all.

"But our lovemaking was out of this world. It was never like that with anybody before.... And then I did fall in love with you." He paused, "Whether we stay or go, I love you."

Anna said no more. She just wanted that sentence to stay there. To hang there in the sky, undisturbed.

So, she didn't tell him how she had never experienced sex as she did now. That he was the one who had initiated her to sex. With her husband, it had been fine in a sort of familiar way; she had never felt like this before. She would tell him another time.

Anna had stopped running some time back. Her run was over—and the ceiling twirled a little. She had slowed to everyday walking pace. There he was!

The open-shirted Anwar had appeared in the gym door with a book under his arm. (The book he had trouble getting through.)

Anna grabbed the monitor in front of her. "Of course, he's thinking of himself, but so am I— that's the beauty of it," she said out loud.

"Who are you talking to?" Haregewayne laughed. "You look very dreamy," she added after a little while. Haregewayne was getting ready to step onto Anna's treadmill.

Anna straightened up as she jumped off the rubber band. She grabbed her towel and sent Haregewayne a sparkling, joyful smile.

The Author on Lake Tana in 2001

ABOUT THE AUTHOR

Charlotte Schiander Gray, born in Denmark, began to travel widely at a young age; she has been journal writing since twelve years of age. In 1968 she left her study of Danish and Russian at the University of Copenhagen, to go to California with her husband Kenneth Gray. Ten years later, after earning her PhD in Scandinavian Languages and Literature at the University of California at Berkeley, she accompanied her husband to Yemen, and remained overseas in India and Sudan with her growing family for many years. She continued to publish academic articles and book reviews of Scandinavian literature, and while in India, wrote a book on the Danish author Klaus Rifbjerg. While in Sudan, she taught at a women's college in Khartoum.

Returning to California, Charlotte taught literature at UC Berkeley Extension and volunteered for the Friends of the Berkeley Public Library, while raising three sons. She spent fifteen years writing fictional stories of her life in foreign countries, and spends the summer months in her second home on the Danish island of Ærø.

From the Author

I went to Ethiopia in the year of 2000 after my husband signed a two-year contract with UNICEF. My plan was to write. I had long wanted to do sustained, serious fiction writing but had not yet been able to set aside the needed continuous, undisturbed time. There were my three sons and family life, housekeeping, teaching, volunteer work—you name it. This was my big chance away from it all at home. I could begin on a blank page.

Inspired by my new Ethiopian setting, I began to take some notes and write a few lines. I also did some "News from Ethiopia" letters, which I sent home to a group of friends. Of course, there was the distraction of settling in: first a stay at the Hilton while looking for a house, then furbishing the house, getting a car and learning to find my way in a foreign city, joining a French class apart from the Amharic lessons, and starting a reading group. That's not to mention that one son managed to take off a quarter from college to stay with us (and bring his charming girlfriend!), and lots of visitors, who found a chance to visit enigmatic Ethiopia. All of this expected in a normal and active life.

Even breast cancer intervened. That was not expected.

But the biggest time-consumer became my chairmanship of the United Nations Women's Organization. I had joined the organization, and when they asked me to be the Chair, I could not say no. I never was good at saying no when asked to do something, and in this case I felt I could do useful volunteering work in a country that sorely needed it. Board Meetings, management, aid work, newsletter, fundraising store, fundraising gala.

I became increasingly occupied. This didn't leave much time for writing, but it familiarized me with the ongoing aid-work. A good amount of material in my contemporary stories derives from that work and those experiences.

In the midst of all these events, my husband managed to buy an old idyllic thatched roof cottage on a remote Danish island in the Baltic. Unbeknownst to me at the time of the purchase, this island house would become the place for me to write my *Stories from Ethiopia* during summer months there. True to a pattern in my life, my mind was often "somewhere else." Here on this northern, bucolic island of Ærø, I could dwell on my Ethiopian experiences and draw upon them for my fictional writing. Here, I could establish a regular routine of writing in the morning and weeding the flowerbeds in the afternoon.

What can the visitor see and understand, and what can the visitor imagine the locals may think? One of my first strong impressions derived from the beggars in the street intersections. This became the kernel of the first story called "The Beggar." One young handsome beggar, who had one leg amputated below his knee, had especially caught my attention. I had actually planned to meet with him to hear his story but was interrupted by events and my own illness. When I realized that I probably wouldn't get the opportunity, I decided to make up his story. It is now up to the inner workings of the story to convince the reader about its plausibility.

"The Pretty Maid" deals with the AIDS epidemic, which became a prominent feature of our aid efforts. The UN women supported a lot of orphanages created by the epidemic. I also co-led ,with various UN organizations, a drama-writing competition on the AIDS epidemic between some elementary schools. Needless to say, the students were very creative in their responses and they certainly gave me the idea to write my own AIDS story.

"The Terrorist" was not unique to Ethiopia, although I made him Ethiopian in this story. The theme was inspired by the 9/11 terrorist attack, which took place while I was in the process of writing these stories. I tried to bring forth all the reasons, some young person—almost always young, and almost always male—would plan a suicide attack. What was he like, the one who becomes estranged from everybody? The one who no longer belongs? I made him Muslim because that was the case in 9/11; there are terrorists of all persuasions. Incorporating some features from the Egyptian Mohammad Atta, who became the pilot of one of the planes that flew into the World Trade Center Towers, I wanted to make "my" terrorist both personal but also "typical."

"The Guard" borrows from my own domestic setting with an enclosed, even claustrophobic villa surrounded by a small garden ruled by the meticulous guard. The young American woman grows bored and fills her vacuum with sexual fantasies about her guard and Amharic teacher.

"The Girlfriend" deals with the love and failings in a relationship between an American man and his Ethiopian girlfriend. Is the girlfriend of the Western man "the other," the one he can't quite relate to, or take serious, or live up to?

Inspired by my own immigrant story, I have always been interested in new beginnings, immigrant settings and psychology. In "The Immigrant," the young Ethiopian woman is keen on taking up American ways, while her husband tries to uphold traditional male authority. The story explores the impact on their marriage.

In "The Rich Man," I take a little break from the serious issues to poke fun at the volunteering efforts of the international community. In this "farce," the characters are more stereotypical than realistic.

"The Tourists" takes up the subject of a sister and brother seeking adventure in foreign lands. The young siblings exude the inexperience and ignorance of many a tourist.

Finally, in "The Lover" a middle-aged American woman exercises on a treadmill while thinking about her much younger Ethiopian lover; age; health; disease and death. She is in the midst of it all.

In the process of writing the contemporary stories, I became more and more interested in Ethiopia and its history. I felt like deepening my superficial knowledge of the country. What was the history of that proud and intriguing people, who had managed to stay independent for all of its history?

My curiosity brought me to the Doe Library (the graduate library) of the University of California at Berkeley—my home town. The eight months of the year that we were home in America while I was writing, I frequented the library. Amazingly, Doe had about any book I looked for in their big underground storage space. I dug in and took notes, not to become an expert but to find the stories that I could create out of that vast canvas of history; stories that appealed to me. I read about the various Ethiopian rulers and their times and chose the settings and events from which I could create my historical fiction.

In "The Dreamer," the fictional Pero joins Father Alvares and other famous Portuguese explorers in search of the mystical ruler, Prester John, in far-away Abyssinia. The early explorations in the beginning of the 16th century laying the foundations for colonial times—although Ethiopia is unique in that it did not become a colony. Pero's experiences alternate between hopeful dreams and (cruel) reality.

"The King," apart from being that very individual of King Tewodros, who ruled from 1855 to 1868, also represents a recurring narrative about the ruler, from successful beginning to frustrating resistance and obstacles, to final abuse of power, and ultimately, defeat. The almost archetypal story of extreme ambition and the real limits of concrete life.

"The Diplomat" also has a fictional character, Pietro, whose intro-duction to diplomacy and politics took place during the rule of King Menelik (1889–1913). Pietro is forced to make a choice when he real-izes that *you cannot play the political game without dirtying your hands.* Motivated by his love of an Ethiopian woman, he is not ready to give up his idealism.

In "The Emperor," I focus on Hailie Selassie's struggle to save Ethi-opia from the onslaught of the Italian fascist Mussolini. It became a David versus Goliath story. David was victorious in this case but not before many victims had suffered a tragic death. The victims—who do not survive to hear about the possible "good ending." The victims—who are left alone to face their often painful death.

"The Ideologue" takes place under the rule of the dictator Mengistu, in power from 1977–1991. In this last historical fiction, I experiment with the structure and characters of a folktale: a peasant, a soldier, and a student. The form seemed well suited to convey the ideological times of a dictator.

Like the contemporary stories, the historical fiction is woven from the interaction between locals and foreigners, natives and visitors. The intercourse between the familiar and the unknown, the rooted and the far-away, was the driving force behind *Stories from Ethiopia*. This interplay between my own familiar world and curiosity of the unknown proves a lasting source of creativity for me.

www.ingramcontent.com/pod-product-compliance
Lightning Source LLC
Chambersburg PA
CBHW020910200626
46814CB00001BA/263